CRITICAL
FEDERAL SPACE BOOK 2
DESCENT

ZACHARY JONES

Copyright © 2020 Zachary Jones

All rights reserved. No part of this novel can be reproduced or used in any manner without the written permission of the copyright owner, except for quotations in a book review.

ACKNOWLEDGMENTS

Well, this novel has been bit of a a project. Countless hours of writing, rewriting, and even more rewriting until I started to go a bit crazy.

Fortunately for me, and my sanity, I didn't have to go it alone. I would like to start by thanking Global English Editing for both editing and proofreading Critical Descent. Their work was invaluable in turning a rough manuscript into a professional quality work.

I would also like to thank the folks at Damonza for their work in crafting the cover that gained your interest in the book in the first place, as well as converting the manuscript from Word to the appropriate formats for E-book and Print-On-Demand.

To you, the reader, I hope you enjoy the adventure waiting for you in the following pages. If you enjoy Critical Descent, or if there is anything you feel I can improve on, please leave a review on Amazon or Goodreads.

Happy Hunting,
Zachary Jones

PROLOGUE

Ants were fascinating creatures.

From a low squat, Jerome watched hundreds of individual ants working together as a collective whole to achieve a single goal, which in this case was the consumption of a piece of caramel candy he had placed half a meter away from the entrance to their nest.

It had not taken long for the ants to find the precious lump of sweet calories resting right on their doorstep. Within minutes, a trail of workers had formed to harvest the candy, each ant breaking off a small piece and taking it back into the nest.

Unlike many of the flora and fauna that had been introduced to Starport Armstrong to bring a bit of nature into the vast artifice of the station, the ants were an invasive species. They were intruders that had stowed aboard in a poorly sanitized piece of cargo and had managed to make themselves a part of the station's internal ecosystem, despite all efforts to eradicate them.

Jerome was struck by the parallels between the ants and his own people. Workers, soldiers, drones, and queens all working towards the survival of the colony. For the Ascended, too, each had a role to play. Not just for the betterment of their own people, but for all life. But where the ants' goal was the collection of calories, the Ascendency's was the collection of knowledge.

The sound of small claws skittering against bark drew Jerome's attention upward.

Above him, in the branches of the tree that loomed over the ant hill, a pair of squirrels chased each other around the tree's trunk. Unlike the ants, the squirrels had been deliberately introduced. Many humans found the small rodents, with their bushy tails, appealing, despite their tendency to become pests whenever they did anything other than act as living decoration.

Jerome looked up higher, through the tree's canopy, towards the blue artificial sky projected on the curved ceiling of the torus two hundred meters above him.

Not for the first time, he found it curious how humans needed to bring a piece of Earth with them just to feel at home. It was an inefficient use of biomass. Though it did give him the chance to study animals and insects that he otherwise would only know of as entries in the Ascendency's shared database. To see actual living creatures in a facsimile of their native environment was a rare privilege. Jerome was, not for the first time, grateful that he had been born an emissary.

A signal from his warform bodyguards, accompanied by the image of a middle-aged human female in a crisp black business suit, alerted Jerome to the approach of a visitor.

Jerome signaled to his bodyguards to relax and let his friend through.

The human female was Mayor Ari Delois, the elected leader of Starport Armstrong. Though useful in keeping Starport Armstrong's citizens under control, Jerome had developed a fondness for her—which made the actions the Ascended would have to take after the transgressions by the Earth Federation even more regrettable.

Jerome turned to face the mayor. "Good afternoon, Ari. Is that for me?" He gestured to the small black box she carried, held closed by a white ribbon.

"It is. A gift in gratitude for your lenient treatment of my people," Ari said, holding out the box.

Jerome accepted the box. "May I open it?"

"Of course."

Jerome pulled on the end of the ribbon and the bow unraveled and fell away from the box. He tucked the ribbon away into a pocket of his robe and opened the box. Inside was a gray polymer data stick resting inside a soft foam interior.

"From my personal media library," Ari said. "My selection of novels and short stories written in the last two hundred years from across settled space. I've already sorted them in the order I would recommend."

Jerome smiled. "That is very kind of you, Mayor. That must have been quite the task."

Ari shrugged. "Benefits of a misspent youth as a literature teacher. Putting together reading assignments is second nature to me."

Jerome replaced the lid on the box and tucked it away into his robe. "A gift I will cherish, Ari. Hopefully, a sign of our two peoples' future cooperation."

"Indeed," Ari said with forced sincerity.

Though she had been cooperative from the moment the first Ascended had set foot on her station, Ari had made no secret of her disapproval of the actions taken by the Ascended. It was unfortunate that her home happened to orbit a planet of vital strategic importance to the Earth Federation, and thus was the first target in the Ascendency's pacification campaign.

The fact that Ari and her people would have to bear the brunt of the retaliation against the Earth Federation made Jerome's heart ache. He agreed with the course of action, of course. The Consensus always chose the right course of action. But it meant hurting a friend. Such was war.

"Is there something wrong, Jerome?" Ari asked. "I can change my reading recommendations, if you want."

"No, it's not that, Ari. Your gift is a fine one," Jerome reassured her. "It just pains me that I have to reply to your gift with bad news."

Ari wasn't surprised. She was an intelligent human. She knew there would be consequences for her people after the Earth Federation's attack. She set her jaw and straightened her posture. "Well, no point waiting. What's going to happen to us?"

Us. Not referring to Jerome and her, but to her people. Her constituents on Starport Armstrong and the millions of other Jovians on hundreds of stations currently under occupation by the Ascendency. Despite their friendship, Jerome knew he would always be "other" to Ari.

Humans were always good at turning their own kind into others. It would be even easier for them to do such to the Ascended. He supposed he shouldn't judge her too harshly on that. He thought of humans as the other as well. Since they were. The Ascendency were created to be separate and distinct from humanity. To erase the boundary between human and Ascended would be to betray the intentions of the Visionaries.

"We can no longer ensure the safety of Jupiter's civilian population. Not after the Earth Federation demonstrated their willingness to attack our forces around Jupiter, despite the chances of endangering millions of their own citizens. Therefore, we will be evacuating the entire Jovian population."

"That's quite the logistical task," Ari said. "Mind telling me how you intend to do that, and where we will be going?"

"You will be sent down orbit towards the inner solar system," Jerome said.

"Has Earth Fed agreed to this?" Ari asked. "What you're stating is going to require thousands of transports. Not to mention a ceasefire."

"There is no ceasefire," Jerome said. "And as for transports, we have solved that problem."

"Solved? How?"

"May I connect to your brainset, Ari? I have something to show you."

"I'm open," Ari said.

Jerome nodded, and connected her to an external feed of Starport Armstrong. The first time in months any human aboard the station had gotten to see the exterior of their home.

"What the hell are you doing to my station?" Ari said after a moment. "Those look like rocket boosters."

"They're self-contained, prefabricated long-burn drives," Jerome said. "There are thirty-six attached to strongpoints across Starport Armstrong. And thousands more have been attached to every other civilian station around Jupiter."

"You're going to push us out of orbit," Ari said breathlessly. "How much delta-v do those pushers give us?"

"Just enough to send your stations on a parabolic trajectory through the inner solar system, with perihelion right between the orbits of Earth and Venus," Jerome said.

"Parabolic? You're not just de-orbiting us—you're sending us on an escape-trajectory out of the solar system."

"Not if the Earth Federation elects to catch you."

"I don't understand," Ari said. "With the delta-v you're expending, you could put all our stations into a simple transfer orbit."

"Time in this instance is far more important than fuel, Ari," Jerome said. "And we have an abundance of it due to our control of Uranus and Neptune. This way, your stations will reach the inner solar system in months rather than years."

"And then we pass on by and back out of the solar system," Ari said.

"Only if the Earth Federation doesn't stop you," Jerome said.

Ari snorted. "Yes, catching hundreds of billions of tons worth of space stations would just be a walk in the park for Earth Fed."

"How they accomplish that will be up to them."

"Also rather conveniently rids you of a burden."

"You have been no burden, Ari," Jerome said. "It has been a great pleasure to get to know you and your people and learn all that I have. Hopefully, once this war is over, we might continue this."

Ari crossed her arms, her face stern. Jerome suspected she used the same expression back when she had been a teacher disciplining a recalcitrant student. "You're using my people as a weapon."

"Nonsense, we've made every effort to make sure none of your station will end up on a collision course," Jerome said.

"That's not what I meant, and you know it. You're using my people to create a refugee crisis," Ari said.

"You'll be the best provisioned refugees in history," Jerome said. "Starport Armstrong, and all the other stations around Jupiter, are fully stocked with supplies. You will not starve before your government has a chance to rescue you."

"Yes, and I'm sure the commitment of ships and fuel to accomplish such a rescue is just a bonus for you."

Jerome sighed. "It's true, we're using your people. In war, one must use all tools available in order to secure victory as swiftly as possible, with as little suffering as possible. I know this will affect your people harshly, but in the end it will be worth it."

"Maybe to you it will. If you excuse me, I need to tell my people and prepare. I'm sure you would hate for anyone to get injured once you ignite those pusher engines." She turned to leave but paused to glance over her shoulder at Jerome. "I hope you enjoy your reading."

"I will, Ari. Farewell."

"Not with any help from you," Ari said, and departed.

Jerome nodded to his bodyguards and left the park. It was time to depart the station for the last time.

A shuttle was already waiting to take him and the last of the Ascended from Starport Armstrong. After linking with the shuttle pilot's sensor feed, Jerome saw similar events playing out across Jovian space. Shuttles by the hundreds were flying away from Federal civilian stations to waiting starships.

Jerome's destination was *Victorious Intent*, a kinetic weapon combatant that the Federals had termed a battlecruiser. An evocative, if archaic, name originally used to refer to an unsuccessful type of wet-navy capital ship. It betrayed the limited, Earth-bound thinking of humanity.

As the shuttle pulled into *Intent*'s small shuttle bay, Jerome automatically linked into the starship's local Consensus. Two hundred Ascended greeted his return after so long among the humans. He opened himself to the Consensus, sharing his experiences with his eager comrades.

Crew and pilots never got to venture off their ships, and like all Ascended were extremely curious. Like the ants Jerome had gifted candy to, the Ascended swarmed around his awareness, taking a copy of his experiences to add to their own.

They were particularly eager for the data stick hidden away in the pocket of his robes.

That, he would have to connect directly to a data port, after due diligence to make sure there was no malicious software inside, though Jerome doubted Ari had the intent, let alone the means, to do such a thing.

But that would have to wait.

Jerome left the shuttle, his robes floating about him as he moved down the tubes that ran through *Intent*. The crew, with their micro-gravity adapted hand-like feet, scuttled around him, reminding him not for the first time of the ants back on Starport Armstrong.

Each one flashed a short greeting to him through the Consensus before continuing. Like all Ascended, save for emissaries, they had no mouths, their faces featureless save for their eyes. They didn't need mouths, since they did not talk, or eat, or breath. Their narrow bodies were perfectly adapted for life in space.

Jerome soon arrived at his destination, the control core of *Intent*, where the disembodied brain of *Intent's* navigatrix rested in an armored sphere, connected by tendrils of fiber-optic cables to the ship's various systems.

The navigatrix was analogous to the captain of a human ship, but not the same. On a human ship, the captain's word was law; the Ascended had no laws. They had the Consensus. The navigatrix's role was to bridge the gap between the virtual world of the Consensus and the world outside *Intent's* hull.

"Hello, Emissary Jerome. I see you brought some new content to share with the ship," Navigatrix Constance said.

"Indeed, I have, Constance," Jerome replied, pulling the box containing the data stick out from his robes. "Shall I connect it to *Intent's* network?"

"Maybe later. We're about to ignite the pusher motors, and I would like to remain free of distraction," Constance said.

"Understood." Through the Consensus, he saw what Constance, and all the other Ascended aboard *Intent*, saw. Through the *Intent's* sensor arrays, the Ascendency fleet took position down orbit of the main belt of stations that orbited Jupiter just outside the orbit of the moon Callisto.

Then, all at once, the drives lit up, and stations started to gain speed, slowly bulging out of their orbits until they would no longer be bound by Jupiter's gravity. But the pusher engines would do more than simply shove the stations out of their orbits. They would continue to burn for days until all Jovian stations were on a trajectory that would have them passing through Inner Sol at the same time.

It was unfortunate that millions of Jovian citizens would have to be displaced from their homes. But if the suffering of millions brought about the swift victory that Jerome and every Ascended so desperately wanted, then it would be worth the price.

CHAPTER 1

Jessica's mission was to find the trail that led to where the Ascendency came from, and there was only one place in the universe where that trail could have started. Earth.

There was just the small matter of getting past the Ascendency forces occupying Outer Sol. And not dying of boredom along the way. There wasn't a lot to do aboard FSFV *Dakar* as the cruiser made the one-week trip from Procyon to Sol.

The only indication *Dakar* was moving was the faint buzz that ran through the hull of the ship as capacitors dumped power into the starship's drive-keel to initiate a jump. A hundred billion kilometers at a time, every ten minutes. That buzz was the root of an affliction colloquially known as jump-insomnia, which afflicted some spacers. These were spacers who had grown up on planets, and thus were not fully inoculated to the noises of living in space.

The typical solution was a set of noise-canceling earplugs so the afflicted could sleep in blissful silence. Jessica would've been one of them except all she had to do was turn her ears off when she went to sleep. Being a full-body cyborg had its perks.

Another perk was the fact that decapitation was merely inconvenient rather than fatal.

Jessica rubbed her neck at the memory, when Mason had, at her insistence, cut her head away from her broken body after she had been run over by an automated garbage truck. That's what she got for trying to cross a road without looking.

Still, it wasn't all bad. Mason proved to be good company.

A ship-wide announcement went through the speakers after another buzz passed through the hull.

"All crew, this is the captain speaking, we're one jump out from Sol. The habitat module will be spun down and retracted into the hull in five minutes. All personnel are to evacuate to the main hull."

Jessica sighed and started to finish the last of her coffee with a long sip. The few off-duty officers that shared the small wardroom with her finished their own drinks and snacks before getting up and throwing drink packets into recycling chutes, and soiled dishes and cutlery into the cleaning station.

Jessica squeezed the last of the coffee from her packet until there were only scattered droplets of liquid a shade of brown darker than her skin adhering to the clear plastic. She got up and tossing the flaccid bag into a recycling station along the way to the center of the habitat module.

Dakar's habitat rotor was a spinning, barbell-shaped module with two cylindrical habitat modules at each end. A bank of elevators ran up the center of both modules, and up the arms of the rotors into the main hull of the ship.

There was an orderly crowd of officers and enlisted spacers waiting for the next elevator. *Dakar*'s crew was well practiced in the art of getting into line and awaiting their turn. Each elevator that arrived was filled precisely with ten spacers before the doors closed, the maximum occupancy as per safety regulations. There was no cutting in line or attempts to crowd as many bodies into an elevator as possible. And the queue made no allowance for rank. Your place in line was determined simply by when you took your place in the queue.

The line moved quickly, and Jessica boarded an elevator within two minutes of getting in line. The doors closed, and the elevator started to ascend. Some of the officers and crew chatted among themselves as the elevator moved closer to the center of rotation, and the spin-gravity gradually faded away.

Jessica was using a toehold to hold herself to the deck when the elevator arrived in the hab-rotor hub with the barest fraction of a g pulling down. As soon as the elevator doors opened, everyone inside jumped out, crossing the threshold between spinning rotor and the rest of the ship.

As a passenger rather than part of the crew, Jessica's place was a wardroom one level below the command deck. She climbed her way up from the habitation section of the ship, climbing deck after deck through ladder wells, usually with the feet of another spacer hanging in front of her.

"Now hear this, hab-rotor evacuation complete, beginning spin down and storage procedure."

Jessica arrived at her assigned deck and pushed herself off the ladder, catching the handholds on the opposite walls. From there, it was just a matter of launching herself, one handhold over the other, flying over the dark high-traction coating of the deck until she arrived in the small wardroom nestled below the bridge, located right up against the ship's drive keel.

The wardroom was empty when she arrived; all the other officers aboard *Dakar* had something to do. She strapped herself into one of the acceleration seats and tilted it back to the optimal angle for dealing with high-gs. A cruiser like *Dakar* could pull 4gs in combat, and, even with her cyborg body, a fall in acceleration of that kind could cause serious damage not easily remedied without a cyberneticist on hand.

She understood why her place was in the room. Other than the bridge, this was the best protected part of the ship, with the most possible armor and hull between her and empty space. But that placed her right next to the star drive, an almost solid spear of space–time-bending technology that ran the length of the ship and doubled as her keel. There was no documented evidence of star drives having any effect on a ship's crew, beyond transporting them instantly across space. But Jessica always felt a little uneasy being so close to one during a jump.

In a few minutes, capacitors that were busy soaking up all the energy *Dakar* could generate would spill their power into the drive keel in a single burst of energy. And from the point of view of everyone aboard the ship, all that would happen is the star drive would get hot, and the ship would begin the process of dumping the heat into the radiators.

But if one looked outside, they'd notice they were hundreds of billions of kilometers from where they were just an instant before.

Well, not quite an instant. The actual jump took a very tiny amount of time to complete. An infinitesimal fraction of a second. Jessica had watched slow-motion recordings of what happens during a ship jump. All the incoming light rapidly red-shifts as everything around the ship falls away—like the expansion of the universe is suddenly kicked into overdrive. The red-shift continues until, for the briefest moment, the starship hangs in an empty black void. And then the process reverses, the universe collapsing back around the ship, the stars blue-shifting back to normal as the starship returns to normal space.

Return might be the wrong word. When Jessica was first taught the basics of what a star drive did to move a ship across space, her teachers insisted that the ship didn't go anywhere. It had just transitioned from the point of departure to the point of arrival; that the inky darkness was just the result of the tiny delay it took light to penetrate through the bubble of space–time the star drive had punched into the universe.

All that said, Jessica could never shake the feeling that the ship did travel somewhere between departure and arrival, going somewhere cold, dark, and dead before returning to the universe she knew in a flash of light.

This was why she hated being a passenger during faster-than-light travel—without a pile of data to occupy her attention, she started to overthink things.

"Just one more jump, Jessica. No need to worry," she said to herself, though that was a lie.

She stole one last glance at the bulkhead that separated the wardroom from the star drive, and then decided to direct her attention to the outside. As an intelligence officer in the Special Purpose Branch, Jessica, with the captain's permission, had privileged access to *Dakar*'s suite of sensors.

She connected to the ship's sensor AI via her brainset and was greeted by an all-encompassing view of space around the starship. Sol was directly ahead, the brightest star in the sphere of sky surrounding her. From a hundred billion kilometers out, *Dakar*'s sensors picked up the faint echoes of four-day-old long-burn drive emissions, encrypted comm chatter, and the thermal radiation of thousands of stations and one heavily industrialized planet.

But there were none of the telltale flashes of nuclear detonations, no signs that there had been major fighting four days in the past. She hoped that remained true.

"This is the captain speaking. We're about to jump into Sol. Hopefully, there will be friendlies waiting for us at the arrival point, but we might have to fight our way into the inner solar system," Captain Shiro said.

Jessica didn't favor *Dakar*'s odds if the 1st Fleet wasn't there to cover them as they appeared in the Sun-Jupiter L5 Lagrange point. A single kinetic kill vehicle fired from the spinal gun of a Cendy battlecruiser could split *Dakar* in half like a bullet through a tree branch.

A countdown timer appeared in Jessica's HUD, or heads-up display, showing her the final countdown to jump. In the last seconds before the jump, she tried to calm herself, grateful that her artificial heart was not susceptible to her anxiety. Then the buzz of a large angry insect vibrated through the ship as power flooded into the star drive not five meters from her. And then, in a flash, *Dakar* went from over a hundred billion kilometers from the Sun, to a little under a billion, right inside the Jupiter-Sun L5.

There were dozens of contacts waiting nearby, all in deep blue, friendly federal icons. Jessica let out a sigh of relief as she read off the names of the ships.

Two 1st Fleet carriers, FSFV *Goshawk* and FSFV *Hyena*, loitered a few million kilometers inside the Sun's jump limit, a spherical zone centered around the star where its gravity prevented star drives from functioning. In and around the Lagrange point were a couple of squadrons of Federal Lightnings, powerful fighters ready to drop torpedoes on any Cendy warship that might jump in.

A sudden 1g acceleration pulled Jessica into the gel of her acceleration chair as *Dakar* ignited her long-burn drive and accelerated towards the two carriers guarding the Lagrange point. Shifting to a more comfortable position in her seat, she expanded her awareness further, almost a billion kilometers away in the direction of Jupiter.

She lurched forward when she saw a trail of icons millions of kilometers long streaming away from Jupiter, each displaying the spindle-shaped icons of space stations.

"Bloody hell…"

An incoming message icon popped up in the periphery of her vision. A simple text message from Captain Shiro ordering her to report to the bridge.

She had a pretty good idea what he wanted to talk to her about.

Replying that she was on her way, Jessica released her seat restraints and stood up out of the seat. With *Dakar* accelerating, it was an easy walk to the nearest ladder well and a quick climb up to the control deck.

She passed the guards flanking the heavy hatch leading into the circular amphitheater of *Dakar*'s bridge. Two tiers of control consoles surrounded the central holotank, the crew at the station facing towards the center of the bridge, where *Dakar*'s captain sat looking up from at the projection of Jupiter and the string of space stations falling away.

Jessica walked down to the holotank and snapped a salute. "Lieutenant Sinclair reporting for duty."

Shiro nodded towards the holotank. "Any insights into what the hell is that?"

"Ah…" Jessica looked up at the holotank and the string of stations. "How many stations are there exactly?"

"Based on what Captain Lafferty aboard *Goshawk* said when I spoke with her, all of them," Captain Shiro replied. "Seems a week ago, the Cendies started pushing every civilian station in orbit of Jupiter onto an escape trajectory that will take them down below the orbit of Earth, and then back out of the solar system."

"That's quite an achievement."

"That's one way to put it, Lieutenant. Any insights as to why?"

"Well, I've only just got here, sir, but if I were to venture a guess, I would say this is retaliation for Operation Autumn Fire."

"Seems disproportionate," Captain Shiro muttered.

"The civilian stations are a drain on the Cendies' resources, Captain," Jessica explained. "We demonstrated that the civilian stations no longer had value as deterrents against attacks by us. By doing this, they're off-loading a burden and placing it on us."

"They had to use a lot of fuel to do that," Captain Shiro said.

"They control Outer Sol, sir. So they have plenty of it… which we don't."

"Sounds like something just occurred to you, Lieutenant."

"The Cendies just neutralized much of what's left of the 1st Fleet's fuel reserves," Jessica said.

"I don't follow, Lieutenant."

"Sir, the 1st Fleet used a lot of their fuel reserves during Operation Autumn Fire." She pointed to the holotank. "And now they have twenty million people about to fall through Inner Sol. They'll be using the rest to rescue those people before their station flies off into the void."

Captain Shiro stared at the holotank for a moment, then turned back to Jessica. "I hope you're not the first person to notice that."

"I would hope there are people down orbit who have come to the same conclusion," Jessica said.

"I would imagine the local Special Purpose Branch officers are gearing up to scour as much intel from the Jovian stations as possible," Captain Shiro said.

Jessica looked at the holotank and noticed there were no Federal ships inbound on the station just yet. "Are any there, sir?"

"No, the stations are currently too close to Cendy-controlled space."

"Then I need to get to those stations as fast as possible, Captain."

"It would take three days at full burn for my ship to get there, Lieutenant. And I'm not sure what value a detour to those stations will have for your mission."

Jessica pointed at the stations. "The people on those stations have had direct contact with the Cendies for months, sir. There's a good chance they know something that will help narrow down were I have to look. And besides, I wasn't thinking of having *Dakar* fly there. I was thinking of something faster."

"Like a destroyer?"

"Like a Lightning, Captain" Jessica said. "Could you get in contact with the carriers and see if I can't borrow one of their pilots?"

⁂

It wasn't hard for Jessica to get a pilot. Every pilot who was in space volunteered, and it came down to the senior-most pilot pulling rank to decide who would get to carry Jessica to the falling Jovian stations.

The chosen Lightning pulled into *Dakar*'s small hangar bay, squeezing into the space between the cruiser's two assault shuttles, wings folded in, in order to fit.

Jessica had pulled on a space suit while waiting outside the hangar airlock for the fighter to arrive. Her artificial body could survive several minutes of vacuum exposure, but it was only for emergencies. A space suit was critical for anything longer.

Pincer arms unfolded from the celling of *Dakar*'s hangar bay and clamped onto strong points on the Lightning's wings, locking the fighter into place.

The cockpit canopy opened; the opaque metal panel, almost invisible while closed, swung up to show the pilot in a black hardsuit waving to Jessica to get inside.

Jessica jumped and floated towards the fighter, catching herself on the lip of the cockpit and pulling herself towards the passenger seat at the back of the cockpit. The passenger seat was primarily for picking up stranded fighter pilots but could also be used for passengers who were in a major hurry, like Jessica.

She strapped herself into the gimballed acceleration chair and plugged her space suit directly into the fighter's power supply. Lightnings lacked built-in life-support systems, relying instead on those contained in hardsuits and space suits.

After plugging herself in, she connected to the fighter's near-field communications network with the fighter's pilot.

"Welcome aboard, Lieutenant Sinclair. I'm Flight Lieutenant Sienna Armitage and I'll be your pilot for this flight."

"A pleasure, Flight Lieutenant. Thank you for volunteering for this task. What's your callsign?"

"Marbles, Lieutenant."

"Well, Marbles, I'm as ready as I'm going to be," Jessica said. "At your pleasure."

"Will do. You'll want to switch to subvocal for the rest of the flight. We'll be pulling 10gs the whole way there."

"I have the same g-tolerance you do, Marbles. Don't worry about me," Jessica reassured her.

"Good to know."

A tremor passed through the fighter as the clamps released, and there was a gentle forward pull as Armitage backed out of *Dakar*'s hangar bay with a push from the nose thrusters.

Once clear of the cruiser, Armitage swung her fighter towards the line of stations falling away from Jupiter almost eight hundred million kilometers away.

"Brace yourself, Lieutenant," Armitage said.

"I'm ready, Marbles."

The long-burn drives activated, and a full g pulled Jessica into her seat, then the pull gradually increased as Armitage opened the throttle. Two more Lightnings took up flanking positions off either wing of Armitage's fighter.

<Friends of yours?> Jessica subvocalized as the pull of acceleration increased.

<Couple of pilots from my squadron, Giggles and Fishtail. They'll be providing us with an escort.>

<How thoughtful of them.>

<They seemed to think flying with us would give them a better chance of killing some Cendies.>

<If it's all the same to you, Marbles, I hope the Cendies don't see a trio of Lightnings as worth the trouble of intercepting.>

<To each their own.>

Armitage pushed her fighter to full cruising burn. Ten gs pulled down on Jessica, pressing her body into the acceleration gel of her seat. She dialed down her pain receptors to a comfortable level, until the weight pressing down on her was resting in the periphery of her awareness.

<I'm going to go into hibernation, Marbles. Wake me when we get there.>

<Rest well, Lieutenant.>

Activating her hibernation mode, Jessica's consciousness started to fall away. Her last thought was a wish for an uneventful flight.

CHAPTER 2

Mason could really use a vacation.

The closest thing he'd had to a break in a long while were the days he'd spent in the hospital of the Alpha Centauri Fleet Base while his leg wound was fast-healed. He would have thought that after helping achieve Earth Fed's first real victory against the Ascendency that Federal Command could have given him a few days' leave.

Instead, he'd got a promotion and a new mission. To put together a new squadron to replace the loss of the 4th Special Operations Fighter Squadron. The Void Knights.

Of the sixteen pilots who made up the squadron, only six survived the mission to recover FSFV *Independence*. And those six pilots were now heroes, too visible to be useful for covert operations, and too valuable to be risked in combat missions.

Mason had survived the mission with his life, anonymity, and therefore, expendability intact. That thought did nothing to help the tension headache pulling at the strands of his central nervous system.

"Good morning, Colonel Shimura," Mason said.

"Good Morning, Squadron Leader Grey," Colonel Shimura replied. "Ready to get started assembling Osiris Squadron?" A tall, solid woman wearing the olive-drab jumpsuit of a trooper, she'd been a spy longer than she'd ever been an infantry officer, Mason was pretty sure, though even after months working with her, he still had only the most superficial knowledge of her past before she joined the Special Purpose Branch.

"Osiris Squadron?" he asked.

"Named for the ancient Egyptian god," Colonel Shimura explained.

"I know who Osiris is, sir, Mason replied. "I just don't understand why we're naming a squadron after him."

"What do you know of Osiris, Squadron Leader?"

"He had to get sewn back together after getting cut to pieces."

"Correct. An appropriate code name, given where we're going to be recruiting our pilots from."

"Ah, yes, I see what you mean. Cendies left plenty of broken squadrons on this station waiting to be harvested for spares," Mason said. "So, is Osiris Squadron the official name, sir?"

"No, the official name is the 77th Special Operations Fighter Squadron."

"Sounds like the Special Purpose Branch has a lot of spec op squadrons," Mason observed.

"We don't. The number is randomly chosen in order to obfuscate the true number of special operations squadrons that are active at any given time."

"Well, sir, it's working. I sure as hell don't know how many squadrons you have."

"*We*, Squadron Leader. You are part of the team now."

"Uh, yes, sir. Apologies," Mason said. "Still hasn't sunk in."

"You're going to have to get it sunk in, then, Squadron Leader. It won't be too long before you're leading missions for the Special Purpose Branch."

"In that case, sir, I should get started."

"Where do you intend to start, Squadron Leader?" Colonel Shimura asked.

"I need an XO, sir," Mason said. "And I know just who I want for that."

Flight Lieutenant Zinash Yordanos was a tall woman who matched Mason in height and had a muscular build that her black jumpsuit did little to conceal. She kept her frizzy black hair cut short, and her dark skin contrasted sharply with her perfect white teeth when she smiled at Mason and shot him a smart salute.

Mason returned the salute, and then shook her hand firmly. "Belts and zones, it's good to see you, Zin."

"You too, Mason." She released his hand. "I must say, I was surprised to see your message. I had feared you died when *Eagle* was reported lost."

Mason suppressed a shudder. "It was damn close, I won't lie."

"I don't suppose you'd be willing to tell me what happened?" Zin asked. "It's not every day someone returns from the dead with an extra bar pinned to their jumpsuit."

"Yeah, so, that's actually related to why I contacted you," Mason said. "I'm working with the Special Purpose Branch."

Zin nodded. "I see. That would explain why you were quiet for so long. Would it be a mistake to assume you're here to recruit me?"

Mason shook his head. "Not at all, Zin. I'm putting together a new special ops squadron, and I want you to be my Executive Officer."

"I hope this isn't just because we're friends."

"It's a part of it. I'm new to this whole commanding-my-own-squadron thing and I need an XO I can trust," Mason admitted. "And… I know you're between squadrons right now."

Zin nodded solemnly. "I guess it's no coincidence you showed up right after my squadron got disbanded."

Mason shook his head. "It's in fact one of my criteria. I wasn't going to steal you from an active combat squadron."

"So, you're cannibalizing from dead ones instead."

"Effectively, yes. I won't lie—the job I'm offering is high risk."

Zin chuckled. "You're not selling this very well."

"I'm telling the truth," Mason said. "And besides, I know you, Zin. You want to see action. And I can tell you from experience, spec ops squadrons do not lack for it."

Zin crossed her arms, cocked her head to one side, and smiled. "You're right, you do know me. More appealing than waiting for a new squadron assignment to conjure itself out of the ether. Okay, Mason. I accept."

Mason shook Zin's hand. "Welcome to the 77th Special Operations Fighter Squadron, Zin, otherwise known as Osiris Squadron. The two of us currently make up the entirety of it."

Zin smiled. "Well, let's not waste any time in remedying that."

Flight Lieutenant Tanner Dominic was an anomaly among pilots in the Federal Space Forces, and not just because he was much older than the typical flight lieutenant. Fully twice Mason's age, Tanner's junior rank relative to his age was not due to poor performance, but because he didn't join the Federal Space Forces until he was in his fifties after a successful civilian career.

He had the distinction of being one of the few pilots in the Space Forces who could afford to buy his Lightning outright if the Federal Legislature ever authorized the fighter for private sale.

Flight Lieutenant Dominic waited for Mason alone in the ready room reserved for the remains of the 60th Fighter Squadron, which consisted of a total of six pilots, including Dominic himself, who was the senior surviving officer.

Dominic stood up and snapped a salute at Mason as he entered. A short, solidly built man who had elected to allow his hair to gray naturally, though modern medicine had kept the more deleterious effects of aging at bay.

Mason returned the salute. "At ease, Flight Lieutenant."

Dominic nodded and sat back down, resting his left foot on his right knee. "So, you're here to take over the ragged remains of my squadron, sir?"

"No, I already have a squadron. And I'm looking to recruit you into it," Mason said.

"Right to the point." Dominic smiled up at him. "Is this optional or is your recruitment mandatory?"

"It's all volunteer."

"All volunteer, eh? Well, sir, with all due respect, I know very little about you other than the fact that you were, until very recently, MIA," Dominic said. "Might I ask what you were doing all that time?"

"I've been working with the Special Purpose Branch," Mason said. "That's all I can say at this time, I'm afraid."

"Oh? I don't suppose you were at all involved in the recovery of that battlecarrier Earth Fed had squirreled away on Amalthea?"

"Again, I'm not at liberty to discuss any activities I might have participated within the Special Purpose Branch. But if you were to join me, you might find out."

"Oh, tempting, sir. Though may I ask why me? I'm just a rich guy enjoying his adventure retirement with the Space Forces. Why would a pilot with the Special Purpose Branch want me?"

"Because, despite your service being 'adventure retirement', you also happen to be among the best pilots currently available to me on this station."

"I know I have a good record, but I know of several other pilots who have better."

"Most of whom are already spoken for."

"I'm not?"

"Not for much longer. The 60th are going to be disbanded and their pilots sent to fill out openings in other squadrons," Mason told him.

Dominic sighed. "Well, that is no surprise." He opened his mouth to ask another question, and then stopped as a thought occurred to him. "You're putting together a special operations squadron."

"Not a big leap, given I'm working with the Special Purpose Branch," Mason said.

"Special operations are about as high a risk profession as one could ask for in the Space Forces," Dominic said.

"Does that worry you?"

"No, quite the opposite, actually. Seems far more exciting than waiting for Earth Fed to decide what to do with me. May I ask what the criteria are you're looking for?"

"Simple. Direct combat experience against the Cendies. You got more than your fair share defending Jupiter from their first invasion," Mason said. "And not being attached to any active squadrons."

"What do you need me to do?"

"You'll be leading my squadron's third flight. Spec Ops squadrons have four flights rather than three, like regular squadrons, so you'd be next in line behind my XO in the squadron's chain of command. You'll also have your pick of pilots to serve with you in your flight, pending my approval."

"There are some pilots in the 60th I'd like to keep flying with, if that's all right, sir."

Mason nodded. "I'd be more than willing to review who you have in mind."

Dominic pushed himself out of his seat. "Well, sir, when do we get started?"

∽

The last pilot to fill out the senior officers of Mason's squadron was not staying in the pilots' barracks. Instead, she was staying in the main hospital center of the Alpha Centauri Fleet Base, in the physical rehab section.

When Mason arrived, he found Flight Lieutenant Xelat Sabal on a treadmill, running at a brisk pace.

Her running form was strong and fluid, her breathing deep, but not labored, like the well-conditioned athlete she was supposed to be. One could be forgiven for wondering why someone in such good shape was undergoing physical rehab at all, if it were not for the fact that the legs sticking out from her loose Space Forces' regulation running shorts were a pair of matte-gray prosthetic legs. The legs moved like normal human legs, but every time her feet hit the ground, there wasn't the soft padding of flesh, but the hard thump of hardened plastic.

Her condition was directly related to why Mason was here to recruit her into the 77th. She had lost both her legs flying against the Cendies during their surprise attack against Jupiter. A bit of shrapnel had penetrated the cockpit of her Lightning and sliced off both her legs above the knee.

Flight Lieutenant Sabal had managed to not black out from her sudden amputation while her jumpsuit's inner gel layer sealed around the stumps. She then continued to fly her fighter, scoring one more kill against the Cendies before returning to her carrier when 10th Fleet retreated from Outer Sol.

Ever since, she had been at Alpha Centauri Fleet Base learning how to use her newly installed prosthetics. The Space Force's standard procedure for treating amputation was tissue regrowth but growing two whole legs would take eighteen months at minimum. So, Sabal had chosen to have prosthetics installed instead, and not the temporary kind for people waiting for tissue regrowth. Her new legs were the permanent kind, grafted directly onto the remains of her femurs, making her new legs just as strong as her old ones.

Sabal's pace slowed to a stop on the treadmill. Grabbing a towel hanging from the handlebars, she wiped the sweat from her brow, and turned around.

It was only then she noticed Mason.

Dropping the towel, she snapped to attention, her artificial ankles clicking together.

"At ease, Flight Lieutenant," Mason said.

She relaxed, but her expression was still contrite. "My apologies for not being ready for your arrival, sir. I had lost track of the time."

"You were busy breaking in your new legs," Mason said. "Nothing to be sorry for. How are they doing?"

"Thighs barely ache anymore," Sabal said. "Doctors say almost flight ready."

Mason nodded. "I talked to your doctor. He's had to order you to dial back on your conditioning because he was concerned you might injure yourself."

"There's a war on, sir. One that we're losing. I'd like to get back to the fight before it's over."

"Are you worried that you're not doing your part?"

"That would require me to care what anyone thinks, sir," Sabal said. "I just want to get back to doing my job."

"Which just so happens involves killing people and breaking their ships."

"Yes, sir."

"Well, I might have the job for you, Flight Lieutenant."

"You have an opening in your squadron that you want me to fill, sir?"

"As a matter of fact, I do. I'm looking for someone to take command of my fourth flight, and I'd like that to be you."

"May I ask which squadron and ship you're from, sir?"

"No ship currently. As for the squadron, we're still in the process of putting it together. If you accept my offer, you'll be part of the 77th Special Operations Fighter Squadron."

"Special operations? You're Special Purpose Branch?"

Mason nodded. "I am, Flight Lieutenant."

"Were you one of those pilots involved with recovering that battlecarrier out from under the noses of the Cendies?" Sabal asked. "Because I don't recall seeing your name included with the Void Knights."

"I wasn't a member of the Void Knights, Flight Lieutenant," Mason said. "And whatever involvement I might have had with *Independence*'s recovery would be classified."

"Fair enough, sir," Flight Lieutenant Sabal said. "Though I have to say, the Void Knights took a hell of a beating getting *Independence* away from the Cendies."

"You're right. A lot of Void Knights didn't make it out of Jovian space alive," Mason agreed. "What I'm offering you would also be extremely high risk."

"Lots of action?"

"Oh yes," Mason said.

"Well, where do I sign up?"

"We'll deal with that after you're discharged, Flight Lieutenant."

"That could be a while. Doctors seem more interested in fussing over me rather than giving me back my flight status so that I can get back to the war."

"I think I can pull some strings to get it expedited. Your first task won't need you in flying shape anyway."

"And what would that task be, sir?" Sabal asked.

"Choosing the pilots who will fill out your flight, Flight Lieutenant."

CHAPTER 3

Jessica woke up from her hibernation with ten standard gravities crushing her into her seat, far away from any of the falling Jovian stations.

<Sorry to wake you early, Lieutenant, but we have a problem.>

A window appeared in Jessica's HUD showing a squadron of ten Cendy fighters burning on an intercept course.

<I was really hoping they'd think three Lightnings weren't worth the trouble,> Jessica replied.

<If their pilots are anything like ours, they'd never give up the chance to rack up their kill scores if they can get away with it.>

<Any chance we can tell them we're not interested?>

<Speaking for yourself, of course, Lieutenant.>

<On your own time, Marbles. I have a mission that does not include getting into a scrap with Cendy fighters,> Jessica said.

<Well, the Cendies don't seem to share that sentiment.>

<More's the pity,> Jessica said. <I see we're still on approach to the Jovian stations.>

<We've still got a few minutes before the Cendies reach interceptor range.>

<Could we cut our braking burn, and instead do a shorter, harder braking burn when we get to the stations?> Jessica asked.

<We could, but the Cendies would still reach us about a minute before we could dock with the closest station,> Armitage replied. <I did the math before waking you up.>

<Any way we can delay the Cendies?>

<Giggles and Fumbles are more than willing to cover us while we dock,> Armitage said.

<Two against ten, that's not very good odds.>

<No, they're not, Lieutenant, but any fighter pilot worth their wings is more than willing to face those odds.>

<Very heroic, but you'll excuse me if I don't want to have the deaths of a couple of fighter pilots on my conscience.>

<You have an alternative in mind?>

<Not just yet but give me a moment and I'll think of something.>

The first step was to see if any of the stations would be willing to let a fighter do a combat docking. They were close enough to the stations for real-time communications, so she pulled up a window to see the nearest of the falling stations.

Some of the closer stations were starports, stations that specialized in handling cargo and passengers from starliners and starfreighters and handing them off to intra-system passenger liners and haulers. They would not be lacking docking facilities.

She looked over the nearest starports, and one stood out to her. Starport Armstrong, Mason's home station. Seemed as good as any to start.

<Starport Armstrong, this is Lieutenant Jessica Sinclair aboard Federal Lightning Lancer Four. We have hostile fighters on approach and request permission for a combat docking.>

Just a few seconds later, Jessica got a reply.

"Lieutenant Sinclair, this is Starport Armstrong STC. If you can get here ahead of the Cendies, you're cleared for docking."

Jessica would've jumped with joy if there hadn't been 10gs pulling down on her. <Thank you, Starport Armstrong, we'll take care to get there before the Cendies catch us.>

<We will, Lieutenant?> Armitage queried. <I hope you have a plan to manage that.>

<We don't need to fight the Cendies, just delay them. Right?> Jessica said. <If our escort were to launch all their interceptors at extreme range, and then bug out, you think that could work?>

<Those interceptors won't kill anything, but they might do the job

of holding the Cendies off until we reach Starport Armstrong,> Armitage said. <Have you ever felt 18gs before?>

<I have the same g-rating you do, Marbles,> Jessica reminded her.

<But you've never actually been in a Lightning during an emergency burn before, have you?>

<First time for everything, Marbles.>

<Well, that's encouraging. You better brace yourself, Lieutenant. It's not going to be pleasant,> Marbles warned. <Giggles, Fishtail, I've got orders for you.>

<We're listening, Marbles,> Giggles said.

<You two are going to dump your interceptors and then bug out. Don't get into a furball. If either of you dies heroically, I will take your posthumous medals and melt them down into paper weights. Is that clear?>

<Crystal, Marbles,> Giggles said, <moving to engage.>

The long-burn drives on Giggles' and Fishtail's Lightnings flared and the fighter accelerated away until they were just a pair of bright stars against the black of space.

At the same time, Armitage cut her long-burn drives, leaving her Lightning in freefall. The weight pressing down on Jessica vanished, and for a moment, she had trouble telling which way was down.

<So, what now?> Jessica asked.

<Now we wait and see if those two get the job done,> Armitage said.

Giggles' and Fishtail's Lightnings burned directly for the incoming Cendy fighters. Seeing the attacks, the Cendy squadron adjusted their vector to engage the approaching Federal fighters.

At the very moment relative velocity and distance allowed for a fire solution, Giggles and Fishtail launched all eight of their interceptors, and they immediately flipped and burned. Their long-burn drives flared with emergency power as both Lightnings fought to redirect their vectors away from the Cendies.

The Cendies scattered to evade, firing their own retaliatory interceptors towards the Lightnings.

As predicted, the Federal interceptors, firing at the edge of their engagement envelope, failed to hit anything. The Cendies didn't even need to expend any of their own interceptors to deal with them.

But the brief battle had bought time—enough, Jessica hoped, for her to reach Starport Armstrong before the Cendies could get a firing solution.

For several minutes, Armitage drifted her Lightning at high speed towards Starport Armstrong. The incongruity of being in a high-speed pursuit while being completely still from her frame of reference was not lost on her.

<Hang on, I'm about to ignite the drives at emergency power. Clench your teeth so you don't bite off your tongue,> Armitage advised.

<Noted.> Jessica clenched her teeth.

<Here we go!>

Violent acceleration crashed down on her with a blunt force that brought up unpleasant memories of the moment she had been run over by that automated garbage truck. Her lips stretched taut and her eyeballs sank into their sockets. The tight bun she'd put her hair into felt like it had a lead weight inside it.

And it hurt, a full-body ache that felt like she had fine needles being driven into her by a sadistic acupuncturist. She ended up switching her pain receptors off entirely to spare her any more discomfort. How the hell did Mason put up with this?

The Cendy fighters were gaining rapidly as the acceleration of Armitage's braking burn added to their own acceleration. But on the maneuvering display, the flight AI calculated they would, just barely, arrive before the sphere of the Cendies' firing envelopes overtook them. Jessica hoped that Armitage was good at docking in a hurry.

<Lancer Four on final approach. You guys better have the doors open for us!> Armitage said over a tightbeam towards Starport Armstrong.

"We're ready for you, Lancer Four," Starport Armstrong STC replied.

<Cutting the drives in three…two…one!>

The g meter dropped to zero in an instant. Jessica didn't feel the sudden transition to microgravity, but just imagining it caused her artificial stomach to twist. Something she never knew was possible until that moment.

Starport Armstrong was still hurtling towards them at a comparatively slow, but still dangerous, velocity.

<We're approaching rather fast, aren't we?> Jessica asked.

Starport Armstrong STC piped in to echo her concerns. "Lancer

4, you're approaching well above maximum safe docking velocity. Slow down now."

<No time for a slow dock, Armstrong STC. I'll bring my bird to a stop before I hit anything,> Armitage replied. <And no back-seat driving, Lieutenant.>

"Lancer 4, lower your approach vel–"

<Did you just cut him off?> Jessica asked.

<He was distracting me,> Armitage said.

Starport Armstrong's northern docking bay barreled towards them like the maw of some great space-faring beast about to swallow their tiny strikecraft in one gulp.

The Cendies continued to burn inexorably towards interceptor range.

Armitage's Lightning passed through the entrance to the docking bay. The speed at which the walls of the docking bay flew by gave Jessica an emphatic reminder of just how fast she was going.

And then Armitage fired the fighter's maneuvering thrusters. Exhaust from the long-burn drives would've incinerated the interior of the docking bay, but the maneuvering thrusters were far cooler.

They were by no means gentle, however. As Armitage's Lightning came to a hard stop, the blast from the maneuvering thrusters blew through the docking bay like a hurricane, blowing ablative panels off the station's interior and rocking the station's internal cranes and docking arms in their mounts.

Then, Armitage cut the maneuvering thrusters, leaving her Lightning motionless just a few meters short of the back end of the docking bay.

"Now I know why you're called Marbles. You clearly lost them a long time ago," Jessica said.

"No, Lieutenant," Armitage said. "I never had them in the first place."

CHAPTER 4

Mason stood before the assembled pilots of Osiris Squadron, his squadron, ready to conduct his first briefing with the Special Purpose Branch's newest spec ops fighter squadron.

They weren't going to like their new assignment; he sure didn't.

"Our first mission will be a two-day flight down to Liberty, where we'll land at Akira Planetary Base. I'm sure you all have questions."

"Yeah, Hauler. Last I checked, there weren't any Cendies down that way," Sabal said.

"You're right. We'll be spending a week on Liberty doing refresher training for air-to-ground combat," Mason said. "We'll also have some familiarization training done on a new toy the Special Purpose Branch is going to give us."

"Air-to-ground?" Dominic queried. "That would imply we're going to bomb someone."

"Yes," Mason said.

"Did we find a Cendy planet or something?" Dominic persisted. "I thought they don't do planets."

"If that's changed, no one's told me about it," Mason said. "All I know is that this is our next assignment. I don't yet know why they decided they need us to go planetside to train at bombing things."

"Well, this isn't as exciting as I thought Spec-Ops' flying was going to be," Dominic said.

"It will only be a week," Mason said. "After that, I suspect we'll be headed to wherever the Special Purpose Branch wants us to bomb. I'm sure it will prove plenty entertaining for you when we get there, Silverback."

"Well, at least Liberty's northern hemisphere will be lovely this time of year," Dominic said.

"Don't think anyone's going to get a lot of time to enjoy the nice weather. Once we're down on Liberty, the only times we won't be with our fighters is when we're sleeping or eating," Mason said.

∽

Mason shut down the long-burn drives and flipped his Lightning around to meet Liberty's atmosphere head-on.

The thousands of lakes that dotted the planet glistened with sunlight as Mason flew towards the sunrise. Liberty had no oceans, just millions of lakes fed by countless twisting rivers. The land below was covered in a molted green and brown carpet of genetically engineered plant-life that kept the planet habitable. Akira Planetary Base was visible from space as a dark gray patch on the shore of Lake Akira, the second largest lake on the planet.

His Lightning shuddered as it hit the first wisps of atmosphere. He had entered the atmosphere at just under three times the speed of sound, slow enough not to cause the shock heating of a ballistic entry. Retrorockets fired, pulling him forward as he worked to keep his fighter from gaining more speed on descent through the atmosphere.

The retrorockets stopped as soon as he hit the stratosphere and the air became thick enough to slow the fighter through drag alone.

As they descended, he trimmed his fighter for atmospheric flight and switched his engines to airbreathing mode. Control surfaces along the wings unlocked and started to flutter to keep the fighter stable while intake vents opened to feed supersonic air into turbines that directed the air into heating elements around the fighter's reactors, superheating the air and spewing it out the back to generate thrust. The sound of the turbines was a soft whine, as opposed to the harsh growl of the long-burn drives.

"Akira ATC, this is Osiris Leader, my squadron is atmospheric and descending towards you. Request landing clearance."

"Clearance granted, Osiris Leader. Follow the pattern to Runway 27."

"Roger that, Akira ATC, Osiris Squadron entering landing pattern."

Behind him, fifteen other Lightnings trailed in a snake over a hundred kilometers long, with his fighter the head of the snake.

The landing pattern was a wide spiral that circled around the base, starting five thousand meters above the eastern end of the base and ending on the ground at the western end of the base's main runway.

Mason slowed to subsonic speeds before entering a lazy left-hand turn, spiraling down a thousand meters with every loop around the base. After the fifth loop, he lined up with the runway, flaps extended to their landing configuration and undercarriage lowered. Flying low and slow, his fighter felt like it was floating through the air as he approached the runway.

Just before touchdown, he idled the engines and pulled up the nose to flare the fighter, slowing down his descent until his wheels kissed the runway with only the slightest squeak. The flight AI deployed the airbrakes, and Mason tapped the wheel brakes to slow down enough to turn off onto the first exit to the taxiway, clearing the way for Osiris 2 behind him.

The rest of Osiris Squadron circled above, Osiris 16 entering the top of the spiral just as Mason rolled off the runway. Rolling to the parking area, he followed the guidance of a spacer waving a pair of glowing batons toward an empty corner of the tarmac.

Once stopped, he killed the turbines and shut down the reactors. Osiris 2 was pulling up just as he popped open the cockpit, the shrill whine of the idling turbines buzzing in his ears.

Climbing down, Mason traded salutes with the senior ground crew before taking position in front of his fighter as he waited for the rest of his fighters to park, keeping his helmet on, both to protect his ears from the deafening turbines and to ease his anxiety at being outside without anything overhead to keep the air from being sucked out into space.

Once Osiris 16 pulled up, Mason had a row of huge aerospace fighters dwarfing the people standing around him. Despite flying Lightnings for the better part of a decade, he didn't often get a chance to appreciate the scale of the things. Down on the ground with their wings folded up, the fighters loomed large in front of Mason.

Most of his pilots started popping their helmets off, though Mason continued to keep his on; he intended to keep it on until he got inside.

"All right, folks. Hit the showers and get something to eat. This will be our only day off before we start training in earnest tomorrow."

"No rest for the weary, eh, Hauler?" Zin said as she passed.

"Nope," Mason said and proceeded to walk towards the pilots' barracks a few hundred meters off the flight line.

Once inside, Mason finally popped the seals on his helmet and pulled it off. Airconditioned air washed over his face, cooling the thin layer of sweat covering his skin. He proceeded to his assigned quarters, marked down helpfully by his brainset.

Inside was a bare room with a cot, a desk, a small kitchenet, and, most important of all, a private bathroom with a shower.

He commanded his hardsuit to open, and it broke apart, pulling itself off his body and letting him slip out the back. Unzipping his jumpsuit, Mason wasted no time in washing the last two days of space flight off him.

※

"Today will be familiarization training," Mason said. "We'll be taking turns by flight blowing up wrecked vehicles on the shooting range on the far west side of the base. Your loadouts have already been selected."

Flight Lieutenant Sabal scoffed. "Holly hell, Hauler, how did you convince the bean counters to give us so much ordinance for training?"

"Look again, Hardball. Most of the stuff you're carrying will be dummy loads. I want everyone to get used to flying bombed-up Lightnings in atmosphere. Each fighter will have just one fully loaded Atlatl pod and two scimitars mounted on the internal launchers."

"Ah," Sabal said, deflating a bit. Clearly, she had been excited at the prospect of carrying enough ordinance to take out an armored division.

"Hauler, I noticed that some of the Atlatl pods are filled with simulated Skylances," Zin said. "Are we going to engage in air-to-air training?"

"Lightnings usually carry anti-air ordinance while flying ground attack, Shutdown," Mason responded.

"That doesn't answer my question, sir."

"Your point?" Mason said. "Get suited up. Takeoff is in ten minutes."

※

Federal Space

Mason pulled on the stick and his Lightning lifted off the runway. He could feel every last kilo of both dummy and real mentions loaded inside the weapons bay and hanging off the wings.

Minutes after taking off, the rest of Osiris Squadron formed around him as he orbited the planetary base, dividing into four flights of four Lightnings apiece.

Though well outside the paved expanse of the main base itself, over a thousand square kilometers of the land around the base was owned by the Space Forces for use in air-to-ground training.

Mason turned toward the first waypoint, flying directly for the shooting range several hundred kilometers away. They crossed over Lake Akira, and over vast expanses of unoccupied land. The whole area had been used as a live-fire ground for the Space Forces for two hundred years and bore the scars of thousands of mock battles. Craters and rusted hulks of vehicles littered the ground below.

As they came within two hundred klicks of the shooting range, they entered the range of the Scimitar cruise missiles.

"Osiris Squadron prepare standoff launch. I'm uploading targets to the datalink," Mason ordered. "Fire on my mark."

Each pilot got a target. It was simple matter of using the coordinates provided to lock a target into the guidance system of their cruise missile and launch.

Mason selected his own target, a simple bullseye painted into the side of a hill.

"Fire!" Mason said as he hit the release button on his joystick.

The doors on the belly of his fighter swung open and the Scimitar missile fell out, firing its small jet engine a second after falling away and accelerating away from his Lightning.

Fifteen more missiles flew off in formation, quickly devolving into dots in the sky.

A minute later, the distant hillside flashed with the impacts of sixteen warheads. Mason would review the accuracy after the battle, but it seemed they were all on target. A good sign, but Scimitars, being standoff fire-and-forget missiles, were one of the easier air-to-ground weapons to use.

"All right, transition to secondary objective and prepare to practice some close air support," Mason said. "Fourth Flight will engage first while the rest provide overwatch. Then Third Flight will get their turn, followed by Second. My Flight will engage last."

"Roger that, Hauler," Sabal said. "Engaging targets."

Sabal took her flight low, her Lightnings splitting into pairs and separating until almost twenty kilometers separated them.

Their attack against the drone vehicles was fast and brutal. Each Lightning fired all six live Hammer air-to-ground missiles, and twenty-four ground drones were turned into flaming wrecks.

As Sabal's flight disengaged, the firing range reset, more drones rolling out of protected bunkers to act as prey for Dominic's flight.

After Zin's flight finished, the shooting range was awash with burning vehicle wrecks. Yet more drones rolled out to meet their fate and Mason took his flight low to launch their own attacks.

As Mason assigned targets to the pilots in his flight, the back of his mind was counting down to the little surprise he had waiting for the pilots doing overwatch above him.

"Contacts bearing 065 incoming fast," Zin said.

A dozen yellow wedges appeared on the tactical display, low-flying aircraft resolving against the clutter on the ground below.

The Lightnings on overwatch, on the other hand, were high and easy to spot against the empty sky.

Seconds after Zin announced the contacts, missile launches were detected, and the yellow contacts turned red as the combat AI reclassified them as hostile.

"Missile's incoming, going defensive!" Zin shouted. Her fighter turned hard towards the incoming missiles, as did the rest of the fighters on overwatch.

Mason shook his head. They were reacting like they were still in space.

They fired their own simulated Skylance missiles, most focused on the air-to-air missiles burning in on them. But where space combat gave you minutes to react against an attack, aerial combat gave only seconds.

Many simulated missiles were intercepted and destroyed, but the Lightnings that were foolishly relying on their own missiles to defend themselves were left vulnerable to the incoming missiles that escaped interception.

Thirty seconds after the first missile launch, ten Lightnings were marked as simulated kills.

By the time Mason aborted his attack run to join the rest of his squadron, it was too late. The overwatch fighters were knocked down for no losses by the attackers.

A few seconds later, Mason's fighter was "killed" along with the rest of his flight as the attackers launched another overwhelming wave of air-to-air missiles that closed the distance and wiped them out in a matter of seconds.

CHAPTER 5

A TREMOR RAN through Jessica's buttocks as the Lightning's maglocks secured the fighter to one of the docking pads of Starport Armstrong. The Lightning was the sole ship inside the otherwise empty and deserted docking bay. All the other docking pads were empty, and all the arms and cranes that surrounded all the pads were still.

Jessica was relieved when the docking pad started descending into the hangar beneath.

Once sealed, the hangar started to pressurize. As soon as the atmosphere was at Earth sea level, a hatch opened, and a group of station police officers in deep blue uniforms floated in.

A dozen of them. None carried guns, but Jessica could see collapsible batons and stunners clipped to their belts.

"Quite the welcome party," Armitage murmured.

"Indeed. Could you be a dear and pop open the canopy, Marbles?" Jessica asked.

"I think I can do that."

Air hissed as the slight pressure difference between the hangar and the fighter's cockpit equalized, and the canopy swung up.

Jessica hit the release on her seat restraints and floated out, crawling from handhold to handhold over the Lightning.

"You the pilot?" asked one of the officers, a bald, dark-skinned man with a full beard and calm eyes. His name tag had Omenuku written on it.

"No, I'm the passenger." Jessica jerked a thumb over her shoulder. "The pilot's back there in the cockpit. Could I speak with someone official?"

"I'm the chief of police on this station. That count?" Omenuku said.

"It's a start," Jessica said.

"Well, good for you. The mayor wants to speak with you. I'm here to get you to her without causing much of a fuss," Chief Omenuku said.

"How would my presence cause much of a fuss?" Jessica asked.

"That fighter behind you is the only functioning spacecraft on this station, and there are a lot of people who want to get off."

"It'd be kind of a tight fit," Jessica said.

"That won't stop some people from trying. Come. There's a private elevator that will take you to the government center without having to cross through any public corridors. We use it for VIP visitors."

"I'm flattered," Jessica said. "You coming, Marbles?"

"If it's all right with you, I'd rather stay with my fighter."

"Got it." Jessica nodded to Omenuku. "My pilot wishes to stay with her fighter."

"I've no issue with that. The fewer Federal officers I need to babysit the better."

Half the police officers, including Chief Omenuku, gathered around her and followed her out of the hangar with the remainder staying with Marbles' Lightning.

The corridor was deserted, save for the police officers guarding every intersection to make sure Jessica's approach to the spin hub was safe. They passed through a hatch and stopped in front of a slowly moving wall with rows of windows that looked like a train coming into a station but was actually a bulkhead separating the rotating inner ring of the station's northern habitat ring from the non-spinning spine of the station.

Jessica reached out and grabbed a railing that ran along the side of the wall and let the rotation pull her away. The miniscule spin-gravity pulled her feet to the deck while the police escort followed behind her.

Through another hatch, and Jessica found herself in an elevator lobby with two more police officers guarding it.

"We'll be taking the middle elevator, Lieutenant," Chief Omenuku said.

They squeezed into the surprisingly small elevator, with barely enough room for Jessica to stand in the middle of the elevator without touching the six officers surrounding her. The doors closed, and the elevator started to climb up one of the habitat ring's four spokes.

Jessica arrived inside another elevator lobby, like the one she had seen before, complete with police guards. The only difference was the full standard gravity pulling her down.

Taking a step forward, Jessica stumbled, and would've hit the deck if the officers hadn't caught her.

"Are you all right, Lieutenant?" Chief Omenuku asked.

A quick diagnostic revealed the problem. One of the sensors used to control her balance was off, probably a result of the heavy-gs Jessica had just experienced. She reset the sensors and felt herself become immediately steadier.

"Apologies. I'm still recovering from the hard-burn it took to get here," she said.

"You did seem like you were in quite the hurry," Chief Omenuku said.

"I am," Jessica said. "Where's the mayor?"

"Right here, Lieutenant," said a tall, attractive, middle-aged woman. "Mayor Ari Delois, at your service." She held out a slender hand.

Jessica took it and gave it a firm shake. "A pleasure, Mayor Delois."

"You seemed in quite the rush to get here, Lieutenant."

"Yes, well, you're the first people with direct experience of talking with the Cendies that I've had a chance to talk to. Didn't want any intel you have to go stale," Jessica explained.

"So, you're just here to debrief us—is that it, Lieutenant?"

"I'm afraid so," Jessica said. "Though I'm certain the Earth Federation is organizing a rescue operation as we speak."

"I know, I've been in communications with Federal Station since we regained control of our communications systems," Mayor Delois said. "Seems they intend to evacuate us."

"And that's good, right?"

"Lieutenant Sinclair, I know Starport Armstrong may seem like just another space station to you, but to me and my constituents, it's our home. Evacuation means abandoning it to drift off into the void."

"Maybe it'll be salvaged later," Jessica suggested.

"Maybe," Mayor Delois said, her tone far from sanguine. "But that's not your problem. You want to know what we know about the Ascendency. Well, you're in luck, I got a chance to get to know Emissary Jerome quite well."

"Is that the same one who did all the interviews after the invasion?"

"The same."

"And what can you tell me about him?"

"He's extremely well read."

"Define 'extremely'."

"He has apparently read every piece of literature that we torture our students with in secondary school. Everything from the Epic of Gilgamesh to Neil Gupta's Chronicles of the General War."

"That's… comprehensive."

"For the most part, though it's clear he did not have access to more recent works," Mayor Delois said.

"How recent are we talking?" Jessica asked.

"Chronicles was published in 2695, shortly after the founding of the Earth Federation. As far as I could see, he had not read anything published after 2700."

Jessica's artificial heart skipped a beat. "Oh, that's brilliant!"

Mayor Delois cocked an eyebrow. "And that would be why?"

"I know when the people who created the Cendies left Federal Space, or at least the span of time that they did," Jessica said.

"Belts and zones!" Mayor Delois muttered, using the trademark Jovian expression. It reminded Jessica of Mason who was fond of the term. Not for the first time, she remembered how much she missed him.

"There weren't that many major colony efforts at that time," the mayor went on. "The solar system was still recovering from the devastation of the General War."

Jessica cleared her throat and focused on the task at hand. "I'll need to pass this on to the Special Purpose Branch down orbit. They can scan through all the known colony expeditions at the end of the 27th century. I'll have to ask you not to speak about Emissary Jerome's reading habits."

"I'll be circumspect." She sighed. "I take it you'll be departing soon?"

"Not that your station isn't lovely, but I am in a hurry," Jessica said.

"The sooner I pin down out who made these bastards, the sooner we can figure out where they've come from."

"Well, be sure to pass on one thing when you speak with your superiors," Mayor Delois said.

"That is?"

"Emissary Jerome showed me the Space Forces' attack to recover that starship they had stashed away down on Amalthea."

"Is that a problem?"

"That Earth Fed worked to recover a warship instead of liberating their people? Almost certainly for others, but not for me. I had a different concern," Mayor Delois said. "I know Earth Fed doesn't have enough fuel left to both recover my people and keep the 1st Fleet fueled."

Jessica shrugged, though she had come to the same conclusion. "I'm not sure what I can say about that."

"You don't have to say anything," Mayor Delois said. "Safe travels, Lieutenant. I hope Earth Fed has something up its sleeve to counter the Cendies' current move. Otherwise, my peoples' freedom from their occupation may prove brief."

Jessica nodded and left the mayor's office.

Upon returning to the hangar, Marbles' Lightning was waiting. She found the pilot still in the cockpit waiting for her.

"That didn't take long," Marbles said.

"Got what I needed," Jessica said as she climbed back into the cockpit.

"So where to now, Lieutenant?"

"Earth."

"We'll need to refuel if we want to make it there with a cruising burn."

"I'll see if I can't arrange an in-flight refueling," Jessica said. "At least this will take us further from Cendy territory."

"A shame too," Marbles said. "I'm not much for flying passengers."

"And there I was thinking I was good company." Jessica locked herself into her seat and inspected her restraints to make sure she was ready for a high-g flight. "Well, chop-chop. We only have the fate of humanity resting on us."

CHAPTER 6

BEING AMBUSHED AND killed to the last was probably not the way any of his pilots thought their first live-fire mission as special operations pilots would end.

The flight back to Akira Planetary Base was silent save for the bare minimum of chatter between pilots and Akira's air traffic controllers. Flying above and behind them were the twelve sleek T-1011 trainer jets that had killed them.

One by one, they landed on the main runway at Akira Planetary Base, Mason being the last.

The T-1011s landed while Osiris Squadron parked their Lightnings.

As Mason climbed out of his cockpit, Zin approached, her helmet held at her hip, and her face sporting a deep frown.

"Squadron Leader, sir," Zin said as Mason's feet hit the tarmac, using the stiffly formal tone of voice she used with superiors she was annoyed with. Which, for the first time in his life, was him.

"Yes, Zin?"

"Could I have a word in private?"

"Follow me to my office."

"Yes, sir."

Entering his office in the pilots' barracks, Mason popped off his helmet and placed it gently on the desk. In the visor he could see Zin's disgruntled reflection.

"Permission to speak freely, sir," Zin asked.

Mason turned around to face her. "Granted."

"What the fuck was that, Mason?"

"Training, Zin," Mason said.

"Training? You arranged to have us bounced by an aggressor squadron without telling us and you call that training? What exactly were we supposed to learn from that?"

"How deficient we are in air-to-air combat, Zin," Mason said. "After flight school, we don't do much air-combat training. I looked back in the training logs of all our pilots. You know how many flight and sim hours were spent doing air combat?"

"Not a lot, I'm guessing," Zin said.

"Less than five percent," Mason said. "Earth Fed goes to all that trouble teaching us how to fly in atmosphere, and then doesn't make sure we maintain those skills."

"Can't say I like how you went about making that point," Zin said.

"It worked."

"Yes, and now your pilots won't trust you."

"They'll get over it," Mason said.

"Really? And how long did it take you to forgive commanding officers who pulled shit like you just did?" Zin asked.

"Fair point," Mason said. "It's a good thing I have an XO my pilots do trust."

"I'm glad you have so much faith in me, Mason. But I think you're going about this wrong," Zin said.

"I respect your opinion, but my point still stands. Our pilots, when faced with air-to-air combat, tried to fight like they were in space. That got them killed fast, by craft that are far less capable than Lightnings."

"I would say that the conditions were artificial," Zin said.

"I disagree. The conditions were quite realistic," Mason countered. "I know from experience that the Cendies like to attack at the worst possible times."

"Mason, in real life, those fighters would be spotted from orbit. We'd have ample warning before they arrived."

"Zin, that assumes we have orbital superiority. And I think you're underestimating how hard it is to detect and track low-flying aircraft, even from orbit. Atmospheres are very good at concealing things."

"You don't know if the Cendies will do that. Hell, we don't even know if their fighters are rated for atmospheric flight!"

"But we don't know that they're not, or if they have specialized combat aircraft."

"You can't prepare us for everything, Mason."

"No, but I can patch the holes in our skillsets before we're deployed to wherever the hell Federal Command intends to send us."

"Am I interrupting something?" a woman in a black jumpsuit enquired. She was a slender woman of average height, with short brown hair.

"Not at all, Crash. I was just discussing the mission with my XO before we debrief the rest of the squadron," Mason replied. "Zin, this is Squadron Leader Mary Landing, 20th Training Squadron. She's the newest instructor down here."

Zin turned and took Landing's hand in a gauntleted hand. "I've heard of you, sir. You were part of the 4th Special Operations Fighter Squadron."

"What was left of it," Landing said. "And just call me Crash. My skin crawls every time someone 'sirs' me."

Zin smiled. "Understood, Crash. Your squadron was quite efficient in killing us."

"Yeah, I shared Hauler's doubts about his pilots' air-to-air skills. We got so good at killing things in space that we forgot how to fly where things like lift and drag are an issue."

"Apparently," Zin said. "So, I take it you will be helping rectify that problem?"

"That's right," Landing said. "I've got a vested interest in making sure the squadron that takes the 4th's place is up to spec. So, my fellow instructors and I are going to be working with your pilots for the next week. By the time the Special Purpose Branch ships you off to whatever hellhole they intend toi, the 77th Squadron will be the finest air-combat pilots in the Space Forces."

"I hope there won't be any more ambushes," Zin said.

"Not until after my people teach yours how to properly react to getting bounced," Landing said. "First thing's going to be re-teaching them proper atmospheric missile-evasion tactics."

◈

The next few days were hour upon hour of flying Lightnings against T-1011s, re-learning the ins-and-outs of atmospheric missile evasion.

Trying to shoot down an air-to-air missile while in was a recipe for suicide. There wasn't enough time to attempt to shoot down incoming missiles.

That didn't mean air-to-air missiles were harder to defeat; they just required a different technique.

The missile alarm sounded in Mason's ears as soon as a pair of Landing's T-1011s flew over the ridge of a mountain and launched a salvo of virtual missiles at his real Lightning.

Mason fired a pair of Skylances at the T-1011s before flipping his fighter over and pulling hard on the stick to get his nose pointed towards the ground.

The Lightning shuddered and its frame groaned as aerodynamic forces attempted to rip his wings off in the 10g turn.

Mason could feel the air grow thicker as it plummeted down to the deck, the incoming missiles adjusting their course to try to intercept his fighter, driving themselves even deeper into the thick air, quickly draining the energy imparted by the brief burns of their solid-fuel motors.

Pulling up, Mason leveled out his Lightning a hundred meters above the ground, roaring over the rough ground at just above the speed of sound, flying laterally into the path of the missiles. His combat AI dropped them off the threat board as their energy became too low for them to intercept his fighter. The virtual missiles arched down and impacted the ground, disappearing from the tactical display.

Mason turned back towards the T-1011s, who had similarly dodged his missiles. He locked more Skylances, and fired, depleting the virtual stores of the Atlatl pods on top of his wings. The T-1011s moved to evade, and his combat AI's estimated kill probability plummeted, but the missile attack wasn't to try to kill them but to put them on the defensive.

Mason opened the throttle and quickly gained altitude. His fighter's chief advantage against the T-1011s was raw power. Low and slow, the tiny trainer jets would fly circles around his massive aerospace fighter.

He needed to keep his speed up and maintain his energy advantage.

Leveling out at 10,000 meters, Mason depleted another Atlatl pod, sending another six Skylances burning down towards the T-1011s.

The two jets evaded again, forcing Mason's missiles to chase them through the thick air below, wasting their energy.

But it kept them low while Mason set up his attack.

Flipping his Lightning over, he turned and drove his fighter towards the lead trainer jet.

The T-1011 had just started to regain altitude after dodging Mason's missile, igniting its afterburner to climb as fast as possible. Mason lined up his nose with an icon ahead of the trainer and squeezed the trigger.

His fighter buzzed with simulated firing of his main gun, and the combat AI registered a fatal hit on the T -1011. Mason pulled up and rocketed straight up faster than the leader's wingmate could keep up.

Two more missiles rocketed up after him, but Mason kept climbing at full throttle.

The missiles gained on him for several seconds after burning out their motors, but while his Lightning could fight gravity indefinitely, the missiles could not. A couple of hundred meters short of his tail, they slowed to a lower speed than his fighter and fell back to Liberty's surface.

Mason pulled on his stick, topping out in the stratosphere before diving back down on the last "live" T-1011. The little trainer jet's pilot had elected not to follow him, staying low and fleeing into the mountains to try to bait him into a low and slow dogfight against which Mason's Lightning would be all but helpless.

Pulling back his throttle to keep from over speeding as he hit the thick air of the lower altitude, he dived on the maneuvering T-1011.

The trainer jet turned towards him while he tried to line up a gun shot, and Mason was flying too fast to bring his gun to bear before the trainer shot past him. Rather than turn to try to get on the T-1011's tail, Mason gently pulled his fighter out of its dive and kept his engines throttled up, opening the distance to the trainer while it turned to get on his tail; but it didn't have the speed to follow him up.

No missiles came chasing Mason; the trainer had expended its light load of virtual Skylances. All it had was the virtual gun that the trainer jet didn't really have.

Mason turned and dove on the T-1011 again, and again the trainer jet turned towards him to evade, but Mason anticipated the maneuver. He opened his Lightning's airbrake and his fighter trembled as its brake bit into the air.

Lowering his fighter's flaps to get extra lift and using his fighter's thrust-vectoring for all it was worth, he forced the nose of his fighter ahead of the trainer jet for the barest second and the combat AI let off a short burst from his cannon.

The trainer jet "died" as a stream of virtual bullets merged with it.

Leveling out, the T-1011's pilots wiggled her wings to salute his victory. Mason took up position next to her and wiggled his wings back at the aggressor pilot.

"That was some inspired flying, Mason," Zin said after he returned from his own simulated combat. It was only two days since the 77th's embarrassing defeat at the hands of Squadron Leader Landing's aggressor squadron, yet they were already getting the better of the aggressor pilots as they refreshed their skills on properly using a Lightning in air combat.

Half the squadron was still in the air, each pilot going up against a pair of aggressors to put their skills to the test.

So far, the results had been encouraging. Tomorrow, they'd be doing the same against ground-based missiles. After that, the rest of the week would be focused on reteaching his pilots on the particulars of dropping bombs and launching air-to-ground missiles.

"Thanks, Zin," Mason said. "I'm sure I'd feel proud of myself if my brain wasn't mush."

"Starting to get sick of the training?" Zin asked.

"Yeah, I should complain to the squadron's CO," Mason said. "Oh wait, that's me."

"Go to the officer's lounge and take a break, Mason," Zin said. "I can keep an eye on our pilots as they come back in. It's pretty much just debriefings and chow for the rest of the day."

"Thanks, Zin, I think I'll do that."

After a shower and a change into a fresh uniform, Mason headed to the officers' lounge in the barracks.

He found Squadron Leader Landing sitting at the table, dark circles under her eyes as she nibbled on a donut with minimal enthusiasm.

"You look like I feel, Crash," Mason said as he sat down with his coffee.

"If you think what you're doing is hard, you should try aggressor training," Landing said. "At least you and your pilots will get to put those skills to use against the Cendies."

"It already eating at you?" Mason asked. "It hasn't been that long."

Landing grunted. "Long enough. I was a spec-ops pilot for three years with the 4th. Never happier in my career. I was looking forward to the day I'd get to lead my own special ops squadron. Instead, I get to lead an aggressor squadron while a guy who was recruited to play truck driver gets his own special ops squadron." She grimaced at him. "I admit to being more than a little envious."

"Fair," Mason said. "I do appreciate your working so hard to get my people into shape."

"Well, given what I know of the Special Purpose Branch, you and your pilots are going to need all the help you can get," Landing said. "They don't assign their people to training just for giggles."

"Yeah," Mason said. "How ready do you think my pilots are?"

Landing shrugged. "I haven't the faintest fucking idea. They're good pilots. All of them. But I have no insights beyond the obvious about where they intend to send you. Frankly, it's bizarre that they'd send you down here to blow holes in the ground."

"You ever do atmospheric missions?" Mason asked.

"A few times, but never an Earth-like planet outside of training," Landing said. "Had a couple of missions in the atmosphere of gas giants to take out high-value targets like gas skimmers and aerostat stations."

"Well, given the nature of our training, I think we can rule out the Branch sending Osiris Squadron to ruin Cendy gas-mining infrastructure," Mason said. "Makes me even wonder if we're being sent against the Cendies."

"What makes you think that, Hauler?"

"As far as we know, the Cendies don't currently occupy any planets," Mason said. "So why would they be training us to bomb targets unless they intend to send us against someone who does have planets? Someone other than the Cendies."

Landing sighed. "Wouldn't be the first time the Branch sent us against someone we weren't at war with."

"Care to elaborate?"

"That's about all I can say on the matter," Landing said. "No offense, Hauler, but just because you're a part of the Special Purpose Branch doesn't mean I can share information that you don't need to know."

"I'm sure the Branch appreciates your discretion."

"I also don't want to spend the next decade inside a prison cell on Mercury. There are better places I can be than Sol's second shittiest planet."

"Fair enough." Mason took a long sip of his coffee, taking the time to think. "Of course, that presumes we manage to keep the Cendies out of Inner Sol."

"Call me an optimist," Landing said as she stood up from her seat. "I need to sleep. I suggest you do the same, Hauler. Get a good long rest while you still have the chance."

CHAPTER 7

Jessica's two-day flight from Starport Armstrong to Earth was not anywhere near as eventful as the flight from *Ankara* to Starport Armstrong had been. After transmitting her report down orbit, the analysts of the Special Purpose Branch had started searching for exosolar colony ships that had departed Sol in the five-year window between 2695 and 2700, suggested by the gap in Emissary Jerome's reading.

One colony ship came up unaccounted for. The conveniently named *Ascension*, built by Xia Spaceworks over Luna under the sponsorship of the Pinnacle Foundation.

Jessica pulled open a window of the SV *Ascension* and was surprised by the sheer scale of the vessel.

She was a 3000-meter-long cylinder, with drives at one end and an open front at the other. The tip of the drive keel protruded through the open front. According to the schematics, the open forward bay was a construction hangar. Behind that was a pair of contra-rotating internal centrifuges with enough living space to comfortably house the 500 colonists aboard her. Save for some cargo holds and hydroponics bays, the rest of *Ascension's* interior was taken up by fuel tanks. Enough to give the vessel a 200-light-year range using its star drive. Almost four times the range of a modern Federal warship. The people who built her were keen on getting as far away from Sol as possible. Given the time that the ship was built, she couldn't blame them.

The Earth Federation had only existed for twenty years when *Ascension* launched, formed in the aftermath of the devastating General War, when the old nations all but destroyed the solar system's orbital infrastructure and caused a sudden interruption in interstellar trade.

And the peace that came from the Earth Federation's founding was about to come to an end. Less than five years later, the Earth Federation would attack the newly formed League of Sovereign Systems and be soundly defeated at the First Battle of 61 Virginis.

Jessica barely noticed the drive cut, but she did notice the powerful force pressing down on her disappear.

<Are we there?> she asked.

<Ah, you're awake, Lieutenant,> Marbles said. <We're coasting into the docking bay of Ariane Orbital Gateway.>

Jessica patched into the external view and found herself floating high above the Earth in geo-stationary orbit. She saw a simple double-ring station with a cavernous docking on each end of the central axis. A multitude of intra-system haulers and trans-atmospheric shuttles were either lined up for docking or flying away from the station.

Armitage slipped past the queue of waiting spacecraft into the maw of the hangar. All around the interior of the cylinder were occupied docking pads. A moment later, she set her Lightning down on the docking pad and shut the fighter down.

"Last stop," Marbles said.

"Thank goodness." Jessica sighed as she unstrapped herself from her seat. Her artificial body didn't ache. But it would go numb and prickly after she had spent an extended period with her peripheral nervous system dialed down for comfort.

She wouldn't immediately dial it back up to normal. She had learned the hard way when she first had her brain transferred into an artificial body that the brain would quickly adapt to whatever sensitivity setting she set her body to, and so dialing it up too fast would result in her becoming overstimulated. Instead, she would slowly dial up to normal over the course of the day. In the meantime, she would just have to deal with feeling like she was moving through a tank of acceleration gel.

Marbles popped the cockpit and pushed herself out, floating towards the airlock adjacent to the docking pad. Jessica followed behind her, floating into the airlock and coming to a stop by the control panel. She hit the button on the control panel, and the outer hatch of the airlock swung shut.

Jessica popped off her helmet as soon as it was safe to do so and took a gulp of fresh station air. The air didn't feel any different, her senses were too dull for that, but she still savored the feeling of freedom in no longer being trapped inside a helmet.

Armitage popped off her own helmet, and Jessica was surprised to see a young woman under the black plates. Shimmering blue hair fanned out around her head in the zero gravity. She was significantly shorter than Jessica, shorter even than Jessica had been before she upgraded her height.

"Feels good to be out of this thing," Armitage said.

"No kidding. You've earned a leave, I think," Jessica said.

"If the powers-that-be would be so kind."

"I'll put in a good word."

"Much appreciated, Lieutenant."

"Jessica, please. I think after four days stuffed together inside a Lightning, we should be on a first-name basis, Sienna."

"I suppose that's fair, Jessica. Though only my mom calls me Sienna."

"Then you'll just be Marbles with me," Jessica said.

"Thanks, Jessica. So, what now?"

"Now? Now, Marbles, I have a meeting to go to."

◈

Armitage's docking with Ariane Orbital Gateway was not an arbitrary decision. The station was the first and last stop for Special Purpose Branch personnel traveling to and from Earth. Branch headquarters was on Federal Station itself, in the Earth-Sun L5, but the Branch had offices both in orbit and on Earth's surface.

Jessica passed through the security gate leading into the Special Purpose Branch offices and to the local commanding officer.

Captain Tiberius Adakai was a tall man in a Fleet-blue uniform like Jessica's. He had long black hair tied back in a ponytail and gray eyes.

"Lieutenant Sinclair, thank you for reporting in. I know you must be tired from your flight," he greeted her. "Please take a seat."

"Actually, I found the flight quite restful," Jessica said, sitting down. She only exaggerated slightly. She indeed had spent much of the flight asleep. But her body still needed time to recover.

"Perks of a prosthetic body," Captain Adakai said. "Well, our colleges down on Earth have done some digging into the history of the Pinnacle Foundation."

"Find any interesting nuggets, sir?" Jessica asked.

"Yes, one of the sponsors is still alive, after a fashion."

Jessica leaned forward. "Really, sir? Please explain."

"Miriam Xia, founder of Xia Spaceworks." Captain Adakai uploaded a data packet containing her dossier to Jessica.

She didn't need to read the dossier to know the basics about Miriam Xia. Xia Space Works was one half of what would become Earth Fed's largest starship builder, Xia-Macintyre Interstellar.

"Her dossier says right at the start she died in 2711," Jessica said.

"Her biological body died," Captain Adakai said. "She had a digital copy of herself created shortly before she passed away."

"I see. Where would I find this digital copy?"

"Singapore."

"Then I'll have to go down there to speak with her."

"That won't be straightforward. Her estate controls access to her digital consciousness, and they are not known for letting anyone other than her direct descendants speak with her. And even then, it takes a lot of convincing."

"Who represents the estate?"

"A big legal firm that specializes in representing the estates of digitized people. The Viduus Group."

"Have we contacted them?"

"Earth Fed's made a formal request while you were in-flight. They said no."

"Can't we force the issue?"

"Legally? Eventually, but the Viduus Group has a long history of tying up legal requests to speak with their clients for years."

"Years we don't have."

"No."

"So, the legal route is out. What about extra-legal?"

Captain Adakai sighed. "Well, that depends. Are you willing to engage in an off-the-books mission?"

"Sure, what's a little black op between friends?"

"I wouldn't be so flippant, Lieutenant," Captain Adakai said. "You get caught, you'll be disavowed by the Special Purpose Branch."

"Then I won't get caught," Jessica said. "What do I need to do?"

"Study up, Lieutenant. I understand that you're an electronic warfare specialist with some of the best hackware available. I'm sure with the intelligence we provide, you can figure something out. I do ask that you keep the number of people you work with to a minimum."

"I'll be discreet. When's the next flight down to Singapore?"

"It just so happens that there is a shuttle flight from Ariane to Singapore leaving inside the hour. That will get you down to Singapore at around 1300 local time."

"Best that I get going, then. What discretion do I have?"

"Full. Just don't get caught, Lieutenant. I'm afraid we have no get-out-of-jail-free cards available."

"Noted," Jessica said. "Just point me in the direction of the shuttle."

CHAPTER 8

AT THE CONCLUSION of their training at Akira Planetary Base, the assembled pilots of Osiris Squadron and Landing's aggressor squadron had a farewell party, holding a cookout near the flight line before the pilots of Osiris Squadron had to board their fighters and make the long hard flight back to Centauri Fleet Base.

Mason was glad to leave the base behind, though sad to say goodbye to Squadron Leader Landing. The way she stared at his fighters made it obvious that she wanted nothing more than to hop into one of them and join Osiris Squadron on whatever adventure the Special Purpose Branch had in mind for them.

But Landing was a hero, and Federal Command hated letting heroes die.

As he flew up orbit in a 10g cruising burn, Mason browsed over the latest news. The training on Liberty hadn't left much time for anything but the most cursory glances at the latest news coming out of Inner Sol.

Evacuation of the Jovian stations was starting in earnest. The 1st Fleet had sortied to guard the stations while everything from troop transports to civilian shuttles were swarming the stations, taking their inhabitants down orbit to either Earth or one of the thousands of habitats that filled the Earth-Sun L4 and L5 Lagrange points.

No effort was being made to save the stations themselves. The effort to slow them down into a stable orbit around the Sun would be too costly, even if Earth Fed wasn't experiencing a critical fuel shortage in Inner Sol.

The stations would be abandoned, the homes of twenty million Jovians left to drift off into space after swinging around the Sun. There was the possibility of salvaging the stations later, but that wasn't going to happen until after the war was over, and no one knew when that was going to be. Or if Earth Fed would be victorious.

At least his parents were safe, still aboard Alpha Centauri Fleet Base as far as he last knew, guests of the Federal Space Forces until they were given a chance to find a more permanent place to stay.

He couldn't see either his mom or dad deciding to settle down planetside. They were both born and raised Jovians; their total time spent on inhabited planets could be counted in hours. Mason suspected they'd head to Procyon, the only system in the Earth Federation with a totally space-based population. Procyon was like a larger version of the outer solar system with its population living in stations and habitats orbiting gas giants that had been infused with helium 3 and other valuable elements by Procyon's bright main star, and by the death of the B star when it evolved off the main-sequence eons ago. A pair of experienced hauler pilots like them would have little trouble finding work there.

As Osiris Squadron approached the end of their burn, Mason could make out details of the starships around the station. One starship was an enormous vessel that dwarfed the two fleet tenders flanking her. A cylindrical scaffold had been wrapped around the hull of the ship to aid in the repair of the damage she had taken when Mason had helped rescue her from the hidden base drilled into the icy rock of Amalthea where she had been built. She had been a secret weapon meant to take the League by surprise and turn the war decisively in the Earth Federation's favor.

But that was before the Ascendency showed up and turned the universe on its head.

"Osiris Squadron match my vector as I adjust course," Mason said.

"Is there a problem, Hauler?" Zin asked.

"Negative, Shutdown. I just want to get a closer look at *Independence* before we dock."

"Not above a little sightseeing are you, Hauler? I would advise not taking too much time. Your pilots won't appreciate delaying them from their hot showers, soft beds, and real food."

"Not to worry, Shutdown, it's just going to do one flyby," Mason said.

The flyby wasn't that close. Even for a squadron of Federal fighters, he had to keep his fighters outside of a hundred kilometers of *Independence* lest he annoy the destroyers guarding the warship.

But for a fighter designed to detect and track targets millions of kilometers away, a hundred kilometers was practically touching.

While the flight AI guided his fighter on approach to Alpha Centauri Fleet Base, Mason examined a magnified view of *Independence*. The scaffold only partly concealed the starship's hull; her lines were clear to see. She looked more a battleship than a carrier, with her sharply pointed armored nose and pair of super-firing turrets on the dorsal and ventral surfaces. The only hint that she wasn't simply a very large battleship were the dozens of large doors divided into two belts that wrapped around the hull behind the hidden habitat ring. Each door covered a hangar bay large enough to fit a full-sized strikecraft.

That was what made her so special. A single hull that combined the firepower and survivability of a battleship and the reach and flexibility of a carrier. And after the battering Earth Fed had taken during the Battle of Jupiter, losing the 9th Fleet's entire battle line, she went a small way towards filling the gap left by those lost ships.

The flyby of *Independence* also lined his squadron up with Alpha Centauri Fleet Base's Number 1 docking bay.

Like all fleet bases, Alpha Centauri Fleet Base was a twenty-kilometer-long armored cylinder that tapered at the ends. At each end was an open maw of a massive docking bay.

After receiving clearance to dock, Mason shut down his long-burn drives and coasted into the docking bay at an easy 20 meters per second. Using just his maneuvering thrusters, he matched the slow spin of the station and aligned to land on his assigned docking pad.

He touched down gently on the docking pad; his fighter held down by the light spin gravity. A wheeled tractor drone trundled onto the docking pad, unfolding a stout arm with a burly pincer on the end that clamped around the strut of the nose gear. The tractor rolled his Lightning off the docking pad, towards an airlock big enough for his fighter to fit inside. The tractor then disconnected from Mason's fighter and rolled out of the hangar before a large hatch closed to seal the hangar off from the vacuum of the docking bay. Air started seeping in at a rapid pace, and after a minute, the pressure outside his cockpit reached 1 atmosphere.

Mason popped open his cockpit and waited a moment for the inert gas that filled the cockpit to dissipate before popping his helmet off. He took in a deep breath of heavily filtered, recycled air, grateful to finally have something more substantive than dumb mass keep the air from being sucked out of his lungs. His favorite part of planetside assignments were their conclusions. For all the toil his squadron's visit to Liberty had involved, at least it had been brief.

Of course, given what they had been training to do—well, he hoped all the training was just for a simple airstrike. In and out without ever having to set foot on solid ground with the big empty sky looming above him.

Mason shuddered a little at the thought. He was a creature of space. Living on planets was for his long-dead ancestors.

<Zin, you docked yet?> Mason asked over a subvocal channel.

<Tractor just pulled me in, Hauler,> Zin replied. <What do you need?>

<See about getting the squadron squared away. I have a meeting with Colonel Shimura at the station's HQ building.>

<You think she has our mission ready for us?>

<That's what I'm about to find out.>

"Welcome back, Squadron Leader. I trust training went well down on Liberty?" Colonel Shimura asked.

"Yes, sir, though my pilots aren't exactly happy that the first thing they did as special forces pilots was to blow holes in the ground," Mason said.

"I imagine they're curious what that was all about."

"As am I, sir," Mason said.

"Well, you're in luck, Squadron Leader. After your training finished, I received our new marching orders directly from Admiral Moebius. We'll be embarking aboard FSFV *Amazon* in two days."

Even before the ship's information popped onto his HUD, he knew just by the name that she was an orbital assault ship, built for landing troops and equipment onto hostile planets. The information also told him that she was an old ship, a Spartan-class orbital assault ship that was in Alpha Centauri's mothball fleet.

At least until just recently.

Mason cocked an eyebrow. "Who are we invading, sir?"

Colonel Shimura shook her head. "No one yet. *Amazon*'s going to serve as a mobile base of operations for the duration of our mission."

"What happened to *Mervie*?" Mason asked.

"I don't know, Squadron Leader. She left the system shortly after we recovered *Independence*. Besides, *Mervie* doesn't have the capacity for all the personnel equipment that we'll be lugging along. Something an orbital assault ship has an abundance of."

"So does a carrier."

"Of which there aren't any available for the use of the Special Purpose Branch," Shimura said. "But a surplus assault ship should suit our mission just fine."

"And what mission is that, sir?"

"Defending the planet Triumph."

"Did I hear you right, sir?"

"Have you been struck by a sudden case of deafness, Squadron Leader?"

"No, sir," Mason said. "It's just I never thought I would be defending the capital world of the League. I thought we'd be taking part in driving the Cendies out of Outer Sol."

"We will be doing our part to oust the Cendies from Outer Sol, but not in Sol," Shimura said. "You should know by now that the Special Purpose Branch rarely goes about solving problems in the most direct fashion possible."

"So how does defending Triumph accomplish that, sir?" Mason asked.

"By securing a source of fuel for the Space Forces, while denying it to the Cendies."

"The League is going to share fuel with us?" Mason asked, incredulous.

Colonel Shimura nodded. "In exchange for our help in defending 61 Virginis, yes. Given the layout of the system, you have to control Triumph in order to control the part of the system that matters."

"Do we have intel on when the Cendies are going to attack Triumph?"

"Not precisely, but we've seen movements to suggest they're gearing up." Colonel Shimura gestured, and an icon appeared on Mason's HUD. "Here's the briefing package. It includes information taken from one of our reconnaissance ships examining systems close to League space."

Mason opened the package and browsed through the files to examine the reconnaissance ship's report. Information about what ship had gathered the intel was not included. But it did include the location of the system, and the Cendy ships gathering in it.

There were a lot of them. Over a hundred and fifty warships. Fusilier-class battlecruisers and Katyusha-class arsenal ships. Since recovering *Independence*, the Special Purpose Branch analysts had come up with code names referring to each new class of Cendy starship. There was also a smattering of utility ships. Freighters, tankers, and refinery ships needed to keep the fleet fueled.

There was also a single massive contact Mason had never seen before.

"What the hell is a Monolith?" Mason asked.

"A giant starship used by the Cendies. Beyond that, we can only speculate."

"What's the speculation, sir? More to the point, is my squadron going to have to deal with one of those when we're trying to keep Triumph from falling to the Cendies?"

"Maybe, Squadron Leader. Some analysts think it's a giant starfreighter the Cendies use to carry supplies. Others think it's an enormous capital ship."

"I will hope for the former then, sir."

"In any case, you're not likely to be dealing with a lot of Cendy space-based assets once we arrive on Triumph. Though I'm afraid there are even more unknowns involved with that."

"Like if the Cendies even bother with invading planets, sir?"

"Yes. There's a possibility that the Cendies will just bomb the planet before moving on down orbit to take the inner system's gas giants," Shimura said. "But we doubt that. Triumph's defenses are exceptionally resilient. Even if they sterilized the surface, there would still be a vast network of planetary defenses that they would have to contend with if they wanted to take the inner 61 Virginis system.

"Not to mention those Leaguers manning those defenses would be looking to get some revenge on the Cendies for glassing their homeworld," Mason said.

"Like I said, we believe a wholesale bombardment is improbable, if for no other reason than it wouldn't neutralize the planet as a threat. That would require a ground assault."

"How do we know that?" Mason asked.

"Because that's what we believe the Space Forces would have to do in order to take Triumph and neutralize its defenses."

"I don't think we have enough troopers to do that."

"We don't, but the Cendies might for all we know."

"I guess we'll find that out the hard way," Mason said.

"Learning the hard way is practically the Special Purpose Branch's motto, Squadron Leader."

"Sir, I do think I need to make the point that if the Cendies make a determined attempt to take Triumph, my squadron isn't going to be able to hold them off by ourselves."

"Osiris Squadron isn't expected to hold off the Cendies alone," Shimura said. "Your mission will be to help the League defenders on Triumph hold off the Cendies until Earth Fed can muster reinforcements."

"When will those reinforcements arrive, sir?"

"When they arrive, Squadron Leader."

"That's rather vague, sir."

"If you're looking for specifics, you're in the wrong industry."

"So, we're just going to roll with whatever punches the Cendies throw at us, sir?" Mason asked.

"That's why I wanted you to lead the 77th, Squadron Leader. I already know you can adapt to bad situations on the fly."

"Well, that's encouraging," Mason said. "So, what other assets will we bring?"

"A regiment of Raiders including Major Hauer's company." Shimura said. "*Amazon*'s holds are going to be stuffed to the gills with as much space and air-launched weaponry as possible. As well as some extra equipment. You won't be arriving on 61 Virginis lacking firepower, Squadron Leader."

"That sounds intriguing. What is some of that extra equipment?"

"We'll be bringing along an experimental weapon for your fighters,"

Shimura said. "As a special operations squadron, you get to field-test new toys."

"Like the Stiletto pods," Mason said.

"Correct. I will upload a data packet with information on some of the weapons and equipment that will be made available to your squadron."

"Guess I have some homework to do, sir," Mason said.

"Make it a cramming session, Squadron Leader. We're departing for Triumph inside of a week."

"Belts and zones, Colonel, I only just got my squadron together!" Mason protested.

"We're all scrambling, Squadron Leader. Fact is, the Space Forces has been on a timer ever since the Cendies decided to deorbit most of Jupiter's stations."

Mason sighed. "In that case, sir, I'd better get some coffee. I think I have some long nights ahead of me."

"You and me both, Squadron Leader, you and me both."

CHAPTER 9

THE SHUTTLE TOUCHED down on the wet runway at Changi Air and Space Port with a light squeak.

As the engines idled, the pitter-patter of raindrops against the shuttle's skin filled the passenger compartment. It was the middle of monsoon season in Singapore, and the world outside Jessica's small window was obscured by a wet mist.

She had dressed for the occasion. Leaving her uniform back in orbit, she had chosen a pair of snug black pants and a dark-gray jacket with matching shirt that well with her dark skin.

She was not on Earth as Lieutenant Jessica Sinclair, but under a false identity of her own creation. It was illegal for the Special Purpose Branch to conduct operations in Federal territory. That was the jurisdiction of the Federal Marshal Service, and the only thing they hunted with more zeal than foreign spies were domestic ones.

Wartime or not, if Jessica got caught, she would face a court-marshal and a long stay in one of the Earth Federation's more secure military prisons.

But she wasn't all that worried about getting caught. Infiltrating secure computer networks was exactly the kind of thing she was trained and built for, though she doubted anyone in the Special Purpose Branch thought she would use her training and hackware to attempt to get into the virtual domain of a dead woman's digitized consciousness.

Now, it was just a matter of getting to where she needed to go.

The shuttle pulled up to the terminal, and Jessica disembarked with the rest of the passengers, carrying just a small personal bag with her. She didn't have any special gadgets inside, just a change of clothes and toiletries. Most of the hardware she needed was in her body. And the rest would not be hard to source in a city as large and prosperous as Singapore.

A short train ride took her directly into downtown Singapore. Walking out of the train station, Jessica pulled up the hood of her jacket before walking into the heavy rain. She took a moment to enjoy the white noise of rainfall splattering against her hood. It had been a long time since she had experienced a good downpour. It brought back some of her more pleasant childhood memories, watching one of London's frequent rainstorms from the comfort of he bedroom window.It also gave rise to some unpleasant memories. She didn't normally like thinking about her childhood. Her parents' rejection of genetic engineering or modern cybernetics had left her trapped in a broken body for almost twenty years. She hadn't even been allowed a brainset and had had to wait till she came of age and could get one implanted regardless of her parents' wishes.

Jessica pushed the unhappy thoughts away, and the anger that boiled inside her. She was on a mission and dwelling on her childhood would do nothing to help it succeed. What would help was access to the network that connected to Miriam Xia's digital mind, and she had an idea for that.

To prevent wealth from being concentrated among a few immortal digital oligarchs, the Earth Federation had instituted the Rubicon laws, which separated the digital world from the biological. Digitized consciousness were treated as separate from the people who uploaded their minds, a legal and philosophical position helped by the fact that mind-uploading was non-lethal. Indeed, Miriam Xia didn't die until a week after uploading her mind.

Uploaded minds did have rights, but they were different from those of biologicals. They couldn't own real-world property, nor could they exercise any authority over biological people. For their part, biological people couldn't interfere with the goings on of digitized people. The two may as well exist in different universes, which was not far from reality. Most digitized minds, both as a matter of cost-savings and convenience, were heavily underclocked, experiencing time at one percent that of biological people by default.

Though Miriam Xia had been dead for over two hundred and fifty years, she had only experienced about two-and-a-half years since she was uploaded, which, Jessica hoped, meant that her memories would be fresh. It was just a matter of connecting to her and clocking her up to normal time. She couldn't underclock her brain to Miriam's frame of reference.

Before departing Arianne Gateway, Captain Adakai had given her access to a preset crypto-currency account filled with various denominations popular with Earth's underworld.

She stepped through the door of a shop located below a pachinko parlor. The front presented the image of a clean and modestly stocked second-hand electronics store, mostly dealing with wireless brainset accessories. It was a front for a black-market dealer who thus far had stayed off law-enforcement radar, but not that of the Special Purpose Branch.

"Good afternoon, miss. How may I help you?" asked a middle-aged woman with dark skin and dyed turquoise hair. She sat behind a glass desk showcasing some of the shop's choicest items.

"I'm here to see Clarence. I have an appointment," Jessica said.

The woman's smile vanished, and she pressed a button on the desk. The store's front door locked.

"Follow me," she said.

Jessica followed the woman into the back room, where a bald, heavily built man lounged in a small chair. Hired muscle, no doubt.

The woman grabbed a wand and turned to Jessica. "Arms up. Pull anything, and my man over there will throw you out. In pieces."

Jessica shrugged off her jacket and held up her arms. "I've got nothing to pull."

"We'll see," the woman said. She waved the wand over Jessica, Jessica's cybernetic body's sensors picking up the emissions coming off the wand, helpfully identifying the kind of scanner it was. It was the wrong type for detecting her cybernetic nature. It was just looking for bugs or weapons, of which Jessica had none.

The woman finished and nodded to the muscle, who got up and opened a door that led down a flight of stairs.

The woman disappeared without a word, while the muscle waved her through.

Jessica gave the muscle her best smile before descending the stairs.

Reaching the bottom of the stairs, she passed through a door and her brainset immediately lost its connection to the local network.

Glancing around, she saw the wall behind the racks of illegal goods covered in wiring. The proprietor of the black-market shop had built a Faraday cage. A good way to avoid detection by authorities.

A solitary man stooped over a workbench with his hands stuck into the guts of what looked like a stolen police quad-rotor drone.

"You Clarence?" Jessica asked.

"Clarence is just a code word for anyone who wants to come down here to see my special inventory," said the man. He was an older man, built long and lean. He had a pointed goatee and a shaved head that proudly displayed intricate tattoos that disappeared down the collar of his dark shirt. "To what do I owe the pleasure, miss?"

"I need something stealthy that I can use to hack into a closed network," Jessica said.

"I have plenty of stealthy drones down here. Do you need something that can swim, walk, or fly?"

"Walk," Jessica said. "And jump, and climb."

"I might have something that fits that description," he said, abandoning the police drone on the bench and walking over to a trunk. He opened it and pulled out a drone with a body that looked like a headless, tailless cat, its legs tucked under its body.

Judging by the way he handled it, it looked lightweight.

Jessica walked up to get a closer look. The drone was about the size of a small dog. Small enough to fit into a large handbag.

"Looks like one of those rescue bots I've seen fire departments use for search and rescue," Jessica said.

"Same platform—things that make a robot good for getting into a collapsed and burning building are also rather good for getting into guarded places," the proprietor said.

"Does that include remote hacking?" Jessica asked.

"It can with the right modules, though those cost extra."

"I'd like to take a look at what you have."

He nodded and pointed to the rack. "Those are what I have right now."

Jessica glanced over the rack, noting the selection of hackware modules that she wouldn't need since she had those covered. What she needed was a hard connection to the network Xia resided on.

Jessica pointed to a module that looked like a cable pully. "How much fiber-optic wire is that?"

"Five hundred meters," the proprietor said.

Jessica nodded. That should be more than enough.

"Does the drone come with a universal connector?"

"It does," he said.

"Then that's all I need," she said.

"No hackware, or jammers? Without those all the drone is good for is making hardwire connections," he said.

"That's all I need. I already have everything else."

"I hope you got them from someone good."

"The best."

After a brief bit of haggling and an exchange of crypto-currency, Jessica walked out with a sturdy black duffel bag and her purchased drone inside.

Now was just a question of getting within five hundred meters of a network node, which meant she had one more place to visit.

⁂

It was raining even harder when Jessica stepped off the tram adjacent to a tower that stabbed into the wet gray sky. The tower was a mixed-use property. It had floors of offices, retail, and apartments climbing a kilometer into the overcast sky, but what Jessica was looking for was well below her feet.

She had changed into more formal clothing. A finely cut black jacket, white blouse, and a tight black skirt that flattered her figure and contrasted nicely with her brown skin. She completed the look with a pair of glossy black heels that clicked on the tile floor as she walked.

Adjusting the strap of the bag hanging over her shoulder, she felt the weight of the drone inside shift. It was a large, expensive bag of dark brown leather decorated with brass buckles. More importantly, it was large enough to carry the drone without bulging out the sides. Oversized handbags were currently fashionable, so the large bag shouldn't draw any attention.

She walked through the main entrance of the building.

There wasn't any special security. The first floor was dedicated retail space, and Jessica blended in with the people filing in to get out of the rain. Once in, she headed directly for the public elevator banks, boarding an elevator with a group of shoppers and residents. The public elevator didn't go down to the basement, but the elevators that did didn't stop at the ground floor. So, she took the elevator up, watching Singapore's skyline fall away as the elevator climbed up the side of the tower.

She got off near the top, the highest publicly accessible floor. The only floors above her were penthouses for wealthy residents who wanted a residence that loomed over Singapore.

The private elevators were in the center of the building rather than the sides.

Security was fully automated, operated by a vigilant AI. But no matter how smart the AI, its decisions were only as good as the data it was given, and Jessica was determined to give it nothing but an unending stream of bullshit.

The AI scanned her brainset and downloaded the falsified credentials she had made during the flight down. A green light appeared with a ding and the doors parted. Jessica stepped in and hit the button for the sub-basement level.

She looked around the elevator, noting the expensive wood paneling and marble floor. This was no utility elevator.

After a long descent in the finely furnished box, the elevator doors parted, revealing an opulent lobby. A woman sat behind a desk directly in front of the elevator, her black hair tied in a tight bun held in place by lacquered sticks.

The woman smiled. "Hello, miss, how may I help you?"

"Hello, I'm Estell Dari. I'm here for the tour," Jessica said.

The receptionist smiled. It was all a formality. The security AI would've already told her Jessica's false identity, and her reason for coming.

"You're just in time. Your group is gathering in the waiting area just down the hall," the receptionist said. "Feel free to help yourself to refreshments while you wait."

"Thank you," Jessica said, heading to the waiting area.

There were six people in the room, four men and two women. Most looked like they were getting on in years, their advanced age indicated by the wrinkles and gray hairs that even the best life extension couldn't keep at bay. The other two were a middle-aged woman and, to her surprise, a young man who looked like he was in his early twenties.

Most of the people were relaxed, even excited to be there, but the young man looked pensive.

Jessica sat down in front of him. The man perked up, the look in his eye indicating he was grateful to have an attractive young woman to look at rather than some old fart.

"You here to tour the facility?" Jessica asked with her best smile.

The man nodded, giving her a nervous smile. "Ah, yes I am."

Dark hair, dark eyes, tanned skin. He looked like a bog-average representation of the multi-ethnic population of Singapore. He wore a simple t-shirt and pants rather than the business clothing everyone else was wearing, making him stand out even more.

If Jessica had to guess, it was almost like he had come here on a whim.

He picked at his shirt. "Yeah, I didn't have time to get a suit before coming here. Don't have a lot of leave."

"Are you in the Space Forces?" Jessica asked.

He nodded. "Spacer 2nd class."

"Been in the service long?" She knew the answer was no but didn't want to give away the fact she was in the Space Forces by recognizing what his rank meant.

"I've been in a year, including my time in basic," he said.

"What's your name?"

"Shin Bao. Yours?"

"Estell."

"That's a pretty name," Bao said.

"Thank you," Jessica said. "So why did you decide to spend your limited leave time down here."

He shrugged. "Isn't it obvious? I'm thinking about getting my mind copied."

"Aren't you a little young for that?" Jessica asked.

"Maybe. Might not live to old age given how the war is going," Bao said.

"But on a Spacer's salary?"

"I've saved most of what I've made. Enough to get a slot in the public server. Seems like a better investment than what my crewmates are blowing their salaries on."

"You're from Singapore?"

He nodded. "My parents live here. I'm staying with them during my leave. Getting my affairs in order."

"You really think you're going to die?" Jessica asked.

Bao took a deep breath. "After the Cendies pushed all those stations around Jupiter towards us, scuttlebutt is that the 1st Fleet won't have enough fuel both to effect a rescue and to fight back a determined push by the Cendies. Everyone I know seems to think so."

Jessica had no idea morale was so bad. The nature of her profession limited her contact with rank-and-file members of the Space Forces. And if a Spacer 2nd class had a good grasp of the situation his fleet was in, then she could only imagine what the mood must be among the crews of their ships.

"Didn't Earth Fed score a big win getting that carrier out of Jupiter?"

"Yeah? I'm not sure what good that's going to do," Bao said.

Well, all the ships *Independence* destroyed on her way out weren't around to threaten Inner Sol anymore, but Jessica wasn't going to voice that point and break her cover as a clueless civilian.

"I suppose," Jessica said. "So, you want to make sure you leave something behind?"

"Yeah," Bao said. "I know it won't be me. Not really. Just an AI with my memories. But at least some part of me will continue since it doesn't look like the Cendies are going to let me live long enough to have kids. Maybe even see the end of the universe if I'm—I mean my copy—is lucky enough."

"Well, I for one hope that you are lucky enough to live a long, happy life, with as many kids as you want," Jessica said.

Bao chuckled. "I can agree with that sentiment, Estell. Maybe we can talk more over drinks?"

"I'm afraid I won't have time for that, Bao. But I'm very flattered," Jessica said.

"Eh, worth a shot."

"Ladies and gentlemen," said a smartly dressed man as he entered the waiting area. "If I can have your attention, the presentation is about to start. Please direct your attention to the screen in the back."

The large screen came on with the Ataraxia Incorporated logo appearing first, a stylized A superimposed over a similarly styled X. Jessica was towards the back of the room relative to the screen.

As all attention was facing away from her, she reached into her large bag and pulled a fine fiber-optic wire out and connected it to a port behind her left ear. She adjusted her hair to keep the port out of view and woke up the drone in her bag.

The drone came to life in complete silence, its little motors heavily quieted. A screen appeared in her HUD showing what the drone saw, which wasn't much given it was still in her bag.

On its own, the drone used a pincer on one of its legs to grab the zipper and pull it open. Jessica's teeth clenched as she heard the faint ripping of the zipper coming undone, but no one heard it over the presentation.

Barely sparing any attention to the room Jessica was in, it skittered out of the room, leaving an almost invisible guidance wire behind, the soft pads on its feet silencing its steps. The small box it had sat in in her bag ensured that the bag did not collapse as it left.

Jessica guided the drone to the main server room. She couldn't guide it wirelessly because the security AI would pick up the signal and trigger an alarm. But though the wire was hard to see, it wasn't completely invisible. If someone stumbled across it... well, she'd better get this done quickly. The presentation would end in thirty minutes.

The drone quickly climbed the wall like an enormous insect using the smart adhesive pads on its feet. The drone's active camo would make it difficult to pick up on camera, but even a fleeting glance would be enough for the security AI to trigger an alarm.

Jessica guided the drone to the air vent indicated by her stolen map. The drone, designed for crawling through debris, was more than small enough to fit into the vent. It was just a matter of getting it open.

There was no sign of an alarm on the vent cover. Probably because the vent was too small for a person to fit through and no one considered someone using a wire-guided drone to get in.

Anchored to the wall with three legs, the drone's right foreleg was raised by Jessica and its built-in multitool deployed. She quickly loosened the screws, careful to collect each one and attach them to a magnetic pad on the drone's belly before pulling the cover off.

The drone moved inside while still holding onto the vent cover, keeping it still while the rest of the drone moved in. Then, the drone pulled the vent cover back into place behind it.

Since the wire spooled off the drone, it didn't matter if it got caught on something. Jessica just had to be careful about moving herself.

The drone proceeded down the vent, turning left at an intersection, optics tuned to spot any kind of security measures.

She didn't run into any when she reached the vent leading into the server room.

Reaching through the air vent, the drone removed the screws and pulled open the vent, leaving one of the bottom screws in place to allow it to hang from the wall.

The server room had none of the opulence of the public spaces. Just bare metal walls and rows of tall, thin server towers.

The drone climbed down to the floor and crept over to the maintenance console, climbing onto an empty chair in front of the console. A data port became visible. Jessica ordered the drone to connect to it, and a thin arm deployed from the drone, a wire with a connector at the end extending and inserting itself into the port.

And with that, the drone's job was finished, giving her a hard connection to the servers that Miriam Xia's personal afterlife ran on.

Her hackware got to work, isolating the control console from the security AI without alerting it. She searched for Miriam's server address, and it came up, along with data on what she was doing.

To Jessica's relief, Miriam was alone in a private instance of some kind rather than networked with other minds. She'd be less likely to miss Jessica's communication request.

Jessica sent the request and hoped Miriam would reply before the presentation ended.

CHAPTER 10

FSFV *Amazon* was just about the ugliest starship Mason had ever seen. She was a bullet-shaped vessel, round nose at the front and five engines in the back in the standard quincunx pattern of Federal Space Forces warships.

An old Spartan class assault ship, she had been designed to deliver a regiment of troopers along with an armored company onto a hostile planet, but she was more than a simple-troop transport. Numerous gun turrets covered her hull, mostly point-defense guns meant to protect her and her assault shuttles from ground-based fire. Four larger turrets were mounted in pairs on the top and bottom of the hull, each carrying a pair of stubby bombardment cannons. Each weapon had a muzzle energy comparable to that of a battleship's main gun. But where a battleship launched a relatively light and fast-moving KKV, bombardment cannons fired rods that were both an order of magnitude heavier and an order of magnitude slower—perfect for penetrating a planet's atmosphere to pulverize ground targets. Backing up her weapons were thick layers of armor protecting the ship's vital spaces.

All that said, Mason still wasn't sold on the idea of using an old assault ship as a mobile base of operations. But no one in the Special Purpose Branch asked him his opinion.

"*Amazon* Control, this is Osiris Leader. Request permission to dock."

A deep female voice replied loud and clear. "Osiris leader, this is *Amazon* control. Permission granted. Proceed to docking bay eight."

"Roger that, *Amazon* Control. Osiris leader proceeding to docking bay eight."

Docking bay eight, part of the middle ring of docking bays circling just behind the ship's round nose, was rather inconveniently on the side of the ship facing away from him. He coasted his Lightning past the ship, maintaining a two-thousand-meter clearance from the assault ship. Mason used the close flyby to get a detailed look at the orbital assault ship, looking for any signs of modifications made by the Special Purpose Branch to modernize the ship. He was dismayed to see no high-tech gadgetry bolted to the ship's hull. Just technicians in space suits and repair drones flitting around the starship's hull as they scrambled to get her ready for deployment.

The doors for docking bay eight were already open when Mason came around the side of the ship. With a couple of pulses from the maneuvering thrusters, he brought his Lightning to a stop relative to *Amazon*, and then slewed his fighter to the side to line up with the hangar bay. Having lined up, he folded his wings, lowered his landing gear, and then fired one last pulse to drift into the hangar bay. After drifting inside the hangar, magnets on the bottom of his landing gear activated and pulled his fighter down to the landing pad.

There was a slight bump as the shock absorbers of his landing gear buckled under the impact of the one-hundred-ton fighter hitting the deck at half a meter per second. The doors were already closing behind him as he shut down his Lightning and heard the reactors spool down.

Once his fighter was shut down, he started to depressurize his cockpit, sucking the nitrogen gas out and into storage tanks. After a couple of minutes, the cockpit was close to the vacuum of the hangar bay, and Mason opened the canopy.

Hangar techs floated out into the hangar, flying towards his fighter guided by puffs of cold gas from their suits' built-in maneuvering rigs. Taking special care to keep their distance from the Lightning's still-hot engines, they started attaching tubes and cables to the fighter. One of them opened the small cargo compartment under the right wing and pulled out the sealed hardshell container holding Mason's belongings.

Mason leapt from his fighter and used his hardsuit's thrusters to guide him towards the main airlock. He grabbed a handhold near the airlock controls to arrest his momentum. Checking to make sure the outer hatch was clear, he pulled the safety cover off the control lever and pulled it down to start the cycle.

The outer hatch closed, and air started pouring into the airlock. The airlock finished cycling and the lights flanking the inner hatch shifted from red to green, and the inner hatch swung out into the corridor beyond.

Mason launched himself from the handhold and stuck the toe of his boot into a foothold on the opposite bulkhead. Hanging from the foothold, he hit the release on his hardsuit's helmet and popped it off.

A refreshing wave of cool air washed over his face. *Amazon*'s atmosphere was cool and dry and carried the familiar antiseptic smell of recycled air. The smell of home. Out of the corner of his eye, he saw someone in an orange jumpsuit floating towards him, a short man with dark hair.

"I didn't know you were aboard, Chief," Mason said. "Thought you were still aboard *Mervie*."

"No point in having me aboard without fighters to maintain, sir," Chief Rabin said. "I go where there are fighters."

"Fair enough, Chief," Mason said, shaking Rabin's hand. "It's good to work with you again. You still working with the same people?"

"Yes, sir. *Mervie* unloaded all her hangar techs before departing. We've been cooling our heels until we're told to pack up and transfer over to this ship."

"I hope *Amazon*'s not too much of a downgrade for you, Chief."

"Hardly, sir. *Amazon*'s not as flashy a ship as *Mervie*, but she's got much better accommodations for enlisted crew than *Mervie* did. Not that you would know, being an officer and all."

"Rank has its privileges," Mason conceded.

"It does, sir," Chief Rabin said. "I actually was asked by the colonel to meet you when you docked. She wanted me to show you one of the new weapons we're going to be carrying."

"Oh, that's something I'm very curious to see."

An alarm bleated through the corridor.

"All crew now hear this, long-burn drive ignition in one minute. All crew prepare for transition to thrust gravity."

"Not wasting any time to get underway," Mason said.

"Your squadron was the last thing *Amazon* was waiting for, sir."

A minute later, a rumble traveled through *Amazon* and a fraction of a g pulled his boots down to the deck. Over a period of thirty seconds, the acceleration increased until a full g pulled Mason down to the deck.

"Next stop, Triumph," Chief Rabin said.

"Yeah, I'm weirded out by that too, Chief," Mason said. "Now, where's that new weapon?"

"One level down, sir. We repurposed one of the vehicle hangars for munitions storage. Got it packed between racks full of air-to-ground missiles."

Mason stopped in his tracks as he walked into the ground vehicle hangar and found himself staring down the barrels of a pair of massive guns.

Colonel Shimura stood tall between the two weapons and looked positively tiny in comparison. The weapons stood taller than she did on their mounts, the outer diameter wider than her torso at their widest points.

"Welcome aboard, Squadron Leader," Colonel Shimura greeted Mason.

He gave her a quick salute. "Thank you, sir. So, what are those?"

The colonel walked over to the gun on her left and gave it an affectionate pat.

"These are the first two Raiden Mark 0 recoilless cannons to be deployed for field testing. They're intended as a replacement for the slugger torpedoes we normally use for disabling starships."

Mason looked at the muzzle, noting the relatively small diameter of the bore compared to the rest of the barrel. It looked barely wider than the conventional main gun of a Lightning.

"This some kind of higher velocity weapon, sir?" Mason asked.

"That is correct, Squadron Leader," Colonel Shimura said. "The intent is to create smaller weapons that match the velocities of main guns found on cruisers and battleships. The projectiles these things fire aren't all that much larger than the rounds your Lightning's regular guns fire but are launched at a vastly higher velocity."

"I'm assuming when you say 'recoilless' that there's some kind of system to cancel out some of the recoil?" Mason asked.

"There is. Follow me to the rear of the weapon."

Mason walked down the length of the weapon, counting his paces as he did.

It was at least thirty meters long by his estimation.

The back end of the Raiden was a revolving cylinder like that of an Equalizer pistol, and a cone like a long-burn drive's engine bell.

"That cylinder contains five propellant charges that detonate in sync with the cannon, canceling out the recoil," Colonel Shimura explained.

"So, I just get five shots out of this?"

"Yes. There's a redundant safety system to prevent the weapon from firing without a charge. Otherwise, the recoil would rip the weapon off its mounts when it fired."

"Speaking of mounting, sir, how the hell is a Lightning going to carry one of these? It's almost as long as the fighter itself."

Colonel Shimura tapped a button on the rack's control panel, and the barrel of the weapon telescoped into itself.

Mason watched with interest as the barrel segments withdrew into each other, the rear segments expanding to fit the segments before them, until the weapon was about a quarter of its original length, short enough to fit into the weapon bay of a Lightning.

"The weapon is designed to be mounted in the weapons bay of a Lightning using a retractable mounting system that will lower the weapon. This way the weapon can be carried by a Lightning in a stowed configuration without compromising its aerodynamics."

"Can the weapon be used in atmosphere?" Mason asked.

"It's ineffective if fired in substantial atmosphere. Shock heating will melt the projectile within a couple of thousand meters. You shouldn't be firing this thing in anything more than .5 percent Earth sea level."

"Basically, this is a space-only weapon?"

"Or very high altitude on an Earth-like world, Squadron Leader," Colonel Shimura said. "For air-to-ground, the Lightning's conventional cannon is more than sufficient. The Raiden is essentially a giant anti-materiel rifle for use against hard targets in space."

"Like Cendy warships."

"Among other things, yes."

"So, what do the powers that be intend us to use these for, sir?" Mason asked. "Because they don't seem to fit the expected mission profile."

"I think they intend us to figure that out, Squadron Leader," Colonel Shimura said. "They're more space-efficient than Slugger torpedoes. And they give your Lightnings a viable non-nuclear anti-starship weapon."

"I take it the Leaguers aren't going to let us land any with any torpedoes or space bombs in inventory?" Mason asked.

"No, Squadron Leader, they were quite specific about no Federal nukes on Triumph."

Mason sighed. "I suppose the League will have plenty of their own nukes."

"If the estimates of their stockpiles on Triumph are any indication, they'll have more than enough."

"So why are we going, sir?" Mason asked. "Because as far as I can see, we're just a token force."

"There are ways we can be helpful beyond simple firepower, Squadron Leader," Colonel Shimura said. "All of Osiris Squadron's pilots have experience fighting the Cendies. The same can't be said for all the League pilots who will be defending Triumph. Further, I have confidence that everyone aboard *Amazon* will find clever ways to punch well above their weight."

"I hope you're right, sir," Mason said. "Because I don't know how an assault ship carrying a regiment of troopers and a squadron of Lightnings is supposed to make a difference."

"Neither do I, Squadron Leader," Colonel Shimura said. "But I'm sure we will find some way after we make planetfall on Triumph."

CHAPTER 11

Underclocked to one percent of real time, Jessica knew it would take a couple of minutes at least before she could expect Miriam Xia to reply.

As the minutes ticked by, the presentation exploring the virtual amenities that would be provided to client's uploaded minds passed the halfway point and entered its final act. Jessica was only vaguely aware what was going on around her, her attention focused on her hardwired connection to the server.

Then, precisely four minutes after Jessica sent her request, she got a response.

Miriam Xia had accepted her request and was dialing up to real time.

Jessica mentally sighed with relief, and after a brief pause to note how much time she had left in the presentation, she made a connection to the server, and the room fell away.

She found herself standing on a beach of brilliant white sand. To her left was an empty sun chair resting in the shade of a parasol.

Jessica was in uniform, much to her annoyance. She looked down at her blue sleeves and scoffed. When had she set her uniform as her default virtual appearance?

Footprints in the sand led to the rippling blue water. It appeared that Miriam Xia had been taking a swim before Jessica interrupted her. There was a dark shape beneath the rippling water swimming towards shore. Jessica walked up to the water until the rolling tide kissed the tips of her boots.

A young woman erupted out of the water in front of Jessica, nude and dripping. She wiped back her wet black hair with her hands, revealing the face of a young Miriam Xia.

The young, nude Miriam Xia was stunning to behold. Slender and fit, but not so beautiful as to be uncanny. And clearly quite comfortable with her nudity.

Standing in front of Jessica with her feet in the water, she wrung her hair out while her dark eyes regarded Jessica.

"Hrmm. I see the Space Forces' taste in uniforms hasn't progressed much in the last two hundred years."

Jessica wasn't sure if it was a good thing or a bad thing she was in uniform. Miriam Xia had made much of her fortune building starships for the nascent Federal Space Forces.

"Ah, yes." Jessica glanced at her uniform. "To be fair, they're quite comfortable and functional."

"And they do flatter the figure," Miriam said as she stepped out of the water and strutted past Jessica, exaggerating the motion of her hips.

Whatever the outcome of this meeting, at least Jessica was getting a good show.

Miriam sat down on the beach chair under the parasol and held out her hand.

A man in a stark white t-shirt and white pants appeared out of nowhere to hand Miriam a colorful drink with a straw and an orange slice sticking out of the glass. Miriam took a long sip of her drink as she regarded Jessica.

"So." Miriam set her drink down. "How may I be of service to you, Lieutenant Sinclair?"

Jessica was surprised Miriam knew her name, and then was annoyed with herself at being surprised. Her uniform had her surname embroidered in white lettering above her left breast, and a woman who spent a decade working with the military would of course be familiar with Space Forces' rank insignia.

"Oh, bloody hell," Jessica said. "This is what I get for forgetting I left my uniform as default."

"There's nothing stopping you from changing into something more comfortable," Miriam said. "Unless you're here on official business. Which would be very curious given digital people aren't supposed to do business with biologicals."

Jessica picked at the collar of her jumpsuit, considering switching to something more informal. Though not as informal as Miriam's outfit.

"Well, I suppose I'm here on unofficial official business," Jessica said. "I'm with the Special Purpose Branch."

Miriam set down her drink. "You're a spy? How exciting! I'm afraid any information I have is a couple of hundred years out of date. I don't really keep up much with the outside world."

"I take it you're aware there's a war on?"

"Yet another dust up with the League. I'm not sure what you expect me to do about it."

Jessica waved her hand around. "How long have you been in this instance?"

"Before your interruption? Just over four days," Miriam said.

Four days for Miriam would translate to over a year in the real world. She had been skinny-dipping and sipping cocktails in her private paradise completely unaware of the Ascendency's invasion and occupation of the outer solar system.

"Well then, I should inform you that the war with the League is over," Jessica said.

"Well, good. I hope it wasn't too bloody," Miriam said. "Who won?"

"Neither," Jessica said.

"Stalemate?"

"No, the war was interrupted when the Ascendency attacked," Jessica said.

Miriam set down her drink and sat up. "The who?"

"The Ascendency. They're a post-human species that has, among other things, invaded and occupied Outer Sol. Their goal is the dissolution of the Earth Federation and the League."

"Really? That doesn't seem so bad," Miriam said. "The Earth Federation vs League paradigm grew stale a long time ago. It's good to see there's finally been a change."

"You're not worried about what they'll do if they take Earth?" Jessica asked.

Miriam shrugged. "I suppose that would depend on what their attitude is towards digitized minds, but given you said they're post-human, I would assume they wouldn't take issue with me."

She was probably right, though thus far the Ascendency had said nothing about how they would treat the Earth Federation's digital citizens. Given they seemed entirely interested only in the physical universe, she couldn't blame Miriam for being unworried.

"What if I told you that they might be related to the Pinnacle Foundation in some fashion?" Jessica asked.

Miriam paused, the first crack in her carefree demeanor forming. "What makes you think that?"

"After interviewing someone who got to know one of their emissaries, it was revealed that the Ascendency have a two-hundred-year gap in their reading," Jessica said. "Working back, the window in which their creators could've left Sol coincided with the departure of the Pinnacle Foundation's colony ship. It's further reinforced by the fact that the colony ship's name was *Ascension*."

"That could be a coincidence," Miriam said.

"I don't believe so," Jessica said. "And I don't think you believe that, either."

Miriam crossed her arms under her breasts, a strong, authoritative pose despite her nudity. "You haven't a clue what I think. This Ascendency and the Pinnacle Foundation have nothing to do with each other."

"And what makes you think that?"

"Because creating an army of post-human invaders was not the goal of the Pinnacle Foundation."

"Two hundred years is a long time for someone to change their goals."

"It would take a lot more than a little time to change the goals the Pinnacle Foundation had," Miriam said firmly.

Jessica held up her hand, and a package appeared in it. "This is everything we know about the Ascendency and what they've been up to."

Miriam quirked an eyebrow. "You don't expect me to open strange data, do you?"

"There's no security safeguards on it, so you can scan it for malware at your leisure."

Miriam reached out and took the virtual package without opening it. "You've gone to a lot of trouble to speak with me, Lieutenant Sinclair."

"Jessica, please. There's no need to be so formal."

"Hard not to be formal with you so overdressed," Miriam said. "How about this? I'll see about e-"

The connection broke, and Jessica was back in the conference room, surrounded not by other potential customers but by half a dozen security personnel in gray jumpsuits. One of them held the end of Jessica's connector in her hand, the tip dangling limp in front of her face.

"Uh, how may I help you?" Jessica asked sheepishly and tried to move, only to find her hands cuffed behind her back. It seemed they had taken the precaution to restrain her before pulling her out. She gave the handcuffs a quick tug and concluded that her artificial arms would break before they did.

"You're under arrest," said the woman holding the connector. "Police are already in the building and are on their way down to arrest you. I have to say, using a drone to plug directly into the sever was clever. Security AI didn't have a clue what you were up to until one of the guests almost tripped over the wire sticking out of you head.

Jessica had accepted the risk of getting caught, but it still hurt her pride that they had managed to catch her in the act. She adjusted herself in her seat as much as her cuffed hands allowed and cleared her throat. "I decline to answer any questions until I have a chance to speak with an attorney."

"Ah, well, that might help with criminal charges but know that the Viduus group is already hard at work getting ready to sue you into non-existence," the guard in charge said. "You probably haven't a clue how many terms of service you just broke pulling this."

Jessica knew perfectly well. Preventing the downfall of the Earth Federation seemed worth the risk of being sued into bankruptcy a thousand times over. She sat there, silent, staring off at the wall until half a dozen police arrived and took her to the surface, where an armored police van waited for her.

CHAPTER 12

"Squadron Leader Mason Grey, report to the bridge." An artificial voice echoed through the suit-storage chamber as Mason's hardsuit closed around him.

There weren't a lot of reasons for Mason to be called to the bridge as he was suiting up to climb into his fighter, and he doubted any were good. Just a single jump out from 61 Virginis, he was pretty sure *Amazon*'s deep scan had revealed something they didn't like.

"Get everyone to their fighters, Shutdown," Mason instructed.

"Got it, Hauler," Zin responded and added as Mason exited the room, "Be sure to let us in on the good news when you get back."

"Thinking positive, I see."

"Always."

Amazon was not accelerating as she prepared for her final jump, so Mason floated through the assault ship's corridors and "down" several decks to reach the command deck. He passed through the bridge's armored hatch to find it fully staffed by a couple of dozen very tense-looking spacers. He set his jaw, steeling himself for what he knew was going to be bad news.

Colonel Shimura, Major Hauer, and Captain Alvarez, the stout swarthy man who commanded Amazon, hovered around the central holotank as it showed a representation of the 61 Virginis system. A collection of angry icons clustered around the inner system confirmed that something bad had happened.

"Belts and zones!" Mason exclaimed as he took in the information, coming to a stop next to Colonel Shimura.

The colonel turned towards him, her eyes glancing briefly at his hard-suit. "Sorry to interrupt you in the middle of flight preparation, Squadron Leader, but as you can see, the situation with 61 Virginis has deviated from expectations."

"Looks like the Cendies have already taken the system," Mason said.

"Not quite," Major Hauer said. "Triumph is still unoccupied. It appears the Cendies instead set up shop around a large asteroid belt called 30 Skeksis."

The holotank focused on the asteroid of 30 Skeksis, its orbit near its closest approach to Triumph. Fusiliers and Katyushas formed a halo around the asteroid, while a tight cluster of icons representing unknown contacts hugged close to the rock. The holotank zoomed in some more, until 30 Skeksis resolved into a lumpy, oblong nickel-iron shard. An icon representing one of the Cendies' massive Monolith-class vessels appeared to be touching the asteroid right at the center of rotation.

"It appears the Cendies have brought along one of their Monoliths and parked it on the surface of 30 Skeksis. Best guess is that they're mining the asteroid to make supplies for the fleet," Captain Alvarez said.

"What about those unknown contacts?" Mason asked.

"I've gone ahead and given them the provisional reporting name of Turtleback. Beyond that, they're about the size of cruisers and make up about half the composition of the Cendy fleet," the colonel answered.

"Any idea what their function is, Colonel?" Mason asked.

"Best guess would be troop transports, assuming the Cendies intend on assaulting the planet itself. I suppose we'll find out if that guess is correct soon enough."

Mason frowned. "What about the League fleet defending 61 Virginis?"

Colonel Shimura reached into the holotank and pinched her fingers to make it zoom into the inner 61 Virginis system. Three hot-gas giants made up the inner reaches of 61 Virginis: Inferno, Ember, and Ash.

"What's left of the League battlefleet retreated to Ash, taking up defensive positions to prevent the Cendies from penetrating down into the system to attack the gas-mining infrastructure of the inner gas giants. They're relying on Triumph's formidable defenses to keep the Cendy fleet at bay."

"So that means our mission has failed, then, sir?" Mason gestured towards the holotank. "Because it looks to me like the Cendies have beaten us to the punch."

"The mission hasn't failed, Squadron Leader, merely changed," Colonel Shimura said. "We need to find a way to get past the Cendy fleet."

"It won't be with *Amazon*, Colonel," Captain Alvarez said. "She's tough, but 1g of acceleration isn't enough to evade any Cendy warships sent to intercept us."

"What if we pre-accelerated before the jump?" Colonel Shimura asked. "It would give us a few hundred kilometers per second head start."

Captain Alvarez shook his head. "If we were going fast enough to outrun any Cendy ambush at the jump limit, we'd overshoot Triumph and not be able to slow down before reaching the other side of the jump limit, where I have no doubt we would have a flotilla of Cendy warships waiting for us."

"In other words, you'd need twice the acceleration *Amazon* is capable of to slow down," Mason said.

"More like triple. I wouldn't start decelerating immediately after we jump, given there'll probably be a force of angry Cendies trying to run us down," Captain Alvarez said. "There's no way I can push *Amazon* that hard."

"But we could push the assault shuttles and Lightnings that hard," Mason said.

Colonel Shimura looked hard at Mason. "You're suggesting we launch our assault shuttles and fighters outside the jump limit, Squadron Leader?"

"Yes, sir. Just like we did for Operation Autumn Fire," Mason said. "*Amazon* burns her engines to give us a few hundred extra-KPS before jumping just short of the jump limit. Then we launch and proceed down orbit while *Amazon* turns around and jumps out. We use the greater acceleration of the small craft to come to a stop over Triumph."

"That means only one trip with the shuttles," Colonel Shimura said.

"We would have to leave most of our stuff behind, sir," Mason said.

"But we'd at least get something down to Triumph to help the Leaguers defend the planet."

"That kind of acceleration's going to be hard on your people," Captain Alvarez pointed out. "Fighter pilots can handle it just fine, but what about the troopers and support personnel?"

"My troopers can handle hard gs," Major Hauer said.

"How much acceleration are we talking about, exactly?" Colonel Shimura asked.

"I haven't mathed it out, sir, but I would say 5g to be on the safe side," Mason said.

"Then start mathing it out, Squadron Leader," Colonel Shimura said. "And I'll start making decisions on what and who we leave behind.

~

Mason's guess of 5gs turned out to be right after he sat down and let an AI crunch the numbers. While he worked on getting the fighters ready from an improvised station on the bridge, he let Zin handle getting the Osiris Squadron pilots ready, making sure they got their belongings transferred from the quarters to their fighters.

Colonel Shimura walked up to Mason's station. "Squadron Leader, could I have a moment?"

"Of course, sir. I've just finished figuring what I'm loading aboard my fighters."

"Good. I'd like to add one more item to your fighters."

"What is that, sir?"

"Passengers."

"I can do that, sir," Mason asked. "May I ask why?"

"That's sixteen people we don't have to load onto the assault shuttles—which is that much more cargo we can load aboard the shuttles," Colonel Shimura said.

"Seems reasonable," Mason said. "Who are my pilots carrying?"

"Myself, Major Hauer, and a couple of squads of troopers."

Mason nodded. Troopers had the highest g-tolerance of anyone other than fighter pilots. If they ended up tangling with Cendy Outrider fighters on the way to Triumph, he wouldn't have to worry too much about killing his passengers during hard maneuvers.

"You can ride with me, sir. I'll see that Major Hauer and his troopers are assigned seats with the rest of my fighters,"

Colonel Shimura nodded. "Good. I also have an inventory of the cargo the shuttles will be carrying down to Triumph along with personnel."

The inventory appeared on Mason's HUD and he opened it. He scrolled through it, noting most of the extra gear consisted of spare missiles for his fighters, weapons and ammunition for the troopers, a couple of the experimental Raiden cannons, and not a kilo of extra food.

"We're not bringing extra food with us?" Mason queried.

"Nothing other than personal rations," Colonel Shimura confirmed.

"I hope the Leaguers are in a generous mood then."

"I'll make sure they don't give us any spoiled rations, Squadron Leader."

"How long until we jump?" Mason asked.

"Captain Alvarez will finish the approach burn in an hour. I intend on having him charge the star drive as soon as *Amazon*'s long-burn drives go cold, so everyone and everything needs to be loaded and ready to launch by that time."

"Well, sir I've finished everything that I can do here. I'll head up to the hangar bays and see to the last of the preparations."

Colonel Shimura nodded. "I'll see you up there shortly, Squadron Leader."

Mason got up and departed the bridge. With 1g of thrust gravity, he decided to use one of *Amazon*'s elevators to take him up to the hangar-bay level towards the bow of the ship.

He pinged Chief Rabin and found him in Hangar Bay 22, where one of the assault shuttles was loading up with personnel. Mason proceeded there, passing through the open airlock and into the pressurized hangar. The assault shuttle rested on its docking pad with its tail ramp open, troopers and hangar techs hard at work loading crates into the assault shuttle.

Chief Rabin directed the loading operation wearing an orange pressure suit, the visor of his helmet open to the air.

"Hello, Chief. How are preparations going?" Mason asked.

Rabin nodded to him. "Going well, Squadron Leader. Making sure we fill every bit of space aboard this assault shuttle before launch. I've already inspected all your fighters. Nothing should fall off once you start burning hard."

"Thanks, Chief. I get the sense we're going to miss you on Triumph."

"That's heartwarming, sir, but I wouldn't make your goodbyes just yet." Rabin gestured to the assault shuttle. "I've got a seat on that shuttle."

"You're going to Triumph with us?" Mason asked, surprised. "That could very well be a one-way trip."

"You think I don't know that, sir?"

"I'm sure you're perfectly aware, Chief. I just want you to know that you don't have to."

"Yeah, I do, sir," Rabin said. "If you intend on having League ground crews working on my fighters, then you better have me down there to direct them. I'm not going to have some Leaguer over-torqueing a mounting bolt or loading a kinetic round backwards because they've never worked on Federal equipment. Bad enough I have to leave most of my people here on *Amazon*."

"You're bringing some of your people?"

"Just a couple of my most senior techs, sir. I'd bring more if there were room. God knows I'll need as many experienced eyes as I can looking after the knuckle-draggers the League is likely to assign to taking care of my fighters."

CHAPTER 13

Something made the Singaporean police exceptionally cautious with Jessica. It probably had something to do with her prosthetic body actively jamming their attempts to scan her. Their response was to put some truly beefy cuffs of hardened steel over her wrists and elbows and place her feet in shackles before sitting her in a cell with a heavy door and a pair of chairs.

After attaching the hobble chain to the floor, the police departed the room—she assumed to get in contact with a Federal Marshal. She glanced at the door, noting the dents left by one of the room's previous occupants who had clearly attempted to batter down the door bare-handed. This was one of the cells reserved for heavily augmented criminals, and the overkill restraint they gave Jessica was part of it.

For her part, Jessica waited for her chance to call her lawyer. Not just to get representation, but to pass along what she knew to the Special Purpose Branch. They would disavow her, of course, so there was no point in asking for their help. But with what she knew, she hoped someone luckier than she was could follow up with Miriam Xia.

After thirty minutes, the door to the cell opened again, and a portly detective in a rumpled suit walked in, followed by a tall, vaguely familiar man in a finely cut blue suit that no detective could afford.

The well-dressed man gave her an appraising look before glancing at the detective. "Take her out of those ridiculous restraints."

"Sir, our procedures…"

"Are for augmented criminals. She is augmented, yes. But she is no criminal, as I have explained to you ad nauseum. The Viduus Group has already dropped their charges. I see no reason for her to remain in those restraints any longer."

"Mister Harper, she's a fully prosthetic cyborg. She can potentially tear us apart bare-handed," the detective said.

She couldn't. Her body was strong, but only in relation to what a fully biological human her size would be. The kind of strength the detective was worried about would require her body to be so overbuilt she would weigh almost double what she currently did.

The man named Harper held out his hand. "If you're so afraid of her, I'll free her while you remain safely outside."

The detective glanced at the man, then pulled a key out and left the room. The door shut and locked with a clang.

The man named Harper glanced at the key and walked over to Jessica. "So, you're the one who all this trouble is about." He stood half a meter away from her, key dangling from the tip of his index finger.

"You said you were going to uncuff me," Jessica said.

"After you answer my questions."

"If this is some ruse to get me to waive my rights, then I will have to refuse."

"Do I look like an inspector to you?"

"If you are, you are a very well-dressed one."

Harper chuckled. "I suppose I should introduce myself. My name is Henrick Xia Harper. I'm the great-grandson and current executor of the estate of Miriam Xia."

Jessica cocked her head to one side. "So, what's with your bullying your way past that inspector and tempting me with my freedom?"

"Well, while I was having my afternoon tea, I got a very curious call from the digital ghost of my long dead great-grandmother stating that I needed to get you out of prison. Which is the first time since I became her executor that she has spoken with me. I had thought she had completely checked out of the affairs of the physical world, but you seem to have piqued her interest."

"So how did you convince the detective to let you in here?" Jessica asked.

"Simple. I marched in here with an army of lawyers stating that you're a penetration tester I hired to test the security of my great-grandmother's digital personage."

Jessica glanced up at the camera in the corner of the ceiling.

"We're not being recorded," Henrick said. "The army of lawyers I brought along have seen to that. Now, since neither of us is risking incriminating ourselves in front of Singapore's finest, how about you explain what the fuck is going on?"

Jessica cleared her throat. "It's a matter of Federal security."

"Federal? How interesting. Explain."

"I believe your great-grandmother Miriam might have insights into the Ascendency," Jessica said. "She was involved with an organization known as the Pinnacle Foundation, which I believe might have been run by the people who created the Ascendency."

"Pinnacle Foundation? You mean that bunch of scam artists?"

"You've heard of them, I take it."

His face darkened. "Yes. Their leader, Doctor Julian Marr, charmed my great-grandmother out of a couple of billion stellars, before adjusting for inflation, to build that ridiculously huge colony ship that he loaded up with his followers and took into the void."

"By charmed, do you mean…?"

He shook his head. "No, no evidence of that, thank God. He sold her a pack of goods about making a better human race out in the stars. She apparently was quite taken with the idea."

"Well, the Ascendency might very well be the product of those endeavors," Jessica said. "How about you uncuff me and we can discuss this further somewhere that's not a police station?"

Henrick walked behind Jessica and unlocked the cuffs, letting them drop to the hard floor. As she stood up, she rubbed her forearms.

"Thank you," she said.

"Don't mention it," Henrick said, handing Jessica the key to let her take care of her leg restraints herself. "Seeing as how you have not immediately torn me to pieces, I think it's time I escort you out of here. I have a limousine waiting for us out front."

Jessica stood up from opening her leg cuffs. "That seems a much better place."

Henrick knocked on the cell door, and it opened to reveal the inspector and a couple of more officers in armor, submachine guns clutched to their chests.

"We're leaving," Henrick told them. "I presume my lawyers have already cleared all the paperwork?"

"She's free to go," the inspector said. "Next time you should inform us if you're going to be testing security."

"That would defeat the point of the exercise. Good day, Inspector."

Jessica followed Henrick out of the holding area and through the lobby. It was still raining outside, water coming down in sheets through the station's glass front.

Standing near the door was an elegantly proportioned servant robot, its black and white color scheme evoking the suit butlers wore. It stood erect, boxy head held high. Its hands rested on the handle of a large umbrella, tip resting between its feet.

The robot turned to them with a crisp movement. "Good afternoon, sir. I see you will be bringing a guest with you. Shall I inform your house servants?" It spoke with a British accent that was more refined than any Jessica had heard from a flesh-and-blood Englishman.

"Please do. Have the usual prepared for me," Henrick said. "What would you like waiting for you when we arrive at my home, Lieutenant?"

"You're taking me to your home?"

"Yes, my great-grandmother would like to speak with you and my home is the only place outside of the Viduus building where that can happen."

"Some black tea and muffins would be splendid."

"I shall inform the kitchen staff, sir," the servant robot said. "Your refreshments will be waiting in the lounge upon arrival."

"Thank you, Nigel," Henrick said, before approaching the door.

Nigel held the door open for Henrick and Jessica, before following them out and opening the large black umbrella held in its hand, big enough for two people.

Henrick walked with Jessica straight to a large gray limousine that bore little decoration beyond a stylized L on the front. The passenger door opened as soon as the rim of Nigel's large umbrella loomed over it. Henrick climbed inside the car and made room for Jessica. Not so much as a drop of rainwater landed on them as they climbed inside. The door closed, and Jessica was plunged into silence. She couldn't even hear the rain hitting the roof of the limo. Henrick sat across from her, in the seat facing towards the rear. She was surrounded by polished metal and hand-stitched leather. Jessica saw Nigel sit down in the driver's seat, separated by a tinted glass partition.

The car started to move; the whine of its motor was barely audible.

"Nice car," Jessica said. "Very tasteful."

"Thank you. I find that wealth is best used for maximizing personal comfort rather than to show off to peers," Henrick said. "Which ironically makes this vehicle stand out all the more at social functions."

"I do appreciate the comforts. I feel like I'm wrapped in a leather cocoon that the troubles of the world cannot penetrate," Jessica said.

"That's rather the point," Henrick said. "We should arrive at my home in thirty minutes. There's a small refrigerator in the center console with some cold water if you're thirsty."

"That's very kind of you," Jessica said, helping herself. The water was not in a disposable plastic bottle or packet, ubiquitous in space, but in a clear glass bottle with a metal twist cap.

She twisted the cap off with a snap and took a long sip. The water had a slight alkaline taste.

"Prior to today, the only other time I met my Great-Grandmother was in 2892 when I was ten years old. Somehow my parents managed convince her to dial-up to real-time so she could meet with the latest generation of her descendants. I think that meeting lasted maybe forty minutes."

"What was it like?" Jessica asked.

"It was strange. The children all met her in turn where she would gush about how cute the babies were, or how big and strong the older children like me were. I got the impression that she was trying hard to pretend that she cared about her descendants."

"You don't think she did?"

Henrick shrugged. "She never spoke with any of her family in the sixty years since before today. I think she just decided to drop the pretense and enjoy her afterlife. At least before you came along."

"I suppose I should feel flattered,' Jessica said. "I hope that doesn't make you jealous."

Henrick pinched his thumb and forefinger together in the air. "Perhaps a little."

"And yet when she asked you to help me, you didn't hesitate," Jessica said. "Not to sound ungrateful, but it does seem seem like an odd thing to do for a dead woman who doesn't care about you."

"My great-grandmother's fortune has ensured that I and the rest of my family, and our descendants, get to live lives of leisure and comfort," Henrick said. "Her digital construct might not care about me, but after twenty years as her executor, its clear to me that the living Miriam Xia did care about the welfare of her descendants. To put it simply, I owe her a lot. Helping her digital construct in an… unusual situation like this seems more that reasonable. And besides, your situation is damn *interesting*. There are few things to a man who has everything that are more valuable than having something interesting happen."

Jessica picked up her bottle in a mock toast. "Well, I'm grateful to have your interest."

Henrick smiled and nodded, then turned to look out the window.

They spent the rest of the trip traveling through the streets of Singapore in comfortable silence. Just under half and hour later,

the car pulled into an underground garage at the base of a tower so tall its top floors disappeared into the soggy sky above. It came to a stop in front of an elevator, and by the time Jessica had undone her safety belt, Nigel had opened the door. She hadn't even noticed him get out.

"Welcome home, sir." Nigel said. "And I do hope you enjoy our hospitality, miss."

"Thank you, Nigel," Jessica said.

They rode the elevator up for several minutes before the doors parted at the top floor. Jessica found herself staring out over the clouds, broken only by the tops of other massive towers.

"Blimey!" Jessica breathed.

"Yes, quite the view, isn't it?" Henrick said. "Does keep one nicely above the worst of the monsoon weather."

Nigel took Henrick's coat and handed it to another, less advanced-looking servant robot that disappeared with it.

"No human staff?" Jessica enquired.

"None here. I can't abide paying a human being to engage in menial labor," Henrick said.

"Serving your personage is hardly menial, sir," Nigel said.

"Of course, you would say that. You were built for it," Henrick said.

"Quite well too, if I may say so, sir," Nigel said. "Is there anything you need before I retire?"

"Not yet, Nigel. Feel free to return to you charging station and get that update that's been waiting for you," Henrick said.

"Very good, sir." Nigel gave his master a slight bow. "Enjoy the rest of your evening. Don't hesitate to ask if you need anything."

"Thank you, Nigel. Come along, Lieutenant. Let's not keep my great-grandmother waiting."

Jessica followed him. The lounge sat towards the middle of the penthouse, away from the vast windows that looked out over Singapore's soggy skyline.

When Henrick opened the door to the lounge, Jessica heard the authoritative ticking of a massive clock. As she entered and turned her attention to the clock, she saw Miriam Xia standing facing the clock, her back to the door. Far more dressed than when Jessica had met her inside her virtual world, she wore a dark blue pantsuit cut to show off her figure, though not nearly as well as her birthday suit had. She was slightly transparent, a holographic projection. Jessica could barely make out the glare of the laser projectors in the ceiling.

"I see you've kept this thing running, Great-Grandson," Miriam said.

"Not easily," Henrick said. "There aren't a lot of clockmakers to go around these days."

"Entropy doesn't like letting things last." She turned around to face Jessica. "Ah, my great-grandson's penetration tester."

"Was that your idea?" Jessica asked.

"As much as I would love to take the credit, it was Henrick who thought of the lie," Miriam said. "I'm afraid I haven't kept up with the latest security protocols in the last two hundred years."

"It would cut into your nude sunbathing time, I'm sure," Jessica said.

"Quite. You should give it a try some time," Miriam said.

"I'll keep that in mind, but I'm afraid I am here for business," Jessica said.

"Ah yes, the Special Purpose Branch was never big on fun."

"Isn't that the bloody truth," Jessica agreed.

"Well, take a seat—might as well enjoy my great-grandson's hospitality while we get down to business."

Jessica sat down on a deep-brown leather couch that was tasteful and very comfortable. Henrick sat down in a large chair that looked made specifically for him.

Miriam walked over to Jessica and sat down next to her, which looked somewhat bizarre as her weightless holographic body didn't sink into the cushions but just kind of floated on top of them. Crossing her legs and wrapping her hands around her top knee, Miriam leaned forward and turned to Jessica, letting her long black hair hang down.

Bloody hell, she is attractive, Jessica thought. In life, Miriam Xia had paid for the finest of cosmetic surgeries and gym trainers to keep her among what the media at the time dubbed the most beautiful women in the solar system. She had ranked up with the likes of supermodels and movie stars, though she had no interest in modeling or acting herself. She wanted the world to know her for one thing first and foremost: a shrewd businesswoman and industrialist.

"I take it you've caught up with current events?" Jessica asked.

"Yes. It's very distressing. It's almost embarrassing that I was lounging on a beach while the Earth Federation was facing an existential crisis. Tossing all of Jupiter's stations out of orbit was a brilliant strategic move. The First Fleet's not going to have enough fuel to both evacuate them and fight of a push from the Ascendency."

"No, which is why we're in a hurry trying to secure fuel from other sources," Jessica said.

"The League, namely," Miriam said. "I saw that Triumph is still the League's main fuel production center."

"A couple of hundred years is nowhere near enough time to deplete the reserves of three gas giants," Jessica said.

"I suppose not. It's ironic that Triumph would become important for the Earth Federation's survival. Considering Earth Fed's history with that world."

The Battle of 61 Virginis during the climax of the First League War had been, up until very recently, the greatest defeat the Federal Space Forces had ever experienced, practically wiping out every operational Federal warship at the time. If the League had had the capacity to invade Federal space back then, it would have been the end right there.

Even so, the defeat and resulting loss of confidence in the centralized Federal government had almost led to it falling apart, until a new administration and a lot of diplomatic compromise averted the total dissolution of the Earth Federation barely thirty years after its founding.

"Under normal circumstances, I'm sure the League would be more than happy to see the Ascendency take down the Earth Federation," Jessica said. "Unfortunately, the Ascendency also wants to destroy the League, so our fates are currently linked."

"Yes, if I were in charge of the Ascendency, I wouldn't have declared war against both the Earth Federation and the League," Miriam said.

"The flaw in that logic is that we don't actually know why the Ascendancy decided to attack," Jessica said. "I was hoping that you might have some insights."

Miriam sighed. "If the Ascendency is the result of Julian's work, then I'm afraid I'm as lost as you are."

"You know what he intended to do?" Jessica asked.

"Yes. He wasn't a grifter, like some in my family believed." Miriam gave her great-grandson a pointed stare. Henrick for his part just shrugged and sipped his tea.

"So, what was his plan?" Jessica asked.

"Well, if they are a result of his work, then they are not doing what he intended them to do," Miriam said. "Julian wanted to create a post-human species that was beyond vulgar things like warfare. They were supposed to, above all else, value knowledge. He wanted them to be explorers, not conquerors."

"It seems that they've turned into the latter, sadly," Jessica said. 'Do you think Doctor Marr changed his mind at some point after his departure?"

"I doubt it, but I can't say for certain," Miriam said. "There's only so much faith I can put into the promises a dead man gave a dead woman."

"We know that Julian gave a falsified destination for his ship," Jessica said. "Would you know where he intended to go?"

"I was aware his stated destination was false," Miriam said. "But I don't know precisely where he intended to go. I don't believe he even knew where he was going at the time the *Ascension* departed."

"You mean the *Ascension* didn't have a destination in mind when she set out?" Jessica interjected.

"That's right," Miriam said. "But while I can't tell you where he was going I can tell you where he did *not* intend to go."

"Which was?" Jessica prompted.

"To any main sequence star, particularly any that were charted," Miriam said. "He was just going to travel a hundred or so light-years away from Sol and then look for an acceptable place to put down his roots. He knew his project would take centuries and he didn't want it to be interrupted by human expansion. His idea was rather radical. Find either a rogue planet or brown dwarf far away from Federal Space and use the resources there to start his project. It's all in the manifest. The real one, not the one made publicly available."

"Where would I find this secret manifest?" Jessica asked.

"I have it," Miriam said.

"Might I look at it?"

Miriam nodded, and an icon appeared on Jessica's HUD.

The manifest was a simple plain-text file that took an instant to download. Jessica opened it and started reading through it. It was comprehensive.

There wasn't a single piece of equipment carried aboard *Ascension* that would be of any use trying to establish a planetary colony. But there was plenty of gear for mining and construction of space-based infrastructure, including an army of construction drones.

What Jessica saw was not the manifest of a colony ship, but a massive, long-range factory ship, not unlike current vessels used to build space stations over distant stars.

"There must be a space station out there where the Ascendancy got started," Jessica said.

"That was what I was led to believe," Miriam said. "Though my knowledge is two hundred years out of date."

"And there's nothing you know that would suggest Doctor Marr's creation, the Ascendency, would become a threat to humanity?" Jessica probed.

"Doctor Marr, for all his vision, was a very pessimistic man when it came to humanity," Miriam said. "He was certain that even after reaching the stars, humans would find some way to drive themselves to extinction, be it through a self-destructive war or earning the ire of an advanced alien civilization. If he had his way, humanity would never have learned of the Ascendency's existence. At least not until all the biologicals had died off."

"That's what you were waiting for, wasn't it? For humanity, its biological members at least, to die off?"

Miriam shrugged. "Julian's conclusions seemed logical, and with the time compression, I didn't think I'd have to wait more than a few decades of subjective time before whatever apocalypse ultimately befell the human race came and went."

"And what would you do if the Ascended dug you up from the rubble?" Jessica asked.

"Learn what they discovered," Miriam said. "They were made to be explorers, Lieutenant. There's a lot they could learn over the centuries."

"Well, it seems they decided to run up the timetable of their return."

Henrick set down his teacup, having quietly observed the conversation. "So, this is the story Marr sold you to get you to help finance his little adventure. That he'd make a race of monsters to explore the cosmos until the filthy apes died off."

"I wouldn't put it that way," Miriam said. "There was a possibility, however unlikely, that humanity would naturally evolve out of its self-destructive nature."

Henrick snorted. "Seems to me, Great-grandmother, that the Cendies decided not to wait for either outcome."

CHAPTER 14

"Launch! Launch! Launch!" shouted Captain Alvarez, and *Amazon*'s catapult tossed Mason's Lightning out of the hangar.

The assault ship was already hurtling towards 61 Virginis at several hundred kilometers per second when she jumped, appearing fifty thousand kilometers short of the jump limit.

Lightnings and assault shuttles launched in sequence behind Mason's Lightning, shooting out of the hangars at nearly two hundred kilometers per hour, opening the distance in seconds.

Mason ignited his long-burn drives and oriented his fighter towards 61 Virginis, a gentle 1g pulling him into his seat. Behind him, *Amazon*'s maneuvering thrusters burned bright as they pushed to flip the massive starship over.

"Good luck out there, Colonel," Captain Alvarez said over the local channel. "We'll loiter out in deep space providing updates to Federal Command."

"Thank you, Captain. Stay safe out there," Colonel Shimura responded.

"Thank you, Colonel. *Amazon* out."

"How's it looking on your end, Squadron Leader?" Colonel Shimura asked Mason.

"Looks much the same as the deep scan, just better resolution," Mason said. "What's left of the League's 1st Battlefleet is huddled down near Ash while the Cendies are loitering around that big asteroid up orbit from

Triumph, staying out of effective range of the planet's missiles. It'll be a few minutes before their closest units detect our jump flash."

"Then let's open up as much distance as we can. Throttle up the long-burn drives, Squadron Leader."

"Will do," Mason said. "All ships, commencing 5g burn on my mark. Mark!"

He pushed the throttle forward, sending a tactile command to his Lightning's flight AI to increase thrust.

Over the course of a minute, the output from his fighter's two long-burn drives multiplied until the thrust gravity became mildly crushing. At least by fighter pilot standards, 5gs was nothing too strenuous. Too much for standing up and walking, but perfectly reasonable when resting in an acceleration seat. No hardsuit or g-tolerance implants required.

Of course, most of the people aboard the assembled small craft burning towards Triumph weren't fighter pilots.

Mason glanced at the status display of the sixteen fighters and eight assault shuttles burning hard towards Triumph, and their pilots. Everything appeared normal with both the ships and their pilots, but the information panels told him little of the state of the passengers and cargo who were also being subjected to the high acceleration.

<How are you doing back there, Colonel?> Mason asked, subvocally. Five gs was just a little too heavy to make oral communications comfortable.

<Not my first experience with heavy gs, Squadron Leader. But your concern is appreciated,> Shimura responded.

<I wouldn't be a very good pilot if I didn't keep an eye on my passengers, sir>

<Is that from your background as a hauler pilot, Squadron Leader?>

<It wouldn't do to have you stroke out while I'm not paying attention, sir>

<I'll try not to do that. Now if you don't mind, I think I'm going to go under for a bit. Wake me if anything disastrous happens.>

<Sleep tight, sir>

Colonel Shimura's vitals settled into the rhythm of induced sleep, leaving Mason alone in his cockpit as the collection of small craft fell past the jump limit.

Five minutes after *Amazon*'s departure, a Cendy picket force of two Fusilier-class battlecruisers and one Katyusha-class arsenal ship jumped in with bright arrival flashes. The range and relative velocity was too high for even the arsenal ship's missiles, so the Cendies didn't bother with pursuit. Instead, the picket force loitered at the edge of the jump limit as if to block off their most direct line of escape.

Ahead, the Cendy fleet inside the system had yet to be paying any mind. Triumph and its powerful Planetary Defense system were a far greater threat than a couple of dozen fighters and assault shuttles.

When Mason was halfway done with his approach burn towards Triumph, his sensors picked up the launch glows of thousands of chemical boost rockets. The glows were soon replaced with the vastly hotter exhaust of long-burn drives as the torpedoes that had been launched from Triumph's surface reached safe ignition altitude.

The torpedoes accelerated hard for 30 Skeksis and the Cendy fleet arrayed around it. With nothing else to hold his attention during the flight to Triumph, Mason watched as the torpedoes made their six-hour flight towards the Cendy fleet.

The Cendy fleet was spread out in a loose formation thousands of kilometers across, centered on 30 Skeksis. Hundreds of Cendy Outrider fighters maintained a screen between the Cendy warships and Triumph, with more fighters launching to reinforce the screen against the oncoming torpedo attack.

In the last minutes before impact, the Cendy fleet and fighter screen erupted with interceptors, point defenses, and jamming to blunt the attack. The heavy planetary torpedoes responded with countermeasures of their own, making random vector changes while launching decoys to confuse the Cendy defenses. And, while the Cendy fleet was spread out, the torpedoes focused on the ships on the Cendy flank.

Torpedoes winked off the screen in a rapid succession of flashes as Cendy defenses found their mark, dwindling in number at an exponentially increasing rate as they closed the range.

The battle concluded with a single huge flash as a solitary long-burn torpedo survived the gauntlet to get into detonation range of a Cendy battlecruiser.

<Leaguers sure put some big warheads on their torpedoes,> Flight Lieutenant Sabal subvocalized.

When the glow faded it left an expanding field of debris that used to be a Fusilier-class battlecruiser.

<I sure hope they don't shoot any of those at us when we enter the range,> Flight Lieutenant Dominic responded.

<They know we're coming,> Mason said. <We just need to get past the Cendies.>

<How do we intend to do that, Hauler?> Squadron Leader Dominic asked.

<We'll approach from the day side,> Mason said. <Triumph seems to be doing a good job holding the Cendies at bay right now. Might as well try to put that planet between us and them…>

A ping from his combat AI notified him of a change in vector from the Cendy fleet. The AI highlighted a group of icons burning hard in the rough direction of Osiris Squadron. Forty Cendy Outrider fighters vectoring on an intercept course.

<You seeing that, Hauler?> Zin asked.

<I see it, Shutdown,> Mason said. <Intercept in twenty hours. Looks like they want to catch us before we get too deep into Triumph's missile envelope.>

<What's the plan, Hauler?> Zin asked. <We ask the League for help?>

<I'll send a tightbeam, but I wouldn't assume that they will,> Mason said. <They might not have the fighters to spare.>

<So, we should prepare to fight our way through them?>

<Exactly, Shutdown,> Mason said.

CHAPTER 15

Captain Adakai was stoney-faced on the monitor as Jessica gave her update.

"So, it seems most likely that *Ascension* set up shop around a distant brown dwarf or rogue planet," Jessica finished. "Somewhere out of the way that still had the resources for them to develop their project."

"How likely do you think Doctor Marr's expedition is the source of the Ascendency?" Captain Adakai asked.

"Ninety-nine percent, sir," Jessica said. "The clues don't point anywhere else."

"The problem is, we don't know where *Ascension* went," Captain Adakai said.

"But we know where it didn't go," Jessica pointed out. "And we have the information provided by Mister Cordial during Colonel Shimura's mission to Fomalhaut. They go back some time."

"I'll get my analysts to work on it. See if we can't narrow down the places we need to search," Captain Adakai said. "Good work, by the way, Lieutenant. I'm glad we didn't have to disavow you."

"Me too, sir," Jessica said. "Though I'm afraid Miriam Xia didn't help me purely out of charity."

Captain Adakai sighed. "What does she want?"

"I think that's best for her to discuss with you," Jessica said.

"Hello, Captain Adakai," Miriam said.

"Mrs. Xia," Adakai said.

"Miriam, please. 'Mrs.' just reminds me how many husbands I've had," Miriam quipped. "I would like to ask a favor in return for my help. One that, in the long run, might prove useful in your efforts to discover where the Ascendency came from."

"I'm listening," Captain Adakai said.

"I wish to accompany Lieutenant Sinclair as she tries to find where the Ascendancy came from."

"Do you now? And what would you give in return?"

"Besides my knowledge of the Pinnacle Foundation and its members? How about over a century of life experience? I would be a valuable asset, and I'm not even charging a consulting fee."

"What do you think, Lieutenant?" Adakai asked.

"I think it would be a good idea to have her on hand," Jessica said. "She has insights into what the Ascendency was supposed to be, which can be useful in determining what they actually are, and what their ultimate goals are."

"And how, may I ask, do you intend to bring Miriam with you?" Adakai asked. "Last I checked, her mind resides in a computer buried a kilometer below Singapore."

"I already have a mobility rig that I can upload to," Miriam said.

"You realize you'll be risking your life," Adakai said.

"I'll have a local backup on pause while I'm away," Miriam said. "Should I meet an unfortunate end, I'll just have missed a little bit of subjective time. And if I survive, well, it's been a while since I've had a real adventure."

"I'll need to get a special pass for you, Miriam," Adakai said. "There are quite a number of laws that prohibit what you're suggesting, but exceptions can be made."

"I know, my great-grandson's lawyers have already pointed out as much."

"Then I'll see about getting approval. When I get that, you will be under Lieutenant Sinclair's authority."

"Oh? Do I get a rank?" Miriam asked.

"No," Captain Adakai said. "Lieutenant Sinclair, see to getting your… consultant ready for travel."

Jessica nodded. "I will, sir."

"Good. See you topside." Captain Adakai closed the connection.

"Well, I suppose we'll need to get you a mobility rig," Jessica said.

"I already have something lined up," Miriam said. "I'm finishing uploading to it right now."

"Where can I find it… or you, as would be the case?" Jessica asked.

"I'll find you, just wait," Miriam said before fading away.

Jessica sighed and made herself comfortable looking out over the monsoon-drenched skyline outside the windows.

Soft footsteps alerted her to someone's approach, and she turned to see a high-end mobility rig walking towards her. Her breath caught in her throat.

"I take it you like?" Miriam said. The mobility rig had a fully expressive face. It didn't have Miriam's face, instead opting for a stylized feminine face that blended well with the rest of the body.

Jessica stood up. "Feminine without going full fem-bot—nice. I'm surprised you didn't get one modeled after yourself."

Miriam did a little pirouette, showcasing all the lines and curves of her new body. It was light-years ahead of the boxy and functional mobility rigs that Jessica had the displeasure of using. "I didn't have time for a custom order, so I had to get something off-the-shelf, so to speak."

"Whoever you got it from does fast deliveries."

"My great-grandson charged the expedited delivery fee to my estate."

The mobility rig was a work of art that evoked the sculptures of classical Greece. Long slender arms, a modest bust, with a subtly concave waist, generous hips, and broad legs. The mobility rig was alluring without being lewd. The way it was colored and textured served to deemphasize sexual characteristics, making everything blend into the body as a whole. It almost looked like a well-tailored hardsuit.

"Well, I'm feeling a little jealous. I've only had the economy models," Jessica said.

Miriam looked Jessica up and down with subtly glowing gold eyes. "You don't look like an economy model."

Jessica touched her chest. "Oh, not this, of course. This body is a prized piece of military hardware."

"Oh? What can it do?"

"That is classified," Jessica said. "But you might get a chance to see what I can do when you're working with me."

"I look forward to that," Miriam said. "But the Earth Federation seems to have made sure they gave you a body that serves you well. If you don't mind my asking, how did you end up losing your biological body?"

Jessica shrugged. "There wasn't much to lose. My parents were big into things like nature and purity. So, they didn't bother with any of the pre-natal care that would have caught, and corrected, the tetra-amelia syndrome I was born with. Further, they refused to correct it post-natal for some rubbish reason. I couldn't get it fixed until after I turned eighteen and my parents no longer had a say in the matter."

"Oh, that's horrid. I take it your parents didn't take it well?"

"I haven't spoken to them in over a decade, so no," Jessica said.

"Well, I won't dig any further," Miriam said. "So, where do we go, boss?"

"Boss?"

"Your CO made it clear you're my boss. So, where do we go?"

"A shuttle's waiting for us at the spaceport," Jessica said. "Think your great-grandson could spot us a ride?"

CHAPTER 16

"Osiris Leader, Triumph Planetary Defense Central Control. We acknowledge your call for assistance and will vector fighters to help," said a gruff, accented male voice over the tightbeam.

Mason felt more than a little relief. He wouldn't have to face the incoming Cendy fighters without support.

"Relief fighters will take position along your vector at this point."

A waypoint appeared, and Mason's heart sank. The League fighters would remain close to Triumph, millions of kilometers short of the point where the Cendy fighters would intercept his squadron.

<Belts and zones!> Mason exclaimed.

<That good, huh?> Zin asked. They were over the command channel, with Dominic and Sabal.

<Well, the good news is that they are sending help,> Mason said. <But their fighters aren't flying too far from Triumph. Probably don't want to risk losing whatever they have left.>

<Fuck the League! We'll deal with the Cendies ourselves,"> Sabal said.

<We're outnumbered over two to one,> Dominic said. "We're going to take losses.>

<Risk is part of the job, old man,> Sabal said.

<Not just our lives we'll be risking, Hardball,> Dominic said. <We've got passengers to think of.>

Mason glanced at Colonel Shimura's vitals. She was still in a deep induced sleep while the hard-burn continued. <Silverback's right. We need to take precautions to minimize our losses as much as possible.>

<What's the plan, Hauler?> Zin asked.

<I'm open to suggestions.>

<We could burn ahead and counter-intercept the Cendies before they get close enough to shoot at the assault shuttles,> Sabal suggested.

<That doesn't exactly work towards keeping us alive,> Dominic pointed out. <Any chance we could directly ask the League fighters for help?>

<What? Out of a sense of solidarity?> Sabal said. <Even if they were willing to risk their necks for us, which I doubt, they probably have orders not to fly off away from Triumph.>

<No, but maybe we can use bits of both plans,> Mason said.

<You've got an idea, Hauler?> Zin asked.

<We'll push ahead of the assault shuttles and engage the Cendies early, like Hardball suggested,> Mason said. <But before anyone gets too excited, we're not going to engage in a protracted fight. We're loaded with a lot of interceptors. We'll leverage that with a high-speed missile volley.>

<And the assault shuttles?> Zin asked.

<We'll get them to adjust their vector to make them move them further away from the intercept point.>

<The Cendies can easily adjust,> Zin said.

<Yes, but if we do this right, they'll have to pass through the area of space the League fighters will be occupying,> Mason said.

<Assuming they're there to help,> Zin muttered. <What if they're not?>

<Then instead of a flyby, we engage the Cendies at a low relative velocity and tie them up in a dogfight until the assault shuttles make it to safety.>

<Roger that, Hauler,> Zin said.

Against forty Outriders, the chances of survival weren't what Mason would prefer. In fact, he guessed better than even odds that all his fighters would get wiped out. It was a near certainty they would suffer heavy losses. But there were hundreds of people aboard the assault shuttles. Counting the passengers in every Lightning, the loss of Osiris Squadron would amount to 32 deaths, including practically every trooper officer and senior non-commissioned officer.

Mason opened the display reporting the vitals of all the passengers they were carrying. Troopers were supposed to have the same g-tolerance as pilots, but they didn't spend much time in extended high-g flights. That meant less time for any flaws in their augmentations to present themselves.

He put the worries out of his mind. The Outriders had to be dealt with. If he survived, that's when he'd deal with the problems any casualties would present.

<All fighters form on my wing and prepare to go hard-burn,> Mason ordered.

Fifteen Lightnings gathered around his in four loose, uneven chevrons.

<On my mark. Three…two…one…mark!"> He pushed his throttles forward, and the acceleration doubled, and then tripled. Fifteen gs wasn't for long-burns, but he wouldn't have to keep it up for long.

Osiris Squadron flared across the EM spectrum, their drive glows brighter than even the main star of 61 Virginis.

The assault shuttles in contrast cut back their drives and changed their vector, setting up to fly past Triumph rather than stop. The line of their predicted vector passing close to the League fighters.

The Outriders turned to face the incoming Lightnings, their long-burn drives glowing bright at full throttle.

The time to range was less than half an hour. Mason started working out target selection. He intended on launching every interceptor his squadron carried in the first pass. He had twelve interceptors per Lightning, just short of two hundred in total. Enough to send five interceptors against almost every Outrider.

Of course, each of the 40 Outriders carried up to eight interceptors. Over three hundred in total.

Belts and zones! he thought as he did the math. Twenty interceptors for each Lightning. And that was assuming the Cendies didn't concentrate their fire.

A chill ran through Mason's body. It wasn't the first time he'd had that many interceptors homing in on him, but his experience had done little to inure him to the danger.

The stiletto pods and their tiny stiletto interceptors were his main advantage in the upcoming fight. They had proven to be exceptionally good at defending against incoming interceptors. But the Cendies had had months of exposure to them and were no doubt developing countermeasure.

Mason just hoped that the fighters who were about to try to kill him and his squadron didn't have any yet.

He chose his targets, picking Outriders towards the edge of the formation, and then uploaded the targets to Zin.

<We're only engaging sixteen of them? That's fewer than half,> Zin said, using the direct private channel.

<We don't need to kill them all, just bloody their noses,> Mason said. <This will give each of us one target to focus all our attention on.>

<Roger that, Hauler,> Zin said. <I'll pass it down to the rest of the squadron.>

Zin switched to the Squadron Channel. <Good news, you each get a Cendy to kill today. Every fighter has one Cendy to focus all their tender loving attention on.>

<Just one, Shutdown? We're not going to kill even half of them focusing our fire like this,> Sabal protested.

<You have your target, Flight Lieutenant,> Zin said.

As Zin handled passing down his order, Mason switched his attention to Triumph. Rising from the planet and riding long trails of superheated long-burn drive exhaust, his sensor AI resolved a full squadron of twelve League Asp fighters pulling 10gs to get to the rendezvous point.

Mason sighed in relief. Whatever happened, the Cendies wouldn't be able to engage the assault shuttle without running afoul of a squadron of League fighters. Now all he had to do was survive the next thirty minutes.

His orders given and targets assigned, there wasn't much more for Mason to do than fly his fighter into harm's way.

He picked the leader of one of the Cendy squadrons for himself. He didn't know how Cendy fighter squadrons handled things like chain of command, but whatever it was, he doubted it would work as well when Osiris Squadron's interceptors started cutting links.

All twelve Javelin Mark IV interceptors showed green on his weapons display, their seeker heads booted up and lapping up the targeting data fed to them by his Lightning's sensors. All twelve of them here singularly focused on his target the way only machines could be.

He wondered how many Cendy seeker heads were locked on his Lightning, waiting for their chance to come out and meet him as soon as he entered the engagement envelope.

The Cendies fired first, launching a volley of three hundred and twenty interceptors. All appeared to be tracking reliably. Even before they launched, the combat AI got to work using dazzle lasers and jammers to throw off their locks, joined by those of Osiris Squadron's other Lightnings.

Mason's target started to blur as the Outriders' jammers and dazzle lasers activated, the two forces throwing gigawatts of disruptive energy at each other.

<Osiris Nine ready to fire,> Sabal said, her subvocalized voice carrying her eagerness to fire.

<Wait for my order,> Mason said. They couldn't afford to fire their interceptors too soon. He wanted the Cendies deep inside the Javelin's engagement envelope.

His thumb started to ache as it hovered over the firing button in 15gs of gravity, waiting for the range to close just a bit closer, just a bit closer.

<Fire!> Mason mashed the button on his stick.

The four interceptors on the wings simply popped off with the force of explosive bolts and flew off. The rapid-fire rotary launcher in his fighter's belly ejected the remaining eight, one at a time in half-second intervals.

All his interceptors flew true, bearing down on his target. The Cendies were not slow to realize they had interceptors bearing down on them and flared their drives, pushing past 20gs as they started to evade.

Mason took a glance at his tactical screen. He had twenty interceptors bearing down on him. He should do something about that.

He pushed his long-burn drive to emergency power, piling five more gs on him. Every inch of his body went from aching to straight up hurting. The gel layer of his hardsuit felt like iron against his back. The skin of his face stretched taut, and his eyeballs squeezed down into their sockets.

All the while, the twenty interceptors his combat AI were tracking changed their vectors to remain on a collision course with their prey.

But he wasn't alone. The rest of his flight stayed on his wing and formed into a vertical diamond formation, providing overlapping defenses.

Each fighter in his flight had twenty Cendy interceptors of their own chasing them.

The combat AI of each fighter got hard at work trying to come up with a strategy that maximized the chance of survival of the flight, potentially sacrificing one of his pilots to save the others.

Mason was not one of the sacrifices. His fighter had both the mission's overall commander and the leader of the squadron aboard. The combat AIs would prioritize the survival of his fighter over those of the junior pilots around him.

The privilege of command. Thinking about it made Mason's stomach churn, the queasy feeling exacerbated by the heavy gs.

As time to impact closed, Cendy interceptors started to lose lock, either fooled into chasing imaginary targets or blinded by dazzling lasers.

Steadily, missiles fell away from the flock of munitions burning through space towards his squadron, a steady attrition as the time to impact counted down.

Mason didn't need the combat AI to tell him it wasn't enough.

A dozen Cendy interceptors made it into the engagement envelope of Mason's Stilettoes before the combat AI fired. Twenty-four of the little interceptors flew out of the wing-mounted pods, launching perpendicular to the wings before turning to engage their targets.

Stilettoes short-burn drives only had a few seconds of fuel aboard, just enough for the small missiles to place themselves between the interceptors and their targets.

The Cendy interceptors attempted to evade, making violent turns to get around the Federal interceptors. Most didn't succeed, and were vaporized by direct collisions, but there were still four bearing down on Mason.

Eight more Stilettoes left the pods in the last moments before impact.

Two interceptors flashed out of existence.

The other two continued on track.

The pop of the countermeasure launchers was the last thing Mason registered before a flash blinded his sensors.

Though blind, he didn't feel any impacts, just the continuing 20g pull.

When his sensors recovered, Mason could see the universe around him again. The Cendy interceptors must have struck the decoys his fighter dropped, the flash of their nearby impact blinding him.

There were four Lightnings glowing an angry red. Izumo in Osiris 2, Dominic in Osiris 9, Yardley in Osiris 4, and Kazan in Osiris 15.

Thousands of kilometers away, there was a staccato of flashes as Osiris Squadron's interceptors found their targets. Fifteen Cendy fighters dropped off the threat list, turned into expanding clouds of gas and debris that glowed on the thermal imager.

And just like that, the fight was over, the Cendies receding into the distance faster than any weapon Mason had at his disposal.

Free from danger for the moment, Mason cut his long-burn drives to 1g and almost passed out from relief.

Collecting himself, he checked the vector of the Cendy fighters. Their formation was reorganizing after scattering to evade his squadron's interceptors, but their vector didn't yet intersect with the assault shuttles. Further in the direction of Triumph, the League fighters waited, the assault shuttles just about to fly by them.

<Hauler, report,> Zin said over the direct channel.

Mason shook himself and checked her status display. Zin and Second Flight seemed undamaged.

<I'm here, Shutdown. What is it?>

<Just checking in with you. We're picking up a beacon from Silverback's cockpit. Looks like he ejected after his fighter got hit,> Zin said.

Some good news for once. <What about the others?> Mason asked.

<Nothing, sir.>

Mason took one more look at the Cendies as they grew more distant. They were still accelerating, but their changing vector was moving away from the assault shuttles, bending back towards the outer system. It appeared that after their little scuffle with Mason's squadron, they'd decided they'd had enough.

<Get someone to pick up Silverback's cockpit. I'm going to check the wreckage of Osiris 2,> Mason said. <Who's checking on the others?>

<Osiris 8 is already moving to grab Silverback's cockpit,> Zin said.

<Osiris 3 is moving to examine Osiris 4's wreckage. Hardball and her flight are checking in on their casualty.>

Mason locked onto the remains of Osiris 2, picking out the largest piece. It looked like the fighter had broken into three large pieces, the engine nacelles and wings moving on separate trajectories from what remained of the fuselage.

From a distance, the forward fuselage looked mostly intact.

Mason resisted the urge to feel hope. The rescue beacon wasn't working. Those were supposed to activate automatically if a damaged fighter still had a live pilot aboard. But no one entirely trusted them, and the last thing Mason was going to do was abandon one of his pilots to the mercies of empty space.

Mason locked onto Osiris 2 and burned towards them, canceling out most of his velocity a few kilometers away, and then coasting the rest of the way using the gentle pulses of his fighter's maneuvering thrusters. Firing the braking thrusters a few hundred meters away, he activated his external search light and shone it on the broken remains of Osiris 2.

The severed frontal half slowly rotated along its long axis; the fighter was neatly severed just behind the cockpit canopy. The line of blackened metal was perilously close to where the rear of the cockpit would be.

But he had to know.

Extending the grappler arm from the nose of his Lightning, Mason eased his fighter up to Osiris 2 until he was just in reach. Then he reached out with the arm and caught the nose of the spinning wreck.

His fighter bucked under the impact and maneuvering thrusters hissed and popped as the flight AI killed Osiris 2's remaining momentum.

<This is Hauler, I've made hard contact with Osiris 2. Going EVA to investigate the cockpit,> Mason said.

Colonel Shimura was still asleep, oblivious to the battle that had just happened. Mason saw no reason to wake her but made sure her suit was sealed before he depressurized the cockpit and opened the canopy.

Releasing his restraints, he pushed himself out of the cockpit, floating a few meters free of his Lightning before activating his suit thrusters.

From outside, he saw his fighter locked into an awkward embrace with the broken frontal half of Osiris 2's fuselage.

Using the pulse of the suit thrusters, he pushed himself towards Osiris 2, moving slowly enough to grab a handhold near the cockpit and anchor himself to the fuselage. He pulled open a panel, exposing an emergency release handle and a pressure gauge that showed the cockpit was depressurized.

Mason pulled the handle.

A shudder ran through Osiris 2 and the canopy floated away.

Mason braced himself for what he was about to see.

It didn't help.

The light from his helmet revealed the charred interior of Osiris 2, and its occupants.

Major Hauer and Flying Officer Izumo were mummified in the semi-molten remains of their hardsuits. There was a small comfort in knowing that the jet of plasma that had charred and melted the exterior of their hardsuits would've killed them before they knew what had happened.

<This is Hauler. I've opened the cockpit. There are no survivors,> Mason said.

<Understood, Hauler,> Zin said. <Osiris 8's picked up Silverback's cockpit and has it locked up inside their weapons bay. Both he and his passenger are unharmed.>

<That's good.> Mason said and sighed heavily. <Not much left for us to do here. I'm going to place Osiris 2 into graveyard orbit. We'll recover them when we leave the system.>

His grim task finished, Mason ordered Osiris Squadron to re-form and rendezvous with the assault shuttles. Between the hard-burn from the jump limit and the fight with the Cendies, fuel levels were starting to get low. It was enough for a 1g cruising burn to Triumph, but only just.

The assault shuttles were proceeding to Triumph on their own, under escort of the League fighters that had loitered while his squadron almost died. He felt a pang of anger. If they had helped, three of his pilots and their passengers would probably still be alive.

The assault shuttles and their escorts entered low orbit over Triumph. As Mason closed the range, a transmission came from the lead League fighter.

"Osiris Leader, this is Centurion Leader," said in an authoritative female voice. "You are to enter formation with my squadron and follow us down to Citadel 44. Do you copy?"

"I copy, Centurion Leader. Vectoring to match orbits now," Mason said.

He locked onto Centurion Leader and set his flight AI to make intercept.

It was about time to wake his passenger up and give her the bad news. He started the wakeup procedures and watched Colonel Shimura's vitals as she was roused out of her induced sleep.

"Fuck me!" were the first words out of her mouth as she came back to consciousness, feeling the aftereffects of the extreme gs he had subjected her body to. "What happened, Squadron Leader?"

"We got intercepted by Cendy fighters," Mason said.

"Clearly we got the better of them," Colonel Shimura said. "Losses?"

"Four fighters. Three with their passengers and crew. Including Major Hauer," Mason said.

"I see," Colonel Shimura said. "That is unfortunate. How about the assault shuttles?"

"All intact and waiting for us in low orbit," Mason said. "We're on our way to meet them and their escorts now."

"Escorts? Did the League help deal with the Cendies?" Shimura asked.

"No, sir," Mason said.

"Well, this is off to a poor start," Colonel Shimura said. "Thank you for waking me up, Squadron Leader, and for getting all the assault shuttles through, despite resistance. I'm going to check in with the assault shuttles."

"Understood, sir," Mason said.

They formed up with the assault shuttles a few minutes later, orbiting just five hundred kilometers above the surface of Triumph.

The planet itself was about two billion years older than Earth. It was a world of low mountains and vast shallow seas that, despite its age, had never achieved more than the most rudimentary forms of life.

There were three mid-sized continents divided by three oceans, each of which rivaled the Pacific Ocean in size. The continents combined had slightly less land area than that of the Eurasian continent on Earth. The interiors of each continent were a mix of equatorial deserts and temperate forests at the higher latitudes. Urban centers were concentrated along the coasts, massive archologies surrounded by farmland, each one connected by networks of roads and highspeed rail.

It looked a lot like any developed world Mason had ever orbited over.

A waypoint appeared in the center of the continent of Stoneland, Citadel 44.

"We'll be descending into the atmosphere in twenty minutes, Squadron Leader. Are all your fighters ready for atmospheric flight?" asked the leader of the League squadron.

"We are, Centurion Leader," Mason said. "Lead the way."

Minutes later, the League fighters fired their retro thrusters, lowing the periapsis of their orbit into the atmosphere of the planet. Mason matched the maneuver, as did the assault shuttles and the rest of Osiris Squadron.

From there, it was just a matter of letting gravity and momentum carry them the rest of the way in.

CHAPTER 17

There was a great bustle of traffic around Ariane Orbital Gateway as Jessica's shuttle drifted into the docking bay. There was an even mix of passenger haulers, personnel capsules, assault shuttles, and civilian aerospace shuttles streaming to and from the station, almost all probably involved with transferring evacuees from the Jovian stations down to Earth's surface. There were lines much like it around all of Earth's orbital gateways, and at every near-Earth habitat as part of the effort to transfer twenty million people to safety.

Fortunately, her shuttle was given priority, so she didn't have to wait in the long queue of vessels awaiting their turn to dock.

Millions of kilos of fuel were being burned every second by all the ships involved in the evacuation, draining the First Fleet's fuel reserves like sand out of an hourglass. Jessica could calculate down to the hour when the evacuation efforts would exhaust the 1st Fleet's fuel reserves. After that, without a prompt resupply, the war was as good as over.

In the seat next to her, Miriam pressed her face against the small viewport in the side of the shuttle, taking in the sight of the massive station and the long lines of space traffic filing into it.

"I could connect you to the shuttle's external cameras if you want to get a better view," Jessica said. She had been plugged into the shuttle's external cameras since it took off from Singapore.

"Oh, I'm quite satisfied with the view I have from here," Miriam said.

"I've always loved to look out of a window when flying. It's been a long time, both objectively and subjectively, since I've gotten to experience it."

"How does modern space flight look to you?" Jessica asked.

"Much like it did two hundred years ago—which looked not that different from two hundred years before that. Mature technologies tend not to change very much."

"And yet you're still staring out that window," Jessica remarked.

"It's the wonder of it," Miriam said. "The vast majority of human history was with our feet firmly planted on the ground. It's the privilege of our generation to get to experience life beyond it."

"Our generation?" Jessica asked. "You're ten times my age."

"In relative terms," Miriam said.

The shuttle pulled into the northern docking bay, landing on the docking pad reserved for the Special Purpose Branch.

Captain Adakai was floating outside the airlock when Jessica and Miriam disembarked from the shuttle.

"Lieutenant Sinclair, Miss Xia, I hope you had a pleasant flight up orbit," the captain greeted them.

"It was nice to skip ahead in the queue," Miriam said.

"There are some perks to working with the Special Purpose Branch," Jessica said.

"I imagine I'll be earning those perks in short order," Miriam said.

"That's a good assumption, Miss Xia," Captain Adakai said. "I'm afraid you won't have much time to relax. *Goshawk* and *Hyena* are departing the system. You're going with them."

"If those carriers are departing, who's going to be covering the Sun-Jupiter L5 corridor, sir?" Jessica asked.

"No one, Lieutenant," Captain Adakai said. "There's no more traffic coming into the system, so there's no point in protecting the corridor."

"And what about the 1st Fleet?" Jessica asked. "The Cendies might try to push in with two fewer carriers in their way."

Captain Adakai shook his head. "A pair of carriers out at Jupiter-Sun L5 aren't going to make much of a difference. They'll do more good where they're going."

"And where is that?" Miriam asked.

"To Procyon to reinforce the 7th Fleet," Captain Adakai said.

"So, am I to take Miss Xia to see Admiral Moebius?" Jessica asked. "There's not much she'll get that I haven't already sent in my report."

"Those are your orders, Lieutenant. I'm afraid I can't go into further details since I don't have them. Flight Lieutenant Armitage will be rejoining her carrier. You will go along with her, as will Miss Xia."

"Lightnings only have one passenger seat, Captain," Jessica pointed out. "Unless you mean for her to sit in my lap."

Miriam chuckled. "That would be quite the feat in high-g."

"That won't be necessary," Captain Adakai said. "I know it might seem beneath your dignity, Miss Xia, but your mobility rig can be stowed in the Lightning's cargo compartment."

"Oh joy," Miriam said. "Well, let's get this over with, then."

"Lieutenant Armitage's fighter is waiting in the adjacent docking bay," Captain Adakai said. "I already have a suit ready for you outside the airlock, Lieutenant. Miss Xia, you can board the fighter while Lieutenant Sinclair suits up."

"If it's all right with you, I'd like to wait until Lieutenant Sinclair is ready before I stuff myself into a cargo hold."

"Suit yourself, Miss Xia," Captain Adakai said.

Jessica floated down the corridor to the adjacent suit room. Miriam moved behind her, making the slow and deliberate movements of someone not accustomed to movement in zero gravity.

Entering the suit room, Jessica found a uniform jumpsuit and pressure suit waiting for her, and immediately started pulling off her civilian attire.

"Oh my, you're not modest at all," Miriam said.

"I've never been much for modesty," Jessica said. "And neither are you for that matter."

"A fair point." Miriam floated in the suit room, watching Jessica with interest.

Despite saying she was not big on modesty, Jessica didn't strip down completely, just down to her underwear before pulling on her jumpsuit and zipping it up the front.

Then she pulled the pressure suit over it and pulled the bubble helmet on.

"All seals check out. Looks like I'm ready," Jessica said. "How about you?"

"I'll have to shut down before we enter the airlock," Miriam said. "This mobility rig lacks a vacuum-rated cooling system."

"There are more suits that will fit you," Jessica said. "The main reason I put on a pressure suit is for cooling."

Miriam shook her head. "That won't be necessary. I'm going to be stuffed into a cargo hold anyway, so no point in making the fit any tighter."

"Is there anything you need me to do?" Jessica asked.

"Wake me up when we get there." That said, Miriam curled into a fetal position, wrapping her arms around her legs until she formed a tight ball. Her eyes closed and her face relaxed into a peaceful expression.

"Sweet dreams, Miriam," Jessica said.

Miriam didn't respond; she had shut herself down.

Jessica gently pushed Miriam towards the open airlock and kicked off the bulkhead to follow her inside. She flew past Miriam and caught herself on the far side of the airlock just in time to catch her before she bumped into the outer hatch.

After cycling the airlock, Jessica opened the outer hatch and towed Miriam's curled-up body by the elbow.

Marbles was floating about her Lightning with some hangar techs, inspecting the fighter one last time before the long, hard flight to *Goshawk*.

"How's she looking there, Flight Lieutenant?" Jessica asked.

Marbles looked in Jessica's direction and pushed herself away from the Lightning, using a pulse from her suit thrusters to come to a stop before her. "As clean as the day she left the factory. This your cargo?"

"She's your second passenger," Jessica said. "Mind helping me secure her in the cargo hold?"

"Sure thing," Marbles said.

With Marbles' help, Jessica had Miriam's body secured by a web of elastic straps that would keep her body from bouncing about in the cargo hold during hard maneuvers.

Marbles hit a button, and the hatch in the bottom of the Lightning closed over Miriam. Jessica shuddered at the thought of being inside the dark cargo hold, but she reminded herself that Miriam wasn't aware of what was going on.

"Hope you're ready for some hard gs, Lieutenant," Marbles said. "Gonna be hauling ass the whole way to *Goshawk*."

"At this point, Marbles, I'm almost starting to enjoy high-g flight," Jessica said.

⁓

The flight to *Goshawk* afforded Jessica a high-level view of the evacuation of the Jovian stations.

Each of the four hundred stations had streams of spacecraft moving to them to pick up Jovian refugees, and then scattering away from them towards destinations around the inner solar system.

Most were headed to Earth and the habitats surrounding the planet, with the rest headed to the habitats in the Earth-Sun Lagrange points.

The bulk of the 1st Fleet maintained its orbit in the Earth-Luna L3, the second most powerful concentration of firepower in the solar system. The most powerful loitered high above it all around Jupiter where three hundred Ascendency warships waited for the Federals to expend their fuel reserves and then drive down towards Inner Sol to run a dagger right through the beating heart of the Earth Federation.

After two days of hard-burning, little had changed that paradigm. Marbles finished her braking burn and killed the fighter's main engines, coasting at a safe docking velocity towards FSFV *Goshawk*.

Like all Lion-class carriers, *Goshawk* had a large boxy superstructure at the front of the otherwise typical Federal starship design. That superstructure had dozens of covered openings, each one a hangar large enough to carry a full-sized strikecraft. *Goshawk* had fifty in total. Enough for the standard complement of three squadrons of Lightning aerospace fighters and one squadron of Conqueror space bombers, plus a couple of assault shuttles for good measure. With her sister ship, *Hyena*, *Goshawk* and the cruisers and destroyers escorting them represented a powerful concentration of Federal firepower that was about to abandon Sol.

Marbles slipped the Lightning into one of *Goshawk*'s hangar bays and set it down on the magnetic docking pad.

"Don't get out of your seat just yet, Lieutenant. *Goshawk*'s going to ignite her engines and start burning for the jump limit," Marbles warned.

Moments later, the gentle pull of thrust gravity pressed Jessica down into the gel cushion of her seat. The thrust gravity increased gradually until the pull of gravity reached a full standard g.

The cockpit canopy swung open, flooding the cockpit with the bright overhead LEDs of the hangar. Jessica released her restraints and climbed after Marbles out of the fighter. As soon as her feet hit the deck, she turned her attention to the Lightning's cargo hold.

The hangar techs had already opened it and were in the process of extracting Miriam's balled-up form, unfolding her mobility rig and laying her flat on a stretcher.

As they started rolling her, Jessica walked up beside them.

"Where are you taking her, Spacer?"

"*Her*, sir?" the tech asked.

It occurred to Jessica that they didn't know who they were carting. They were unaware that the mobility rig contained the digitized ghost of a famous industrialist. Captain Lafferty probably didn't want that getting around on her ship. As far as they were concerned, it was just an unusually pretty mobility rig.

"The mobility rig, where are you taking her?" Jessica asked.

"Ah, on account of the rig's feminine appearance, I get you, sir," the tech said. "We're supposed to take her to the habitat ring. Guess they'll have someone who knows their way around mobility rigs check it out."

After a quick airlock cycle, Jessica was able to pull off her helmet and breath in the crisp air of *Goshawk*'s interior. She was an old ship. The wear on her high-traction deck coating and the faded stains on the ballistic fabric spall liner made that evident. But the air had the clean smell of properly working air recyclers. Despite her age, *Goshawk* had been well maintained.

Jessica followed the gurney that bore Miriam to the elevator banks that ran up the spine of the ship. They descended towards the engines, coming to a stop at the habitation level roughly halfway between the carrier's blunt prow and engine cluster.

The habitation ring had been spun down, so it was just a matter of walking across one of the spokes that ran from the center of the hub out to the ring. The spoke terminated at a joint in the ring, where the gurney turned right into one of the gimbaled modules that made up the habitation ring like a necklace made of oblong beads.

The module Jessica found was a two-level habitation module filled with officers' quarters. The techs wasted no time in departing, scurrying away from officer country as quickly as they could and closing the hatch behind them.

A few minutes later, a lanky woman in a Fleet-blue jumpsuit, curly fair hair, and a prominent nose walked in. Jessica saluted, recognizing Captain Hera Lafferty by the name embroidered on her jumpsuit and the captain's bars on her collar.

"Welcome aboard *Goshawk*, Lieutenant Sinclair," Captain Lafferty greeted her.

"Thank you, sir," Jessica said. "And thank you for letting me borrow one of your pilots."

"Of course. I'm sure Flight Lieutenant Armitage is happy to be back with her squadron mates." Captain Lafftery walked towards Jessica until she was standing next to the gurney. "So, this is Miriam Xia, after a fashion."

"You sound impressed," Jessica said.

"Her company has built a significant amount of the Space Force's equipment since the Earth Federation was founded. It never occurred to me that she would become one of my passengers."

"Would you like me to wake her up so you can introduce yourself?" Jessica asked.

"At your leisure, Lieutenant," Captain Lafferty said.

Jessica reached behind Miriam's right ear and pressed the button hidden behind it. There was a faint whirl of cooling fans spinning up, and Miriam's eyes shot open.

Sitting up, Miriam looked around, taking in her surroundings. "I take it we made it?"

"You have. Welcome aboard FSFV *Goshawk*, Miss Xia. My name is Captain Hera Lafferty, and it's my privilege to be *Goshawk*'s commanding officer."

Miriam swung her legs over the side of the gurney and stood up to shake Captain Lafferty's hand. "A pleasure, Captain. I sense we're under thrust gravity. How long until we make the jump to Procyon?"

"We aren't jumping to Procyon," Captain Lafferty said. "That was a lie to maintain operational security."

"I see," Jessica said. "May I ask where we are going, Captain?"

"Checkpoint Hephaestus."

"Checkpoint Hephaestus? How cryptic," Miriam said. "Any hint on where that is?"

Captain Lafferty shrugged. "That was just the name attached to the coordinates sent with our orders. It's an empty volume of space ten light-years in the direction of League space. All I know is that *Hyena* and our escorts are heading that way as well."

"In the direction of League space?" Jessica queried. "Sounds like we're rendezvousing with other ships."

"That is my guess as well, though I'm not going to speculate on what it is until we arrive,' Captain Lafferty said. "I'll leave the rumors to the enlisted spacers."

"I'm curious—why would we need to go there?" Miriam asked. "I don't know what contribution I'd make to a fleet action."

"Indeed," Jessica said. "My job is to deliver intelligence to Admiral Moebius."

Captain Lafferty shrugged. "All my orders said was that I had to take you aboard my ship before we jumped out for Checkpoint Hephaestus. I suppose we'll both find out when we arrive there in a week."

CHAPTER 18

Atmospheric entry in the age of the long-burn drive was not the dramatic, fiery process that it was back in the days of chemical rockets and freeze-dried ice cream. Long-burn drives were so powerful and efficient that they made the process of entering a planet's atmosphere almost trivial.

Mason just kept his long-burn drives burning as he flew tail-first into Triumph's atmosphere, keeping his descent speed below the point where the shock heating could damage his Lightning. When he was deep enough in the atmosphere for drag to slow him down, he cut the long-burn drives and flipped his fighter over, transitioning to level flight over a rugged landscape of mountains and valleys stretching to the horizon in all directions.

He was right in the middle of the continent of Stoneland, the smallest of Triumph's three continents. The continent was a pair of tectonic plates grinding into each other, creating a vast mountain range in the interior.

Somewhere among the mountains below him was Citadel 44, the icon resting at the top of one of the multitude of peaks stabbing into the sky.

"I have visual on our destination, Colonel," Mason said.

"Good, it will be interesting to see what one of Triumph's defensive installations looks like up close," Colonel Shimura responded, her voice stiff and level.

Mason didn't know Shimura's mannerisms that well, but he did know that the more stressful things got, the more she buttoned up. He suspected Major Hauer's death weighed on her.

"What do you know about their bases?" Mason asked, hoping to direct her mind to something other than grief.

"Not much," Colonel Shimura said. "Most of what we know is the publicly available information about their civilian shelters. They have done a good job maintaining the secrecy of their military bases. All we have are educated guesses."

"Such as, sir?"

"Probably anything that you could conceive, Squadron Leader. Underground strikecraft hangars, munitions depots, surface-to-orbit missile batteries. Probably an entire industrial complex buried under bedrock to keep their defenses supplied," Colonel Shimura said. "We're going to be the first officers in the Special Purpose Branch to set foot in one of their installations."

As the Mason closed on Citadel 44, a pair of parallel runways on a flattened mountain top appeared through the thin clouds.

The base was far away from any of the cities that ringed the coasts of Stoneland. Road, rail, and a few scattered towns and farms nestled in the valleys between mountains were the only signs of civilization below him.

He suspected that the League had made a point of placing his squadron as far away from any major population centers as possible, minimizing the number of civilians who could have to see the triangular shapes of Federal Lightnings soaring overhead.

"Osiris Leader, this is Centurion Leader. Enter the holding pattern around Citadel 44 and await landing instructions," said the leader of Mason's escort.

The Asps broke formation, climbing to higher altitude, both to provide cover for the landing Federals, and to remind them whose planet they were flying over.

"Roger that, Centurion Leader," Mason said. He connected to Citadel 44's air traffic control channel and cleared his throat. "Citadel 44, this is Osiris Leader, request landing instructions."

"Osiris Leader, this is Citadel 44," said a gravely male voice in accented Federal. "Maintain orbit at current altitude while assault shuttles land. Will contact you once runway is clear."

"Roger that, Citadel 44," Mason said. "You get that Osiris Squadron?"

"Loud and clear, Hauler," Zin said. "We'll stay in formation until they call us down."

The assault shuttles started descending, entering a shallow spiral towards Citadel 44.

The eight assault shuttles extended their wings to full forward sweep and lowered their flaps to landing configuration. Fully loaded, the assault shuttles would need all the lift they could generate to do a runway landing without assistance from the landing thrusters.

In pairs, the assault shuttles touched down on the parallel runways, slowing down quickly before turning off the runways and onto the taxiways.

"Osiris Leader, you are cleared for landing approach," Citadel 44 said.

"Roger that. Osiris 8, you land first. I'm sure Silverback wants to get out of that cockpit as soon as possible," Mason said.

"Roger that, Hauler, making my descent now," Osiris 8 said.

"Zin, I'll land with Osiris 8. The rest of the squadron will land in sequence. Understood?"

"Roger that, Hauler," Zin said. "See you on the ground."

"Safe landing, Shutdown," Mason said, then banked right to start spiraling down, following a kilometer behind Osiris 8.

With all his interceptors gone and his fuel tanks almost empty, his Lightning handled lightly, almost gliding with his engines just above idle power.

"Citadel 44, Osiris 8 on final approach."

"Osiris 8, land on runway 08L," Citadel 44's ATC said.

"Osiris Leader, on final approach," Mason said.

"Osiris Leader, land on runway 08R."

Mason lined up to land on runway 08R and pulled his throttle back to full idle and lowered the flaps, feeling his big wings bite into the air.

Though capable of landing vertically, the down blast from his Lightning's landing engines would create hurricane-force winds for hundreds of meters in all directions. Enough to flip over light vehicles and turn bits of clutter into deadly projectiles.

Osiris 8 flew just to his left, ahead and below his fighter. Her landing gear was already deployed, and her wings set to full landing configuration.

Mason lowered his landing gear just as Osiris 8 touched down, the tires of her landing gear letting off puffs of smoke as they touched the tarmac.

Despite the routine nature of a runway landing, Mason's heart beat a little faster. Flying in space was simple compared to a runway landing in atmosphere. In space, the only thing affecting your ship was its own engines. Here, he had gravity, air, and weather to contend with, along with all manner of mountainsides he could plow his fighter into if he wasn't careful.

The end of the runway was marked by a black splotch of leftover rubber from countless prior landings. Mason touched down right on top of it, his tires squeaking as they hit the runway. Deploying the airbrakes, the deceleration pulled him forward. He felt his fighter's weight settle onto the landing gear as he bled speed and Triumph's gravity asserted itself.

With a gentle application of the wheel brakes, he slowed his fighter down enough to turn right onto the first exit, towards the rows of squat armored hangars that ran parallel to the runways. The four assault shuttles were already lined up, their tail ramps opened and disgorging cargo and passengers.

Following instructions from Citadel 44's tower, he parked his Lightning next to the last assault shuttle in the line.

"And we're here, sir," Mason said as he stared the shutdown procedure, his fighter spinning down from idle power.

"Thank you for the ride, Squadron Leader. Mind opening the canopy?"

Mason unbuckled his restraints and pulled the switch to open the cockpit canopy.

Sunlight flooded into the cockpit as Colonel Shimura climbed out, walking over the chines that ran along the sides of the Lightning towards the boarding ladder and climbing down to the tarmac.

Mason stood up to follow, the g-meter on his HUD displaying .97g.

Colonel Shimura pulled her helmet off and shook her head, running a hand through her short black hair. She turned her face up at the bright blue sky and sighed with relief. Mason kept his helmet on, waiting to get indoors where there would be a solid roof between him and the big empty sky above.

He walked to the first Lightning in the line, where Osiris 8's pilot was already busy lowering Silverback's ejected cockpit out of her fighter's weapon bay. She'd had to jettison her fighter's rotary missile launcher to fit the cockpit in her fighter, but there was a 3D printer that could fabricate a spare packed in one of the assault shuttles.

The cockpit touched down on the tarmac just as Mason got close.

He walked up to the cockpit pod as the pylons that had held it inside the weapons bay retracted back into the fighter. He knocked on the opaque canopy twice, and the panel started to swing open.

Inside, Dominic and Sergeant Cane were free from their restraints and had started climbing out of the cockpit.

Mason reached in. "Need a hand?"

Dominic took the hand. "Sure. Thanks for the pickup, sir."

"You're welcome," Mason said. "How about you, Sergeant?"

In answer, she launched herself out of the cockpit and landed on the tarmac with a thud against the hard ground. He heard the servos in her hardsuit strain from the impact.

"I can help myself, sir," she said.

"Status, Sergeant?" Colonel Shimura asked.

Cane pulled her helmet off and saluted the colonel. "I'm ready for action, sir."

"Good. Go join your platoon. I'll be with you directly."

"Sir!" The trooper marched off towards the assault shuttles.

Dominic took his helmet off and rubbed his gray beard. "Ah, that feels nice. Good to see Triumph's mountain air is as refreshing as Earth's. Not going to give it a try, sir?"

"Not if I can get away with it, Flight Lieutenant," Mason said.

"If you insist, sir," Dominic said.

"Curious," Colonel Shimura said.

Mason turned to her. "What, sir?"

"No welcoming committee," Colonel Shimura said. "I don't even see guards."

Two by two, the rest of Osiris Squadron landed and taxied off the runway to park next to his fighter. Their engines, muffled by his helmet's hearing protection, were little more than a dull roar.

The last fighter from Osiris squadron landed and pulled into line short of the hangars, and still no League personnel had come out to meet them.

Then Mason heard a roar behind him and turned just in time to see the dagger nose of an Asp flying low and fast towards him. He ducked by reflex as the Asp roared overhead, his chest vibrating in response to the engine noise.

More Asps flew over the line, buzzing the Federals on the ground before swinging around in a tight turn, rapidly dropping their speed before lining up to land.

Colonel Shimura didn't duck, but she did cover her ears with her hands. As the Asps started to land, she uncovered her ears. "That must be what counts as a welcome around here."

The Asps landed in rapid succession, each pair clearing the runways within seconds until all twelve fighters were rolling two abreast down the taxiway. Each fighter rolled and parked facing Osiris Squadron's Lightnings, lining up like a rank of soldiers.

Mason took a moment to study the Asps. It was the first time he'd got to see any so close that weren't broken wrecks.

They had long, thin fuselages that reminded Mason of the shape of a particularly pointy dagger, bulging at the rear where the main long-burn drive was, and tapering to a needle-point nose.

Where Lightnings dropped their missiles from belly-mounted weapon bays, Asps fired them out the front of a pair of missile tubes tucked under the roots of each wing. The short reverse-geometry wings were each tipped by a pod, each containing a turbine engine with a small long-burn drive nested inside. The pods could swivel 360 degrees on their mounts, giving the Asp unique maneuvering characteristics in both space and atmosphere.

The canopies of the Asps opened as one, and their pilots climbed out.

The pilot of the Asp parked at the front of the line, directly across from Osiris 8, walked directly up to Mason and Shimura.

She pulled off her helmet to reveal an oval face with dark hair bound in a tight bun over the back of her head, the insignia of a League lieutenant commander etched on the front of her chest plate.

"Which one of you is in charge?" she asked in clear, if accented, Federal.

"I am. Colonel Shimura."

She nodded. "Welcome to Triumph, Colonel. I'm Commander Erica Serova, commanding officer of Battlefleet Fighter Squadron 90, the Centurions. Who leads your fighters?"

"I do, Commander," Mason answered.

She looked at him and grimaced. "Our air not good enough for you, Squadron Leader?"

Mason sighed in resignation. Rather than try to explain his anxiety about going outside without a space suit, he swallowed his discomfort and popped the seal on his helmet.

Cool mountain air, quickly warmed by the unfiltered sunlight, hit him right in the face as he pulled his helmet off. He felt a shiver run through his body and had to clench his mouth shut to keep his teeth from chattering.

Mason cleared his throat. "Apologies, Commander. The air is just fine. I just wear these things so much that I forget they're on sometimes. Anyway, I'm Squadron Leader Mason Grey. CO of the 77th Special Operations Fighter Squadron."

"Hrmph. You'll be reporting to me while you're down here."

"Uh, Colonel Shimura's my commanding officer, Commander," Mason said.

"And while your fighters are on my base, they are under my authority, Squadron Leader," Commander Serova repeated.

"Wait a minute–" Mason began.

"That will be fine," Colonel Shimura said, cutting him off. "We're here to provide any assistance we can."

Commander Serova nodded. "Thank you, Colonel." She looked at Mason. "Will there be any problems with that, Squadron Leader?"

Mason glanced at Colonel Shimura, who gave him a hard look in return.

"No, Commander. I look forward to working with you," Mason said.

"Good," Serova said.

Flight Lieutenant Xelat Sabal, who had walked up from her fighter in time to hear the end of this exchange, turned to Mason and spoke in none too low a voice, "Wait a fucking second, we're going to follow *her*? She just sat there while we almost got shot to pieces!"

Mason rounded on her. "Not now, Flight Lieutenant," he hissed.

"But, sir—"

"I know you're pissed. I am too, but now is not the time to start fights with our hosts," Mason said. "Get your gear from your ship and do what Shutdown tells you."

She nodded, her jaw clenching hard as she gave Commander Serova a venomous look before turning back to return to her fighter.

Mason nodded to Zin for her to keep an eye on Sabal, before turning back to Serova.

"Will you be able to keep your pilots under control?" Commander Serova asked coldly.

"It was a hard flight, Commander. For all of us," Mason said. "We could have used some help with the Cendies."

"If there was help to spare, you would have had it," Serova said. "Unfortunately, the Ascendency didn't leave a lot for us to spare. Follow me to the down below. Ground crews will be up shortly to transport your fighters to the hangars."

Mason glanced at the three squat armored structures. Big as they were, they didn't look quite large enough for all his fighters and the League Asps.

"You'll have to stack my fighters on top of each other if you want them to fit in there, Commander," Mason said.

"Those aren't hangars, Squadron Leader; those are armored housing protecting the aircraft elevators. The hangars are below us."

"Underground base, neat! I brought a few Federal spacecraft techs with me," Mason said. "Whoever is in charge of your ground crew should coordinate with Chief Rabin."

"I'll pass the word along, Squadron Leader," Serova said.

Soon, League personnel started pouring out of the hangar and control towers. The sheer number of them more than the size of the building suggested. More evidence that most of the base was under his feet.

There was a whine of electric motors, and a dozen drone tractors rolled onto the tarmac, heading directly for the Asp fighters to lock onto their nose gears.

A group of League ground crew headed towards the Lightnings

but were blocked by Chief Rabin and the techs he'd brought with him from *Amazon*.

Sensing an argument about to happen, Mason jogged up to Chief Rabin in time to hear him say to one stony-faced League tech, "These are my fighters, got it? You can't just roll up and start messing with them without my go-ahead."

The tech said nothing, probably because he didn't speak Federal. "We got a problem here, Chief?" Mason asked.

"Just a bunch of Leaguers who don't know their way around Federal equipment and are about to do God knows what to my Lightnings, sir," Rabin said. "Does he know what I'm saying?"

"Their brainsets can translate," Commander Serova said.

"Ah, thank you, sir," Rabin said. "Are you in charge here?"

"I am," Serova said.

Rabin gave Serova a smart salute. "A pleasure, sir. I would recommend, for both the safety of your people and my birds, that you let my techs show yours the basic ins-and-outs of our fighters."

"I've already agreed to it," Commander Serova said. She nodded to one of the techs. Not the man Rabin had been talking to, but a small, middle-aged woman standing apart from the group. "You can confer with my crew chief there."

"Ah." Rabin glanced dismissively at the tall man he had been talking to and walked up to the smaller woman Serova had pointed out.

"Come along, Squadron Leader, we'll take the elevator down with the first of my fighters," Serova said.

Mason nodded but turned towards Zin and made a subvocal call to her.

<What is it, Hauler?> she asked.

<I'm heading down with Commander Serova. Can you mind things up here?>

<I can. Try not to anger our new hosts.>

<Same to you, Zin,> Mason replied. He turned to Serova. "Lead the way, Commander."

The large doors to the nearest hangar were already open as the first of the Asps rolled inside. Mason followed Serova into the hangar, where she walked straight towards a large elevator that took up most of the floor space.

There, they waited at one corner while Citadel 44's ground crews got to work loading up Asps onto the elevators. The sleek League fighters had their reverse-geometry wings folded up to make room, but there was barely enough room to fit all of them.

"Lightnings have a larger footprint than Asps," Mason said. "Might be a challenge to fit six at a time on these elevators."

"We'll adjust as needed," Serova said, unfazed.

Once the last of the Asps were secured on the elevator, the ground crew left, leaving Mason alone on the elevator with Serova and the six Asps.

A retractable fence rose out of the floor along the perimeter of the elevator, painted in spirals of black and bright yellow, clearly marking the area that was about to become a pit trap.

There was a jolt, and the elevator started moving. A wall of concrete rose around Mason as they descended into the floor of the armored hangar. But it was soon replaced by dark rock as the elevator descended into the mountain itself.

"How deep does this elevator go, Commander?" Mason asked.

"Deep, Squadron Leader," Commander Serova said. "Below the foot of the mountain."

"Below? Belts and zones, that's like three thousand meters!"

"This place was designed to survive a sustained orbital bombardment by the entire Federal Space Forces, if needed," Serova explained. "Putting it under a mountain was necessary."

"Well, I hope it works as well against the Cendies as you intended it to against us," Mason quipped.

"Me too, Squadron Leader."

Eventually, the elevator opening above was just a dot at the end of a very, very long tunnel. Markers every hundred meters showed the depth.

There was a lot of rock around Mason and there was something unsettling about that. He had been inside asteroids far, far larger than the mountain, but for all their apparent mass, Mason couldn't feel it like he could here.

It was the gravity, Mason concluded. Almost a standard g pulled down on the millions and millions of tons of rock surrounding him. Ready to come crashing down at any moment.

They had just passed fifteen hundred meters, halfway down the mountain, when Serova said, "You're looking pale, Squadron Leader. Are you well?"

"Oh, I'm just a bit out of my comfort zone, nothing to worry about," Mason said.

"You are space-born, aren't you?" Serova asked.

"Jovian."

"Never spent a lot of time on planets, I take it."

"Oh, plenty of time on them, Commander. Not so much under them."

"Ah, yes. A lot of League space-born feel the same way when they first find themselves in one of our citadels."

"I take it there are more places like this?" Mason asked. "The fact that this place is Citadel 44 would seem to give that away."

"A fair assumption," Serova said. She did not elaborate. The nature of Triumph's defenses was one of the League's best kept secrets, and she didn't seem too keen on spilling them.

"So, I take it you grew up on a planet, then?" Mason asked, trying to distract himself by making conversation.

"This one, specifically," Serova volunteered. "Though not on this continent."

"So, it never bothered you being underground?"

"Oh, it did, just not as acutely as it seems to be bothering you. Are you usually this nervous when you're outside your comfort zone?"

"You mean am I going to get all jittery while trying to fight off a possible Cendy invasion? Is that what you're asking, Commander?"

"Is fighting off a planetary invasion something you've done before?"

"No. But I am very used to doing my job while in stressful situations."

"Good. I'm sure the Ascendency will provide you with plenty of stressful situations to practice with."

"Oh, they've given me plenty already, believe me," Mason said.

A further fifteen hundred meters of descent later, and the elevator reached the bottom of the subterranean base, the elevator pad resting flush with the coated floor.

Serova stepped off the elevator as ground crew walked on, complete with six electric tractors for pulling the fighters off the elevator.

Mason found himself standing inside an enormous squat dome. From the base of the dome to the top ran heavy metal girders, with interweaved cables stretched between them. He could barely see the rocky ceiling through them.

"What's with all the cables?" Mason asked.

"It's to catch rocks that get knocked loose by any bombardment," Commander Serova said.

"Are they any good?"

Serova shrugged. "Hopefully. Though the net has never been tested in battle. I would keep an eye on the ceiling when the Ascendency starts to bomb this place."

"Belts and zones!" Mason breathed.

"I don't understand that expression," Commander Serova said.

"It's a Jovian exclamation of surprise or frustration," Mason said. "It references Jupiter's bands."

"Oh I see," Serova said, not sounding as though she saw at all.

"You never grew up with Jupiter just outside your window," Mason said.

"A fair point."

The first of the Asps rolled past them. After the last one rolled off the elevator, the safety fence rose, and the elevator started to ascend again. This time to bring down the Federal craft, Mason assumed.

With the Asps for scale, Mason got a sense of just how big the dome was. There was room for a hundred strikecraft with room to spare. As it was, he saw only two squadrons of twelve Asps apiece. There were also several squadrons of parked tilt-rotor aircraft sharing the hangars with the aerospace fighters. Large bulbous transports and smaller, sleeker gunships. There were also a few League assault shuttles scattered about.

But what stood out most to Mason were the empty parking spaces. The dome seemed barely a quarter filled.

"This place looks a bit empty, Commander,' Mason observed. "How many squadrons are assigned here?"

"Three squadrons of aerospace fighters, including yours, Squadron Leader. We also have a regiment of Espatiers detached from the battlefleet, along with an aerial assault regiment from the Planetary Defense Forces, with an attached squadron of gunships for close air support."

"And how many squadrons were here before the Cendies arrived?"

"Fifteen."

"Belts and zones!"

"Indeed, Squadron Leader," Serova said as she came to a stop in front of several empty spaces marked out on the dome's floor. "This will be where your fighter and assault shuttles will be parked."

Mason looked to the elevator and back to the parking spaces. "Clear way to the elevators."

"These spaces are reserved for the ready alert. But as you can see," Commander Serova swept her arm at the empty spaces, "we don't have to worry about who gets to have direct access to the elevators." All the strikecraft that were in the dome were located near the elevators.

"Are any strikecraft kept topside?" Mason asked. "It'd take a while for those elevators to ascend."

"They can, but not now," Serova said. "Anything on the top base will be easy targets for orbital bombardment."

"Well, in that case, how would you launch anything once the surface base gets destroyed?"

"The surface base is not the only place to sortie from the base, though it is the only one where a rolling takeoff can be done," Serova said. "Come, I'll show you."

At the far side of the dome was a wide tunnel that looked big enough for a pair of Lightnings to roll down two abreast, with their wings folded. The floor of the tunnel had the same high-traction gray coating as the rest of the dome.

Serova pointed down the tunnel. "That tunnel leads to a network of auxiliary launch facilities hidden around the mountain. There are four such tunnels spaced evenly around the circumference of the dome." She turned and pointed to a group of bright-yellow construction vehicles. "And should the tunnels collapse, we have equipment for digging them out, even making new exits if we have to."

"Huh," Mason said. "This place was made to be hard to destroy."

"Almost impossible, in fact," Serova said. "The planet's surface could be completely sterilized, and this place and its defenders could still fight."

Mason turned to Commander Serova. "You really planned to fight that long?"

"Yes," Serova said. "Though we assumed the Earth Federation would give up before that happened. Too many resources with too long supply lines."

"Just seems extreme to me," Mason said.

"Good deterrents usually are."

"The Cendies don't seem too deterred to me."

"Not yet," Serova said.

CHAPTER 19

There were a lot of empty beds in Citadel 44's subterranean barracks, and the Leaguers had been kind enough to clear out the belongings of the former occupants. The barracks were located beneath the hangar dome, in crisscrossing tunnels cut into the rock.

They were basic. Rows of cots with trunks for personal belongings and partitioning curtains for token privacy. On one side was a communal shower and restroom. On the other, combination offices and private cabins for senior officers.

Mason and Zin got the private rooms, while the rest of the squadron got their pick of the bunks.

The private room was larger than what he had on ships, but bare. Just a cot on one side, a desk on the other, and a small private bathroom. Hot water was the extent of the luxuries. Still, it was a safe place for his pilots to sleep. With kilometers of rock between them and a soon-to-be-hostile sky.

While he was getting his little desk set up, Zin knocked on the open door and leaned in.

"Come in, Zin. Got good news?"

"I suppose. Everyone's getting settled in and resting," she said. "I also touched base with Chief Rabin. All our fighters are parked above us and are being serviced. Apparently, the Leaguers are figuring out how to maintain them pretty fast."

"I'm sure they'll be debriefed on every last detail on how our Lightnings operate," Mason said. "How about ordinance?"

"Mixed," Zin said. "The munitions we did bring were unloaded from the assault shuttles. We've got enough air-to-air and air-to-ground ordinance to fully equip our fighters for at least three full sorties, assuming we fire everything off. But we have no Javelin interceptors left, and only a handful of Stilettoes."

"So, we're not capable of effective space combat," Mason said. "At least until we figure out how to adapt League interceptors to our ships."

"You think they'll let us?"

"I'll bring it up with Commander Serova in the morning. Right now, I'm too damn tired."

"You look it."

"As do you, Zin. You should get some rest."

"I agree, but there's one more thing. The pilots we lost. I'd like to hold a memorial service for them. I think that would help morale."

"Tomorrow," Mason said. "Let's give everyone a chance to rest first."

"Understood. Rest well, Mason. I'll see you tomorrow."

"Thanks, Zin. Close the door please."

She nodded, and closed the door behind her, leaving Mason alone in his room.

Pulling off his jumpsuit, he tossed it over the back of the chair and lay down on the cot.

The stiff foam mattress wheezed as his weight forced the air out, sighing in resignation as it was forced to endure carrying Mason's weight. Once the mattress finished complaining, there was just the sound of the ventilation system in his room. He couldn't hear any of his pilots outside. They were probably all busy sleeping off the strain of two days spent in high-g flight, and then several minutes at even higher gs as they fought for their lives.

Mason glanced at his hardsuit, which stood in the corner of the room like a headless statue, the helmet resting on the desk. The suit had its back to him. He made a mental note to examine it in the morning to make sure it was in good working order. There were only a few spares and the hardsuit maintainers they did bring along would be occupied keeping the troopers' hardsuits working.

He supposed they could enlist the help of the League allies, but that would require training. Training required time. And what time they did have was completely up to the Cendies.

Mason stared up at the ceiling. Beyond the three kilometers of rock, a hundred or so kilometers of atmosphere, and millions of kilometers of empty space, the Ascendency invasion fleet waited for their time to strike. Hundreds of ships manned by an enemy whose planetary invasion tactics were unknown to him.

Shaking his head, Mason cleared his mind. It was time to sleep, not dwell on thing that were outside of his control.

Sighing, he drifted off to sleep.

❦

Mason bolted upright as a familiar alarm echoed through the barracks. He had heard it before aboard LCS *Fafnir*. A battle alarm.

With a signal from his brainset, he ordered his hardsuit to open. The hardsuit's back split along several seams at it stooped forward, clearing the way for Mason to climb inside. He shoved his legs in first before shimmying his torso inside and shoving his arms through the sleeves. Another signal, and the hardsuit closed around him, hugging him tight.

The acceleration gel felt cold and sticky to his skin. He realized that, in his rush, he had forgotten to put his uniform on and was only wearing his regulation boxers and t-shirt. There was no time to be bothered by that. Mason grabbed his helmet and burst out of the door of his room at the same time as Zin did.

They nodded to each other and entered the barracks proper.

The pilots of Osiris Squadron were all suited up, most with their helmets on.

"What's the word, Hauler? I hear the alarm, but I don't see any notifications on my brainset," Dominic said.

"We haven't had a chance to integrate our brainsets into the local network. I'll figure out what's going on," Mason turned to his XO. "Shutdown, get everyone to their fighters."

Zin nodded. "On it, Hauler. We'll be ready for whatever's got the Leaguers agitated."

Mason headed for the Command Center, which like the barracks was under the dome level. He saw a lot of Leaguers and more than a few Federals rushing around. A lot of the Federal personnel had lost expressions on their faces.

One of them was Chief Rabin, who came to an abrupt halt at the sight of Mason. "What's going on, sir?" he asked.

"I'm going to find out, Chief. Head upstairs and get our Lightnings ready to fight."

"On it, sir," Rabin said and continued on his way, his subordinates following behind him.

The guards outside Citadel 44's Command Center blocked Mason's way. He held up his hands. "Hey, guys, I'm just here to report to Commander Serova."

The eyes of one of the guards became distant as they seemed to be communicating with someone via brainset. He then nodded and waved Mason through.

Inside, he found the Command Center bustling with activity. There were rows of manned control consoles like pews in a church, all facing a massive screen that was currently projecting a tactical display of the space around Triumph.

Colonel Shimura stood at the back of the Command Center with her arms crossed, studying the screen with an impassive expression. Like she was interpreting a particularly abstract painting.

Commander Serova stood in the middle of the Command Center, leaning over the shoulder of one of the operators sitting at a console.

Mason walked up and exchanged salutes with Colonel Shimura. "What's all the excitement about?" he asked.

The colonel nodded up at the screen. "The Cendies just made their next move, and it's a big one. Their arsenal ships unloaded a massive volley of missiles. Ten thousand in total. They've also sortied two thousand fighters to provide escort for them."

Mason felt a shiver run down his spine as he thought about the amount of firepower headed towards him. Ten thousand missiles carrying who knew how many warheads. There could be enough warheads to flatten every city on the planet several times over and throw up so much dust that it would put Triumph into a nuclear winter that lasted decades.

"My pilots are getting their fighters ready," Mason said.

"Good," Colonel Shimura said.

Commander Serova walked up. "Squadron Leader Gray, good to see you were prompt."

"Commander, my fighters are being prepped for launch at this very moment," Mason said.

Commander Serova shook her head. "We won't be needing your fighters for this."

Mason pointed at the screen. "Commander, there are a lot of missiles coming our way. We cou–"

"You have no interceptors, Squadron Leader, and there isn't time to adapt our interceptors to your fighters," Commander Serova said, cutting him off. "I'm glad you're willing to contribute to the defense of my world, but we have no use for you. A squadron of unarmed Federal fighters is just going to put unnecessary strain on our command and control."

"We're not unarmed, sir," Mason said.

Commander Serova gestured to the swarm of missiles bearing down on them. "Your guns aren't going to make a difference against that. Now if you'll excuse me, I need to get to my fighter. You're welcome to stay here and observe events, so long as you stay out of the way." She turned and departed without waiting for a response.

Mason sighed. "Well, fuck."

"My sentiments exactly, Squadron Leader," Colonel Shimura said.

"So, what do we do, sir? I can't believe we went to all this trouble just to spectate," Mason said.

"We're not spectating; we're observing—and remaining on standby to provide whatever help we can," Colonel Shimura lifted an eyebrow. "You think the Cendies are going to stop with just a bombardment? You saw all those ships waiting with their fleet. I'm willing to bet they're troop transports of some kind."

"You think there's going to be a follow-up ground assault?"

"I don't think anything. But it's the only problem that we have the weapons to deal with right now."

Mason nodded. "I'll tell Chief Rabin to start loading up the fighters with air-to-ground ordinance."

Colonel Shimura nodded. "Good."

Mason sent the message off via brainset to Chief Rabin and Zin. They both replied with enthusiasm.

"You're not leaving?" Shimura asked.

"My XO and crew chief can see to the arming of the fighters, sir. I'm going to stay here and see how the situation develops."

"Not a bad idea, Squadron Leader," Shimura said. "You might want to get yourself a drink and a snack while you can. The fireworks start in an hour."

∽

Despite what all the empty parking spots in Citadel 44's hangar dome would suggest, Triumph still could muster a massive force of fighters.

Almost a thousand Asps ascended through the atmosphere and lit their long-burn drives at a hard-burn, rocketing away from the planet towards the incoming attack.

The battle developed as swarms of icons moved towards each other on Triumph's night side.

The Cendy Outriders accelerated ahead of the missiles they were escorting, moving in force against the League fighters they outnumbered over two-to-one.

Mason's stomach tied itself in knots, his recent experience battling the Cendy fighters making his sense of foreboding even more acute.

Both sides launched mass volleys of interceptors. Over a thousand from the League fighters and about double that from the Ascendency.

The Asps immediately started burning perpendicular to bend their vectors away from the Cendies. The missile tracks made it clear that the League interceptors weren't going after the missiles, but Outriders instead.

"They are attacking the fighters," Mason said.

"Probably to prevent the Outriders from screening the missiles against Triumph's ground-based defenses," Colonel Shimura said.

Masses of Cendy interceptors started wandering, signs they were losing the locks on their targets.

"Ah," Colonel Shimura said.

"The League fighters must have upgraded their ECM," Mason said.

"It's not the fighters, it's the planet, Lieutenant," Colonel Shimura said. She pointed to one of the consoles. "That operator over there is directing a long-ranged jamming array at the Cendy interceptors, just like a hundred others on this side of the planet."

"Where did you learn all this?" Mason asked.

"There's a reason I took a position behind everyone, Squadron Leader," Colonel Shimura said. "I've been reading off their screens. The League are up against the wall here and now they're using it to their advantage."

Despite firing a far heaver interceptor volley at the Leaguers, the Cendies had come out the worse. Over three hundred hits were detected on the Cendy fighters, for barely more than fifty on the League side.

The remaining Cendy fighters were scattered by the attack while the Asps withdrew.

Then a swarm of new icons lifted from Triumph's surface.

Tens of thousands of missiles from hundreds of launch sites all over the planet.

Missiles taking off from the far side of the planet turned to move around the planet, while those on the side facing the enemy simply flew straight up towards the Cendies.

The Outriders fired their interceptors against the League interceptors, but it was far less than it could have been if the Asps had not done their job.

Several thousand interceptors disintegrated each other in the space ahead of the missile volley, but many got through.

Just before the interceptors hit, the League missiles started splitting apart.

"They're releasing their submunitions early," Mason said.

Each missile divided into hundreds of contacts, most of which had to be decoys to confuse the interceptors.

The League interceptors crashed into the Cendy missiles like a storm of arrows being shot into a tsunami. There were thousands of confirmed hits, but the Cendy contacts proceeded without slowing.

Additional interceptor volleys launched from ground sites on Triumph firing as fast as their launchers could reload, a constant stream of missiles lashing out at the Cendy attack.

They kept firing even as the Cendy warhead started entering the atmosphere.

"Here goes," Mason said. On the display of Triumph, there was an icon that helpfully showed the location of Citadel 44.

Mason watched and waited for one of the thousands of streaks of missiles to reach where he was standing. He braced for the tremors that were about to rock the base as who knew how many nuclear warheads detonated overhead.

But there were no tremors. The missiles approaching Citadel 44 flew overhead like meteors still thousands of meters above.

Mason blinked and watched more closely. The tracks were headed due east of Citadel 44, concentrated on several icons on the night side of the planet.

"What do those icons represent, Colonel?" Mason asked.

"Heavy missile batteries," Colonel Shimura said. "Those are where Triumph's nukes are kept."

"And those trails are headed right for them," Mason said.

Mason waited as the warhead streaked in, being engaged by surface-to-air missiles as it did. But all the contacts were enveloped in the plasma sheaths of a high-velocity entry. That made them hard to hit and Mason couldn't tell what effect the SAMs were having.

Then the first contacts disappeared over their targets. No detonation or other signs of impact. They were just gone.

"What the hell!" Colonel Shimura exclaimed. Even she could be taken by surprise, it seemed.

Confusion spread through the control centers as the operators tried to find detonations that hadn't happened.

All that effort by the Cendies, and all that was the result were some streaks of smoke in the sky. That was anticlimactic.

Then the calls came in over the emergency band. Mason didn't understand Exo, but the panicked voices he heard were quickly translated into Federal by his brainset, which superimposed the text over his HUD.

"Intruders?" Mason turned to Colonel Shimura. "Sir, this is a ground attack."

"They're trying to take out the anti-starship missile batteries," Colonel Shimura said. "Get to your squadron, Squadron Leader. I think our opportunity to make a difference has arrived."

"You think the Leaguers are going to let us do that?" Mason asked.

"Leave that to me, Squadron Leader."

Colonel Shimura walked forward, barking in Exo at the League personnel. Whatever reservations the Leaguers had about having a Federal officer shout orders at them melted before her authoritative demeanor.

As she got the Command Center into motion, she spotted Mason and made a "Go!" movement at him.

Mason nodded, saluted, and charged out of the Command Center.

CHAPTER 20

Mason's boots thundered against the bare stone floor of the hangar dome as he sprinted towards his squadron's fighters.

Each Lightning, save one, had their pilots doing final inspection of all their weapon mounts. Each fighter had eight Atlatl pods attached to their external hardpoints.

There was more activity beyond the Lightnings. Hundreds of soldiers, with more than a few Raiders among them, gathering around the tilt-rotor transports.

Zin walked from underneath Mason's fighter and saluted him.

"What's the word, sir?"

"The missiles were carrying soldiers, not nukes," Mason said.

"Explains why they're loading up soldiers in the transports," Zin said. "You know where we're going?"

Mason pointed at the gathered soldiers. "Where they're going. Everything ready?"

Zin nodded. "I took the liberty of inspecting your fighter myself, Hauler. All we need is the word to mount our fighters and get them powered up."

"Consider the word given."

"Understood, Hauler," Zin said. She turned and cupped her hands around her mouth. "Mount up, we've got a job to do!"

The pilots of Osiris Squadron started pulling on helmets and scrambling up the sides of their Lightnings.

Mason ran over to his own fighter while pulling his helmet on.

Climbing up the fighter's retractable ladder, he dropped down into the seat and buckled himself in before closing the canopy, shutting out the buzz of priming reactors and the whine of spooling turbines.

A few minutes later, both of Mason's reactors were at idle power and all his systems came up green. Flight, combat, and sensor AIs all reporting normal.

He connected his brainset to the fighter's systems, and the cockpit vanished as his Lightning's sensors became his eyes and ears.

The two surface access elevators started their long climb to the surface fully loaded with tilt-rotor transports.

A call came in from the Command Center. When Mason answered, Colonel Shimura was on the other line.

"Report, Squadron Leader."

"All fighters are fully armed and ready to fight, sir," Mason said.

"Good, because we've got one developing. There's another Planetary Defense installation three hundred klicks east of us that's under attack. It's a missile base housing ten anti-starship missile batteries. It's currently under attack by Cendy ground forces along with all other missile bases on the continent. Citadel 44 is sending its ground troops as reinforcement. A few of my Raiders are embedded with them to act as forward controllers for you. They'll liaise with the Leaguers and point out targets for you to destroy."

"Got it, sir," Mason said. "When is our next turn on the elevator?"

"After the League gunships get aboard, Squadron Leader," Shimura said. "Your fighters are a lot faster than they are, so should arrive at the target area before them, regardless."

"Understood, sir," Mason said.

"Good hunting, Squadron Leader. I'll give you updates on the strategic situation when you get back."

After the elevators disappeared into the ceiling, drone tractors rolled up to the Lightnings of Osiris Squadron and took a hold of the nose gear of each fighter with their heavy pincers.

As soon as the elevator returned, the drones rolled the fighters onto the two platforms in quick order.

Mason's Lightning shuddered as the elevator started rising. He occupied himself going over his pre-flight checklist while the elevators carried his squadron up the shaft, trying not to think of the mayhem the Cendies were causing while he was still underground.

When the elevators reached the top, tractors towed the fighters off, instantly lining them up just outside the protected elevator bunkers. The drone tractors then detached themselves and formed into a single column as they rolled back to the elevators.

Mason opened the intakes and got the turbines spinning, feeding air into heat-exchangers around the reactors, superheating the air and expelling it out the back to generate thrust.

With just the barest bit of throttle, Mason started rolling forward, followed by the rest of Osiris Squadron.

As soon as Mason rolled onto the runway, he pushed his throttles to takeoff power. The acceleration pulled him back into his seat as his Lightning screamed down the runway. In just a few seconds, he was going fast enough to pull up his nose and lift his fighter off the runway.

The rest of Osiris Squadron took off in good order and formed up around him in a large chevron formation. Climbing to an altitude of five thousand meters, they were soon well above even the highest of Stoneland's peaks.

Mason went supersonic in the direction of Heavy Missile Base 20, overflying the tilt-rotor transports and gunships in minutes.

"This is Osiris Squadron to transport flight. Who can I coordinate with down there?" Mason asked.

"That would be me, sir," Sergeant Cane said. "Transports are Mule Squadron. The gunships are Shuriken Squadron."

"What do you need from my pilots, Sergeant?" Mason asked.

"I'm uploading our landing zone to you now, sir. If you could clear it before these big vulnerable transports get there, that would be greatly appreciated."

"We'll get it done, Sergeant. Osiris Leader out," Mason said. "All right, everyone, set your Hammers to airburst and follow me. Time to put that practice on Liberty to good use."

Mason pushed the throttle forward and increased his speed to over

Mach 2, Osiris Squadron keeping up behind him. Within minutes, Heavy Missile Base 20 peaked over the horizon, columns of smoke rising into the air.

"Well, this looks like the right place," Mason said. The sensor AI was picking up a lot of chatter from below, but it was indecipherable and most of it in Cendy. If the Leaguers manning the base were still alive, they were hunkered down.

The base itself was a kilometer-wide concrete slab stretching across the flattened top of a hill. The dozens of heavy doors covered the tops of surface-to-space missile batteries.

Under magnification, Mason could see flashes of gunfire, and more than a few bodies scattered across the ground, both those of League defenders and the long lanky forms of Cendy soldiers.

"All right, we've ten minutes to clear the landing zone and inflict some attrition on the Cendies," Mason said. "We'll go in by flights. Stay outside of ten clicks of the base. We don't know what kind of air defenses they brought."

"Roger that, Hauler. We'll fly in after you make your run," Zin said.

"Roger that. First Flight follow me in and engage at will," Mason called. He pulled back his throttles and dove his fighter to low altitude, slowing to subsonic speeds as he lowered his altitude to five hundred meters.

He armed his Hammers, forty of the weapons lighting up green in his weapon bay and wing-mounted Atlatl pods. He set the Hammers to airburst mode, where they would be most effective against infantry.

The sensor AI detected a dozen concentrations of Cendy soldiers around the landing zone. Mason locked them and distributed the targets among the three other fighters of his flight.

As soon as he entered range, he fired the Hammers out of his Atlatl pods first, sending eight Hammers against each marked ground target. He then turned his fighter away and pulled up.

Once launched, the Hammers didn't need any further guidance. They burned out their rocket motors within seconds and coasted the rest of the way on pure momentum.

In the terminal phase, the missiles did a pop-up maneuver, entering a steep climb, bleeding off most of their energy before tipping over and falling straight down onto their targets.

At the set altitude, they detonated their shaped-charge warheads, sending a cone of shrapnel straight down onto the heads of any Cendy soldiers unfortunate enough to find themselves under them.

As the debris cleared, Zin's flight rolled in. Mason picked up some sign of movement from the surviving Cendies around the landing zone, and his sensor AI shared that information over the squadron datalink.

Zin's flight launched another volley of Hammers, and more of the missiles detonated in the air.

"Hardball, you're off the leash. Start patrolling around the perimeter and engage any targets you come across," Mason ordered.

"Will do, Hauler."

Third Flight dropped to a thousand meters and peeled off to the north to start their search-and-destroy.

Mason maintained his orbit over the facility. Any Cendy soldiers that got within a thousand meters of it got a Hammer chasing after them for their trouble.

"Hauler, I'm getting a lot of movement below," Sabal said.

"What do you mean?" Mason asked.

"The Cendy troopers are doing a good job keeping themselves concealed, but I'm picking up enough trace thermals that my sensor AI thinks there is an infantry division down there."

That set Mason's mind racing. A division was ten thousand troops. If there were that many attacking Heavy Missile Base 20, then there were nine other facilities like it under attack.

"Belts and zones! Hardball, cancel search-and-destroy and return to an overwatch position. Everyone else, don't fire unless you're guaranteed to kill a bunch of Cendies. If there's a division down there, we're going to have to be economical with our munitions. Sergeant Cane?"

"I copy, Osiris Leader. What's the situation?" Sergeant Cane responded.

"Emissions suggest there's at least a division's worth of Cendies around the missile base. You're going to be outnumbered by a fair margin when you land."

"I'll pass the word along, Osiris Leader," Sergeant Cane said. "There's a

Planetary Defense armored regiment with supporting mechanized infantry rolling in to provide reinforcements. ETA thirty minutes after we land."

"We'll try to tilt the odds in your favor until they arrive," Mason said.

"That would be greatly appreciated, Osiris Leader," Sergeant Cane said. "Shuriken Squadron's gunships are about to make their first run. Mule Squadron will start landing troops approximately one minute after that."

"Roger that," said Mason. "We'll be on standby for your calls."

The gunships flew in low and fast, their rotors in full puller configurations as they let loose with volleys of rockets and bursts of cannon fire from their chin turrets, their massive rotors stirring up smoke as they flew through it.

Missile alert sounded as a SAMs streaked out of a ruined building, detonating off the right wing of one of the gunships, blowing its starboard engine pod off.

The gunships went spinning out of control, and the pilot and gunner ejected.

"They have SAMs. Watch out!" Mason warned.

From his position high above, he saw the parachutes from the fallen gunship's crew deploy. Moments later, the chutes, and the pilot and gunner dangling helplessly from them were perforated by gunfire, a dozen muzzle flashes lighting up on the ground below them.

"Motherfuckers!" He queued up another couple of Hammers set to airburst and sent them where he saw the muzzle flashes. The missiles detonated and blotted out the ground with clouds of smoke and debris.

The gunships turned hard towards the building where the missiles came from, dropping lines of flares in their wake, and laid into it with rockets until the already burning building collapsed.

The transports of Mule Squadron came in, rotating their engines up to hover position and tilting their noses up into the air to come to a rapid halt until they touched down onto the ground.

League Espatiers and Federal Raiders charged down the ramps of the transports, emptying the craft in seconds before the transport gunned their engines and took off, preemptively dropping flares as they fought to gain speed and altitude.

More surface-to-air missiles flew from the tree line after them, but the transports at least knew they were coming.

Most of the missiles went after the flares, but one found its mark, detonating in a burst of black smoke just over one of the empty transports. Smoke billowed from both engines, but the transport didn't immediately drop out of the sky. Instead, it struggled to stay in the air as it turned away from the fighting area.

The gunships responded by staffing the tree line with rocket fire.

"Osiris Leader, this is Cane. Me and my troopers will be calling out targets while the soldiers push their way into the missile base."

"Roger that, Sergeant. We've got you covered."

League Planetary Defense infantry squads moved forward, diving for cover as Cendy soldiers opened fire on them.

True to her word, Sergeant Cane started designating targets.

"This is Sergeant Cane, I'm marking a building that I need knocked down," she said, a laser from her hardsuit painting the target.

"Osiris 4, rolling in," Zin said, launching a Hammer as instructed.

The Hammer popped up, and crashed through the roof of the building, detonating a split second later. The building, and the Cendy soldiers firing from inside it, disappeared in a cloud of smoke and debris.

"Kills confirmed," Sergeant Cane said.

More callouts came as Espatiers and embedded Raiders hit resistance, gaining ground with every Hammer missile strike by Osiris Squadron and strafing run by Shuriken Squadron's gunships.

By the time the Planetary Defense soldiers reached the base's main entrance and started forming a defensive perimeter, Osiris Squadron had expended three-quarters of their Hammers.

The League gunships looked like they had used up their rockets, because they were only using their canons as they strafed Cendy positions.

Another gunship took a hit from a Cendy missile. The pilot managed to keep control of the crippled aircraft and crash-landed inside the defensive perimeter.

The nearby Espatiers threw smoke grenades to conceal their movements and they went to get the pilot and gunner out of the fallen aircraft.

"This is Sergeant Cane. We have heavy Cendy contact inside the base facility. Looks like they're trying to hold us off until they can break into the underground facility. I request a danger close gun run at the designated position!"

Mason saw the designated area just in front of Cane's position. "This is Osiris Leader, rolling in for a gun run."

Diving in at a steep angle, Mason knew he would be in range of Cendy SAMs as he made his run. His big aerospace fighter would be an irresistible target.

"Cover me while I make my run," Mason called. He put his aiming reticle right on Cane's designator and closed the range to less than five thousand meters.

He started dropping decoys preemptively a couple of seconds before he squeezed the trigger.

His Lightning trembled under the recoil of its gun, the retort of the weapon reverberating off the ground as he peppered the target with hypervelocity projectiles.

As he pulled away from his run, still dropping a trail of decoys behind him, a pair of SAMs rose after him.

Mason pushed his throttle to full and gained speed as his fighter shot straight up.

The rocket motors of the missiles ran out and the weapons quickly lost speed, falling away as Mason climbed past their maximum engagement altitude.

"Good shooting, Osiris Leader. We're clearing the last of the Cendies now," Sergeant Cane said. "Now we just need to hold it."

"Roger that, Sergeant," Mason said. "Keep the callouts coming, and we'll keep delivering fire."

"I got a lot of movement around the facility. I think we pissed them off!" Sabal said.

"We don't have a lot of ordinance left, only fire on callouts. The troopers know better than we do the best place for our missiles," Mason said. "Maintain speed and altitude."

A surge of Ascendency soldiers came storming around the facility from all angles. The entrenched Espatiers started firing, and callouts from the embedded Raiders started pouring in.

Two at a time, Lightnings swooped high over the battlefield, hitting designated targets with Hammer missiles while the remaining tilt-rotor gunships strafed the Cendies from low altitude.

The forest around the missile battery became a burned-out hellscape of craters and smoldering tree trunks.

The Cendies pushed hard, enduring horrific casualties as they were held back by Espatiers on the ground and blasted from above by Lightnings and gunships.

Mason fired his last Hammer missile at a Cendy squad attempting to charge through a gap in the defense perimeter, blasting several apart, and sending the survivors scattering.

A glance at his squadron's status display showed that his squadron had used up almost all their missiles. Only four missiles shared among twelve fighters.

The Cendies were still pushing hard, and the gunships were withdrawing due to damage and lack of ammo. Pretty soon, his Lightnings would start strafing the Cendies with their guns, exposing themselves to their short-range SAMs.

The little missiles probably couldn't down a Lightning in one hit. But the damage would keep it under repair for days, days where that fighter might be sorely missed.

Fortunately, just as his squadron was out of guided munitions was when the League Planetary Defense armor rolled in.

The tanks had positioned themselves on a hill overlooking the base, using it as cover as they fired down on the Cendies.

The Cendy soldiers didn't panic or scatter in confusion like most people would do when tanks showed up and started gunning down their friends. Instead, those that had anti-tank weapons turned and fired their missiles, while those that didn't took cover.

The tanks' point defense systems shot down most of the anti-tank missiles, and those that did hit struck the tanks on the front of their heavily armored turrets.

Caught between an armored regiment on one side, dug-in infantry on the other, and air support above, the Cendy position was untenable.

And they seemed to realize that quickly, as Cendy squads scattered into the woods around the base. Mason watched them run, clocking their running speeds at fifty kilometers per hour.

"They're running! Permission to engage!" Sabal said.

"Denied. We'll let the tanks deal with them. Sergeant Cane, my fighters need to return to base to rearm."

"Understood, Squadron Leader. Espatiers are going to hold tight until relieved by the mechanized infantry. My guys might catch a ride to the other areas to provide forward control when you get more missiles."

"We'll be there when you need us, Sergeant."

Mason led his squadron up to ten thousand meters to fly back to Citadel 44 at Mach 2.

"Citadel 44, this is Osiris Leader. We're inbound and about to rearm. ETA, ten minutes," Mason said.

"Osiris Leader, this is Colonel Shimura. The League fighters have returned from orbit and are themselves being rearmed for air-to-ground combat, so things are going to be pretty busy when you get back."

"Understood, sir. What's the strategic situation?" Mason asked.

"Dire," Colonel Shimura said. "The Cendies took out nine planetary missile batteries before Planetary Defense could respond. The one you just defended was the only one that survived."

"I take it we can expect more Cendies on the ground, sir?" Mason asked.

"Yes, Squadron Leader," Colonel Shimura said. "Many more."

CHAPTER 21

With a last effort by *Goshawk*'s star drive, the carrier jumped into the sphere of empty space marked out by Checkpoint Hephaestus.

Only, it wasn't empty.

"Blimey," Jessica said.

"Something interesting out there?" Miriam asked. She had not been granted access to *Goshawk*'s external sensors, so couldn't see directly through them like Jessica.

Jessica activated a monitor with a tactical display on it for Miriam. "Seems there's a fleet gathering here, and I have a pretty good guess which one is the flagship."

At the center of the collection of starships, in formation with four Saturn class battleships, was FSFV *Independence*, the battlecarrier that she had helped rescue from the clutches of the Ascendency fleet occupying Jupiter.

The fleet tender FSFV *Onager* was docked alongside the battlecarrier, a clear indication that she was still having repairs done.

Someone really wanted *Independence* out here if they had gone to the trouble to bring a fleet tender with her just to help with repairs while underway.

Miriam squinted as she studied the monitor. The face of the high-end mobility rig made the movement seem completely natural despite the rig's obvious artificial nature. "That's a lot of dots. How many starships are out here?"

"A hundred and twenty-seven total," Jessica said. A notification appeared on her HUD; it was a call from Captain Lafferty.

<Yes, Captain?>

<I just got a call from *Independence*. You and Miss Xia are to head to Hangar Bay 50. The assault shuttle there will take you to *Independence*.>

<May I ask who gave the order?> Jessica asked.

<Your boss, Lieutenant. Admiral Moebius.>

<I see. I'll proceed to Hangar Bay 50 at once. Thank you for getting us out here, Captain.>

<You were model passengers, Lieutenant,> Captain Lafferty said. <Good luck aboard *Independence*.>

<The same with you and your ship, sir,> Jessica said. The call ended, leaving Jessica alone with Miriam.

"You were staring off into space for a while. What's happening?" Miriam asked.

Jessica sighed. "We've got a shuttle to catch."

*

Independence was starkly different from when she had last been aboard her. For one, there were no bullet holes in the walls, or desperate civilian workers crowding every compartment and corridor.

There was plenty of activity. As Jessica floated up from the hangar bay, teams of technicians with patches identifying them as part of *Onager*'s crew floated about the ship carrying bits of equipment to repair one system or another.

No one seemed to pay any mind to the luxury mobility rig following Jessica through *Independence*'s corridors. They were too busy preparing *Independence* for battle. The smell of fresh paint and sealant gave the ship's atmosphere an astringent smell.

After riding an elevator down one of the spokes of *Independence*'s internal habitat ring, Jessica found herself standing outside a guarded hatch with Miriam. The module was reserved as a working space for flag officers and their staff.

One of the troopers guarding the door waved them through. "You're clear to enter. The admiral is waiting for you both in her office."

Jessica nodded and entered.

The Flag Officer module was essentially a two-level office building inside the battlecarrier. A place where the admiral could manage a fleet outside of combat.

A flag bridge located on the level above the main bridge was reserved for flag officers while in battle.

Admiral Mobius had helpfully had her name stenciled over the closed hatch to her office. Jessica walked up and pressed the call button on the door. The door opened as she approached, revealing Admiral Mobius behind her desk.

Her office aboard *Independence* was tiny compared to the office she had on Procyon Fleet Base, but large for an office aboard a warship: a hundred square meters of floor space dominated by a large desk. The walls were decorated with pictures of starships and photos and certificates from Admiral Moebius' long and eventful career in the Space Forces. It seemed the admiral intended to use *Independence* as her flagship for the long term.

Jessica stopped in front of the admiral's desk and saluted. "Lieutenant Sinclair reporting, sir. May I introduce you to Miriam Xia."

Admiral Moebius stood up and returned Jessica's salute before walking around the desk to shake hands with Miriam.

"A pleasure to meet you, ma'am," Admiral Moebius said.

"Miriam, please. Ma'am just reminds me how old I am," Miriam replied with a smile.

"Well, thank you for making your way all the way out to the middle of nowhere with Lieutenant Sinclair," Admiral Mobius said.

Miriam shrugged. "It's been a while since I've last bumped elbows with Federal flag officers. It's a nice change of pace from lounging on the beach or attending weekly orgies."

Admiral Moebius chuckled. "Oh, I can see why you'd want a change of scenery, then." She gestured to chairs in front of her desk. "Take a seat, both of you. Based on the report you sent me, I think we have quite a lot to talk about."

"That we do, sir," Jessica said, taking the guest seat to her right while Miriam sat to her left.

Admiral Moebius sat down behind her desk and planted her elbows on the surface while resting her chin on her steepled fingers. Her attention was focused on Miriam. "So, you were involved with the people who created the Ascendency?"

"I suppose helping fund the Pinnacle Foundation does count as involvement, so yes," Miriam said.

"And you were in the confidence of their leader, who let you in on their secret plans?"

"Apparently not as much as I thought. Nothing Julian said suggested he wanted to create something that would attempt to conquer humanity."

"Either he was lying, or something changed after they left," the admiral said.

"I very much doubt he was lying to me, Admiral," Miriam said. "The latter seems much more likely to me."

"Well, at the very least, we now know where not to look to find the Cendies' home system," Admiral Moebius said. "Though right now, we have more immediate concerns than where they came from."

"Is that what this fleet is for, sir?" Jessica asked. "To relieve Inner Sol?"

Admiral Moebius nodded. "Yes, but not directly. I'm sure you were somewhat surprised to see *Independence* out here."

"A bit, though it's clear she still has some repairs left to be done," Jessica said.

"*Onager*'s crew has been worked to the bone getting *Independence* into a battle-ready state," Admiral Moebius said. "I don't suppose you noticed some of the other ships in the fleet?"

"I admit *Independence* was holding my attention pretty firmly, sir," Jessica said.

"Taskforce Red isn't a simple battlefleet, Lieutenant. Once we've finished gathering our forces, fully a third of it will be made up of tankers."

"And those tankers are full of fuel that we're going to take to Inner Sol, sir?" Jessica asked.

"No, they are quite empty. We'll be heading to 61 Virginis to fill them."

"The League's agreed to let us take their fuel? What's the catch?"

"The catch, Lieutenant, is that Triumph is currently under siege," Admiral Moebius said. "Our objective will be to break the Cendy siege of the planet before filling our tankers and escorting them to Sol to refuel Inner Sol."

"How many Cendy ships are in Triumph?" Jessica asked.

"Hundreds, though only about three hundred space-based combatants."

"Only three hundred, sir? That's three times as many fighting ships as we have here."

"We'll be leveraging Triumph's defenses and what remains of the League fleet in 61 Virginis to balance out the Cendies' numerical advantage," Admiral Moebius said. "But that's not the biggest concern. That would be the other ships making up the majority of the Cendy fleet."

"What do you mean?"

"They're believed to be landing ships. Massive ones. It appears the Cendies intend on taking the planet by invasion."

"Invasion, sir? That would take an enormous army for a planet like Triumph."

"Given the size of their landing ships and their numbers, they seem to have just that."

"Blimey!" Jessica breathed.

"This just doesn't make any sense," Miriam interjected.

"What doesn't, Miss Xia?" Admiral Moebius said. The admiral clearly couldn't bring herself to use Miriam's first name, despite the invitation.

"Giant fleets, planetary invasions. Armies. Everyone the Pinnacle Foundation sent aboard *Ascension* were doctors and scientists. There wasn't a single soldier among them."

"What's the point you're trying to make?"

"The point I'm trying to make, Admiral, is that there wasn't anyone who could teach them how to wage war," Miriam said.

"I don't believe anyone needed to teach them, Miriam," Jessica said. "I think they reinvented it when they decided to attack Federal Space. The way they approach space warfare is very different from our approach. They put the emphasis on range and overwhelming firepower with specialized starships. Our ships, on the other hand, are made with versatility and survivability in mind."

"And you think that will apply to their approach to ground warfare as well, Lieutenant?" Admiral Mobius asked.

"I think the people defending Triumph are learning that the hard way," Jessica said.

CHAPTER 22

The airbase on the top of Citadel 44 was crowded with Asps, their reverse-geometry wing unmistakable from above. It looked like, rather than bring the fighters down to the subterranean base, they had brought the munitions up to the fighters. Tractors pulled trailers piled with weapons out to the waiting fighters to be loaded by gangs of ground crew.

Citadel 44 was scrambling to provide air support for Planetary Defense Forces who were still dealing with the remains of the Cendy raid.

It was hard to think of an operation that involved landing a hundred thousand troops as a mere raid.

While the Asps were all being rearmed, the runways themselves were clear. All twelve fighters of Osiris Squadron landed before the first of the Asps started taxing for the runway.

Taxiing off the runway was a much more challenging affair than it had been the day before. The base bustled with activity, and Mason had to bring his fighter to a stop more than once to let taxiing Asps or gaggles of ground crew go by.

Citadel 44's ATC directed Mason to a clear area of concrete reserved just for his squadron. There he found Chief Rabin standing among a group of League ground crew. Behind them were large containers mounted on trailers, each filled with a hundred Hammer missiles. That was one-third of all the Hammer missiles they had brought along. Another third had just been expended.

Mason rolled his Lightning to a stop and opened the canopy. He unbuckled his seat restraints, climbed out of the cockpit, and dropped down to the tarmac. Chief Rabin walked up and saluted him.

"I see you've been busy, sir."

"That I have, Chief," Mason said. "Cendies gave us a lot to shoot at."

"Yeah, that could be a problem."

"I know. We have what? Maybe one more full reload after this?" Mason asked.

"For the Hammers, yes," Rabin said. "We still have all of our Scimitars."

"It would be a waste to use cruise missiles against infantry," Mason said. "We'll have to see about trying to adapt League munitions to our fighters."

"I've been touching base with Tech Sergeant Chicane, my opposite number with the League. She thinks we could start adapting their freefall bombs to our fighters."

"Bombs? Please tell me they're guided, at least."

"Afraid not, sir. Most of the base has simple iron bombs that can be fitted with guidance kits. Unfortunately, those kits aren't compatible with our fighters. At least not yet."

"Well, better than just our guns when we run out of Hammers," Mason said. "When do you think you can get that done?"

"Once we're not busy servicing fighters, a few days. Just need to use the base's 3D printers to make the adaptors."

"Some good news, for once."

"Probably not from that one, sir," Rabin said, pointing behind Mason.

Turning around, he saw Commander Serova marching towards him. Her helmet was tucked under her left arm, revealing a face bearing her habitual grim expression.

"Squadron Leader Grey," she said.

"Commander Serova," Mason replied and waited for a reprimand from the stoney-faced commander. It didn't come.

"You did good work providing air support for our missile battery. I can say without reservation that your efforts were critical to its survival," she said, her praise taking Mason by surprise.

"Yeah, too bad that wasn't the only base that got hit," he said.

"Yes," Serova said. "Seems we have underestimated the Cendies again.

Our planetary missile batteries were designed to survive the heaviest of orbital bombardments, not massed infantry assaults. As soon as the Ascendency's soldiers breached the underground complexes, they made short work of the missile crews and demolished the launchers and manufacturing facilities."

"The Cendies are good at hitting us where we don't expect, Commander," Mason said.

"And now this continent has only one missile battery protecting it from the Ascendancy fleet," Serova said.

"Yeah," Mason said. "Just my luck to end up on the continent the Cendies intend landing on."

Serova smiled. "Yes, you seem to have put yourself right in the enemy's path. Is that something that happens to you often, Squadron Leader?"

"More often than I'd like, Commander," Mason said.

"I see you're getting your fighters ready for another sortie. Where do you plan on taking them?"

"Wherever you need us, Commander," Mason said. "We're here to help."

"I suppose you are," Serova said. "Though the irony doesn't escape me that keeping you grounded is what put you in a position to actually make a difference down here."

"Yeah, funny how that worked out," Mason said. "My crew, Chief, and yours have been discussing ways of adapting your weapons to our fighters. Right now, they think they can get dumb bombs adapted in short order, but I would like to ask if you have the resources to get your interceptors adapted."

"I'll see what I can do," Serova said. "Though right now, I need to get back to my fighter. The Cendy raiding forces scattered after destroying our missile batteries and are causing trouble all over the continent."

"Sounds like they're trying to tie up ground forces before the main attack," Mason said.

"That's what I'm afraid of, Squadron Leader," Serova said. "Good hunting. I think the next few days are going to be very difficult."

"Good hunting to you too, Commander," Mason said.

Serova turned around and started jogging back to her parked fighter, pulling her helmet on as she went.

The ground crews finished reloading Mason's fighter shortly after that, and he climbed in and powered her back up, getting his fighter into the takeoff queue to provide whatever support he could.

※

The Cendy raids left fires, figurative and literal, all over the continent that needed putting out.

Where the Cendies had been cornered by Planetary Defense ground forces, it was a simple matter of firing a few air-bursting Hammers into their hiding places. But in most areas, it was a long, drawn-out hunt as Mason's fighters orbited overhead while soldiers and tanks on the ground swept the area for Cendies, often encountering ambushes and calling in air support.

It was a stressful task. Far more stressful than he had ever imagined. Even with the powerful sensors of his fighter, he often didn't detect Cendies until they started firing on the League Planetary Defense soldiers sent to hunt them.

He had to be constantly vigilant, ready to launch a Hammer at short notice, taking care not to catch any friendlies in the blast radius of his missiles.

In ones and twos, Mason fired missiles where they were requested, and continued his orbit. He tried to keep his attention on what was going on below him, but he couldn't help but look up above.

Even through the concealment of Triumph's atmosphere, his ventral sensors picked up the massed long-burn drive glows of the Ascendency fleet burning close to the planet, staying directly over the mostly defanged Stoneland.

There were plenty of missile batteries still on the planet, and they sent constant volleys of anti-starship missiles after the Cendies. But those missiles had to curve around the bulk of the planet, increasing the time it took for them to reach their targets, giving the Cendies more time to deal with them.

After eight hours in the air, the callout for air support stopped shortly before his squadron ran out of missiles. Across the expanse of land Osiris Squadron operated over, the soldiers below were calling the all clear.

It was too much to hope that they had killed all the Cendies. They had probably just driven them away from urban centers and transportation hubs and into the vast wilderness of the continent.

The Cendy soldiers proved to be incredibly mobile for foot soldiers, able to maintain their high running speed seemingly indefinitely, despite the weight of the arms and armor they carried.

With the Cendies gone to ground to await the arrival of the main invasion force, Mason's squadron was finally called to return to Citadel 44.

The surface base was still a hive of activity when Mason's squadron touched down on the runway, but now instead of readying fighters for combat, work was being done as fast as possible to get everything back underground to shelter against the storm that was coming.

Climbing out of the cockpit after parking and shutting down his fighter, Mason took off his helmet. Suppressing his discomfort at the naked sky above him, he took a moment to appreciate the cool mountain air kissing his cheeks, and the vast unspoiled landscape that stretched out in all directions around the mountain Citadel 44 was built into.

Soon, there would be streaks of fire filling the sky, and the ground around would be broken and cratered from sustained orbital bombardment.

Mason sighed. Just getting to this planet had been a challenge. He dreaded the prospect of trying to hold it against a siege. The Ascendency would have to batter Triumph until the defenders were broken or all dead.

"Enjoying the view one last time before we go underground, Mason?" Zin asked.

"I suspect it won't look like this the next time I'm above ground," Mason said.

"Good to see you're still optimistic," Zin said.

"Really? I didn't know that was being optimistic," Mason said.

"You're assuming we'll still be alive to see the world above," Zin said. "Given what is coming, I think that is very optimistic."

"Belts and zones!" Mason said. He turned to Zin. "I'm sorry I got you into this mess, Zin."

"Don't be, Mason. This is exactly where I should be." Zin glanced at the pristine sky above. "Well, not exactly. I would like to get a few thousand meters of rock over my head before the Cendies start bombing this place."

"Good idea," Mason said. The League ground crews were already guiding tractors up to the Lightnings to tow them to the elevator platform. "Let's ride down with our fighters."

After riding the elevators down, Mason and the other pilots of Osiris Squadron made their way off before the groundcrews started unloading the fighters. Sitting on a crate with a smug expression on his face was Flight Lieutenant Dominic. He seemed far too cheerful for a pilot left without a fighter to fly.

"You look like you're in a good mood, Silverback," Mason said.

"I've been productive while you all were busy blasting Cendies off the planet, Hauler." Dominic pushed himself off the crate. "I ran into Chief Rabin and he mentioned trying to adapt League weapons to our fighters. He was already on top of the hardware issue, so I tasked myself with addressing the problem of adapting League software to ours."

"Wait, you've re-programmed League weapons to work with our fighters?" Sabal asked.

"Oh, no. I'm good, but I can't work miracles," Dominic said. "I wrote a patch that should allow our fighters to use some League weapons. Interceptors, specifically."

"Interceptors? So, we can fight in space again?" Mason said.

Dominic nodded. "When Chief Rabin figures out how to mount them on our fighter, yes, sir. Though I'll admit, my patch was a rush job. I'm still working out the bugs and we still won't be able to use the League interceptors to their full potential. No mid-flight guidance, for example, so effective range is going to suffer."

"I can't believe you did this all on your own," Mason said.

"I didn't," Dominic said. "I ran my idea past Colonel Shimura and she got to work finding coders who could help. Turns out there's a fair number of talented League coders under this mountain. The patch should be ready to upload to the fighters in a week."

"Seems like that might be too late," Sabal said. "The Cendies are already moving to invade."

"It will be worth it if we have to launch an attack against space-based targets," Mason said. "Good work, Dominic. Glad to see your old professional skills are proving useful."

"I'm glad I got to occupy myself doing something productive, sir," Dominic said. "The fact it might contribute to keeping us alive is a bonus."

A notification popped in on Mason's HUD. A summons to the Command Center from Colonel Shimura. He hoped she had gotten some sleep since the last time he saw her in there.

"Shutdown, get everyone some food and sleep. We're going to need it," Mason said. "I'm going to touch base with Colonel Shimura."

"Understood, Hauler. Make sure you get a chance for a meal and some sleep yourself," Zin said.

"Oh, trust me, I'm headed straight for the lower level as soon as I'm able to," Mason said.

Zin and the other pilots of Osiris Squadron proceeded in the direction of the nearest stairwell that led to the habitation level. Mason headed for the Command Center across the dome from the aircraft elevators. The guards gave him no trouble as he walked past them.

Colonel Shimura was in the Command Center in the exact same spot she had been some twelve hours earlier. Standing in the center aisle between control consoles, she stared up at the display showing the approach of the Ascendency fleet.

Mason walked up next to her. "Reporting, sir."

"Good work dealing with the Cendy ground assault, Squadron Leader," Shimura said. "That was textbook air support."

"Thank you, sir," Mason said. "Doesn't seem like it was enough, though."

"One missile battery is better than none, Squadron Leader," Colonel Shimura said. "When the Cendies land, they will have some extra attrition."

"We're certain they're going to land?"

"No other reason to use a ground assault to take out ground-based defenses, Squadron Leader," Colonel Shimura pointed out. "They want to take Triumph intact, and that means soldiers."

"You think they'll use the same method as before?" Mason asked.

"No, I don't, Squadron Leader. Look." Colonel Shimura walked over to an empty console and with a few keystrokes, brought up the image of one of the Cendy ships.

"The Turtlebacks? They're troop transports."

"Not just troop transports, Squadron Leader. They're landing ships."

CHAPTER 23

MORE SHIPS JUMPED into Checkpoint Hephaestus, further reinforcing Taskforce Red.

There were now over a hundred warships and fifty massive fleet tankers. A sizable fraction of the Federal Space Forces' remaining fleet was gathered inside a volume of space a hundred thousand kilometers across. And that was starting to concern her. It would only be a matter of time before the Cendies noticed the missing ships, if they had not done so already.

When Jessica arrived in Admiral Moebius' office to further discuss the findings of her investigation, the question still burned in her chest.

"What is it, Lieutenant?" the admiral asked, reading Jessica's troubled expression.

"A fair portion of the Space Forces' remaining fighting strength is out here, sir," Jessica said. "Floating about empty space rather than protecting our systems."

"And you think I'm leaving our systems vulnerable to attack?"

"I think you're doing something to hide that vulnerability, sir," Jessica said. "The false destination you gave *Goshawk* was my first clue. But that wouldn't work in the long run, not with so many ships. Cendy recon ships are going to notice there are a bunch of hulls that aren't arriving at their destinations when they should and are going to start to wonder where they actually are."

"You're right, Lieutenant," Admiral Mobius said. "And given you're a part of my staff, I suppose I should tell you. We're using ships equipped with mimic arrays to take the place of the ships that are making up Taskforce Red."

"When did we have that many?" Jessica asked. From being in the Special Purpose Branch she had a good idea how many ships equipped with mimic arrays they had, and it wouldn't cover a tenth of the ships gathering at Checkpoint Hephaestus.

"We don't," Admiral Moebius said. "Fortunately, the hardware to make a mimic array isn't all that hard to come by. So, I've bolted jury-rigged mimic arrays on every old hulk and star freighter I could find. They're not useful for infiltration and covert surveillance like purpose-built vessels, but they're good enough to fool deep scans. Or that's the hope."

"Well, that's bloody clever, sir," Jessica said.

Admiral Moebius shrugged. "All warfare is based on deception."

"Sun Tzu," Jessica said.

"It's as true today as it was back in his day," Admiral Moebius said. "The Cendies managed to start this war and gain the advantage by using deception. I intend to turn the tide doing the same."

"It's just a small matter of actually beating the Cendies when we get to 61 Virginis," Jessica said. "Have we been coordinating with the League?"

"The League doesn't know we're coming beyond vague assurances," Admiral Moebius said. "We can't risk Operation Turnpike being revealed before it starts."

"It's going to be tricky getting the League to do what we need them to do when we arrive," Jessica said.

"That's why I sent Colonel Shimura ahead of the fleet."

"You sent Colonel Shimura to Triumph?"

"She's already on Triumph," Admiral Moebius said. "Along with a contingent of Raiders and a squadron of Special Operations Lightnings."

"Which squadron is that?"

"The 77th Special Operations Fighter Squadron, under the command of your former colleague, Squadron Leader Mason Grey."

A sudden sense of anxiety welled up inside her, taking Jessica by surprise. "You sent them to hold off the entire Cendy invasion force?"

"No, I sent them to help delay the Cendies and provide coordination between us and the League when we arrive."

"What happens if they're not able to do that, sir?"

"Then we press on with the mission and are probably destroyed in the process."

"That's not much of a backup plan."

"There isn't one," Admiral Moebius said. "We're all-in on this. If we don't secure 61 Virginis' fuel reserves, the Cendies are going to overtake Inner Sol, cutting us off from our industrial heart. Combined with them controlling both Outer Sol's fuel reserves and 61 Virginis', they would be able to leverage that to grind us down."

"Blimey," was all Jessica could say. She had known things were dire but hadn't known how much was riding on just one operation.

She should have, in hindsight. It was all there. The effort to rescue the entire Jovian population, the 1st Fleet's precarious position, the fact that the largest fraction of the Earth Federation's industrial base was concentrated on Luna. The Cendies had slipped a dagger between Earth Fed's ribs and were about to push it the rest of the way in.

"Congratulations, Lieutenant," Admiral Moebius said. "You know something that only about eight other people in the whole Earth Federation know."

"Does Colonel Shimura know?" Jessica asked.

"She doesn't need to know. She's a good solider and smart as hell. She'll do her job."

"We just need to do ours," Jessica said. "Which makes me wonder. What's my job now that I've given you my findings?"

"Continue to chum it up with Miriam Xia's digital persona, learning what you can about the Ascendency's origins," Admiral Mobius said. "I've already had my analysts scouring our charts for every brown dwarf and rogue planet that has been catalogued in the past nine centuries."

"That's going to take a while."

"I'm hoping we'll learn things that will narrow our search. Possibly from the wreckage of the Cendy ships we'll encounter over Triumph."

"Assuming we win."

"If we don't win, then it's all going to be a moot point, Lieutenant."

"You're looking tired," Miriam noted as Jessica entered the common area of the module that served as Miriam's home aboard *Independence*.

"I just learned that the Earth Federation is betting the farm on a single mission," Jessica said. "No biggie."

"I see," Miriam said. "The Ascended were quite clever in how they struck you."

"Tell me about it," Jessica said. "They knew exactly how to hurt us."

"You sound like that's a surprise," Miriam said. "I was aware of that fact two hundred years ago. Earth Fed's dependence on Sol has always been its weakness."

"I suppose everyone thought Sol was too well defended for it to be considered a weak spot," Jessica said.

"Oh, I'm aware of that fact too," Miriam said. "Simply by virtue of being the birthplace of humanity pretty much makes it unavoidable for any state that controls Sol to become dependent on it. It's a reason that the General Conflict was so devastating, when the old nations started tearing each other's space-based infrastructure apart."

"Well, if we survive this war, we'll have to see about distributing Earth Fed's industrial base among the other systems," Jessica said.

"A dangerous proposition," Miriam said. "After all, it would deprive systems like Tau Ceti or Epsilon Eradani of the incentive to stay in the Earth Federation."

"Those systems joined Earth Fed voluntarily," Jessica said.

"Yes, because they were dependent on Sol," Miriam said. "They could get away with that, given their proximity to Sol. But notice, no more-distant systems joined. In fact, some banded together to form the League just to keep Earth Fed out."

"Well, I'd say, given the vulnerability Earth Fed's centralization presents, we might have to find another way to keep the Earth Federation together," Jessica said.

"Why does it have to be the Earth Federation?" Miriam asked.

"Because I'm wearing a uniform with Earth Fed's flag on it," Jessica said. "Swore an oath and everything. I take it you don't feel the same loyalty?"

"My loyalty is to humanity, not particular governments. And I think the whole concept of the Earth Federation is flawed. Has been from the start, from when they decided to include Earth in its name," Miriam said.

"Really? Because I think that's an acknowledgment of reality," Jessica said. "Earth itself has a little under half the Earth Federation's population. It's literally the place where the very concepts we're discussing were invented."

"I sense your bias showing," Miriam said.

"Of course I have a bias towards the world I was born on," Jessica said. "There are parts of the Earth that I quite like. And there are even some people who live there who aren't insufferable gits."

"But do you think that's a basis for a galaxy-spanning civilization?" Miriam asked.

"There is no galaxy-spanning civilization," Jessica said. "Settled space barely stretches more than a hundred light-years in radius."

"On average," Miriam said. "I did some research since leaving my virtual world. There are reports of colonies being set up as far as three hundred light-years away."

"Yeah. There are some people who want to live somewhere out of the way," Jessica said.

"And yet, they only make up a fraction of a percent of the people who set out from their home systems," Miriam said. "Most just emigrate to established colonies rather than building new ones far away."

"You're surprised? It's far more comfortable to settle on a world that has finished terraforming and has such luxuries as a developed electrical grid and running water," Jessica said. "Or in systems with Class 1 Habitat stations that have full spin-gravity and plentiful air rather than some kludge made out of assembled pre-fabricated modules that smell of old farts."

"But don't you see? By having an Earth Federation, by preserving Earth's central place, the Earth Federation has turned the world of our birth into a rock that humanity is chained to. One that doesn't allow most of us to venture forth because we're afraid of losing the comforts staying close to Sol provides."

"Is that one of the things Doctor Marr discussed with you?" Jessica said. "Reducing the importance of Earth?"

"To an extent, but his solution was simple," Miriam said. "Create a people that had no attachment to Earth. They could expand and grow throughout the galaxy without being tethered to one place."

"And yet they came back," Jessica said. "In case you forgot, they have a fleet in the solar system ready to attack Earth as we speak."

"And that's what's so puzzling," Miriam said.

"Do you think Julian changed his mind?" Jessica asked. "Maybe he decided that a race of explorers wasn't what he needed to create, but a race of warriors instead."

"Julian was an anarchist. I don't see him trying to raise an army," Miriam said.

"But his creations did," Jessica said. "Maybe to serve as a means of breaking down the order you're so critical of. To make Earth no longer relevant."

Miriam snorted, a tinny sound from her artificial voice box. "Invading Earth only makes that plan more important. If they wanted to make Earth irrelevant, they'd be throwing asteroids at it. Not Jovian space stations by it."

"A fair point," Jessica admitted. That had been a nightmare scenario for the Federal Space Forces since well before the Ascendency showed up. An enemy putting engines on a few million rocks and pushing them into an orbit that intersected with the Earth. The 1st Fleet could easily destroy one, or even several dozen rocks. But the outer solar system had millions of potential weapons just in Jupiter's Trojan asteroids. They could drop a swarm of deadly rocks that could overwhelm even Earth's defenses.

The fact that they could push four hundred space stations, all of which massed close to that of a good-sized asteroid, on a parabolic trajectory through the solar system showed that they had the technical ability, if not the inclination.

"You see my point? Whatever the Cendies' goals are, Earth is not the end but the means," Miriam said.

"And that end being the dissolution of the Earth Federation," Jessica said. "What comes after?"

"Well, if we're to believe what the Ascendency is saying, a new interstellar order where the Ascendency controls space travel while planets and stations govern themselves internally."

"That sounds a lot like a federation."

"I would call it more of a protectorate," Miriam said. "The Ascendency seems quite keen on controlling space travel. In fact, given the comments they made, I think their goal isn't to simply rule space but to deny its use to humanity."

"You think they want to contain us?"

Miriam shrugged. "Possibly. I think that the Ascendency might just want to have space for themselves, and only let humanity expand on their terms, if at all."

"But you just pointed out that human civilization has been expanding slowly, even after the development of faster-than-light travel through the star drive," Jessica said. "Why would they feel the need to contain us?"

"I don't know. Maybe they found something they felt the need to protect us from," Miriam said. "Or to protect from us."

CHAPTER 24

Mason studied the first high-resolution image of the five hundred inbound Turtlebacks and had to agree with Colonel Shimura that they were landing ships. Immense ones.

They had flattened, aerodynamic hulls that would allow them to skim through the atmosphere like a spaceplane. And they had a mass of cruisers. Mason could only guess as to what was contained within them. Endless swarms of Cendy soldiers? Their equivalent to battle tanks, artillery, and aircraft?

The high-resolution images had been taken by Triumph's array of space telescopes, which were busy gathering all the intelligence they could on the approaching Cendy fleet before they were destroyed. Already, there was a wave of Outrider fighters inbound to do just that.

"Belts and zones!"

"That good, huh?" Zin asked.

"We've got front-row seats to the largest planetary invasion in history," Mason said. "I have to say that I'm a bit surprised that the Cendies have the kind of manpower to pull this off."

"Why? I've read up the reports. They grow their soldiers in tanks, right? They probably have factories growing soldiers by the division. Seems manpower is the least of their problems."

Mason ran his hands down his face. "I'm not cut out for this, Zin."

"Is anyone? You're doing the best you can."

"It doesn't seem like it will be enough."

"That's defeatist, Mason, not a good quality for a leader."

"Maybe because I'm not a good leader."

"Mason, this isn't time for self-doubt. You'll be doing the Cendies' job for them," Zin said. "No one expects us to keep the Cendies from taking the planet all on our own. That's not why they sent us here."

"We're here as a speedbump," Mason said. "I just don't know how much good that will be against the juggernaut that's coming down upon us."

"Well, why don't we do something to tilt the odds in our favor?"

"Like what? The League are already planning on launching a fighter attack against the Cendy landing force. But they're so badly outnumbered, I don't know if that'll do much good."

"Maybe this is a good time to try out those fancy guns Chief Rabin brought down with us," Zin suggested.

"I think we should have brought torpedoes instead."

"League weren't going to let us bring nukes down to their homeworld," Zin pointed out. "And since we're not sure how effective these fancy guns are, we may as well test them out on Cendy landing ships."

Mason sighed. "Not a bad idea. We probably won't get another chance to use the Raidens before the Cendies land. I'll check with Colonel Shimura. Tell Chief Rabin to start loading the guns up on my fighter and yours."

"Why mine?"

"It was your idea."

※

"I'm not sure how I feel about you Federals using our counterattack as a chance to test out your experimental weapons," Commander Serova said.

"The Raiden cannons will be useless against the Cendies on the ground," Colonel Shimura argued. "We either use them now, or we will have wasted the effort in bringing them here."

"Those Turtlebacks, as you call them, are over a hundred thousand tons in mass," Serova said. "I don't see how your pop guns are going to hurt them."

"Commander, do you mind if I use the main screen?" Mason asked.

"Go ahead, Squadron Leader."

Mason tapped commands on the console and brought up a high-res image of a Turtleback.

"I know what that is, Squadron Leader."

"I know, I know, but look closely," Mason said, zooming the image towards the bottom of the Turtleback. "Do you notice how the ventral surface is almost completely black?"

"Yes."

"I think the bottom of the Turtlebacks are covered in an ablative heatshield. Given their current trajectory, I think they're going to make a high-speed ballistic entry, using Triumph's atmosphere to slow to a safe landing speed and using the plasma sheath generated by the entry for protection."

"A clever conclusion, Squadron Leader. Our intelligence analysts believe the same," Serova said.

"Well, the Raidens can punch holes in Turtlebacks' heatshields," Mason said. "If they do that, the plasma from the entry will penetrate into Turtleback's interior, probably destroying them."

"So that's your plan? To poke holes in their heatshields?"

Mason nodded. "It's not something the Cendies will be anticipating. If my fighters can get under them, we can nose up and start shooting into the undersides of those Turtlebacks, maybe knock a few down."

"I think nukes would do a better job."

"The Cendies are going to make an effort to counter any nukes you send their way, Commander," Mason said. "At the very least, while the Cendies are dealing with your nukes, I can sneak under them and start shooting."

"You?"

Mason nodded. "My XO and I will carry the two Raidens we brought. The rest of Osiris Squadron will act as escorts."

Serova glanced up at the large clock, counting down to the expected time before the Cendy Fusilier-class battlecruiser started bombarding the planet.

"You'll have to take off soon, Squadron Leader," she said. "It's almost certain the Cendies are going to hit the surface base in their first round of bombardment."

"My fighters are ready to take off now, Commander," Mason said. "Just give us the word."

"You have it, but on one condition."

"What is it, Commander?"

"My fighters will join yours to provide added escort," Serova said. "If this works, the Cendies are going to see you shooting down their transports and will send a swarm of fighters after you. I'd like to be there to greet them when they do."

Mason smiled. "I'll take all the help I can get, Commander."

"Then let's get out to our fighters, Squadron Leader."

※

Mason pulled back on the stick and climbed into the Triumph's darkening skies. Soon, those skies would be illuminated by the entry of hundreds of massive landing ships. With an untested weapon tucked into the weapons bay of his fighter, Mason wasn't exactly confident that he would make a big difference. But he did look forward to shooting a giant gun at the Cendies.

"All fighters go supersonic. Let's get some distance between us and Citadel 44 before the Cendies start bombing it," Mason called to his squadron.

His Lightning shuddered as it broke the sound barrier as he flew towards the equator. Ahead was an invisible point where the first of the Turtlebacks was predicted to enter the atmosphere. Osiris Squadron would arrive along their predicted trajectory just as the Turtlebacks entered the atmosphere. Mason pulled on the stick and entered a shallow climb to reach operating altitude for the Raidens.

"Look to the east, the first Turtleback is entering the atmosphere," Commander Serova called.

Off Mason's left wing were the first meteor trails of large ships entering the atmosphere at high speed.

"Okay, here we go," Mason said. "Commander Serova, my pilots are at your disposal to provide cover for me and Osiris 5 while we make our attacks."

"We'll make sure to keep the Cendies off your backs, Squadron Leader Grey. I hope your aim is good," Serova said.

"Me too," Mason said. "You ready, Shutdown?"

"Just give the word, Hauler," Zin said.

As soon as he reached the target altitude, Mason armed the Raiden.

The weapons bay opened, and the gun lowered, the telescoping barrel extending forward. Mason felt the extra drag pull on his fighter, but the air was thin at this altitude, and the drag manageable.

"Osiris 5, Raiden is armed," Zin said.

"Osiris Leader, Raiden armed and ready," Mason said.

The combat AI already had firing solutions for him. The Turtlebacks were invisible behind the fireball of their entries, but they would be in the very center, and that's were Mason intended to land his shot.

"Osiris Leader entering climb," Mason said, dialing back on his throttle as he pulled up. He didn't want to get much higher than he already was. Triumph's atmosphere was the best defense against the massed Cendy weapons looming over him.

"Osiris Five entering climb," Zin said.

Mason picked the lead fireball as his first target. The Turtleback was losing speed quickly, dumping its massive kinetic energy into the air.

Taking in a deep breath, Mason let out a long exhale, and pointed his fighter's nose at the lead indicator highlighted by his combat AI.

Then he squeezed the trigger.

The blast of the recoil charge drowned out the sound of the Raiden itself firing, and his fighter lurched under him like it had just been kicked. His shot streaked up into the atmosphere, leaving a faint trail as the round's outer layers burned away. Another streaked into the sky as Zin fired on her targets. The streaks merged with the fireballs of their targets, and the fireballs continued as if nothing had happened.

"Well, that was anticlimactic," Mason said.

Then, a few seconds after the shots were fired, the fireballs disintegrated into expanding fans of flaming debris.

"Okay, never mind, that worked quite well," Mason said. "Fire at will, Shutdown. We have four more shots each."

"I'm already picking my next target," Zin said.

It took ten seconds for the Raiden to charge up for the next shot, during which several Turtlebacks flew overhead untroubled. As soon as the second round was chambered, Mason pulled up, fired, and dived. Another Turtleback broke apart after flying apparently unharmed for a few seconds, the time it took for the plasma to burn through its punctured heatshields and tear it apart.

Zin nailed another Turtleback, and Mason was already preparing to take down another as soon as his Raiden was finished loading the next round. It wasn't until Mason had killed his third Turtleback that the Cendies reacted to what was happening. Turtlebacks that had been flying in straight lines now turned away, leaving curved streaks of fire and smoke overhead. But their attempt at evasion was not enough to get the closest ones out of range of Mason's Raiden. Another pop-up, and another pair of Turtlebacks scattered their wreckage across Triumph's sky.

"Osiris Leader, we have hostile fighters inbound," Commander Serova said.

"I guess that's it for us," Mason said. "Zin and I are diving to the deck."

"We'll send a wave of air-to-air missiles to hold them off and join you," Serova said.

Mason still had two more rounds left in his Raiden cannon, but the swarm of Cendy fighters descending towards him wouldn't be kind enough to allow him time to use them.

"Shutdown, stow your Raiden and follow me to the deck," Mason ordered.

"Roger that, Hauler."

Mason retracted the Raiden back into the weapons bay, cleaning up his fighter before he dived into the thicker air of low altitude. Behind him was a sudden storm of missile launches as Federal Skylance and League air-to-air missiles rocketed into the sky to meet the descending Outriders.

After launching their volley, the combined Lightnings and Asps turned hard and ran for the deck.

Above, the fifty Outriders escorting the Turtlebacks dove down after entering the atmosphere.

Some were taken down by the air-to-air missiles. To the Cendies' credit, they did seem to have a grasp on how to counter air-to-air missiles, pulling out of their dives and climbing higher than the missiles could follow.

They promptly dived back down, chasing after the Asps and Lightnings fleeing towards the deck.

Being outnumbered two-to-one was generally something that made Mason nervous, and truth be told, he was nervous. But his anxiety was greatly relieved as he overflew a highway overpass leading to one of Triumph's equatorial cities. Hiding beneath the underpass was about a dozen mobile SAM launchers. As the Cendies dove in on them, they flew right into the range of the SAM launchers. Missile trails flew out from under the underpass, causing the Cendy fighters to scatter as several were blotted out of the sky, their broken wreckage falling to the ground below. The Cendy fighters cut off their pursuit and turned to climb back to orbit.

"Commander Serova, please tell your colleagues in the Army that their help was much appreciated," Mason said.

"I'll pass the word along once they've finished evacuating the area," Serova said.

A volley of smoke rockets flew into the air, creating an instant overcast cloud to conceal the SAM launchers from orbit. The six-wheeled vehicles then scattered, their massive tires kicking up dust as they got as much distance as possible between themselves and their abandoned firing position.

A minute later, a bright spear of white fire fell from the sky, and the overpass and every building near it disappeared beneath a mushroom cloud as the expected kinetic strike arrived. Mason's heart sank as he saw the size of the mushroom cloud rising into the air. That had to have come from the main gun of a Fusilier. The spinal mount could fling their kinetic kill vehicles to velocities that put Federal capital ships to shame. He couldn't see the icons for the mobile SAM launchers and hoped that was due to interference from all the dust kicked up by the kinetic strike. As it turned out, there was even more interference as he made the turn back towards Citadel 44. On the horizon in every direction, Mason could see mushroom clouds of old kinetic strikes and the flashes of new ones. It seemed like every big gun the Cendies had was now firing on the continent.

Even moving faster than the speed of sound, Mason felt vulnerable.

It was difficult, but not impossible to track low-flying aircraft from space. And with the blast the big guns could create, they didn't have to be precise with their aim to kill them. He wanted to climb to a higher altitude but resisted the temptation. The thick lower atmosphere was what was concealing them from the sensors high above. Climbing higher would make it easier rather than harder for the Cendies to kill them.

"Commander Serova, what are you getting on your tactical channel?" Mason asked.

"Nothing," Serova said. "Everyone's gone radio silent."

"Any other way to tell what is happening?"

"Look outside," Serova said. "We'll be passing Nova Roma in a few minutes."

By the time they reached Nova Roma, the skies had grown dark as night took hold. All around the city were craters glowing from recent kinetic impacts. The city itself seemed untouched. The archology towers still stood tall but, studying his map of the city, it was clear to Mason that just about everything of immediate military value had gotten smashed from orbit. All that was left of the city's main airport was the outline of its perimeter fence and the very ends of the main runway—where the airport terminal would have been was a deep burning crater. All the smaller airports were in similar condition. Mason guessed that it was more important to deprive the defenders of the airports than try to capture them for themselves.

Maybe they didn't need them. He'd find out soon enough, he was sure.

The density of craters became sparser as they flew beyond the city into the more rural parts of the continent. There simply weren't that many targets for bombardments out in the countryside. The Cendies didn't seem interested in bombing farms and hamlets. But as he approached Citadel 44, he could see a large mushroom cloud that was just then starting to dissipate.

It was not a shock by any means to see that the Cendies had hit Citadel 44. But it was disheartening. Colonel Shimura, Chief Rabin, and hundreds of other Federal Spacers were under that cloud.

"They hit Citadel 44. No surprise there," Commander Serova said, her voice tight. "Follow my fighters in, Osiris Leader."

"It looks pretty bad down there, Commander," Mason said. "How do you know if there's still a base?"

"I don't, but I will in a moment," Serova said. "Maintain formation. If there's still a base to land at, I want to do it while the dust could be still obscuring us from orbit."

"Roger that."

Serova and her Asps slowed their speed. Mason did the same, slowing the speed of his fighter below the speed of sound.

"We're approaching one of the auxiliary landing facilities," Serova said. "I'll send a laser beacon and see if I get a response."

As they cruised slowly over the river valley next to the broken top of the mountain Citadel 44's surface facility laid on, Mason kept his attention on Serova's Asp, waiting for her response.

"I got a response! Looks like the underground base weathered the strike. Configure for vertical landing. We're not going to have the luxury of a runway this time."

CHAPTER 25

THE AUXILIARY LANDING facility was an austere thing. Just an expanse of grassland near a concealed entrance to Citadel 44. The landing engines from the Lightnings and Asps would leave pronounced burn scars in the grass. He hoped the Leaguers had a way of covering that up fast.

"This will be a fast landing, so mind your spacing," Commander Serova said.

"Roger that, Commander," Mason said. "All fighters maintain ten meters minimum spacing."

A rocket shot straight up into the air and disappeared into the low cloud layer, where it detonated with a flash. It wasn't a weapon, but a cloud rocket, its warhead adding more particles to the artificial clouds that concealed movement on the ground from space. The Cendies would have to send a ship below the cloud layer to see what was going on, and that would bring them into range of the multitudes of mobile SAM launchers scattered around the mountain range ready to ambush any Cendy fighter that dared fly below the clouds.

Mason lowered his landing gear and warmed up his landing engines.

The engine nacelles on the tips of the Asp wings all tilted up, directing their thrust down. They weren't in a hover, but in a high-angle attack-landing approach to the landing zone.

Downwash from the assembled fighters created hurricane-force winds that scattered rock, dust, and torn tree limbs.

Just before touchdown, Mason flared his engines and pulled his nose up slightly, slowing his descent to a safe rate while killing the remainder of his forward velocity. His rear wheels kissed the ground, and he slowly zeroed out his landing engines, settling his nose wheel to the ground.

The rest of Osiris Squadron landed around him at the same time. The Asps disappeared over the ridge as they landed at a neighboring auxiliary landing facility.

After doing a quick shutdown, Mason popped open his cockpit and climbed out of his fighter, leaping down from the port chine to land on the ground. His boots touched down on ground far harder than he expected. The ground felt more like carpeted concrete than earth. He also noticed that none of the grass was burned, despite the hot exhaust of the landing engines of twelve Lightnings touching down.

Mason knelt and ran his gloved fingers through the grass, his fingertips touching a rough substrate. It wasn't dirt, but pavement. Looking closer at the grass, he saw it was not actually grass but artificial turf, probably made of heat-tolerant polymer. Up close, the green filaments didn't look much like grass. But from up high, it was indistinguishable from the real thing.

The Leaguers certainly went all out when it came to camouflage.

A swarm of automated tractors rolled out of the hidden hangar towards the Lightnings. Mason stepped away from his fighter to clear the way for the squat, black-and-yellow vehicle to attach itself to the nose gear of his fighter. Then it started towing the fighter towards the hangar.

Zin walked up next to him as their fighters were towed into the underground back. "We're going to have to get Chief Rabin's people paint a few Turtlebacks on our noses," she said.

"I suppose we should," Mason agreed. He barely kept track of his kills; his fighter's AI did that for him. But the hangar techs always found time to paint another tiny silhouette on the side of his fighter's nose every time he earned a new kill.

"We should head in and see how everyone weathered the storm," Mason said.

"And make sure we don't get caught out here if a Cendy recon flight shows up," Zin added.

There was a long tunnel where their Lightnings were being towed two abreast at a walking pace. Mason walked behind the Lightnings with his pilots.

"You think it would've hurt to have a couple of carts for us to ride back on?" Sabal said.

"Just think of it as PT, Hardball," Mason said. "A little walk is good for you."

"I did enough of that in rehab," Sabal grumbled.

At the end of the tunnel, they arrived at the guarded entrance to the dome. Two Espatiers and two Federal Raiders in combat hardsuits guarded the far side of the tunnel from a prepared position, one of the Espatiers manning a tripod-mounted heavy machine gun.

One of the Federal troopers walked up to them and held aloft a hand to signal to them to stop. "You're going to have to tell your pilots to put their helmets back on, sir. A lot of rocks got knocked loose during the bombardment, and some of the smaller ones are still falling through the safety net."

"You heard her—helmets back on,' Mason said. He pulled his helmet back on, hoping the twenty millimeters of reinforced plastic and impact gel would be enough protection for any falling rocks that managed to strike his head. After all he'd survived, dying due to a stone caving in his scull would be severely anticlimactic.

After the long walk through thousands of meters of brightly lit tunnel, Mason and his pilots walked out into the main dome of Citadel 44. It was a mess with rocks and dust strewn about everywhere. Crews had erected improvised tents over all the fighters and aircraft to protect them from debris falling from the ceiling. A mix of League Espatiers, Planetary Defense soldiers, Federal troopers, and other personnel were cleaning up the dust on the ground as best they could with brooms and large vacuums. Above, Mason could see boulders suspended from the web of intersecting cables that crisscrossed the ceiling. The safety net was visibly bowed-in from the weight of fallen rocks, and there were more than a few points were cables had ripped free of their anchors and dangled uselessly like vines.

Mason started to feel like his helmet wasn't enough protection.

"The Cendies sure did a number on this place," Zin said.

"Given the Cendies blew up half the mountain over us, I'd say this place is in pretty good shape, Shutdown," Mason said. "I'll check in with Chief Rabin. You get everyone back down the barracks to get some food and rest. I'm sure there will more of work for us to do soon."

"Don't get caught under any falling boulders, Hauler," Zin said.

"I'll try not to, Shutdown."

As Zin led his pilots to the stairs down to the lower level, Mason found Chief Rabin and his people guiding the automated tractors as they towed the Lightnings into tents erected over their parking spots.

Rabin was wearing the same orange construction helmet as the League personnel working on the floor of the dome. Rabin saluted Mason as he approached.

"Welcome back, sir. How did the Raidens work?"

"Like a charm, Chief," Mason said. "How did your people fair?"

"Place shook like a motherfucker for a while, sir," Rabin said. "But everyone in the base was in shelters when the kinetics started falling. As you can see, the safety net kept all the big rocks from falling on us. Just a bunch of pebbles and dust made it through."

"Pebbles? Some of the rocks I saw on the ground were the size of my fist, Chief," Mason said, balling up his right hand to illustrate.

"Eh, there's so damn many of them they all look like pebbles," Chief Rabin said. "Least I didn't get put on cleanup duty. I guess maintaining our Lightnings takes precedence."

"Glad to see your people made it through okay," Mason said. "Have they had a chance to rest?"

"I have my people working shifts, sir," Rabin said. "Half of them are down below getting rack time while the rest supervise the League crews. It'll be my turn to hit the sack in six hours."

Mason nodded. "That sounds like an excellent plan. I think I'll do that myself."

"Sleep well, sir," Chief Rabin said. "Your fighters will be ready to fight again when you wake up."

"I've no doubt about that, Chief."

Entering the stairwell, Mason pulled off his helmet now that he no longer had to worry about falling rocks. The lower level seemed to have fared better than the dome. There was the odd pile of dust or bits of rock knocked loose but, overall, it seemed undamaged.

Mason stopped by the Command Center and was surprised to see Colonel Shimura still standing amid the consoles.

As he approached her from behind, he noticed the slight sag of her shoulders.

"Colonel Shimura?"

She turned around, and Mason could see the bags under her eyes, her pupils dilated from extended stimulant use.

"Ah, Squadron Leader Grey. You did well to shoot down those Cendy landing ships," she said.

"Thank you, sir," Mason said. "You look awful."

Shimura glared at him. "I don't recall soliciting your opinion on my appearance, Squadron Leader."

"You look like you haven't slept since we set foot on this rock, sir," Mason persisted.

"I got plenty of sleep on the flight here."

"Yeah, that doesn't count, sir," Mason said. "You need to take a break."

"That sounds a lot like you're trying to order me, Squadron Leader."

"Sir, you look like you're just a half-step away from a total burnout."

"I assure you, I'm fine, Squadron Leader."

"Then you won't mind if I ask one of the medics to check on you, sir?"

"Oh, so you're my doctor too now?" Shimura said.

"Colonel, with all due respect, you're out of line," Mason said.

"Now I'm out of line? I know you're new to your rank, Squadron Leader, but colonels still outrank you."

"I've never known you to be someone to hide behind anything, Colonel," Mason said, "least of all rank."

Shimura sighed, and turned, gesturing towards the large screen. It was showing a lot of out-of-date information. "Do you know what's happening out there right now, Squadron Leader?"

"Beyond the obvious?"

"The answer is: I don't know," Colonel Shimura said. "This is what I hate about ground operations. There's so much damn clutter that you can't tell what the fuck is going on. At least with space, there's clarity."

Belts and zones, just how many stimulants had Colonel Shimura taken? The officers and enlisted personnel were staring at her, clearly uncomfortable with having an agitated Federal officer in the control center.

"Colonel Shimura, you're not fit for duty right now," Mason said firmly. "I know that's not what you want to hear, but that's the truth. Come on. At the very least, let's get out of here. Give you some room to breathe."

"For the last time, I–"

"Colonel Shimura!" Commander Serova said, marching in, her long ponytail swaying behind her head. "What the hell are you doing in my Command Center?"

"Commander–"

Serova held up a finger. "This is my base, Colonel. And if one of my officers was in as sorry a state as you are, I'd have them sedated and dragged back to their quarters."

"I'm not one of your officers, Commander," Colonel Shimura said.

"You're right, but don't think for a moment that will stop me." Commander Serova glanced at Mason. "And I somehow suspect your subordinates won't get in the way if it came to that."

"But it won't come to that, Commander," Mason said. "Will it, Colonel Shimura?"

The look Shimura gave Mason could bore a hole through the frontal armor of a battleship. She took a couple of deep breaths and for a second Mason thought she was going to strike him.

Then she sighed, swaying slightly as her hand went to her forehead. "My apologies, to both of you. I-I seem to have overstressed myself."

"Then find somewhere to relax, Colonel," Commander Serova said. "I don't want to see you in such a state ever again."

"You heard her, Colonel. Let's get you back to your quarters," Mason said.

Shimura nodded, and followed him out of the Command Center. As she walked beside him, she had a haunted look on her face. Such… vulnerability was not something he had seen from her before. Not something he throught she was capable of.

"I'm sorry once again, Squadron Leader. My behavior was unacceptable."

"We're in a tough spot, sir," Mason said. "All you did was remind me that you are in fact human."

"Don't let that get around."

"Your secret is safe with me, sir"

"Good, I'd have to kill you otherwise."

"Get some rest, sir," Mason said. "The Triumph will still be here for you to save it."

Colonel Shimura shook her head. "I'm not trying to save Triumph. I'm just trying to slow down the Cendies long enough so someone else can."

CHAPTER 26

Mason was summoned to the Command Center by Commander Serova the day after the Cendies landed.

There was a din of constant chatter in both Exo and Federal as the personnel in the Command Center communicated with people all over the planet. Colonel Shimura was nowhere to be seen; she had not left her sleeping quarters since Mason convinced her to go off-duty. He had made sure of it.

Commander Serova was there, however, looking up at the main screen showing a map of Stoneland. Scattered all around the map were dozens of dots, each surrounded by lumpy red splotches.

"That up to date with the latest intel?" Mason asked.

Commander Serova glanced over her shoulder and nodded. "It is. The Ascendency knocked out our satellite communications, but the underground fiber-optic network is still running. What information we're getting is not encouraging."

"How bad?"

"As you have probably gathered, those red areas around the landing zones indicate territory occupied by Ascendency ground forces," Serova said. "In the day since they've landed, there are a hundred such landing zones scattered all over the continent, occupying millions of square kilometers."

"That's a lot of progress in one day," Mason said.

"It is," Serova said. "We knew the Ascendency were bringing a lot of troops down, but the forces we're seeing are more numerous than even our highest estimates. They must have had soldiers stuffed into those craft-like sardines."

"I guess Cendy soldiers don't have the same personal space requirements as human ones," Mason said.

"No, I suppose not."

"How's Planetary Defense holding up?" Mason asked.

"They're doing what they can to slow things down," Commander Serova said. "Mostly hit-and-run attacks. Anyone who tries to stand and fight risks getting hit by an orbital attack. Our aerial units are doing what we can. While you slept, our fighters and tilt-rotors launched over a hundred sorties."

"My fighters are ready to augment yours. Just give us a target."

"Good, we could use your help."

"Name it, Commander."

"One of the Turtleback landing ships you hit with your Raiden cannons crash-landed outside of the enemy landing zones," Commander Serova said. "Isolated as it is, it presents an opportunity for our forces to capture it."

"I doubt the Cendies are just going to let us have it," Mason said. "Why haven't they tried to bombard it from orbit?"

"They have. But the Turtleback fell under coverage of the missile battery you helped defend. It's intercepted everything the Cendies attempted to fire at it and blew up a couple of Fusiliers for their trouble." Serova zoomed the main screen towards the nearest Ascendancy landing zone, where it showed a sharp spear of Cendy forces pushing towards the crash site. "Ascendancy ground forces are right now driving hard towards the crash site. We don't have the forces to hold them off. So, we need to raid the site while we still can."

"What's the plan, Commander?"

"We'll be sending an assault force of Espatiers to secure the crash site and load up with everything they can. Since you're the ranking Federal officer while Colonel Shimura is resting, I thought I'd ask you to provide support by offering your fighters and Raiders."

"I'm sure the Raiders would be more than happy to see some action," Mason said. "How do you plan on getting the ground force there?"

"Tilter-rotor transports. Assault shuttles are too large to safely land at the site. Also, as much as I hate to admit it, your Lightnings are better at ground attack than our Asps, so I want them to engage ground targets while my fighters maintain air superiority."

"We can do that," Mason said. "What are our targets?"

"The Ascendency clearly don't want us to get our hands on whatever's at that crash site. I'll need some of your fighters to work with my gunships to provide close air support while the rest try to slow down Ascendency reinforcements inbound on the crash site."

"I'll tell my crew chief to start loading munitions. What are the rules of engagement?"

"Engage targets at your discretion, Squadron Leader. That includes all civilian infrastructure the Cendy reinforcements can use to reach the crash site. Whatever it takes to buy us the time we need to loot the crash site."

"What about civilians?"

"Any civilians who aren't in their designated shelters have taken their lives into their own hands, Squadron Leader," Commander Serova said. "The mission starts in an hour. I'll leave you to get your pilots ready."

⁓

Mason considered waking Colonel Shimura to consult with her but decided against it. The mission was a simple one. As much as he valued her expertise, there wasn't much she could contribute.

He did check with Lieutenant Major Thorne, the ranking Raider officer after Major Hauer's death. Thorne was more than happy to provide Raiders for the mission. The smash-and-grab nature of the mission was the exact kind of mission the Raiders trained for.

When he arrived at the area reserved for the fighters of Osiris Squadron, he found all the Lightnings covered in ordinance. The dorsal hardpoints were occupied by Atlatl pods, but the four ventral hardpoints each had three League bombs hanging from them. Each bomb had long fines bolted on the sides, and a laser seeker attached to the nose.

"You didn't skimp on the firepower, I see, Chief," Mason commented.

Rabin smiled and glanced at one of the bombed-up Lightnings. "The Leaguers have piles of the things in Citadel 44's arsenals. It's the one thing we have plenty of."

"Good, I get the feeling we won't have any shortage of targets to use them on," Mason said.

"No, sir, I doubt you will. But you've got twelve on the wings and another sixteen in the internal bay, so you'll cause plenty of damage before you need to rearm," Chief Rabin said.

"I see you got the glide kits attached. How many of those do they have left?"

"As many as you need, sir. The kits are made in Citadel 44's 3D printer. The real limiting factor is the seeker heads. There are enough for maybe a quarter of the bombs this place has."

Mason checked the time. "Start pulling the guidance kits off the external ordinance."

"Sir?"

"We can use dumb bombs on the low-threat targets, save the laser seekers for things we need a standoff range," Mason explained.

Chief Rabin sighed. It there was one thing hangar crews hated, it was undoing their own work. "I'll see that it gets done, sir."

"Good," Mason said. "By the way, any progress in adapting other League weapons to our fighters?"

"I've already uploaded the patch Flight Lieutenant Dominic wrote to all the fighters' operating systems, so we should be good to go with firing League interceptors," Chief Rabin said. "They won't perform like our Javelins, but they they're better than just our guns. I think he's now trying to figure out how to get Citadel 44's factory to start making reloads for our Stiletto pods."

"It'll be nice to have those if we have to take on the Cendies in space," Mason said.

"If, sir? Where else is there to do once we kick them off this planet?"

"Always the optimist, Chief."

"If I were an optimist, I'd assume the Cendies would just retreat as soon as their ground invasion fails, sir," Chief Rabin said.

"A fair point, Chief," Mason said. "I'll let you get to work pulling those seekers off."

"Yes, sir!"

Chief Rabin departed and started barking orders to the League ground crew Serova had placed under his command. The techs started grabbing up tools to pull seeker heads and guidance fines off the bombs mounted externally on the Lightnings.

The League crews clearly had been trained in rapidly changing the configuration of their bombs, because it only took just over a minute for them to pull the accessories off all the external bombs on his fighter before moving on to the next.

Zin and Sabal walked up to Mason after they saw crews changing the weapons on their fighters.

"Something wrong with the League bombs, Hauler?" Sabal asked.

"No, I just want to save as many seeker kits as possible," Mason said. "There's a reason I had us practice all that bombing back on Liberty."

"Don't remind me, sir," Sabal said.

"Is bombing things on the ground beneath your dignity, Flight Lieutenant?" Mason asked.

"No, sir," Sabal said.

"Good," Mason said.

"So, what's the plan of attack, Hauler?" Zin asked. "I know the mission in broad strokes, but I've yet to get any details."

"This mission's falling together on short notice," Mason said. "We'll divide into flights as usual. My flight will provide direct close air support for the teams assaulting the Turtlebacks. You two will be engaging in interdiction against Cendy reinforcements. Your objective is to slow them down, not inflict maximum casualties, so err on the side of caution. I don't want to lose anyone to ground fire."

"We'll make sure our pilots keep their distance, Hauler," Zin said. "What are the rules of engagement?"

"Weapons free," Mason said. "You're also authorized to take out infrastructure that can impede the Cendy advance. Roads, bridges, those kinds of things."

"I bet Commander Serova wasn't happy when you asked if we could blow up League targets," Sabal said.

"It was her idea, Hardball," Mason said. "I got the impression that scorched-earth is part of the League's defensive strategy on Triumph."

"What about air attacks, Hauler?" Zin asked.

"Leaguers will be handling air superiority," Mason said. "Lightnings are just plain better in ground attack than Asps."

"Do we have updated information on the League ground force, Hauler?" Sabal asked. "They must have brought some heavy equipment down with them."

"I've not seen any reports of that just yet," Mason said.

"They have to have armored vehicles," Sabal said. "Tanks, armored personnel carriers, combat rovers."

Mason shook his head. "Right now, it just seems to be infantry and lots of it. But don't let that fool you; their ground forces are still deadly. Even when you're dropping dumb bombs, I want everyone to remain at high altitude to avoid Cendy infantry SAMs. Am I clear?"

"Crystal, Hauler," Zin said.

"I'll keep my flight above the fray, sir," Sabal said.

"Good," Mason said. "I want everyone strapped into their seats and warming up their engines in fifteen minutes. We'll roll out to the vertiports as soon as the ground crews finish pulling off the guidance kits."

⁜

Mason rode in his Lightning as the automated tractor towed it through the long tunnel to one of the auxiliary vertiports. The dull whines of dozens of engines idling in the tunnel penetrated the insulation of his cockpit. Hot exhaust gas poured out of the rear nozzles of tilter-rotor transports rolling ahead of him, each filled with a platoon of Espatiers reinforced with a squad of Federal Raiders.

While the engines were running, the rotors were still folded in to make room for the transports to roll down the tunnel two abreast. At a junction, the tilt-rotors divided between two different tunnels leading to separate vertiports while Mason's Lightning proceeded down a third tunnel.

As he neared the end of the tunnel, the doors parted, and he rolled out into an artificially overcast sky dyed the brilliant orange of the setting sun.

The wump of rotor blades somewhere over the ridge signaled the takeoff of the tilt-rotors, and seconds later, Mason saw them lift over the hill line and tilt the rotors forwards as they gained speed.

As soon as his fighters came to a stop on the camouflaged tarmac of the auxiliary flight pad, the automated tractor released from the tow hitch on his nose wheel and rolled away, joining its comrades seeking shelter in the tunnel behind them.

"Osiris Leader, this is Citadel ATC, you're cleared for immediate takeoff."

"Roger that, Control. Lifting off now," Mason said. He added power to the lifting engines, the dull whine turning into a roar as over a hundred tons of thrust crashed down on the ground with hurricane-force winds, and his Lightning carried itself into the air.

The sound of his own engines all but drowned out that of the rest of the fighters of Osiris Squadron, but his brainset, connected directly to the sensor AI, gave him a full view of everything around him.

The eleven Lightnings ascended with him, the blades of fake grass whipping in the exhaust of a dozen aerospace fighters lifting themselves off the ground, the tilt-rotor transports receding in the distance, and the squadron of Asp fighters rising up to the cloud layer.

Mason throttled up the main engines and started flying forwards, quickly gaining enough speed to shut down the lifting engines and let his fighter's large wings do the work of keeping him aloft.

He climbed to just below the bottom of the artificial cloud layer and pushed his speed to Mach 1.5 towards the Turtleback crash site.

CHAPTER 27

"Osiris Leader, this is Centurion Leader, we are five minutes inbound. We're climbing to twenty thousand meters to establish a combat air patrol. We'll keep the Cendy fighters off your backs while you cover the ground forces."

"Roger that, Commander," Mason said. "All fighters split by flight to assigned sectors. Shutdown, Hardball: happy hunting!"

"You too, Hauler," Sabal said. Her fighter banked right and headed in the direction of the Cendy reinforcements, followed by the three other Lightnings in her flight.

"We won't let any of the bastards get past us," Zin said as her own flight turned towards her assigned mission area.

Mason stayed on course, flying low and fast under the concealment of the League smokescreen. Night had set in during the flight to the crash site, but Mason's sensors still allowed him to peer through the darkness to see details of the wrecked starship.

The Turtleback had come down in a region of flat farmland; its massive hull had cut a long and deep trough in the rich dark soil. The Turtleback itself looked like it was in one piece, despite the hard landing—a testament to how tough Cendies built their landing ships.

And his sensor AI was marking the locations of detected Cendy positions as their weapons flashed brightly under image intensification. It appeared most of the landing ship's passengers had survived the crash and were trading fire with the local ground forces that had surrounded the crash site.

The farmland surrounding the crash site was heavily marred by light artillery and partly illuminated by countless small fires, but there were no signs of space impacts. Heavy Missile Base 20 was keeping Cendy starships from supporting the besieged Turtleback.

"Looks like the Cendies are dug-in waiting for their reinforcements," Mason said. "First Flight engage the Cendy positions along the ingress route of the transports. Remember that we're trying to take the Turtleback intact, so be careful where you drop your bombs. Otherwise, engage at will, and keep an ear open for our combat controllers."

His pilots gave him a series of affirmatives before breaking formation.

Mason started hunting for his own targets, his combat AI automatically highlighting groups of Cendy soldiers firing from their foxholes.

"Puck, cover me while I make my bombing run," Mason said.

"Roger that, Hauler."

Mason slowed to just below the speed of sound and lined up with the Cendy firing line. Following the icons projected onto his HUD, Mason held down the bomb release to initiate the combat AI's drop sequence. One at a time, bombs dropped from the rack under his wings, impacting a second later into a fortified Cendy position. Mason left a trail of explosions running parallel to the wreck of the Turtleback, each blast lighting up the crashed starship and the land around it.

The urgent cry of a missile alarm screamed in Mason's ears after he released the last bomb. The missile trail streaked past his tail, his speed being too great for the missile to compensate. The combat AI didn't even drop any decoys to lure the missile away.

"Puck, someone just shot at me. Mind doing something about that?" Mason asked.

"Engaging now, Hauler."

A precious Hammer missile streaked out of one of Osiris 2's Atlatl pods, detonating ten meters above the spot where the missile had come from.

"Good hit, I'm seeing body parts," Mason said.

"Thank you, sir. You got some good hits in yourself."

Behind him, eight burning bomb craters formed a dotted line of destruction. Each blast site surrounded by the remains of unfortunate Cendy soldiers.

"Osiris Leader, this is Sergeant Cane aboard Mule 1, do you copy?"

"I copy, Sergeant. Will you be our combat controller for this fine evening?" Mason asked.

"Indeed, I will. How does it look down there, sir?" Sergeant Cane asked.

"It's crawling with Cendy soldiers, and we've got more inbound from the ground," Mason said. "We're right now in the process of clearing a landing zone."

"Understood, Osiris Leader. Transports will touch down in five minutes."

"All right, folks, start dropping those bombs. I want the landing zone sanitized by the time the transports get here," Mason said.

The sensor AI rendered the friendly ground forces as green dots on the dark ground, but Mason didn't fully trust that all the red dots were Cendies. It wasn't that long ago that League transponder codes automatically came up red. And besides, there could be soldiers down there with broken transponders.

As Mason overflew an area with hostile contacts, he made sure to examine the area under magnification. Cendy soldiers were not hard to identify, with their long, strong frames, and the way they bounded across the ground at speeds no human could achieve.

Comfortable that he was only going to drop his bombs on hostiles, Mason turned and made his run. He kept his altitude as high as he could and still expect to hit with dumb bombs.

No missiles flew up to greet him as he released a pair of bombs that detonated near a dug-in Cendy position, sending geysers of black dirt into the air. As he pulled away, another Lightning flew over the field, dropping more bombs. In the five minutes it took for the transports of Mule Squadron to fly over the landing zone, Mason's flight had thoroughly churned the dark soil twice over with their ordinance.

The cratered landing zone proved to be no obstacle to the tilt-rotor pilots, who set their aircraft down lightly on the ground, staying down just long enough for their passengers to disembark before taking off again. Minigun turrets in their nose and belly spraying green tracers into the night.

"This is Sergeant Cane. I'm on the ground and picking targets," she said. "Request laser-guided bomb on my target. I'm already painting it with my suit laser."

A spot appeared on the screen. From his position, Mason didn't see anything, but that didn't mean there wasn't something there to blow up.

"I copy, Sergeant. One laser-guided bomb coming up," Mason said.

He swung his fighter around, and opened his weapon bay, making sure the seeker head of the selected bomb was tracking on the laser. He released the bomb and pulled away, trusting Sergeant Cane to guide the weapon to her target.

"Good hit, Osiris Leader. I got some more targets for you," she said.

"Keep 'em coming, Sergeant," Mason said.

The Espatiers advanced quickly from the landing zone to the wrecked Turtleback, pausing only when dug-in Cendy soldiers fired on them.

Every time the Cendy opened fire, one of the combat controllers marked the area, and either Mason or one of the other pilots of First Flight flew in and dropped a bomb, silencing the resistance.

"Hauler, we've got a problem," Zin said.

"What is it, Shutdown?" Mason asked.

"Those Cendy reinforcements? Turns out to be a tidal wave of Cendies running over the ground," Zin said. "We're doing what we can to slow them down, but they don't seem to be too intimidated by the bombs we keep dropping on them."

"What about the bridges?" Mason asked.

"I already tasked Hardball's flight with destroying them, but the rivers aren't very wide and the Cendies seem to be pretty strong swimmers," Zin said. "Estimate maybe an hour before they reach the crash site."

"I'll pass that along to the ground forces," Mason said. "Keep up the bombing as much as you can and return to Citadel 44 to re-arm when you run dry."

"Understood, Hauler," Zin said.

Mason checked the feed from Zin's tactical display, and what he saw sent chills through his body. There were tens of thousands of Cendies pouring over the ground, the individual soldiers spaced far enough apart that bombs only took out a few with each hit. When one of Zin's pilots dropped a line of bombs across the path of the advancing Cendy army, the charging soldiers only faltered briefly as they were hit by the concussion, and then continued to charge forwards.

The Lightnings were still inflicting a lot of damage on the Cendy force, and there was a force of League tilt-rotor gunship inbound to inflict even more carnage on the enemy. But Mason knew that available airpower wasn't going to stop the army of Cendies descending on the crash site.

"Sergeant Cane, my pilots say Cendy reinforcements are one hour out and are extremely numerous," Mason said.

"Any chance your pilots can delay the Cendies, sir?" Sergeant Cane asked.

"They're doing the best they can but, like I said, the Cendies are extremely numerous and don't seem all that intimidated by my pilots blowing them to hell," Mason said.

"I copy, Osiris Leader," Sergeant Cane said. "The first squads of Espatiers are about to breach the interior of the Turtleback. We'll grab everything that isn't bolted down and take off before the ground force gets here."

The wave of Cendy soldiers kept coming. The mass of them didn't so much run over the plains leading to the crash site as flowed over it. A flood of gray, armored bodies. Even from above, in a powerful aerospace fighter, the sight of them was terrifying.

Mason could only guess what the soldiers in their path must be feeling.

Air support from Zin's and Sabal's flights pounded the massed Cendies with repeated bombing runs, the Lightnings staying high to avoid the infantry SAMs that rose after them with each attack. League gunships slowed to a hover just outside of SAM range, pelting the Cendies with missiles. But they quickly ran out of missiles, and the SAMs carried among the mass of Cendy soldiers made it too dangerous for the gunships to use their guns.

The charging army slowed when they reached the rivers but didn't stop. Under magnification, Mason saw the Cendies march into the water and disappear below the surface, rising from the water on the other side minutes later.

While the Cendies crossed the river and started charging towards the crash site, the ground force from Citadel 44 scrambled to get as far from the crash site as possible. Espatiers and Federal troopers in hardsuits carried everything they could find to the waiting transports, who kept their rotors spinning the whole time, ready to take off at a moment's notice.

Ten kilometers from the crash site, a blocking force of Planetary Defense tanks and infantry rolled into position, gathering into a firing line ahead of the approaching Cendies. It was a powerful force consisting of half a dozen tanks and twice that many APCs filled with infantry. But it would barely be a hinderance for the mass of Cendy soldiers bearing down on them. A picket fence trying to hold back a rockslide.

"Hauler, both Hardball's flight and mine are empty of bombs. All we've got left are the Hammers," Zin said. "Do you want us to use them?"

"Negative, Shutdown, return to base and re-arm. My flight still has a few bombs; we'll provide close air support until you return."

"Roger that, Hauler. Good luck."

"Thanks, Zin. Get back soon."

As if in answer, Zin's flight climbed to just short of the artificial cloud layer and accelerated to supersonic speeds as it left the battlefield. That left just the four Lightnings of Mason's flight, and a flight of four gunships that had just entered the area to relieve their comrades.

The Cendy infantry were charging towards the entrenched Planetary Defense Forces. Everything from the main guns of tanks, the autocannons of armored personnel carriers, and infantry battle rifles were pointed down range.

A group of contacts on a ballistic trajectory caught Mason's attention. The sensor AI quickly identified them as artillery shells from a battery of self-propelled guns. The shells landed among the Cendies, throwing dirt, rocks, and body parts into the air, laying out masses of Cendy soldiers. But the army kept charging.

The tanks opened fire, firing high-explosive shells into the Cendies. And still they kept charging.

Mason made his first bombing run, dropping his remaining unguided bombs in a line of destruction that shattered the first ranks of Cendy soldiers. And still they kept charging.

The APCs opened with their rapid-fire autocannons, the accurate weapons blowing apart dozens of Cendies in a matter of seconds. And still they kept charging.

Planetary Defense infantry opened fire with their machine guns and battle rifles, pouring gunfire into the massed Cendies, picking off survivors from the rain of artillery and bombs falling among the Cendies. Still they kept charging and even started firing back with their own weapons.

Streaks of rockets erupted from the front ranks of Cendy soldiers, missiles that ran parallel to the ground before popping up to dive straight down on the League tanks.

Point defense guns on the top of the tanks' turrets opened fire, knocking out several of the missiles, but a pair of tanks took hits to the top of their turrets. The vehicles erupted in flames as their ammunition cooked off. Mason could see the crews of the knocked-out tanks bailing out under fire.

The infantry buckled under the barrage of gunfire raining down on them, suppressed by the mass Cendy gunfire.

As the charging Cendies passed within a couple of hundred meters, the League troopers started running back to their APCs, carrying as many of their dead and wounded as they could. The APCs closed their hatches and turned to retreat at full speed, their tracks throwing up black dirt behind them.

Mason made one more attack, dropping a pair of laser-guided glide bombs into the concentration of Cendy soldiers nearest the retreating League soldiers.

Another tank was knocked out and its crew ran out. But as a comrade's tank reversed to pick them up, continuing to pour fire into the Cendies, the dismounted tank crew were overtaken by the Cendies and disappeared in a mass of gray bodies.

The line broken, there was nothing between the crash site and the Cendy army.

"Sergeant Cane, you have maybe five minutes before you have a mass of Cendies crashing down on you," Mason said.

"We're loading up the last of the transports now, Osiris Leader," Sergeant Cane said. "We found some weird shit in that Turtleback."

"I'm sure you did. Make sure you make it back with the weird shit," Mason said.

"You got it, sir," Sergeant Cane said.

Mason felt a wave of relief as the first of the transports lifted off, rising into the air and flying away ahead of the approaching Cendy swarm.

Seeing the transport go airborne seemed to galvanize the Cendy soldiers. Mason didn't know if it was desperation to keep their equipment out of enemy hands, or simple blood lust. Whatever the reason, the soldiers almost doubled their speed beyond what already seemed impossible.

His sensor AI identified several with long tubes on their shoulders. Infantry SAMs. The transports already in the air were safe, flying away too fast for the Cendies to get into range of their missiles. But there were still a few on the ground, lifting off at a painfully slow rate.

"Start hitting any Cendies with a tube on their shoulder," Mason said. "Use whatever guided ordinance you still have!"

His pilots acknowledged, and Hammers started flying from Atlatl pods.

As missile-bearing Cendies charged forward, Hammers flew over them and detonated, erasing them from the field.

But the missile infantry was well spaced. Every blast only killed one or two at a time. Using Hammers to kill individual infantry was dreadfully inefficient, but there was no other way to deal with them before they got into range of the transports.

Mason quickly ran dry of Hammers, and the other fighters in their flight reported the same, and there were still more Cendies.

With just a couple of laser-guided bombs left, Mason picked the frontmost Cendy and painted them with his laser.

Just as Mason released his bomb, the Cendy soldier he was targeting came to an abrupt stop, dropped to a kneeling position, and aimed at a transport that was taking off.

Then the Cendy disappeared as Mason's bomb struck.

The last transport took off with its tail ramp still open, rising into the air as fast as its rotor could carry it. The battlefield was obscured by smoke and dirt thrown up by the bombs and artillery. But the broad-spectrum optics of his Lightning could cut through most of it, and Mason kept an eye out for his sensor AI to call out a target. He had one more laser-guided bomb ready.

All the surviving missile soldiers were charging forward, but they were too far away to catch the last transport before it opened the range.

Then a contact far too close appeared.

Mason focused an optic and saw a Cendy soldier with their legs blown off fumbling with a missile launcher, laying it across their chest as they attempted to aim it.

Mason released a bomb and painted the Cendy, but just before the bomb hit and obliterated the crippled Cendy soldier, a missile flew off towards the last transport.

"Mule 1, you got incoming!" Mason shouted.

The transport pilot barked a word in Exo as the transport banked hard and dove for the ground, Mason's brainset translating the word as "Evading."

Flares erupted from the transport, forming fiery wings that lit up the ruined farmland with orange light. But the missile remained stubbornly locked onto the evading transport, turning with it and detonating directly above the transport.

Black smoke billowed out of both engine nacelles as the transport started to climb, the pilot using the transport's momentum to glide away from the wrecked Turtleback.

Mule 1's pilot started calling out in Exo, Mason's brainset translating. "Both engines hit, losing power. Attempting auto-rotation and emergency landing!"

The pilot managed to elevate the engine nacelles back to a vertical position, slowing their descent as it lost speed.

Mason checked his status display. His flight was down to guns. Zin and Sabal's flights were inbound from Citadel 44.

"Shutdown, Hardball," Mason called, "Mule 1 is going down, and I only have guns. Get here as quickly as possible."

"We can hit Mach 3 if we climb above the cloud layer," Zin said.

"Do it!" Mason said.

"Roger that, we're accelerating now."

The ETA for Zin's and Sabal's flights halved, but despite the best efforts of Mule 1's pilot to put as much distance as possible between them and the Cendies, it wouldn't be far enough.

With both engines out, Mule 1's pilot managed to accomplish a perfect auto-rotation landing, flaring the nose up just before touching down on a massive corn field, crushing the stalks beneath it.

"Mule 1, this is Osiris Leader. Report."

"This is Sergeant Cane, we've made it down with minor injuries," she said. "Pilot says their bird is fucked. Could use an extraction."

"I've already sent word," Mason said. "My flight will provide air cover until help arrives."

"Much appreciated, sir," Sergeant Cane said. "What do you have?"

"Just guns. But I can act as a spotter for artillery."

"That will have to do," Sergeant Cane said. "I'll get set up out here. How long until the Cendies reach us?"

"Five minutes, Sergeant," Mason said.

"Time to get dug in," Cane said.

Mason checked his tactical screen and got the callsign for the Planetary Defense artillery battery.

"Belts and zones! I hope they have their translators working. Banshee, this is Osiris Leader, do you copy?"

Mason got a response in crisp, clear Federal from a female voice. "This is Banshee, what do you Federals need?"

"I have a friendly transport carrying both League and Federal personnel on the ground with enemy hostiles inbound. Request immediate fire support," Mason said. "I'll provide spotting for your shots."

"Understood. Note that we've used up most of our ammunition," she said.

"What have you got?"

"Ten rounds high-explosive each and five rounds of Shrieker shells."

"What are Shriekers?"

"Shells that release heat-seeking flechettes. Meant for use against targets close to friendlies."

"I'll do my best to make sure those rounds count," Mason said.

The Cendies had just reached the crashed Turtleback, several heading inside but most swarming around it and heading directly for Mule 1.

Mason marked the transport. "Banshee, request fire mission on the Turtleback."

"I thought we're not supposed to hit the Turtleback," she said.

"Not relevant anymore; we've got all we need from it."

"Suit yourself. Firing now."

Arching lines flew up from the self-propelled guns set up twenty kilometers away.

It took just under a minute for the shells to complete their arcs and land on the transport. The wreck of the Turtleback was rocked by half a dozen shells, blowing chunks of the wreck into the air and sending a rain of shrapnel in all directions, killing and wounding Cendies for hundreds of meters around the wreck.

"Good hits!" Mason said.

"Keep feeding us targets and we'll keep firing," Banshee said.

"Understood," Mason said.

The Cendy soldiers weren't advancing in a uniform line, but in long fingers extending from the main body as they ran through areas of least resistance.

Mason picked out the fingers he wanted Banshee to cut off.

"Targets locked," Mason said. "Bring down the sky, Banshee."

"Firing."

The self-propelled guns started firing, sending shells on an arching trajectory to the points Mason marked.

With targeting data supplied by his fighter, the Banshee was able to lead the Cendies with their artillery strikes. Mason watched as the Cendies charged beneath the incoming shells.

Six separate explosions marked where the shells struck, meeting the Cendy vanguard, annihilating the soldiers in the front. The Cendies behind them leapt over shell craters and the broken bodies of their comrades as they continued their rapid advance towards Mule 1's crash site.

The troopers and Espatiers who had been aboard the downed tilt-rotor had formed up into a firing line, lying prone with their weapons pointed down range.

"Osiris Leader, I have visual on the incoming Cendies," Sergeant Cane said.

"Understood, Sergeant. I'm connecting you with Banshee. Call them for artillery strikes," Mason said.

"I do love big guns," Cane said. "Making the call."

More artillery fell among the Cendies as they closed into small-arms range.

The Espatiers and Raiders started firing, the muzzle blasts of their battle rifles kicking up dirt with each shot.

The leading ranks of Cendies started firing while on the move. Their fire was inaccurate but heavy. Bullets impacted around the troopers and stray shots perforated the crashed tilt-rotor.

Their advance only faltered when they led headfirst into a wall of air-bursting artillery shells.

"That's the last of the high-ex. Switching to Shriekers," Banshee said.

Mason noticed a new contact moving at supersonic speed from the direction of Citadel 44. It was a Federal assault shuttle.

"Sergeant Cane, this is Colonel Shimura. I'm inbound on your position. ETA, five minutes."

"Good to hear from you, sir," Sergeant Cane said. "Don't suppose you could cut that down by a few?"

"This bird is going as fast as she can in atmosphere, Sergeant," Colonel Shimura said. "Osiris Leader, do what you can to buy us some time."

"Roger that, sir," Mason said. "First Flight, prepare to make gun runs. Start dropping countermeasures preemptively as you make your runs."

The first of the Shrieker rounds arrived. The shells broke up just before impact, releasing a cloud of metal arrows that flew into the Cendies.

Like a swarm of angry insects, the cloud seemed to move with purpose as the individual arrows locked onto Cendy soldiers.

Dozens of them simply dropped to the ground all at once as they were pierced by multiple arrows.

"Good God, that sound is awful!" Sergeant Cane said.

But more Cendies ran past their fallen comrades, continuing forward with single-minded determination.

It was a horrifying sight. Mason didn't know whether it was bravery or the Cendy soldiers simply did not fear death. All he knew was that no matter how hard they got hit, no matter how many were killed, the Cendies refused to falter.

He dove to make his strafing run, setting his cannon to its highest rate of fire.

Opening fire, Mason drew a line of impacts across the mass of Cendies, leaving a blazing trail of decoys in the air behind him as he made his strafing run, illuminating the ground behind him.

His cannon's projectiles didn't have explosives in them, but they were fast and numerous.

As he drew the line of fire over a squad of exposed Cendies, several of them burst into clouds of white mist as they were struck by hypervelocity munitions.

Missiles chased after Mason as he climbed out of his attack, most flying after his decoys, while those that kept locked did not have the energy to catch his fighter in its steep climb. The other fighters of First Flight made their own runs, crisscrossing the ground with their guns, and the sky just over the Cendies with their decoys. Each one had Cendy missiles fired after them. Mason made another run, turning more Cendies into white mist, and outrunning more infantry SAMs as he pulled away.

More Shrieker rounds scourged the Cendies, adding to the carnage the Espatiers and troopers on the ground were inflicting with their weapons. Osiris 2 was about to make another gun run when Cendy missiles launched right ahead of them before they could open fire. Osiris 2 dodged a couple of missiles, but another two closed the distance and detonated just ahead of their Lightning, throwing up a cloud of shrapnel into the fighter's path.

Osiris 2 flew through the cloud and came out trailing smoke.

"I'm hit!" Osiris 2 said. "Losing power in starboard engine. Port engine looks good. Got structural warnin–"

Osiris 2 was interrupted as the fighter's damaged right wing broke off. The Lightning started spinning.

"No control, ejecting!"

Osiris 2's cockpit capsule shot skywards as the Lightning plummeted to the ground, impacting the ground in an explosion of dirt. Lightnings didn't carry much flammable material aboard, so the wrecked Lightning just smoldered on the ground.

The cockpit capsule deployed a parachute and started falling back down to the ground. There were thousands of Cendies below them, and to Mason's horror, several of them stopped to aim their weapons up at the capsule and the helpless pilot within and opened fire.

A barrage of gunfire perforated the capsule, and Osiris 2's vital signs when flat in an instant. The Cendies continued to fire as the capsule floated all the way to the ground, until it was so perforated with bullet holes that it started to look like a cheese grater.

Mason marked the area below Osiris 2's capsule. "Banshee, request a Shrieker on my mark."

"I copy. Sending one on the next salvo," Banshee said.

Six shots arced over the horizon, five heading towards the very front of the Cendy line, directed by Sergeant Cane, but one overflew the frontline, and released its deadly payload where Osiris 2's ruined capsule was settling down.

The Cendies who had killed Puck fell as they were hit by a storm of vicious metal spikes homing in on their body heat.

"I have one more salvo left, and that's it, so make it count!" Banshee called out.

"Banshee, stagger your fire to put down a continuous barrage of Shriekers on my mark," Sergeant Cane said. "That'll hold off the Cendies for a few more minutes."

"Roger that, Sergeant, firing the first salvo now," Banshee said.

Two Shrieker shells flew up and arched down towards the shrinking expanse of ruined farmland between the charging Cendies and the fallen transport. The charge came to a stop as the two shells burst and threw thousands of Shrieker darts into the Cendies.

Another pair launched as soon as the previous shells burst and caught the next wave of Cendies that attempted to charge the last distance.

It was working, the wall of concentrated Shriekers finally stopping the Cendy advance.

Except they didn't stop. Groups of them started wheeling around, flanking around the kill zone created by the falling artillery. The assault shuttle was flying in at twice the speed of sound, but it would be over a minute before it arrived.

"Sergeant Cane, you have Cendies trying to flank around you," Mason said. "Banshee, can you direct fire on my mark?"

"Negative, Osiris Leader. We just fired the last of our shells," Banshee said.

"Fuck! All right, we'll deal with it. All fighters, strafing run on my targets!"

Mason dove his fighter towards the Cendy flanking force and opened fire, pouring kinetic fire into them, throwing up black dirt and white cendy blood into the air.

Osiris 3 started its strafing run as soon as Mason finished his, followed by Osiris 4. Decoys burned in the sky over the battlefield as infantry SAMs flew into the sky after the Lightnings. The strafing run had disrupted the flanking attempt but did not stop it. The assault shuttle and the rest of Osiris Squadron were still too far out. He'd have to risk another strafing run. Mason pulled his fighter up and turned back towards the Cendies to fire again.

More Cendy soldiers were turned into mist a few hundred meters from the crash site. Off to Mason's right, an infantry SAM shot out of the crowd. Before Mason could react, it detonated somewhere below his fighter. The blast knocked out his ventral sensors and everything under his fighter went black. Alarms sounded in his ears as warning icons filled his HUD.

Mason still had control and pulled out of his dive. The maneuver was sluggish, and he had to fight against his fighter constantly trying to yaw to the right.

"Belts and zones! This is Osiris Leader, I'm hit. Looks like I lost the right engine."

Mason pulled up to gain altitude and get out of range of the Cendy infantry SAMs. A quick diagnostic showed he wasn't in immediate risk of crashing. The reactor and long-burn drive in the right nacelle were gone, but the wing itself was holding together despite the damage.

He was out of the fight; all he could do was watch.

Banking to get a functional sensor on the crash site, Mason saw the Cendies continuing the encirclement of the crash site, the pincers closing in on the fallen tilt-rotor like the jaws of a great beast.

"Hauler, we're about to start our bombing runs," Zin said. "Where should we drop them?"

Flying just below the cloud layer, Mason's crippled fighter had a commanding view of the battlefield below. And though his fighter couldn't fight anymore, he could still spot targets.

"I'm marking targets now, Shutdown," Mason said, uploading a live stream of data on the position of the first ranks of charging Cendies.

"Roger that, Hauler. We're going in," Shutdown said.

The eight inbound Lightnings split into two four-ship flights, each flying towards the head of each pincer. The Lightnings flew halfway between Mason and the ground, each dropping a pair of bombs as they did. The bombs struck just as the Cendy soldiers were less than fifty meters from the defensive perimeter surrounding the crashed tilt-rotor. Clouds of dirt erupted from the blasts, and shrapnel scythed through the Cendy ranks. Soldiers that were outside the lethal radius were knocked back by the blast wave. They got up to continue their charge but were themselves blasted by the second bombing run.

The bombing runs stopped the Cendies in their tracks and then pushed them back from the crash site as Osiris Squadron continued to shower them with explosives, opening a clearing just large enough for a Federal assault shuttle to make a combat landing.

"This is Colonel Shimura. We're touching down in thirty seconds. As soon as we hit the dirt, I want everyone to drop what they're doing and evac to the assault shuttle."

The assault shuttle swooped in low over the crash site, wings at full forward sweep, landing thrusters kicking up clouds of dirt as the cannon turret on the nose and minigun turrets under each wing spat continuous streams of fire into the Cendies. The assault shuttle tilted its nose up just as it overflew the crash site and settled onto the ground with its open tail door facing the wrecked tilt-rotor.

The Espatiers and troopers defending the crash site immediately started moving towards the assault shuttle, carrying their wounded and dead with them, but leaving everything else behind, including the captured equipment loaded aboard the tilt-rotor.

Missiles flew from the Cendy lines but were shot down by point defense turrets mounted on the assault shuttle's back. The launch sites of those missiles were quickly obliterated by bombing runs from the Lightnings.

The gun turrets continued to spew an arch of fire in front of the assault shuttle, holding back the Cendy horde, even as Mason saw gunfire spark against the armored hull of the assault shuttle. Then, barely more than thirty seconds after touching down, the assault shuttle's thrusters powered, throwing a cloud of dirt around the shuttle as it lifted off, rapidly gaining altitude and horizontal velocity until it flew out of range of the Cendy infantry SAMs.

Osiris Squadron made one last bombing run as the assault shuttle climbed away, dropping some of their last bombs on the crashed tilt-rotor, denying it and the stolen Cendy equipment to the enemy.

CHAPTER 28

Mason jettisoned most of his remaining fuel, leaving a trail of scattered fuel pellets behind his stricken Lightning. With his remaining reactor and intact thrusters, he barely had enough thrust for vertical landing. Even with the help of the flight AI, his wounded fighter felt heavy and sluggish, barely able to stay aloft.

"You're clear for landing, Osiris Leader. Emergency crews are standing by," said Citadel 44 ATC.

"Understood, Citadel 44, see you guys soon," Mason said. He lowered the landing gear and aimed right for the center of the landing pad.

Two hundred meters from the hidden landing pad, a terrific shudder ran through his Lightning's frame before something burst below him. The fighter tilted to the left, and Mason had to wrench the stick to the right to compensate.

"Ah, fuck!" If he had to work this hard to keep his fighter under control, then the flight AI must be fully occupied keeping his Lightning in the air. He had to tilt the fighter's nose up to keep his descent rate slow enough, but he lost speed quickly. Just as he reached the pad, his fighter stalled, and Triumph's gravity pulled it down to the ground. The landing gear buckled under the impact, and Mason struck hard, knocking the wind out of him. His connection to the fighter's external sensors went dead, leaving him lying staring up at his canopy from his reclined seat.

Moments later the canopy burst open, and a League rescue tech in a reflective suit popped his head in. Mason waved to him and started to unbuckle himself from his seat. The rescue tech helped pull Mason from his fighter, but to his relief, he was able to stand on his own. Mason turned around to look at his Lightning. The fighter was resting flat on her belly, the force of the impact having broken the wing-folding mechanism, and the outer wings were sagging into the artificial grass.

That fighter was never going to fly again. But at least she'd kept him alive.

Mason gave the fighter's space frame an affectionate pat for her good work before letting the medics lead him to a waiting cart.

The medics looked him over, plugging a diagnostic tool into his hardsuit to read his vitals. When they decided the hard landing had not caused any injury, they let him take a seat on the rear bench of the cart before it took off.

Once the cart rolled into the tunnel and the comfort of a hard ceiling, Mason pulled his helmet off and lay back in his seat, feeling the cool tunnel air through his sweaty hair. He tried not to dwell on the memory of Puck's cockpit pod getting ventilated as it floated to the ground.

When the cart entered the main tunnel, he saw the assault shuttle that had rescued the crew of the downed tilt-rotor being unloaded, the wounded and dead being rolled off on stretchers with the help off their able-bodied comrades. The cart came to a stop, and Mason dismounted, taking his helmet with him.

"Squadron Leader, sir," Chief Rabin said, greeting him with a salute.

"Chief," Mason said, "afraid I broke one of your fighters."

"I heard," Chief Rabin said. "My people and I will worry about seeing what we can salvage her. I'm sorry about what happened to Puck."

"Thanks, Chief," Mason said. "I seem to have developed a knack for outliving my wingmates."

"Don't feel bad for surviving, sir." Rabin nodded to the assault shuttle. "A lot of people are alive because your pilots slowed the Cendies long enough for Colonel Shimura to effect a rescue."

"Where is she, by the way?" Mason asked.

Chief Rabin pointed in the direction of the elevators rendered defunct by the destruction of the airbase they were meant to service. "She headed that way, where they're gathering all the crap they pulled out of that Turtleback. Seems they found something she wanted to check immediately."

As soon as Chief Rabin finished his sentence, a message notification from Colonel Shimura appeared in Mason's HUD.

"Well, speak of the devil," Mason muttered, opening the message.

<Welcome back, Squadron Leader. How are you holding up?>

<I'm intact, sir>

<I'm glad to hear it, Squadron Leader. Please join me in the gathering area to view all the Cendy equipment we pulled out of the Turtleback. There are things here that you need to see.>

An icon marking Shimura's position appeared on Mason's HUD.

<I'm on my way, sir.>

Mason walked around the defunct elevator shaft and found Colonel Shimura's icon inside a fenced-in area guarded by League Espatiers carrying battle rifles and wearing combat armor. Scattered personnel loitered around the perimeters, trying to get a look at what had been recovered from the Turtleback before being shouted at by a superior to get back to whatever they were supposed to be doing.

The closed gate, flanked by a pair of Espatiers, marked the entrance into the gathering area. The Espatiers must have been expecting him, because one of them opened the gate for Mason as he approached.

Mason nodded to the Espatiers and walked through. Racks of Cendy equipment organized by type flanked him as he walked inside the fence. Rows of stacked rifles to his left, containers with unknown contents to his right. Down the avenue cutting between racks was a trio of transparent cylinders standing in the center of the enclosure. From a distance, Mason could see the dark shadows of figures inside the tanks, with League techs crawling around one of the tanks. It was also where Shimura's icon was located, directly on the other side of the tanks.

"This is going to be educational," Mason said to himself before walking the rest of the way.

A squad of League Espatiers stood around the tanks, facing inwards with their weapons held at low ready.

Walking around the tanks, Mason took the opportunity to get a good look at what was inside. He instantly saw they were soldiers. Long figures with blank faces and armored plating under gray textured skin. A network of thin tendrils connected the bodies to the top of the tank.

Colonel Shimura stood on the other side, staring up at the Cendies.

"Colonel," Mason said, giving her a salute with his gauntleted hand.

Shimura returned his salute. "Thank you for coming so promptly, Squadron Leader."

"Of course, sir," Mason said. He gestured to the tanks. "I gather this is what you wanted me to see?"

"It is," Colonel Shimura said. "Look down the line. These tanks have been arranged in order of maturity from left to right."

"Maturity?" Mason looked past the leftmost tank with its fully developed Cendy soldier. Each tank to the right contained a Cendy at an earlier stage of development. Just a bit smaller than the last. The Cendy in the rightmost tank was a faceless armored fetus.

"Belts and zones, they're growing soldiers down here!" Mason exclaimed.

"They are, and it makes their choice of landing sights make sense," Colonel Shimura said. "The Cendies concentrated on landing in areas with large amounts of biomass. Biomass that at this very moment is being turned into soldiers."

"Goddamn! Do we know how fast they grow?"

"Given how enthusiastically they're willing to spend the lives of their soldiers, quite fast, I suspect," Shimura said.

Mason walked back down the line towards the developed soldier. He flinched when the thing twitched.

"Shit! Is that thing awake?" Mason asked.

"Dreaming more likely," Colonel Shimura said. "The twitching probably aids in muscle development, but there's more. See that thick wire sticking out the back of the head?"

"I see it," Mason said.

"There's a computer system in there," Colonel Shimura said. "Along with managing the Cendy's growth, I think it's also educating them."

"So that's not just a womb; it's also a boot-camp."

"That would be my guess."

"So, are you waiting for one of them to come out?" Mason asked.

Colonel Shimura nodded toward the tanks at the end of the row to her left with the fully developed soldier. "That one at the end looks ready to come out. Techs think they know how to initiate the birthing process."

"That doesn't sound safe," Mason said.

"That's what all the heavily armed Espatiers are for, Squadron Leader."

"Are you sure you want to stand so close to them, sir?"

"I'll back up when the tanks start to open."

"So, uh, what do you plan on doing with them after they're born?"

"They're prisoners of war, Squadron Leader," Colonel Shimura said. "I'm going to stick them in a cage and start interrogating them."

"I don't see any mouths for them to talk with," Mason said.

"We saw them communicating with humans back on Dagon Freeport. They have to have some way of talking to people."

"More happy memories," Mason said. "You think they'll know anything, sir? I mean, how much would something born today know?"

"Probably enough to kill, Squadron Leader," Colonel Shimura said.

Mason took a deep breath, trying to calm his nerves, feeling grateful that he was still inside the protection of his hardsuit.

A tech said something in Exo that, translated, meant they were ready to initiate the birthing process.

"Stand back, Squadron Leader. I don't want you to get between that thing and the Espatiers in case they have to open fire."

Mason stepped back with Colonel Shimura as the Espatiers stepped forward, forming a wall of armored bodies between him and the Cendies.

Shimura barked an order in Exo to start the birthing process.

The thickest of the cords connected to the Cendy's head detached and withdrew, followed by the tendrils attached to the rest of the body, snaking up through the viscous fluid until they disappeared into the top of the tank.

The Cendy then snapped to awareness, faceless head looking around the interior of the tank before tilting upwards.

The circular hatch at the top of the tank swung open, and the Cendy soldier swam up to the top.

A pair of glistening wet hands reached out of the top of the tank, and the Cendy pulled its head out, dripping with thick fluid.

Pulling itself fully out of the tank, the solider stood fully erect atop the tank, looking down on the armed humans surrounding it.

It showed no sign of either surprise or fear.

Mason stepped back as the creature's face locked onto his, the featureless gray head shining from the slick fluid still dripping from it. Mason was pretty sure its lack of fear was not because it wasn't aware of the peril it was in.

"Get down before you're shot down," Colonel Shimura said. "Only warning."

The soldier seemed to understand Colonel Shimura. It dropped to the ground, landing lightly on its feet. For something that was seconds old, it certainly had the grace of something much more mature.

"I'm Colonel Dolores Shimura of the Federal Space Forces, and you are now a prisoner of war. Do you understand what that means?"

The soldier nodded slowly.

"Good," Colonel Shimura said. "You will be treated in accordance with the Liberty Accords. You will not be tortured or otherwise mistreated. Though it would be helpful if we know what you need."

The soldier balled its fists open and shut as it glanced around.

"If you're thinking of starting a fight, I would advise against that," Colonel Shimura said. "You try anything, these Espatiers with me will put you down with speed and enthusiasm."

The soldier seemed to relax, its hands hanging open at its sides.

"Will you cooperate?"

One of the techs at the far side called out in Exo, "Colonel, I'm picking up transmission from the soldier."

"Trying to communicate with the outside?" Colonel Shimura asked.

The other, less mature Cendy soldiers in the tanks started to move.

"Uh, sir, I think it's talking with its friends in the other tanks," Mason said.

"Shit!" Shimura drew her pistol. "Open fi–"

The Cendy soldier standing on the ground grabbed its neighbor's tank with both hands and threw it directly at Colonel Shimura.

Mason crash-tackled Shimura to the ground as the tank flew overhead to land behind her harmlessly.

The Espatiers opened fire with their battle rifles, gunning down the Cendy soldier as it attempted to duck behind one of the tanks, and shattering the others with gunfire as their occupants attempted to climb out.

The gunfire died in seconds leaving shattered plastic, viscous fluid, and dead Cendies on the floor.

"Thanks," Colonel Shimura said to Mason as she stood up.

"Don't mention it, sir," Mason said.

Shimura sighed and holstered her pistol. "Well, that could have gone better."

"Could have gone worse too, sir," Mason said, turning to see where the tank the soldier threw had landed. "We cou–"

Mason froze. The tank was there, resting at an angle on the racks it had landed on, top resting on the floor, where an expanding pool of fluid was oozing out from the open hatch.

There was no sign of the occupant, beyond wet footprints leading towards the fence.

"Uh, sir, I think we have a runner," Mason said.

Shimura walked up next to him. "Dammit!" She pointed at the footprints and ordered the Espatiers in Exo to follow them. The Espatiers immediately charged through the expanding puddle leaking from the tank and followed the tracks. Mason followed with Colonel Shimura and found the footprints terminated at the fence. Just on the other side was a spatter of clear fluid staining the stone floor where the Cendy had landed after leaping the fence.

Colonel Shimura raised a hand to her temple like she was sending a subvocal communication, and then alarms started to sound. As the klaxons echoed through the chamber, Mason could see doors at the tunnel entrances starting to close, except for one to his right, where there was an Asp fighter halfway through.

It was there that Mason saw a gray body charging for the entrance at a full sprint.

As he drew in breath to call it out, the troopers were already leveling their battle rifles and fired through the fence. The Cendy seemed aware and charged at a group of techs, grabbing a screaming man and holding him up as a human shield.

"Fuck!" Mason ran forward, using the boost of his hardsuit to jump and grab the top of the fence, and then pull himself over. The fence wavered under his weight but didn't collapse, and Mason landed heavily on his feet before he started running at an angle towards the entrance, trying not to get into the line of fire of the Espatiers in case they got a clear shot.

The Cendy tossed its hostage aside when it reached the fighter and leapt up to land atop the fighter and run down its fuselage.

Battle rifles sounded behind him and Mason caught a puff of white mist spew out the side of the Cendy, but it leapt off the back of the fighter and continued down the tunnel.

Mason turned directly for the tunnel, running as fast as his hardsuit could carry him, passing under the wing of the Asp. The Cendy was just a gray speck at the end of the tunnel, too far away for Mason to make the shot without the aid of his helmet. Instead, he kept running after the Cendy, trying to keep it in sight.

<This is Squadron Leader Grey,> Mason said, subvocalizing to conserve breath.

<I have visual on the escapee. It's moving towards the tunnel junction.>

<I'm coming on your left, Squadron Leader,> Colonel Shimura responded.

The colonel rolled up next to him, the motors of the cart letting off an electric squeal.

"Hop in!"

Mason grabbed the top of the cart's roll cage and pulled himself into the passenger seat.

"Thanks for the pickup, sir," Mason said, drawing his Equalizer pistol.

"Make yourself useful and kill that thing," Colonel Shimura said.

"On it." Mason stood up in his seat and rested his arms against the roll cage to stabilize his pistol. Shimura flipped on the cart's high beams, cutting through the dimness of the long tunnel and illuminating the fleeing Cendy.

The cart's electric motors screamed as Mason aimed, the rangefinder in his pistol's optical sight giving him a range of a hundred meters. That was the outer edge of the pistol's effective range.

He fired, and the A.P.E.X. rocket streaked past the Cendy's shoulder. The soldier started to zig zag to throw off Mason's aim.

"Keep shooting at it to keep it evading. We'll catch up to it faster that way," Colonel Shimura said.

"Yes, sir," Mason said, squeezing off another shot that hissed past the Cendy to disappear into the darkness beyond.

Mason fired again and again at the bounding Cendy as it weaved in a serpentine pattern down the tunnel, the range slowly closing.

Mason squeezed the trigger, and the Equalizer gave him an angry beep indicating it was empty. Dropping back down into his seat to reload, he opened the Equalizer to insert an octagonal packet of fresh A.P.E.X. rockets into the cylinder.

As he got back up to fire, he noted markers on the tunnel's ceiling.

"We're coming up to the fork in the tunnel, sir," Mason said.

"Kill that thing before it gets to it," Colonel Shimura ordered.

"Aren't the doors at the end of the tunnels closed?"

"They're designed to keep things out, not in. You want to bet that Cendy won't find a way to open one when it gets to it?"

"Great," Mason said. He braced himself against the roll cage and fired.

His first shot almost hit, flying right past the Cendy's left shoulder as it turned at the last second.

"Fuck!" Mason aimed and fired again. Again, he missed by a narrow margin.

"Just keep shooting at it and we'll catch it," Shimura said.

Mason blew out a calming breath like his shooting instructors taught in basic and squeezed off another shot that flew over the Cendy's shoulder.

When the Cendy reached the fork, it ducked to the side, out of line of sight.

"Keep an eye on which tunnel it goes down, Squadron Leader," Shimura said.

Mason kept his pistol trained on the center tunnel, ready to snap a shot at the Cendy as soon as it tried to run for the tunnel.

Colonel Shimura slowed as they entered the vestibule, just as Mason caught a glimpse in his peripheral vision of the Cendy pointing the muzzle of a fire extinguisher at them.

"To the left!" Mason swung his pistol around just as the Cendy squeezed down on the handle.

The Cendy disappeared behind a spray of white foam and seconds later the foam hit Mason in the face.

His eyes stinging, all Mason heard was Shimura curse as she hit the brakes.

Then the cart hit something and rolled onto its side. Mason found himself flying blind before hitting the ground and rolling.

The hardsuit protected him from the worst of the impact, and he managed to keep a hold on his pistol even as he rolled to a stop.

The impact with the hard ground knocked most of the foam off him, making it easier to clear his eyes even with the heavy gauntlets of his hardsuit.

He looked up and saw Colonel Shimura pulling herself out of her overturned cart.

"You okay, sir?" Mason asked.

"I'm fucking pissed is what I am," Shimura said. "You see where it went?"

"No, sir."

"Shit!" Shimura drew her pistol and started running. "I'll head down the center tunnel. Take one of the others."

The right one was the closest, so Mason moved out of the slick created by the fire suppressant and started running. Someone else could worry about the third tunnel. Mason's hardsuit allowed him to run faster than he could normally, but he wasn't optimistic about running down the Cendy. His best hope was catching it while it tried to figure out how to open the outer door.

There was only the slightest illumination at the end of the tunnel, but it was enough for him to spot the movement of the Cendy at the door. It had gotten further ahead of him than he'd thought.

Mason set his brainset to broadcast <It's at the end of Tunnel 2.> He wasn't sure how far his signal would carry underground. But while he continued to run, he brought up his pistol and started firing.

The Cendy didn't flinch as the shots impacted around it, as it had found what it was looking for. It pulled the lever and the door started to swing out on rollers. The Cendy squeezed out just as Mason fired, the A.P.E.X. round striking the door.

"Fuck!" Mason said aloud before subvocalizing, <It's just gone outside.>

He burst outside into the cool air, his boots clacking against the hard surface hidden under the fake grass. He spotted the Cendy standing at the top of a hill that overlooked the landing site, its face turned to the sky in a silent scream.

Mason skidded to a stop, dropping into a shooting stance and laying his pistol's red-dot sight on the Cendy's torso before squeezing the trigger.

White blood erupted from the side of the Cendy's chest as the A.P.E.X. rocket exploded against it. Mason put two more shots into the Cendy before it dropped to the ground. Running the distance to the ridge, he found the Cendy lying face down, motionless on the ground.

<This is Squadron Leader Grey. I just dropped the Cendy outside.>

<Hold position and keep your gun on it until I get there,> Shimura returned.

All the Cendy did was twitch and bleed until Colonel Shimura came bounding up the ridge from the adjacent flight base.

"Good shooting," the Colonel said.

"Did I get it in time?" Mason asked.

"That's what I'm trying to find out, but I can't talk to anyone inside that damn mountain with my brainset," Colonel Shimura said. "We'll have to wait until someone with League hardware in their head shows up."

A couple of minutes later, Mason heard the whine of an electric cart just before it came trundling out with four armed and armored Espatiers aboard. Loaded as it was, it was no wonder it had taken as long as it had to reach the end of the tunnel.

Colonel Shimura marched down to them, shouting in Exo, which Mason's brainset translated.

"Can you reach the Command Center, Lieutenant?"

The League Espatier officer nodded. "I'm connected to them now."

"Did they pick up any nearby enemy transmissions?"

The League lieutenant nodded. "They detected an ultra-high-frequency burst transmission just a few minutes ago."

Colonel Shimura spun away from the League officer, her face twisting in frustration.

"We're in trouble, aren't we, sir?"

"Yes, Squadron Leader. Yes, we are."

CHAPTER 29

"A large part of the Cendy army advancing towards HMB 20 broke off five minutes after the escapee made their transmission," Commander Serova said.

Mason stood quietly in the Command Center as Colonel Shimura spoke with Commander Serova.

He'd had the damn thing in his sights. If his aim had just been a little better, the Cendy would've died in the tunnels rather than outside where it had the chance to call for help.

No, not help, Mason realized. The Cendy knew it was going to die. It wasn't running for its life. It used what brief life it had to inform the rest of the Ascendency where there were more enemies to kill.

"And what about the fleet?" Colonel Shimura asked.

"Still keeping their distance while Stoneland's remaining missile base is still active," Commander Serova said. "I believe they intend to take Citadel 44 by ground assault."

"How long do we have until they get here?" Shimura asked.

"Given the rate at which those things can traverse over open ground, without having to stop and rest, sometime tomorrow morning."

"Belts and zones!" Mason muttered under his breath.

"You have something to add, Squadron Leader?" Colonel Shimura asked.

Mason wanted to shrink from all the eyes focusing on him. All the people he let down looking at him in judgment.

"Squadron Leader, is something the matter?" Colonel Shimura added.

"I, uh… what's our next move?" Mason asked.

Commander Serova cleared her throat. "When I relayed what we learned from the crashed Turtleback, the League Council held an emergency meeting. They voted in favor of using nuclear weapons against the Ascendency landing zones."

"You're going to nuke them?"

Serova nodded; her jaw clenched. "Yes. As we speak, my crews are dismounting warheads from our torpedoes to mount them on cruise missiles instead. At 2000 hours, our fighters will take off on missions to engage the nearest major landing site. It will be part of a coordinated attack by all remaining League forces on the planet. Since your fighters aren't authorized to carry nuclear weapons, I was going to task your ships with providing fighter cover for mine during the attack. A good role reversal, yes?"

"It's a change of pace."

"Nuking the Turtlebacks doesn't do anything about the armies that are already on the planet," Shimura said.

"No, but it does cut them off from reinforcements," Commander Serova said.

"You can't spare a few nukes for those armies?" Colonel Shimura asked.

"The authorization is very narrow, Colonel," Serova said. "Using nuclear weapons on the armies they have in the field would result in too much damage to Triumph's civilian infrastructure and ecosystem. We'll deal with the Ascendency's armies using conventional forces."

"That's a tall order without orbital fire support," Colonel Shimura said.

"I thought the Special Purpose Branch was in the business of fulfilling tall orders," Commander Serova said dryly. "But we'll worry about that later, after the current mission. Will I still have the services of your pilots, Squadron Leader Grey?"

"You will, Commander," Mason said.

"Then I leave you to prepare your squadron for the next mission," Serova said. "Dismissed."

Colonel Shimura walked up to Mason as he was about to leave. "A moment, Squadron Leader."

"Yes, sir," Mason said.

Out in the corridor, Colonel Shimura leaned close and pitched her voice low so as not to carry. "What's wrong, Squadron Leader?"

"Well, my shit aim's about to get everyone in the mountain killed," Mason said.

Shimura gave Mason an irritated expression. "Are you blaming yourself, Squadron Leader?"

"If I'd managed to kill the Cendy in the tunnels, we wouldn't have a Cendy army about to come knocking down our doors," Mason pointed out.

"You give yourself too much credit, Squadron Leader," Colonel Shimura said. "You were trying to hit an evasive target from a moving vehicle with a handgun. Under those circumstances, the failure of your marksmanship was more than forgivable. Blame the troopers and Espatiers that allowed themselves to get distracted shooting up that Cendy's friends, and the idiot who decided waking those things up for questioning was a good idea."

"Sir, you–"

"Are you about to call me an idiot, Squadron Leader?" Colonel Shimura asked with a cocked eyebrow.

"No, sir"

"Then stop feeling sorry for yourself and get your squadron ready to help the Leaguers nuke some shit."

※

"It's about goddamn time the Leaguers started to use their nukes," Sabal said after Mason briefed them.

"I'm sure the prospect of seeing mushroom clouds rise from Triumph's surface gives you all kinds of happy tingles, Hardball," Flight Lieutenant Dominic said.

"Hey, you think you could adapt some League cruise missiles so our fighters could carry their nukes?" Sabal asked.

"League would never let us carry their nukes on our fighters," Zin said. "Not after they prohibited us from bringing our own with us."

"Not sure why you're disappointed, Hardball," Mason said. "We're going to be flying air superiority."

"Oh, I'm not disappointed at all, sir," Sabal said. "It'll be nice to be a fighter pilot again."

"Good," Mason said. "We'll be flying with a full internal load of Skylances in each fighter."

"External stores?" Sabal asked.

"None. I want our fighters clean," Mason said. "And besides, we don't have enough Skylances to fill a full load of Atlatl pods."

"So, we're going to escort the Leaguers in until they can drop their nukes?" Sabal asked.

"That's right, Hardball." Mason summoned an augmented reality map shared among the brainsets of his pilots. On the map was a green circle some two hundred kilometers from the Cendy landing site. "Our job will be to secure the launch zone for the League fighters until the Asps drop their cruise missiles. After that, we return to base and figure out what the hell to do about the army bearing down on us."

"Leaguers going to spare any nukes to deal with that?" Sabal asked.

Mason shook his head. "It's hard enough for the Leaguers to deploy nukes against one of their planets as it is, Hardball. I wouldn't hope for them to authorize their use to save our hides."

"They'll lose the base's nuke anyway if the Cendies take it," Sabal said.

"What the Leaguers do with their nukes is their concern," Mason said. "Ours is to complete the next mission. And hopefully find some way to survive the aftermath."

"You heard, Hauler," Zin said. "The army's tomorrow's problem. Today's is helping the Leaguers deliver some nukes."

◈

Mason felt bad having to kick Split out of Osiris 11 so he could fly. It was another thing that drove home the losses Osiris Squadron had taken since he'd taken command. Six Lightnings and four pilots gone with no prospect of replacement.

And once again, he was going to lead his people into danger. If the Cendies had any inkling that the Leaguers were about to nuke their landing sites, Mason was certain they would sortie every Outrider they had to stop them.

"You think our internal stores will be enough, Mason?" Zin asked.

Mason glanced at her over his shoulder. Her helmet was off and clutched under her arm like his.

"I'd rather have the extra performance rather than the extra missiles, Zin." Mason nodded in the direction of Commander Serova's squadron. Long thin cruise missiles hung from the center belly hardpoints, each tipped with a warhead taken from an anti-starship torpedo. "And we're not going to be in combat for that long. We just need to keep the Cendies off the Leaguers' backs long enough for them to launch payloads. Then we bug out back to base."

"That's an awful lot of nukes for one target," Zin said.

"Insurance to make sure at least one makes it through," Mason said. "Come on. Let's get mounted up."

"With you, sir."

Mason began the startup process as his fighter was towed down the eastern tunnel by an automated tractor. By the time his fighter rolled out onto the hidden tarmac at the base of the mountain, his turbines were warmed up and humming at idle power.

It was a dark, overcast night when he rolled out onto the vertiport. His Lightning was facing down wind, and he spotted the trail of a rocket flying up to the cloud layer to add another burst of concealing particles overhead.

As the tug detached, Mason connected to Citadel 44's ATC. "Osiris Leader request takeoff clearance."

"Clearance granted, Osiris Leader."

"Taking off," Mason said. He throttled up the lifting engine. The blast from the exhaust flattened the fake grass around him and caused vegetation hundreds of meters away to sway.

He lifted off, clearing the tree line. Just a kilometer away, he saw the first of the Asps lifting away, rotating their wingtip engine pods to the horizontal position as they gained speed, heading in the direction of the setting sun.

Mason turned to catch up with them as the rest of Osiris Squadron took off behind him.

Twenty Asps from Citadel 44's two squadrons formed into five staggered formations of four ships each.

Mason assigned one element of two Lightnings to each.

They burst out of the cloud screen moving at one and a half times the speed of sound, the fastest their airbreathing engines could push them in the thick air of the lower atmosphere.

"This is Centurion Leader to Osiris Leader, we'll be passing over enemy controlled territory in two minutes," Commander Serova said.

"I copy that, Centurion Leader," Mason said. "You watch out for SAMs while we keep an eye out for fighters."

"You watch out for those SAMs too, Osiris Leader,' Serova said. "I doubt the Ascendency is going to discriminate."

"Roger that, Centurion Leader," Mason said.

An alarm from his sensor AI drew Mason's attention to a SAM launch, an infantry-launched missile from some Cendies hidden below, but the fighters were moving too fast and the missile burned out its fuel and fell to the ground behind them.

Mason hoped there weren't any heavier SAMs between them and the launch site. Just because they hadn't seen the Cendies use anything heavier didn't mean they didn't have them.

More Cendy infantry took potshots at them with their infantry-launched missiles, all of which failed to catch the fast-moving aerospace fighters.

Then Mason's sensor AI detected a threat that wasn't a missile. "Contacts Two O'clock high. Bearing Two-Five-Niner at 100,000. ID'ed as Outriders."

"We see them, Osiris Leader," Commander Serova said. "They're directly in our path."

It was just a single squadron of ten fighters. Mason thought there would have been more. But there were dozens of such strikes being carried out at the same time all across the continent. Maybe the Cendy fighters were spread out too thin.

"Moving to engage," Mason said.

"Good hunting, Osiris Squadron," Commander Serova said.

Pulling up into a fast climb, Mason rapidly gained altitude while the engines supplied enough power for him to gain speed as the air got thinner.

"Fire on my mark, two missiles apiece," Mason called, giving each of his pilots one target.

Moments later, he hit the launch button.

The doors of his weapon bay swung open and two Skylance missiles fell away from the rotary launcher. The doors snapped shut just as the missiles ignited their engines and climbed skywards. The fast climb had given the missiles extra energy, extending their range against the high-flying Cendies.

The Cendies replied in kind, firing their own missiles, launching seemingly every air-to-air missile they carried. His sensor AI tracked fourteen missiles homing in on him.

"Break formation and evade!" Mason ordered, dropping his nose and diving back towards the surface.

In the dive he turned hard to the left, his seat reclining as the gs piled up on him. Then he leveled at a thousand meters and reversed his turn, forcing the incoming Cendy missiles to turn again, wasting more of their energy as they had to fight their way through the thickening air.

When Mason turned again, the Cendy missiles had lost too much energy and, unable to match his turn, fell to the ground.

His squadron was scattered across the sky as burned-out Cendy missiles hit nothing but dirt. Black puffs of smoke in the distance marked where his squadron's missiles had found their targets. The Cendies clearly had not given their pilots enough training on air-to-air missile evasion.

The seven remaining Outriders pulled out of their climbs and turned back, climbing away at full speed.

"They're bugging out. Should we pursue?" Sabal asked.

"Negative. Form up with the Asps," Mason said. Those days spent training on Liberty had paid off. He'd have to remember to thank Crash for her help, if he managed to survive this mess.

As they neared the launch point, Mason's sensor AI pointed out contacts in the direction of the landing site. A squadron of Outriders was patrolling high above the launch site. They made no move to engage the incoming League and Federal fighters.

"Splitting formation. Entering final attack phase," Commander Serova said, the five groups of Asps fanning out as they reached the launch site.

Osiris Squadron paired off to guard each League flight, Mason staying in formation above Serova's flight.

"Missile away!" Commander Serova called. In the same moment, twenty Asps dropped their cruise missiles from their belly hardpoints.

The nuclear-cruise missiles lit their engines and dove for the deck as they maintained their supersonic launch speeds, almost disappearing amid the ground clutter.

"We're making our exit; time to impact three minutes," Commander Serova said. "Might want to open some distance before those nukes go off, Osiris Squadron."

"Roger that, Centuriation Leader," Mason said. "We're following you out."

Freed of their heavy cruise missiles, the Asps flared their engines and pushed their speed above Mach 2.

Mason pushed his Lightning to full throttle, feeling the engines battle the drag of flying at low altitude, expending huge amounts of power for small gains in speed.

The assembled League and Federal fighters fled as the minutes counted down, the missiles nowhere to be seen over the horizon. There was no helpful datalink showing where the missiles were, or how they were doing, like there was in space. Just a timer ticking away the seconds to impact. Then Mason picked up a massive emissions spike behind him as the timer reached one minute to impact. It wasn't a nuclear detonation, but powerful RADAR and LIDAR emissions as the defense around the landing site went active.

"Belts and zones!" Mason breathed. He had expected there to be some heavy defenses around the landing site, but what he had detected dwarfed his expectations.

It was like a couple of cruisers blazing away with their full phased-array sets.

There were more energy spikes, as the defenses around the landing site opened fire. For several seconds, the sky in the distance boiled with anti-aircraft fire. And then, seconds before impact, point defenses went silent, and the RADAR switched off.

That wasn't a good sign. The only reason someone would stop shooting at a nuclear-armed missile was because there weren't any left to shoot down.

When the timer hit zero, there was no blinding flash of light from a thermonuclear warhead going off, nor mushroom cloud climbing over the dark horizon.

A cold feeling filled Mason's belly. The Cendies had stopped the missiles.

Commander Serova's Asp broke off, heading back towards the launch site.

"Centurion Leader, where are you going?" Mason asked.

"Scouting the area. I want to know why our nukes didn't go off," Serova said. "My squadron will continue to return to base. I recommend you escort them the rest of the way there."

"Shutdown, you're in command. Escort the Asps back to base," Mason said.

"Roger that, Hauler."

Mason banked hard and turned to follows Serova's Asp as it flew fast and low over the terrain.

"I thought I told you to escort my fighters back, Osiris Leader," Commander Serova said as he formed his fighter up next to hers.

"My XO can handle that," Mason said. "I want to see what's guarding that site too. I'd also like to make sure you make it back to base, Centurion Leader."

"Your concern for my safety is heartwarming, Osiris Leader," Serova said. "We'll take a peek, give our sensor AIs a chance to gather some intel, then bug out at full speed. Maintain radio silence until then."

"Roger that," Mason said. He set his sensor AI to do a full passive search, and then followed Commander Serova as she descended to tree-top level.

Flying low, Mason noted the looted farms and cut-down trees. Intel said there were pastures full of cattle in this area, but there didn't seem to be a single animal in evidence. Even hundreds of kilometers out, the area had been harvested for biomass to feed the Cendy Turtlebacks as they made more soldiers. Like army ants, the Cendies had scoured the area for anything that could be consumed.

He hoped none of the people caught in their path suffered a similar fate.

They passed the launch site without gaining any extra attention. At

Mach 2, the sound of their engines would lag them, but he was sure any Cendy soldiers they overflew would report the sound of the sonic booms.

The Outriders came into view, still patrolling high above at twenty thousand meters. This time, they did react, diving for Mason's and Serova's fighters.

Mason was about to break radio silence when Serova suddenly pulled up.

Yanking back on his control stick, Mason's seat tilted back violently to maintain the optimal angle against the sudden hard pull.

He quickly gained altitude as he followed Commander Serova higher and higher. A flood of contacts poured into Mason's awareness. Dozens of Turtlebacks spread out across the ground of the landing site, their massive size making them look like they were packed tighter than they really were.

The space between them seemed to be crawling with massed formations of Cendy soldiers.

And every Turtleback in sight erupted with SAMs launching from their hull and curving towards Mason.

"Holy shit!" Mason said.

"That explains why the nukes didn't get through," Serova said.

Serova turned and dove for the deck, Mason following close behind her, breaking line of sight with the Turtlebacks.

The missiles must have had guidance of their own, because as soon as they arched down towards Mason, their RADAR went active and they started homing in, their engines still burning. These weren't the tiny SAMs fired by Cendy infantry. These were proper, high-performance SAMs. The kind one would expect from static launchers.

"Centurion Leader, bank right!" Mason called out as he banked left.

She did so without hesitation, and their fighters crossed each other's paths, forcing the missiles to split.

She didn't need him to tell her to reverse her turn, and they scissored again, forcing the missiles to keep weaving through the air, expending their kinetic energy with each turn.

The spent missiles started impacting the ground behind them in a rain of metal as the hard maneuvering robbed them of the energy they needed to run down their fighters.

Mason leveled out just off Serova's left wing and let out a sigh of relief. "Well, that was close."

"That was a waste of perfectly good nukes," Serova said. "Let's return to Citadel 44. We've got an army to fight off."

An army with unlimited reinforcements, Mason didn't add.

CHAPTER 30

"Any chance of trying again?" Mason asked.

Both Colonel Shimura and Commander Serova gave him looks that said no.

"If every squadron of Triumph were to concentrate on one landing site, maybe," Commander Serova said. "But the losses we'd take would mean we'd not have the forces left to resist the armies pouring out of the other landing sites."

"Do we have the forces to do that right now?" Mason asked.

"For a time, Squadron Leader," Colonel Shimura said. "While you were flying your mission, I've had several teams of Raiders forward deployed with Planetary Defense units that are forming a defensive line between us and the incoming Cendy ground forces."

Colonel Shimura turned to face the main screen in the Command Center, and a topographical map of the land around Citadel 44 appeared. A red blob showed that the advancing Cendy army was just a hundred kilometers out. In front of army was a thin line of blue icons.

"Planetary Defense has mustered units of mechanized infantry and armored vehicles," Colonel Shimura said. "But due to Cendy orbital support and their sheer numbers, digging in to stop them is not practical. Therefore, Planetary Defense will engage the Cendies in a fighting retreat. Their goal will be to slow down the Cendies and inflict as much damage as possible without suffering excessive losses themselves."

"I take it the Raiders are going to operate as combat controllers, sir?"

Shimura nodded. "They are, Squadron Leader."

"Then it's back to close air support duty for my fighters."

Colonel Shimura nodded. "That's right, Squadron Leader. Planetary Defense will require around-the-clock air support."

"I'll start dividing up my fighters into shifts," Mason said. "With the pilots and fighters I still have, I can have two fighters airborne at all times, with another four kept on ready-alert status when things get intense."

"I'll organize my fighters to provide combat air patrols over the battle space," Commander Serova said.

"Thanks, Commander," Mason said. "It'll be hard enough without getting bounced by Cendy fighters."

"How long will munitions hold out?" Colonel Shimura asked.

Mason nodded to Commander Serova. "With all the bombs the Leaguers have stacked up in this base, we'll run out of time before we run out of bombs. I'm going to have my fighters loaded up with as many as they can carry with each sortie."

"Then that's your mission, Squadron Leader," Colonel Shimura said. "Get to it."

"I do have one question, sir"

"What is it?"

"All we're doing is slowing the Cendies down," Mason said. "What happens when they get here?"

"Simple, Squadron Leader. We evacuate and continue the fight somewhere else."

Mason nodded, but the answer did not satisfy him. What would happen when there was nowhere else to go?

※

"I'll take the first shift providing air support," Mason said. "Shutdown will lead the ready-alert flight while everyone else gets some rack time. Since we have more pilots than fighters, we will be swapping out pilots on an as-needed basis. I want at least one senior officer up with each support element. Any questions?"

Sabal held up her hand. "Yeah, when's my turn, sir?"

"Since you asked, next flight," Mason said.

"And I remember when you balked at the idea of ground attack, Hardball," Flight Lieutenant Dominic remarked.

"What can I say? I've acquired a taste for bombing Cendies."

"Just remember we're providing close air support. That means staying behind friendly lines and striking targets called out by the Raiders' combat controllers. Avoid flying too close to the enemy. We can't afford to lose any more fighters. Hell, we can't afford what we've lost already."

"I'll drill into these knuckleheads they need to be careful, Hauler," Zin said. "You should do the same."

"I'll try not to make a hypocrite of myself, Shutdown," Mason said.

⁂

As Mason walked out onto the flight line, he saw his Lightning decked out with a frightening number of bombs.

Mason walked up to Chief Rabin as he supervised the loading of another Lightning.

"Those the new bomb-racks, Chief?"

"Yeah, we just had them printed, sir."

The racks were… old school. They wouldn't have looked out of place on a late twentieth-century jet fighter. Each rack on the four ventral wing hardpoints housed six bombs a piece, in two rows of three.

"Got another sixteen bombs loaded up in the weapons bay," Chief Rabin said. "You think forty will be enough for ya, sir?"

"Under these circumstances, Chief, no," Mason said. "But it's as close to enough as we're likely to get."

"At least until the League breaks out the nukes against that army," Rabin said.

Mason shook his head. "The way the Cendy army's spread out, nukes would do more harm than good, Chief. We're just going to have to slow them down conventionally."

"Well, do your best to slow them down, sir. I picked the technician path so I wouldn't have to get into gunfights."

⁂

Mason flew low over the dark mountains with his wingmate, approaching the first line of defense that Planetary Defense set up ahead of the advancing Cendy army.

Everything was cast in shades of green under image intensification. The sun had fully set by the time Mason took off, and the artificial cloud screen above blocked out all the light from the stars and moons above.

But darkness was of little impediment to a Lightning's sensors.

In clearings behind the defensive line rested dozens of tilt-rotor transports, their engines running at idle power ready at a second's notice to pick up the infantry manning the first line of defense and drop them off at the second.

Platoons of tanks and APCs joined, intermingled with the squads of Planetary Defense soldiers and Espatiers, while tilt-rotor gunships buzzed overhead.

Far behind, at the base of the shattered mountain were Citadel 44 rested under, were artillery batteries ready to fire ordinances at the Cendies as soon as they closed into range.

"Osiris Leader on station," Mason said.

"Glad to hear it, Osiris Leader," Sergeant Cane said.

"See you're back to work, Sergeant," Mason said.

"I like to be where the fight is, sir," Sergeant Cane said. "Planetary Defense was kind enough to give me one of their APCs to use as a recon vehicle. You should see my icon ping now."

A blinking icon marked the location of Sergeant Cane's APC. The League APC she was in had an angular, chisel-shaped armored body, with a gun turret on top and six fat wheels on the bottom. Her position was well forward of the firing line.

"You look rather exposed out there, Sergeant," Mason said.

"I have no intention of fighting the Cendies directly, sir," Sergeant Cane said. "Standby for targets. I have a swarm of drones watching the approaches now."

"Understood, Sergeant. I can see plenty from up here."

"I'm sure it's quite the show, sir."

In the vast expanse of dark rolling hills, Mason's sensor AI detected the movement of thousands of warm bodies charging across the planes.

Those Cendy soldiers had been running ever since the one escapee had gotten the signal out and they showed no signs of tiring or slowing down.

There was something both sad and terrifying about the Cendy soldiers. Many that he was about to bomb out of existence were probably only days old, if that. From the moment they crawled out of their birthing tanks, they had known nothing but war, charging over Triumph's surface as they attempted to overrun the planet through sheer force of numbers, completely indifferent to the carnage being inflicted on them.

To be born knowing your purpose was to kill and to have no value placed on your own life… Mason wasn't sure if he should hate them or pity them.

He was ready to kill them in either case. They would do the same to him, and to every last human who stood in their way.

"I've got movement," Captain Crane called. "Cendy squad advancing through the woods. Got a drone tracking them now. Recommend two bombs dropped one hundred meters apart."

The icon appeared on Mason's display off his right wing.

"Understood, Sergeant. Moving in from the west. Two bombs, one hundred meters apart, coming up."

With the telemetry provided by the drone, the combat AI gave Mason a spot to place his bombs where they would have the maximum chance of killing all the Cendies in the advancing squad.

He turned and started to dive towards the Cendy position. He wasn't going to overfly the Cendies and risk having an infantry SAM fired at him. Instead, as he got into range, he pulled up and pushed his engines to full power. The combat AI released the bombs at just the moment where his climb would put them on an arching trajectory towards the enemy. He continued the turn until he was flying away from the Cendies while the two bombs he'd released reached the apex of their flight and arched down towards their targets.

Two flashes and rising clouds of black smoke marked were the bombs struck.

"Good hit, Osiris Leader," Sergeant Cane said. "I've got more targets for you."

"Gummy, you're next," Mason said.

Flashes of gunfire lit up the ground below as entrenched infantry and armored vehicles opened fire on the wave of charging Cendies.

Flashes from around Citadel 44 marked where artillery opened fire, and a few seconds later, fragmentation shells burst above the Cendies.

From far away, the bright glow of large missiles lifted off from the direction of HMB 20. The base was the only thing keeping the Cendy starships sieging the planet from closing in to provide orbital fire support. If that base fell, any kind of large-scale ground resistance would be suicidal.

The gunships started making their runs against the Cendies, flying lower than his Lightning, skimming the treetops while launching rockets and spraying away with their chin turrets.

"Sergeant Cane to Osiris Leader, League Planetary Defense is starting to bug-out to the secondary defense line. We could use some bombing runs to keep the Cendies off our backs while they do that."

"Roger that, Sergeant," Mason said. "Gummy, stay high and wait for me to make my run."

Diving low, Mason turned in until his flight was right between the advancing Cendies and the retreating League ground troops.

Tanks and APCs continued to fire away against the advancing Cendies while the infantry fled to the transports.

Dropping decoys as he made his run, Mason dropped ten bombs in a line. Each bomb landed a hundred meters from the one before, cutting a kilometer-long line through the Cendies. Some Cendies managed to launch their infantry SAMs, but Mason climbed away too fast for the missiles to catch him.

Osiris 2 followed him in and drew another line of explosions with her bombs.

As his wingmate climbed to join him, the tilt-rotor transports took off under close escort from the gunships.

"Infantry is airborne. Armor is starting to withdraw," Sergeant Cane said. "Thanks for the support, Osiris Leader."

"You're welcome, Sergeant," Mason said. "We're returning to base to rearm. We'll be back overhead to provide air support when you reach the next defense line."

"I'll have targets waiting for your bombs when you arrive, Osiris Leader," Sergeant Cane said.

Mason turned towards the truncated mountain of Citadel 44 in the distance, flying low over the tree-covered hills. The hills grew higher and rougher until he reached the closest of Citadel 44's auxiliary vertiports. As he approached to land, carts full of bombs waiting near the tunnel entrance. He opened his weapons bay at the same time as he lowered his landing gear, setting his fighter down on the artificial turf.

As soon as his Lightning's engines idled and the hurricane-force winds died down, the ground crews jumped out of their shelters with tractors pulling the carts full of bombs. Four teams of ground grew descended on the two Lightnings, working together to load up the wings and internal weapon bays of both fighters with all the bombs they could. As soon as the last bomb was fixed to the racks, the ground crew retreated to their shelters.

Mason gave them a little salute and then throttled up his lifting engines, pushing his fighter off the ground with a blast of hot air. It took just a few minutes to fly back over the new position where the League soldiers had set up a few kilometers from their old position. Tank guns and infantry-portable mortars were already lobbing explosives at their previous defensive position as the Cendies overran it.

"Osiris Leader is back on station, Sergeant Cane," Mason said. "Ready to receive targets."

"I got plenty for you, Osiris Leader,' Sergeant Cane said. "Uploading now."

For hours, Mason made dozens of bombing runs against the Cendies. Once the Cendies closed to within a few hundred meters, the Espatiers and Planetary Defense infantry would run to their transports and fly to a next line of defense. Mason used the time between each displacement to load more bombs.

"Hauler, my flight's airborne and on our way to relieve you," Sabal said as she and her wingmate climbed from Citadel 44. Mason had checked the time. Six hours. He had dropped over two hundred bombs had made a total of four rearming runs back to base in that time. "Roger that, Hardball," Mason said. "Returning to base. The Cendies are providing no shortage of ground targets."

"How kind of them," Sabal said. "See you back at base."

"Happy hunting, Hardball."

Mason set down at an auxiliary vertiport minutes later, Osiris 2 landing beside him at the same time.

Automated tractors latched on and towed him back into the mountain.

By the time he arrived in the main chamber, he had powered down the fighter and opened the canopy, reclining in his seat with his helmet off, watching the tunnel's overhead lights go by.

His Lightning came to a stop in its parking spot and, tug detached, Mason jumped down to the deck and, on a whim, glanced at the empty bomb racks hanging from his wings. He had dropped more air-to-ground ordnance in the past six hours than he had during the entire time he had been flying air-to-ground missions. And yet for all the fire and death he had inflicted on the Cendy army bearing down, to them it seemed to be just one more hill they had to climb.

"You look lost in thought, Squadron Leader."

Mason turned to see Commander Serova walking up, her light blue hardsuit contrasting with his black.

"It's been a long day," Mason said. "Thanks for keeping the Cendy air off our backs."

Serova shrugged. "Cendies didn't challenge us for air superiority. They seemed content with letting their infantry deal with us through sheer mass."

"They can certainly absorb the losses," Mason said. "Might as well be dropping those bombs into Jupiter's clouds for all the good they seem to be doing."

"I wouldn't sell yourself short, Squadron Leader," Serova said. "You're buying time."

Mason turned to Serova. "For what, Commander?"

"Every minute the Cendies have an army bearing down on Citadel 44 is a minute that army isn't going after the last missile base we have on the continent or overrunning one of our cities. This fortress we're defending is the thing denying the Cendies full control of this continent."

"I saw how fast your soldiers were falling back, Commander," Mason said. "They'll overrun the western vertiports by tomorrow. The eastern ones probably a day after that. Citadel 44 won't serve much function as an airbase after that."

"We'll evacuate our aircraft before then, Squadron Leader," Commander Serova said. "There are other citadels like this one on the other continents."

"Can't say I'm looking forward to that,"

"You've grown attached to this place?" Serova asked.

"No, Commander," Mason said. "It's just going to be that much more time we have to spend getting ground down by the Cendies."

"Then we'll get ground down," Serova said. "And make them pay for every square kilometer of this planet."

CHAPTER 31

IN THE SECONDS after every jump, the space around *Independence* would shimmer with arrival flashes as the ships of Taskforce Red followed their flagship. A momentary distraction from Jessica's ponderings over what Miriam had said.

The idea that the Cendies were protecting something made more sense to her the more she thought about it. The Ascendency's invasion, and their stated justifications, were consistent with a preventative attack. A check on human expansion.

Earth Fed didn't bother with regulating colony ships that ventured into deep space. So long as the ships were built to standard and everyone aboard seemed sufficiently sound of mind, Federal officials were satisfied to let them depart with little more than a wave goodbye.

And that wasn't counting the colonists that left the League and independent systems. Maybe the Cendies saw the expansion of the human race as a wildfire that needed to be contained before it burned something valuable.

Jessica closed her connection to the external cameras, and instead, brought up a display with a starmap. On it were stars highlighted in red. These were systems known to have permanent human settlement. The frontier extended roughly 200 light-years in all directions, with outliers as far as 300. Then she overlaid suspected encounters with the Ascendancy going back years, marking the systems where they occurred in yellow.

Like a golden finger, the recorded encounters with the Cendies had a definite direction, pointing roughly through the center of the constellation Hydra—far from the official course of the colony ship *Ascension*.

Jessica broke her brainset connection and closed her eyes, freeing her mind of distraction as she imagined Julian Marr leading *Ascension* towards Hydra, just flying out into deep space while they did their experiments, scanning their scopes for any celestial body they could set up shop around.

She wasn't sure how far *Ascension* ended up going, but she suspected 100 light-years was about the outer limit of her range, and they probably settled down somewhere closer.

"You napping on the job, Lieutenant?"

Jessica's eyes shot open and she saw Admiral Moebius looming over her, standing in the .3 gravity of *Independence*'s habitat ring.

"Uh, no, sir. I was just, uh, meditating, I guess you could say," Jessica said.

"Meditating about what, Lieutenant?"

"The Cendies, sir."

"Good to see you're meditating about things relevant to your job, Lieutenant. Any insights?"

"Mostly just feeling out the gaps in our knowledge," Jessica said. "What I've learned from Miriam is helpful, but it also goes to highlight just how little we know about the Ascendency. We have many hints, but few answers. We don't know the full extent of their capabilities, or their motivations, or even have a clear picture of what their culture is like."

"If they even have a culture," Admiral Mobius said.

"They certainly have a culture, sir," Jessica said. "Or at least an interest in human culture, if Emissary Jerome's reading tastes are anything to go by."

"We really need to start feeding more information into that brain of yours, Lieutenant," Admiral Moebius said. "You don't handle boredom well."

"Not particularly, no, sir," Jessica said.

"Good news is that there's going to be plenty of things to learn about the Cendies at 61 Virginis."

"If they don't shoot us all to pieces, sir"

"You're not optimistic about the mission's success, Lieutenant?"

"Too many variables, sir," Jessica said. "Which I don't mean as a criticism. We're headed to 61 Virginis out of necessity, not because our odds of victory are overwhelmingly positive. But there's a chance that when we arrive, it will just be Taskforce Red because Triumph will be conquered and what's left of the League fleet will have either fled or been destroyed."

"You're the only one who seems to think the Ascendency could conquer Triumph so quickly," Admiral Mobius said.

"Anyone who's telling you the Ascendency can't are greatly overestimating their understanding of the enemy's capabilities, sir," Jessica said. "What we have heard about the ongoing invasion has not lined up with predictions. And why should they? All those predictions were made based on our assumptions about planetary invasion. Something I suspect the Cendies care very little about."

"Very little indeed," Admiral Moebius said. "You should take some time to relax, Lieutenant. I want you fresh and ready when there is something to learn about the Ascendency. Consider that an order."

Jessica got up from her seat and saluted. "Well, sir, if an admiral is telling me to relax, then I see no other choice but to obey."

Returning to the pod reserved for just her and Miriam, she found the woman's mobility rig reclined in an acceleration seat, eyes closed. She looked like she was asleep, but of course that wasn't something an AI copy of a dead woman needed.

"Welcome back, Jessica," Miriam said, her eyes still closed. "Come join me, the water is lovely."

"Is it now?" Jessica asked. "You back at your beach?"

"How about you link up with me and find out," Miriam said. An icon appeared, inviting Jessica to connect.

"Well, Admiral Moebius did order me to relax," Jessica said.

"Then get in here."

"As you wish, Miss Xia." Jessica sat down in the neighboring couch, closed her eyes, and accepted the invitation.

Her awareness of the lounge fell away, the cool dry air and buzz of ventilation fans replaced by thick humid air and the chirps of exotic birds.

Opening her eyes, Jessica found herself standing in the middle of a tropical jungle, the thick canopy shielding her from the noon sun. Colorful birds darted between the branches, singing a cacophony of songs that were impossible to tell apart from one another.

Then she heard splashing behind her.

Turning around, she found Miriam, nude as the day she met her, paddling around in a crystal-clear pool of water, fed by a short waterfall.

"You're overdressed," Miriam said. "I thought your admiral ordered you to relax."

Jessica looked down and found she was still in uniform. She really ought to get in the habit of changing her default appearance before diving into VR.

"I suppose I am." Jessica approached the pool while unzipping the front of her jumpsuit, stopping only to remove her boots and push her jumpsuit down to her ankles so she could step out.

Reaching behind her back, Jessica unhooked her bra, and set it atop her folded jumpsuit, along with her regulation boxers.

She turned to find Miriam standing at the edge of the pool, the water just below her belly button. She had a curious expression on her face.

"What? Is there something on my face?" Jessica asked.

"I was just wondering why you undressed instead of just willing your clothes to disappear," Miriam asked.

"How long has it been since you dressed yourself?" Jessica asked.

"With my hands? A while, to say the least,' Miriam said. "There are a lot of basic tasks that I decided to skip after I was digitized."

"I spent over half my life being dressed by nurses and caregiver robots." Jessica dipped her toe in the water. The temperature was perfect. Wading in up to her knees, she held out her arm to show it off. "Once I gained the ability to do it on my own, I learned that I very much enjoyed it."

"I see," Miriam said. "A perspective I never considered." She looked Jessica up and down. "Is that what your body looks like under that jumpsuit?"

"It does," Jessica said.

"A fine piece of work," Miriam said. "Who made it?'

"A prosthetic body manufacturer contracted by the Special Purpose Branch," Jessica said. "One of the privileges was that I got to choose my appearance."

"Hrmm. And you went for almost perfect beauty," Miriam said.

"Yes," Jessica said. "Why not? I take it you approve?"

"Very much so," Miriam said. "I admit to a little jealousy. Your body puts my mobility rig to shame."

"You were quite noted for your beauty in life."

"Beauty that was just as artificial as yours, Lieutenant," Miriam said. "Though in life that was from a combination of cosmetic genetic engineering by my parents, plastic surgery, and an army of dieticians and personal trainers."

"It paid off."

"I do feel like I got my money's worth, yes," Miriam said.

Jessica dove in, immersing herself in the warm clear water. She swam out into the middle of the pool, where the water came up to her navel, then leaned back and floated on her back, letting herself float atop the water's surface.

She always loved the feeling of buoyancy. It was nothing like floating in zero-g. In zero-g, you were basically helpless without a suit thruster. Just one more bit of dust in the vast empty void.

In water, there was a sense of being embraced and supported, able to go anywhere you wanted with just the stroke of a hand.

A movement in the water next to her was the first indication Miriam had floated up next to her. Jessica glanced to her side and found Miriam laid back, her face peeking out of the water while her hair spread out in a black fan around her head.

Miriam's eyes met hers. "It's good to see you finally relax."

"It is nice—though I'm slightly mortified that it took an admiral to order me to do so," Jessica said. "I think the Space Forces have turned me into something of a workaholic."

"It's an easy thing to fall into when the work you're doing is important," Miriam said.

"Anyone had to tell you to relax?" Jessica asked.

"No," Miriam said. "There was never anyone with authority over me to do so."

"You seem to know how to make yourself relax."

"In death," Miriam said. "In life, not so much."

"There must have been things you enjoyed."

"Oh yes. Building the largest ship manufacturer in the solar system after the General War, running various philanthropic organizations when I retired from running the business. Using my vast wealth and influence to help Julian and his colleagues build *Ascension* and fly off into the void. Over a century of hard work, with little in the way of relaxing."

"Do you regret it?" Jessica asked.

"No, curiously," Miriam said. "My life was one of great privilege and even greater achievement. It was never boring, though often lonely."

"Your family and children?" Jessica asked.

"My children were raised by au pairs, nannies, and tutors," Miriam said. "I was a distant figure in their lives. My two marriages were largely strategic in nature, to solidify alliances like the royals of old. There was… little companionship."

"Friends?" Jessica asked.

"A few," Miriam said. "Though I admit, you're the first friend I've made in a very long time."

"You can hardly count the underclocking," Jessica said.

"I haven't made that many friends in the two years I've spent inside," Miriam said. "I spent so much of my time among other people when I was alive that I wanted to spend some of my death by myself."

"That didn't stop you from coming out here," Jessica said.

"Well, I'm curious how the last great project of my life has gone so horribly wrong," Miriam said. "Not to mention, I got to meet a rather fascinating woman in the process."

"You flatter me," Jessica said.

"Yes," Miriam said. "Is it working?"

"It might be," Jessica said.

She felt a shift in the water. She glanced over and saw Miriam standing in the waist-deep water.

"May I touch you, Jessica?" Miriam asked.

"You may," Jessica said.

Miriam laid a gentle hand on Jessica's shoulder to keep her from floating away, and the other on her belly.

The hand on her belly crept up slowly, gliding over her rib cage until it stopped just short of her right breast.

Miriam gave her a questioning look.

Jessica nodded.

The hand glided over her breast, cupping it and giving a firm squeeze before she lifted her hand and let her fingers wrap around the nipple.

Jessica shuddered as the sensual shock ran through her body, causing the water to ripple.

"Sensitive, I see," Miriam said.

"Very," Jessica said.

"Good," Miriam said. She cupped the back of Jessica's head while she continued to play with her nipple and leaned down to kiss her.

Her lips were soft, the kiss gentle.

Jessica stuck her feet to the bottom of the pool and stood up to warp her own hand around Miriam and continue to kiss her.

Jessica's hand found one of Miriam's breasts, the nipple erect. Jessica gave it a pinch and Miriam gasped.

"Hey!"

"Oh, I think I've found a weakness," Jessica said.

Miriam squeezed Jessica's nipple, eliciting a gasp from her.

"A mutual weakness, I think," Miriam said.

One of the things she wanted to do with her new body was get a good fucking in. The digital ghost of a dead woman would have to do. While she continued to play with Miriam's breast with one hand, her other slid down Miriam's neck, following the crease of her back until it disappeared under the water, where it grabbed a handful of Miriam's buttocks.

It felt nice to have someone's ass in her hands. It was something she had wanted to do to Mason the moment she decided she liked him.

She stopped and pushed away.

A look of concern appeared on Miriam's face. "What's wrong? Did I do something?"

"No, no, everything you did was fine, I just…" Jessica's loins burned. A part of her wanted to jump Miriam and continue what they had started.

Another part thought of Mason and his likely battle for survival on Triumph.

"Oh bollocks," Jessica said, sinking into the water up to her chin.

If Miriam seemed annoyed by the sudden termination of her efforts, she didn't look it. Instead, she knelt next to Jessica, her own chin just above the water line.

"This sounds like something you need to talk about," Miriam said.

"You're my therapist now?" Jessica asked.

"No, I just really want to make love to you and whatever's bothering you is spoiling the mood."

"You're hoping I'll continue if we talk it out?"

"At the very least, you might feel better," Miriam said. "So, what's the matter?"

Jessica rested her head on a wet hand. She took a moment to collect her thoughts as the water beaded down her arm.

"I have a friend I'm worried about," Jessica said.

"What kind of friend?" Miriam asked.

"The kind I want to do with what I almost did with you," Jessica said.

"Oh? Do you feel disloyal?" Miriam asked.

"No, it's just, well. I was hoping to… uh, break in my new body with this friend of mine," Jessica asked.

Miriam poked Jessica. "Might I remind you that this body isn't real."

Jessica shuddered. "It feels pretty damn bloody real."

"I understand," Miriam said. "This friend, would they feel the same about you?"

"He might," Jessica said. "He asked me out for coffee."

"I assume for more than just a visit to his favorite cafe," Miriam said.

"It would be disappointing if that's all it amounted to," Jessica said.

Miriam laid a hand on Jessica's shoulder and squeezed. A comforting gesture rather than intimate. "I won't press you any further," she said. "If things don't work out with your friend, you know where to find me."

Jessica smiled. "I suppose I do."

CHAPTER 32

Jessica had first assumed Admiral Moebius chose *Independence* as her flagship because she wanted to command Taskforce Red from the most powerful warship in the fleet. Jessica had been wrong, however. On the outskirts of 61 Virginis, she learned the true reason Admiral Mobius had decided to set her flag aboard *Independence*. The battlecarrier had the most powerful sensor suite of any warship yet built.

It was simply a function of size. The bigger the ship, the bigger the scopes it could mount. And *Independence* had some truly gargantuan ones, drinking photons a hundred billion kilometers out from 61 Virginis.

The object occupying Admiral Moebius's attention was a Cendy Monolith-class vessel. She reached through the holotank to point at the Monolith, the laser light from the projectors speckling the sleeve of her uniform with bright points of light.

"The Cendies have divided their forces between besieging Triumph and protecting their mothership," Admiral Moebius said. "Have our scopes got a clearer picture of the vessels guarding the mothership?"

"Aggregate emissions indicate the Cendies left a quarter of their ships guarding the mothership," Jessica said.

"If we can knock out their ships and the mothership, that would cut into the Cendies' numerical advantage," Admiral Moebius pointed out.

"30 Skeksis is not far from our planned approach, sir," Jessica said.

"Yes, but we would still have to slow down if we wanted to engage in anything more than a flyby," Admiral Moebius said. "And slowing down would give the main fleet more time to prepare for us."

Admiral Mobius folded her arms across her body, touching her index finger to her lips as she stared into the holotank, gears turning in her head.

After a minute of silence, she spoke. "Get me Vice Marshal Singh, I think it will be up to his strikecraft to deal with the mothership and her escorts."

~

Vice Marshal Singh walked through the hatch to Admiral Moebius' office in *Independence*'s habitat ring. He was the tallest pilot Jessica had ever seen, the top of his turban barely clearing the top of the door frame as he walked in.

"You wished to speak with me, Admiral?" he asked.

"I did, Vice Marshal," Admiral Moebius said. She gestured to Jessica. "This is Lieutenant Sinclair, my intelligence officer. There's a major target of opportunity on the deep scan that I need Taskforce Red's strikecraft squadrons to deal with."

"You mean that mothership and her escorts."

"I see you've been going over the deep-scan reports yourself."

"Yes, sir," he said. "I was in the process of making our preliminary plans for our strikecraft for the coming engagement with the Cendies' main fleet."

"I'm afraid you're going to have to delay those plans for the moment, Vice Marshal," Admiral Moebius said. "That mothership and her escorts need to be neutralized, but we can't afford to delay the fleet's arrival over Triumph, nor can we risk having the mothership's escort fleet at our backs when we engage the main Cendy force. Therefore, the attack will have to be done with strikecraft and long-range torpedoes as we fly past them."

"I think my pilots would approve of the chance to strike the enemy without being chained to our starships, sir, no offense," Vice Marshal Singh said.

"None taken," Admiral Moebius said. "Since this will involve primarily strikecraft, you will be in charge of the mission. Lieutenant Sinclair is an expert on the Cendies, and she will provide you with her insights as you formulate a plan of attack."

Singh nodded to Jessica. "I look forward to working with you, Lieutenant. Your work with the Special Purpose Branch was quite impressive."

"Oh? I'm, ah, glad you think so, sir."

Singh chuckled. "I commanded a special operations squadron with the Special Purpose Branch during my time flying fighters instead of desks, Lieutenant. Worked with Colonel Shimura back when she first joined the Special Purpose Branch."

"I'd be very curious to know what she was like back then, sir," Jessica said.

"I'm sure you would," Vice Marshal Singh said. "Maybe she'll even tell you about it after we rescue her."

"I doubt she would refer to it as a rescue, sir," Jessica said. "Merely relief."

"A fair point. One I hope she gets to make soon enough."

"I could not agree more, sir," Jessica said. "So, when do we get started?"

"Right now, Lieutenant," Vice Marshal Singh said. "Come with me."

Jessica glanced at Admiral Moebius when she didn't get up to follow. "You're not coming, sir?"

Admiral Moebius waved her hand. "I have the whole rest of Operation Turnpike to worry about, Lieutenant. Go and come up with something brilliant with him to neutralize that mothership."

CHAPTER 33

Independence was the first vessel to jump into 61 Virginis, flashing into existence at the edge of the jump limit. The other vessels of Taskforce Red followed immediately behind her, treating Jessica to a final light show as the space around *Independence* shimmered with arrival flashes.

And then the strikecraft started launching.

From *Independence*, *Goshawk*, *Hyena*, and the other carriers of Taskforce Red, thirty squadrons of Lightnings and ten squadrons of Conqueror bombers appeared on the tactical display.

As soon as the strikecraft opened a safe distance from their launch vessels, they flared their long-burn drives and rocketed away at 10gs of acceleration. It would take forty minutes for the light from Taskforce Red's arrival to reach the Cendy fleet orbiting Triumph, and Vice Marshal Singh intended to use that delay for all it was worth.

After an alarm echoed off the walls of the flag bridge, thrust gravity started to pull Jessica down into her seat, topping out at a full standard g over the space of thirty seconds.

The drive plumes of three hundred starships lit up the sky around *Independence*.

Taskforce Red was already moving towards the system at several hundred kilometers per second from speed built up prior to jumping in.

Independence passed through the jump limit within ten minutes of arriving, the light from her arrival having traveled a quarter of the distance to Triumph.

Vice Marshal Singh walked over to Jessica, planting his hand on the console in front of her as he leaned forward.

"Are you doing all right, Lieutenant?" he asked.

"Oh, just peachy, sir," Jessica said. "I'm just going to try not to go mad with anticipation while we wait for the Cendies to react."

"There's no point in being anxious, Lieutenant. We have given my pilots the best plan possible with the information we have at hand. It will be up to them to do the rest."

"There's also the Cendies to consider, sir," Jessica said. "If the fleet around Triumph detaches all their fighters–"

"Then my pilots will adapt," Vice Marshal Singh said. "It's the nature of the job, and all my squadron leaders know that. You're just going to have to sit back and let things play out."

"Guess I'm not much for command," Jessica said. "I hate just sitting back and letting things play out."

"Probably a bit of Colonel Shimura rubbing off on you there. She was never one to stay back and let things play out. She always wanted to be in the middle of the action."

"And you, sir, do you still want to be in the middle of the action?" Jessica asked.

"No, I got my fill of that long ago, Lieutenant." He pointed to the icons of the holotank that were pulling away from Taskforce Red. "Now my job is to make sure that those I place in danger have the best chance possible of coming back alive."

"I think I would rather be where Colonel Shimura is right now, funny as that is to say," Jessica said. "As terrifying as it must be to have a Cendy fleet loitering overhead, at least you don't have to wait so bloody long for things to happen."

"It won't be that much longer, Lieutenant. Our jump flash will reach the Cendy mothership momentarily."

Jessica turned her attention to the Cendy mothership and the asteroid 30 Skeksis as the light of the jump flash was about to reach them.

Nothing happened initially, but that was only because lightspeed delay happened both ways. Though it took thirty minutes for the light from Taskforce Redi's arrival to reach the Cendies around 30 Skeksis, it was an hour before Jessica witnessed their response. Ships escorting the mothership exploded with activity. Fusiliers and Katyushas lit their drives to break orbit with the asteroid and move into position to cut off the approach of the Lightnings and Conquerors.

There were no surprises in their reaction. No show of force greater than what was suggested by the deep scan.

The Cendy mothership remained anchored to 30 Skeksis. It was doubtful a ship that enormous could do anything quickly, including decoupling from an asteroid it was mining. No doubt, they had sent a call for reinforcements down orbit on the heels of Taskforce Red's arrival flash.

Ten minutes after the Cendy mothership's escort started reacting, there was a further burst of activity over Triumph as every Fusilier on the scope started launching their Outriders. The Cendy fighters quickly gathered into a swarm of over a thousand strikecraft and started burning hard up orbit towards 30 Skeksis.

Or more precisely, had been burning towards 30 Skeksis for well over half an hour, which Jessica was only seeing now due to the fundamental tyranny of the speed of light.

"Are you sure your pilots are going to be able to adapt to that, sir?" Jessica asked.

"Let's wait and see how the people on Triumph react to the bulk of the enemy fleet's fighter screen departing to defend their mothership," Vice Marshal Sing said calmly.

CHAPTER 34

Mason sat up with a start as the alarm in his brainset went off. Still groggy from the downers he'd taken to get some sleep, he checked the time, and growled in frustration when he saw he'd only got a little under five hours of sleep out of his eight-hour cycle.

<You awake, Squadron Leader?> Colonel Shimura subvocalized.

<I'm up, Colonel,> Mason replied hoping his irritation didn't bleed through his subvocal connection.

<There's been a development. Report to the Command Center immediately.>

Belts and zones, Mason uttered as he got up and walked over to his desk. He popped a blue upper into his mouth and washed it down with cold coffee from the half-empty mug he had abandoned on his desk prior to going to sleep. By the time he pulled on his jumpsuit and zipped up the front, the stimulant had got to work, driving away all feelings of sleepiness.

Minutes later, he walked into the Command Center, finding Colonel Shimura and Commander Serova staring up at the main screen. Following their eyes, Mason saw a map of the 61 Virginis star system, and at the edge of the jump limit, a mass of friendly contacts. That must have been the development the colonel had referred to.

Colonel Shimura glanced over her shoulder at him. "Ah, Squadron Leader Grey, I take it you understand what you're seeing?"

"Yeah, some good news for once," Mason replied.

Commander Serova turned to face him. "Not all good news, I'm afraid, Squadron Leader."

"What's the problem?"

The main screen focused in on the friendly starship formation. It was then that Mason saw the formation of strikecraft icons moving away from the main fleet.

"It appears that your forces have launched a strikecraft attack against the Cendy mothership loitering in our asteroid belt," Commander Serova said. "The Cendies over Triumph have scrambled the bulk of their fighters to reinforce the mothership."

"So, we need to do something to get tie-up for those fighters," Mason said.

"And maybe inflict damage on their starships while their fighter screen is thinned out," Commander Serova said.

"What forces do we have to work with?" Mason asked.

"Just what we have here in Citadel 44," Serova said. "All other forces are engaged."

"So, we need to do something now," Mason said.

"Yes," Serova said. "We'll load up your fighters and ours with all the torpedoes they can carry and launch a prompt attack."

"That won't be enough," Mason said.

"It's what we have, Squadron Leader."

"A torpedo attack by a couple of squadrons isn't going to be seen as a threat by the Cendies," Mason said. "They're only going to call back their fighters from reinforcing the mothership if they perceive the threat to their main fleet as greater than the threat to their mothership."

"If there were more than a couple of hours to organize and attack, I would agree with you, Squadron Leader," Commander Serova said. "But our forces on this planet are almost fully committed. It's only by virtue of the concentration of Planetary Defense ground units around us that we can spare our fighters for anything other than close air support."

"There are enough torpedoes for several attacks stored in this mountain," Colonel Shimura said. "Would multiple sorties be enough?"

Both Mason and Serova shook their heads.

"No, not with the interceptor coverage their arsenal ships provide," Mason said. "It would have to be a massed torpedo launch."

"And we don't have the strikecraft to carry them," Commander Serova said.

"Dammit!" Mason swore. "Hundreds of torpedoes, and they're mostly useless because we don't have the strikecraft to carry… Wait a second. We don't need fighters to carry the torpedoes."

"I'm not aware of us having anything other than our fighters to mount the torpedoes to," Commander Serova said.

"Not mount, carry, Commander," Mason said. "All the torpedoes in this base are stored on wheeled pallets so they can be carted to their launch platforms."

"And?"

"So, how about we just roll those pallets into our assault shuttles and use those to carry the torpedoes up to a safe launching altitude?" Mason proposed. "We have the manpower down here to load up all the assault shuttles before the Cendies are able to break orbit."

"An interesting idea, Squadron Leader," Colonel Shimura said. She turned to Commander Serova. "Would that be feasible?"

"The torpedoes aren't secured to their racks by anything other than webbing straps," Commander Serova said slowly as she thought it out. "If they were dropped at high altitude, they could maneuver off the racks with their maneuvering thrusters before igniting their short-burn drives."

"That sounds like something you could handle over a datalink," Mason said.

"Yes, but your assault shuttles would have to fly close to our fighters in order for them to link up with the torpedoes," Commander Serova said. "Also, I think it's obvious that your assault shuttles will be tempting targets for any Cendy fighters covering the fleet."

"If we load up the assault shuttles with torpedoes, we can arm the fighters with interceptors to defend against Cendy fighters," Mason said. "And the assault shuttles wouldn't have to travel very high. Just pop up above the edge of the atmosphere, and then fall back down to the relative safety of Triumph."

"If those torpedoes aren't targeted in a coordinated fashion, it won't matter how many we fire," Commander Serova said.

"Assault shuttles have a lot of command and control hardware," Mason said. "It should be more than up to the task of coordinating the attack."

"Would one of your assault-shuttle pilots be up to launching a torpedo attack?" Commander Serova asked.

"They won't have to, because I'll be riding in one of the assault shuttles," Mason said.

※

"I don't like it, Hauler," Zin said.

"Which part?" Mason asked.

"Your riding in an assault shuttle filled with armed League torpedoes," Zin said. "I don't see why you can't do that from a Lightning."

"Because I don't want to multitask trying to fly a Lightning and troubleshoot any problems our jury-rigged fire-control system develops. No offense, Silverback."

"None, taken," Dominic said. "Through why not let me ride the assault shuttle? I did the programming."

"Because this is as much an issue of cargo handling as it is programming, Silverback," Mason said. "Need I remind you what I grew up doing?"

"I doubt your parents ever made you work in a cargo hold filled with armed League torpedoes," Zin said dryly.

"I admit this will be a new experience," Mason said. "Look, this isn't up for debate. I've already picked my assignment for the mission. Your jobs," Mason waved his finger indicating all his pilots, "is to keep the Cendies off the assault shuttles until the shuttles release the torpedoes."

"We'll do just that, Hauler," Zin said.

"Good. Get your fighters ready for flight. I have an assault-shuttle squadron to assist."

※

"With respect, sir, we know our job," said Senior Chief Larue, the highest-ranking load master for the assault shuttles.

"With respect, Chief, this is a bit outside your and your fellow loadmasters' skillset," Mason said.

"But not yours, sir?" Chief Larue asked.

"Given that I'm both a licensed hauler pilot and a fighter pilot, I'm about as qualified to drop torpedoes out the back of an assault shuttle as anyone," Mason said.

"Sir, how is this any different from any high-altitude drops?"

"Well, for starters, the stuff your dropping will be going up, not down," Mason said. "And I can tell just by the way you want to secure the torpedoes that they won't be able to separate under their own power."

"Sir, if we don't secure them, the torpedoes will tear off their racks and go bouncing around the interior of our assault shuttles," Senior Chief Larue said. "I don't think I need to explain to you how that might be bad."

"I'm quite aware," Mason said. "It's a risk we might just have to take."

"Sir, our loading procedures are written in blood," Chief Larue said. "Those torpedoes need to be secured by webbing straps in three dimensions. I'm not going to endanger our assault shuttles and their crews deviating from them."

Mason sighed and stared at his boots for a moment while he gathered his thoughts. "Okay, we'll stick to the loading procedures, but let's modify them a bit. Those webbing straps, those can be cut in emergencies, I take it?"

"Yes, sir," Senior Chief Larue said.

"How fast could you cut them?"

"With our strap cutters, I can cut all the straps on one pallet in ten seconds."

"You think you could do that just before launch, Chief?" Mason said. "Run down to the cargo hold with your strap-cutter, slicing straps along the way?"

"That's still going to result in unsecured torpedoes in our assault shuttles," Chief Larue said.

"But only for a few seconds before they're dropped," Mason pointed out. "Would that be acceptable, Chief?"

"Going to make a damn mess of our webbing straps," Chief Larue said. "That might work, but I'd like to try it out once before we start loading up."

Mason checked the time on his HUD. "Once, but as soon as you try it out, we need to get the torpedoes loaded quickly."

"That, Squadron Leader, is something that's well within our skillset."

CHAPTER 35

The assault shuttle shuddered beneath Mason, agitating both his ass and the forty torpedoes occupying the cargo hold behind him.

It was a disconcerting feeling hearing megatons of starship-killing firepower rattling in the racks behind him. But he had insisted on riding in the assault shuttles, so he had no one to blame but himself.

"You're looking worried, sir," Senior Chief Larue said. "This ride too shaky for you?"

"Your concern is touching, Chief, but I'm not the one you should be worried about." Mason jerked a thumb back towards the weapons in the cargo hold.

Chief Larue glanced back as much as his helmet allowed, then looked back at Mason. "I see your point, sir. I hope League torps have good vibration tolerance."

"We'll find out soon enough, one way or another," Mason said.

"Osiris Leader, all Centurion elements are airborne and climbing to your position. What's your status?" Commander Serova asked.

"Bumpy, but nothing an assault shuttle can't handle," Mason said. "We're just waiting for you to join the party." The assault shuttles all flew close together, linked into a closed datalink by a web of comm lasers with Mason's assault shuttle in the center. Once Commander Serova's squadron joined the formation, her fighters would provide Mason with targeting data, which he would pass on to the assault shuttles who would upload the data to the torpedoes. Hopefully, when all the torpedoes dropped, they would know where to go.

After a few minutes the turbulence subsided as the assault shuttle ascended above the storm. By then, Serova's Asps had closed the range enough to join the datalink, followed by the Lightnings of Osiris Squadron led by Zin. On Mason's tactical display, there was a tight ball of assault shuttles and aerospace fighters gradually climbing towards space.

"How's the assault shuttle flying, Hauler?" Zin asked.

"Smooth now we're above the weather," Mason said. "ETA ten minutes to launch altitude. Got any targets for us yet, Centurion Leader?"

"Affirmative, Osiris Leader, but resolution on the passive sensors is not optimal," Commander Serova said. "We'll need to climb a few kilometers more before the atmosphere is thin enough to get good locks for the torpedoes."

"Roger that," Mason said. "Awaiting uploads."

The assault shuttle's own sensors could see the Cendy warship above, registering as tiny splotches of heat thirty-five thousand kilometers above. Unfortunately, the assault-shuttle software wasn't compatible with the League torpedoes, and there wasn't time to patch them, hence the need to rely on data uploaded from Serova's fighters.

"Five minutes to launch," Mason said.

"Osiris Leader, I'm starting to get clear contacts," Commander Serova said. "Uploading targeting information now."

The sky above him lit up with contacts from dozens of Cendy warships in orbit. Far beyond, he could see the exhaust glows of hundreds of Outriders burning for the mothership in the belt, leaving a bare few behind to screen against the torpedoes that were about to come flying up at them.

He uploaded the data into the datalink, and all the torpedoes that were slaved to his brainset happily gobbled up the data.

"Targeting data good. Arming the torpedoes now."

There was a collective hiss in the cargo hold as the torpedoes armed, their seeker heads cooling to operating temperatures. Glancing over his shoulder, Mason could see the articulated eyes of the nearest torpedoes moving in a figure-eight motion behind their transparent nose cones.

The sight made Mason's skin crawl.

"All torpedoes are hot and ready to drop, Centurion Leader," Mason said. "I'll start uploading final firing solutions to you now, Osiris Leader," Serova said.

Mason received and passed on the data to the torpedoes without taking time to review the information. Firing solutions had short shelf lives. The sooner all the torpedoes got dumped out the back of the assault shuttle, the better.

All four hundred torpedoes at his call accepted the firing solution. They would know what to do as soon as the assault shuttles dropped them.

"Hauler, I've got trouble on the sensors," Zin said. "Squadron of Outriders entering the atmosphere on an intercept trajectory."

"Guess they think we're up to no good," Mason said. "How long until they reach us?"

"ETA, five minutes," Zin said.

Mason heard the assault shuttle throttle down its engines as it slowed to below the speed of sound and heard the whine of the actuators adjusting the wings to forward sweep.

"We're at launch altitude, Osiris Leader. Jettison those torps so we can go home," the assault-shuttle pilot said.

"All loadmasters, open tail hatches," Mason said. "That includes you, Chief."

"Yep," Chief Larue said, grabbing a lever adjacent to his station. "Better check your suit seals one last time, sir."

"Got it, Chief," Mason said. All the seals were good. The pressure in his suit was slightly higher than that in the hold. He gave Chief Larue a thumbs-up.

Larue nodded and yanked the lever down. A powerful roar filled the cargo hold as the tail ramp descended, loud enough to trigger his helmet's hearing protection, cutting off his helmet's earphones.

Through the datalink, Mason tracked the squadron of Cendy fighters descending through the atmosphere, riding down on pillars of long-burn drive exhaust. Far above them loitered the Cendy invasion fleet in a single massive formation in a synchronous orbit overhead.

Commander Serova had selected ten unfortunate Katyushas for the torpedoes to home in on, forty torpedoes to a ship.

"All loadmasters prepare to drop on my mark," Mason called out over the datalink. He looked Chief Larue in the eye. "Mark!"

Chief Larue slammed down on the release button.

The rearmost pallet fell away first, tilting backwards and disappearing over the edge of the tail ramp. The second started moving immediately, followed by the third as soon as the second left.

Over the datalink, he saw a line of pallets falling behind the assault shuttles, the torpedoes separating from the pallets a second later, drifting apart as they fell.

Then the first dropped torpedoes ignited their drives, and the night sky lit up with the plumes of short-burn drives.

When the third pallet fell away, Mason looked to the fourth pallet and its lethal cargo in anticipation of watching it slide the full length of the cargo hold and out the back.

It didn't so much as budge.

"Oh fuck!" Chief Larue swore, as he unbuckled himself and got out of his seat.

Mason unbuckled his restraints to follow. "What's the problem, Chief?"

"Don't know yet, sir."

The other assault shuttle reported their drops complete and started diving back towards Triumph.

Behind him, Mason saw ten seeker heads continuing to swerve in a figure-eight search pattern, reminding him that he had a cargo hold full of hot anti-starship weapons.

"Chief?"

"The fucking lock's jammed! All that shaking must have bent something." The loadmaster got up and started walking towards a tool cabinet in the side of the cargo hold.

"Anything I can do to help?" Mason asked.

The loadmaster opened the cabinet and pulled out a prybar almost as long as Mason was tall. "Yeah, you can grab the end of this thing and help me pry this fucker loose."

"Can do, Chief," Mason said.

The prybar was just a couple of meters of steel covered in chipped blue paint, the exposed areas dark from oxidation. Evidence of long years of hard use. Chief Larue jammed the business end of the prybar into the lock, like a spear.

Mason wrapped two gloved hands and started pulling down, almost lifting himself off the floor before he felt something snap.

The pallet slid down the cargo hold and vanished out the back.

Chief Larue sighed, planting the end of the prybar into the floor of the cargo hold with a clink of metal on metal. "Crisis averted."

"Fighters are almost on us. Back to your seats while I dive us out of here," the assault-shuttle pilot called.

"Don't wait on our account," Mason said as he scrambled for his seat.

"Says you, sir," Chief Larue said.

Mason just barely got his seat buckled when the assault shuttle nosed down hard, his stomach floating up to his throat as it went into an almost vertical dive.

"Larue, close the fucking tail before the drag rips the door off," the assault-shuttle pilot yelled.

Chief Larue grabbed the lever and shoved it back up. "Closing now."

"Missiles incoming, going evasive!"

The assault shuttle lurched as it pulled out of its dive and into a hard-left turn. The seat in the cargo hold lacked any kind of gimballing, leaving Mason's stomach free to fall towards his pelvis while his vision darkened, despite the best efforts of his hardsuit to force blood back into his head.

On the tactical display, the Cendy missiles continued to descend, most drawn away from the assault shuttle by the trail of decoys behind it.

One, however, remained locked onto the assault shuttle with stubborn determination.

"Brace!" was all the assault-shuttle pilot got out before the missile hit, and the bulkhead that separated the cockpit from the cargo hold ripped away into the night sky.

CHAPTER 36

Mason found himself looking out over Triumph's night sky, the nose and cockpit of the assault shuttle falling away from him.

He glanced towards Chief Larue, only to find empty air where his seat used to be.

"Oh shit."

What was left of the assault shuttle shook violently as the air grabbed a hold of its ruined fuselage and continued where the Cendy missile left off in tearing the assault shuttle to pieces.

He had to get out of this thing.

Mason hit the emergency release and the airstream tore him from his seat and away from the spinning assault shuttle.

He spread out his arms and legs to stabilize himself. Triumph loomed below him, growing closer and closer by the second. He was still high up, the air quite thin, and his terminal velocity was several hundred kilometers per hour.

The altimeter on his HUD scrolled down with alarming speed. Mason checked his hardsuit's descent system, and it came up green. A good sign that it would work before he splattered into the ground.

He couldn't see the Outriders that shot him down. They were too far away for his eyes or his hardsuit's passive sensors to detect, but he could see flashes below of gunfire marking the perimeter around Citadel 44 and ground forces attempting to hold off the Cendy horde.

Mason checked his trajectory, his HUD helpfully marking his

estimated landing point. It was on the wrong side of the lines. He was going to come down deep in Cendy territory. How the hell was he supposed to get back to Citadel 44 through that?

Of course, that would be a moot point if his hardsuit's descent system failed. Mason tried to relax and enjoy the ride as he waited for his hardsuit to start the soft-landing process.

The first sign that his descent system was working was when the descent module detached from the back of his hardsuit, trailing a pair of cables that attached to his shoulders. Hardsuits didn't have parachutes since there was no guarantee that a pilot would go down over a planet with an atmosphere. As it was, Triumph's atmosphere did most of the work slowing him down, the thicker air of the lower atmosphere slowing his speed to just over 200 kilometers per hour.

That was still more than enough speed to turn Mason into a gooey mess inside his hardsuit on impact. A red bar on his altimeter marked the altitude where the descent module was supposed to ignite.

At three hundred meters altitude, the descent module ignited its thrusters.

The cables on Mason's shoulders went taut and he was yanked up by his shoulders. He glanced up and saw four jets of hot gas spewing from the descent module in an X pattern, marking his position in the sky for anyone to see.

"BRACE! BRACE!" started flashing across his HUD, and Mason unlocked his knees and prepared to hit the ground.

He descended through a cloud of dust kicked up by the descent module until his boots kissed the ground. The module cut the wires and flew away, allowing Mason's full weight to settle on his feet.

He didn't waste time celebrating his return to Triumph's surface. He had survived one danger only to land in the middle of another. Every Cendy for kilometers around would've seen the bright plumes of rocket exhaust and heard the roar of the descent thrusters.

He needed to put distance between himself and his landing zone and fast. He started running roughly in the direction of Citadel 44, his heavy boots crunching through the deadfall below. An icon on his HUD outlined detected movement. Mason had turned away from it before he even saw the Cendy soldiers approaching.

He ran up an incline away from the Cendies as hypervelocity rounds tore through the trees around him. As splinters bounced off his suit, he glanced behind and saw more hostile contacts on his HUD. Then his boot found nothing but air. He screamed as he tumbled off the side of an embankment.

The world spun as he rolled down the steep slope, hitting the water with a crash. He felt himself bounce off the bottom before the current carried him downstream, away from Citadel 44.

He thought about swimming for shore but decided against it. Though the current was taking him in the wrong direction, it was also taking him away from the Cendies that were trying to kill him.

For several minutes, he rode the stream beneath the surface. The longer he stayed under water, the less sure he became of where he was. His internal map was throwing up error messages. All he knew was that he was somewhere east of Citadel 44.

When he finally felt brave enough to pop his head out of the water, he noticed the shore was moving fast, and the water was notably frothier than it had been when he fell into the stream.

White water rapids, that's what they were called, Mason realized. That's what those documentaries on the educational networks called them.

The water kept getting faster and faster, and even with his hardsuit, he was having trouble staying afloat, getting sucked down and dashed against random rocks.

It was like the stream was trying to beat him to death.

When he managed to pop his head above water again, he looked downstream, and saw the reason the water was getting faster. He was approaching a waterfall. What he saw of the stream beyond suggested a long drop.

Belts and zones! Mason started swimming as hard as he could against the current, taking great, splashing strokes with his arms. All his previous swimming experience had been in placid swimming pools and artificial lakes. Swimming in moving water was a new experience for him, and not a pleasant one.

Despite the boost in strength his hardsuit gave him, Mason couldn't contend with the power of the stream. In desperation, he started grabbing at branches overhanging the water, but his weight in a hardsuit, combined with the power of the current, was too much. Every time he grabbed a branch, it tore free to join him on his ride towards the edge.

I can't believe people actually rides these for fun! Mason thought, and then he hit a rock and got spun around.

When he got his bearings, he saw the drop-off just a few meters away and coming fast. He fought against the current, grabbed at branches, and scraped his hands against every rock in reach, but the water continued to draw him closer and closer to the edge.

He was going over the edge. He hoped there was a nice deep pool at the bottom.

He drew in his breath to scream, and then jerked to a stop.

For a couple of seconds, he hung there just over the edge of the waterfall, the current doing its best to pull him over, and something else just as stubbornly holding him in place.

Groping around, he found the torso of his hardsuit wedged between a couple of rocks, the force of the current trying to push him through the gap had stuck him fast.

Mason took a moment to collect himself. The rocks. He couldn't swim against the current, but maybe he could climb.

He took a hold of the rocks he was wedged between and pushed himself free. The current immediately tried to pull him over the edge, but his hold on the rocks held, leaving his feet dangling over the waterfall.

Stone by stone, hand over foot, fighting both the current and his hardsuit's natural buoyancy, Mason crawled along the bottom of the stream, moving towards the shore. The water started to become shallow, allowing Mason to crawl above the water line, until he pulled himself up the sheer rocky edge of the stream.

He lay down on the first dry spot he found, right next to the base of one of the large trees that lined the banks of the stream. Even with the strength-augmenting hardsuit, his battle against the stream had left him exhausted. The heart-rate monitor on his HUD showed a BPM of 152.

Okay, next time I think I'll take my chances with the Cendies, Mason thought.

When he caught his breath, he sat up and looked around. The thunder of battle rumbled in the distance, but he could also hear the chirp of birds and the trill of countless insects calling out in the night. Seemed a little thing like a planetary invasion was no reason to interrupt mating season for the local fauna.

Mason got up on his feet, his muscles aching from the exertion. *Ah, belts and zones,* he groaned. He looked around and tried to get a fix on his location now that he was no longer busy getting knocked around in the current or shot at by Cendy soldiers.

The overcast sky gave him no stars to reference, but the landscape beyond the waterfall was enough for his brainset to estimate his position. He was twenty klicks east of Citadel 44. Thankfully, he would not have to cross the stream he'd just pulled himself out of to get to it—he'd climbed out on the right side. Between him and Citadel 44 was a highway leading to the mountain fortress, and several small towns and homesteads along the way.

Mason glanced at the matte black hardsuit, wishing his had the active-camo system trooper hardsuits had. At least it was dark out. He had another four hours of darkness. Not enough time to sneak through enemy lines to get to Citadel 44, but he could get started.

Mason activated his suit's radio, but on receive only. After almost falling into a waterfall to escape the Cendies, he wasn't about to give away his position through poor radio discipline.

Across all channels, all he got was the high-pitched squeal of com-jamming, with only a few indistinct voices pushing through. Looks like he wasn't reaching anyone even if he did risk broadcasting.

"Guess I'll have to walk," Mason muttered. He fixed Citadel 44's position on his HUD's compass and started walking. He kept the microphones in his helmet tuned to maximum sensitivity, hoping to hear the Cendies before they spotted him.

He didn't hear any Cendy activity beyond the distant sound of weapon fire ahead of him. Just the cacophony of nocturnal calls mixing in with the echoes of war.

As the first rays of the coming dawn started to climb over the horizon, Mason knew he'd have to find shelter to hide in. On his map, there was a group of buildings just a kilometer ahead, well off the main road.

When he came upon the buildings, he found it was a small town nestled in a depression between low mountain peaks.

It looked... like any picture of a planet-side neighborhood that he had ever seen before. Two-lane roads flanked by boxy buildings with steeply slanted roofs. Cars parked on the streets and in driveways. Manicured lawns, trimmed bushes, and decorative fencing.

The only thing that was off was the lack of any people. The residents had probably evacuated to a nearby shelter when the Cendies landed or were huddled inside their homes under a Cendy-imposed curfew.

One of the possibly abandoned houses might have something he could use to contact friendly forces. Maybe help him find a way back to Citadel 44.

He approached the closest of the houses from the side, getting a good view of the tall fence obscuring the backyard.

The fence would provide some concealment, so he made his way towards it. It looked like it was made from solid plywood boards, strong enough to support the weight of his body and hardsuit, so he grabbed the top of the fence and pulled himself over.

The moment his feet landed on the grass on the other side, he was confronted by a pack of barking, growling dogs.

Mason backed against the fence as at least a dozen animals approached him in a semi-circle, staying out of reach as they barked their lungs out. The dogs ranged in size from a pair of thick-coated dogs with pointed ears and long pointed snouts to a fuzzy little thing scarcely bigger than his fist.

The smaller ones seemed to be the bravest, approaching the closest to him.

"Quiet! Quiet!" Mason hissed. "Sit! Heel! Shut up!"

A woman's voice echoed from the back door, and Mason spotted a middle-aged woman holding a light in her hand. She swept the beam of the light over Mason before he could hide.

For a moment, they just stared at each other while the pack of dogs in her yard continued to bark at him.

Then she approached him, laying a hand on the largest dog, who immediately stopped barking, and whined at her. She cooed and whispered to the dogs until they were all quiet, their attention still fixed on Mason.

Then she walked up to him.

"Federal?" she asked in accented Federal. Mason nodded.

She beckoned him. "Come before invaders see you."

Mason tried to follow, but one of the large dogs started to growl again.

"Shush, Reggie!" the woman said. "No more." She turned to him. "Your suit scares them."

Mason nodded, and followed the woman, keeping his movements slow and smooth so as not to startle the animals.

The deck creaked loudly as he stepped onto it and followed the woman through the back door. He entered the lounge that looked out over the backyard. Large glass windows gave an almost uninterrupted view of the outside. The interior of the house was dim, illuminated only by the woman's flashlight and an electric lantern on the coffee table.

The woman started drawing down blinds as she spoke.

"Thought you were more Ascendancy patrolling neighborhood," she said. "Dogs start barking when they come. Must calm them before they start trouble with invaders."

Mason popped the seal on his helmet and pulled it off. "Uh, thank you for letting me into your house," he said.

She smiled at him. "You are welcome. Excuse my Federal. I not speak it since school."

"Uh," Mason gestured towards the pack outside, "those your dogs?"

"Just Neo Shepherds, Reggie and Ronnie." When she realized he didn't know what she was talking about, she added. "Big ones with the pointed ears. All others are neighbors' dogs left behind after evacuation. Government not let people take animals to shelters. I decide to stay and care for dogs." "You stayed to look after you neighbors' pets? They let you do that?"

She nodded as she closed the last of the blinds. "Government does not care about animals. Or those of us who did not evacuate."

"Others have stayed?"

"Yes. Those who could not move quickly enough or hate thought of leaving homes. I could not bear thought of abandoning animals."

Mason walked up to her and held out his hand. "I'm Mason."

She took his hand and shook it, her delicate hand dwarfed by his massive gauntlet. "Angela. Welcome to my home."

"A pleasure," Mason said. "Uh, I don't suppose you have any communications gear I can use?"

She shook her head. "Everything went dark after invasion start."

"How have you survived the Cendies?" Mason asked.

"They leave me alone," Angela said. "Must not think woman with bunch of dogs threat."

"Well, that's good," Mason said.

She pointed towards the gun at his hip. "They might think you are threat."

Mason looked down at the Equalizer pistol hanging from the holster at his hip. Between that and the hardsuit bearing the insignia of the Federal Space Forces, it wasn't hard to tell he was military. "Yeah, well, I suppose they would be right."

"So, how you get here?"

"Shot down."

"Pilot?"

Mason nodded.

"Ah, you fly fighters?"

"Usually"

"I assume you wish to return to unit?"

"That would be helpful."

"Not dressed like that, I don't think. Cendies shoot anyone wearing uniform."

"But they ignore civilians?"

"Yes. Unless they bother them, then…" she pointed her finger at Mason, "Bang!" Her finger recoiled back.

"So, if I don't look like a threat, they'll leave me alone?"

She nodded.

More barking came from the backyard.

After checking the yard, Angela looked at Mason. "Probably another patrol. Might be looking for you. Best you go into basement and get suit off. I'll get clothes after I calm down dogs."

"Uh, right. Where's the basement?" Mason asked.

She pointed to a door before cracking open the back door and going outside.

Mason opened the door, revealing a dark stairwell below. He activated the lights on his helmet and used the helmet as an oversized flashlight as he walked down the stairs, finding himself in a basement that appeared to be furnished as a parlor of some kind, with a large couch facing towards a dark display screen.

Setting down the helmet on a shelf to illuminate the basement, Mason sent a signal through his brainset, and the hardsuit came apart around him. He shimmied his arms out, and then pulled himself out of the suit. He was still wearing his uniform jumpsuit underneath.

Outside, the dogs quieted again to Angela's soft coos, their angry barks subsiding into disapproving whimpers. As they quieted down, he heard the beats of heavy footsteps belonging to multiple individuals.

Shit! Mason grabbed his Equalizer from the holster on his hardsuit and looked for a place to take cover. Then he noticed the hardsuit standing in the middle of the basement.

Belts and zones! Looking for a place to stash the hardsuit, he opened the nearest door and found a closet filled with boxes of home goods. Mason picked up the hardsuit. *Dammit, these things are heavy*, he thought as he struggled to move a suit as heavy as he was without making too much noise.

He got it stashed away into a closet and shut the door.

The sound of the door overhead opening and closing signaled Angela's return inside. Her footsteps rushed from one side of the house to the other, and then back to the top of the basement.

Angela quickly descended the stairs with a bundle of clothes in her arms. She eyed Mason's gun before setting the clothes down.

The dogs started barking again. She nodded to the clothes, signaling Mason to put them on and then ran back up the stairs to quiet down the animals.

Mason dug through the clothes. Angela must have just grabbed the first shirt and pants she came across. Pulling off his jumpsuit, he changed into the civilian clothes.

He settled on a simple brown T-shirt and a pair of blue sweatpants. The T-shirt was loose, and the sweats didn't touch his ankles, but at least the shoes were a good fit and he didn't look like much of a soldier. Hopefully, the outfit wouldn't look too suspicious, or offensive, to the Cendies.

Stuffing his boots and jumpsuit under the couch, Mason crept upstairs. He found Angela in the backyard huddled among the dogs, stroking one of the big ones on the back.

As Mason slid open the back door and walked outside, the dogs turned to look at him. Far from the alarm they had showed earlier, one of the dogs walked up to him with its tongue hanging from its mouth as it brushed up against him.

Not knowing any better, Mason reached down and patted the animal. "Good dog."

The crunch of heavy feet drew the dog's attention, and a low growl left its throat.

"Shh, shh, shh, shh!" Angela walked over and patted the dog. "None of that, Reggie."

"They're close," Mason said.

"Yes," Angela said. Mason moved to go back into the house, but Angela stopped him. "No, stay with me. Will look more natural."

Mason nodded and continued to huddle with her among the dogs. It wasn't hard for him to look the part of a frightened civilian.

Angela walked over to a gate in the fence and opened it. Before Mason could ask what she was doing, a towering Cendy soldier carrying a rifle stepped through. It didn't pay any attention to her as it walked into the yard, barely paying any mind to the growling and whimpering dogs huddled around Mason.

More Cendies followed as Angela walked ahead of the lead Cendy and opened the sliding door to let them in.

She didn't join the Cendies going inside. Instead she joined Mason in huddling down with the dogs.

Mason could feel the muscles under Reggie's fur tense as the Cendies walked by. He himself kept his head down, hoping the Cendies didn't make too thorough a search of the house.

When the Cendies exited the house a few minutes later, they paid no attention to Mason, Angela, or the dogs. They just proceeded to the next house over without so much as closing the gate behind them.

Glass broke as the Cendies forced their way into the next-door neighbor's house, before proceeding to the next one beyond that.

"We go inside now," Angela said. The dogs followed them in, and Angela closed the glass door behind the last dog to enter.

Mason let out a long sigh and settled down in one of the chairs in front of the coffee table.

The Cendies seemed completely indifferent to their presence. As far as they were concerned, civilians were just part of the scenery, like birds chirping in the background.

Angela brought a steaming carafe and a pair of cups from the kitchen and set them down on the table.

"Thank you," Mason said, accepting the cup. She poured steaming brown liquid that smelled of black tea into the cups.

Masson took a sip of the drink and felt himself relax a bit.

"You are safe here," Angela said. "So long as you stay out of way, invaders don't care."

"I saw you open the doors for them," Mason said.

"They break down doors otherwise."

"Ah." Mason took another sip of his tea. "Thank you for the clothes, and for helping me."

She pointed up. "You fight invaders. I should thank you."

"I haven't fought them off yet," Mason said.

"You try at least."

"These clothes yours?" Mason asked.

Angela shook her head. "Son's. With battlefleet. Have not seen him for months."

"I see," Mason said. "I hope he's doing okay."

"Thank you," Angela said.

"Is there anything I can do to help you?" Mason asked.

"Could use more dog food. Do you have any?"

"Not on me personally, I– oh."

One of the little dogs had jumped into Mason's lap.

"She likes you."

"Oh, good," Mason said. He stroked the dog's back, feeling the warm little body under the soft fur. "I, ah, could let people know when I get back to my unit you're out here. At the very least mark your neighborhood as friendly."

"So they don't blow up houses here?" Angela asked. "Please do."

"I don't suppose you'd mind if I left my things down in your basement?" Mason asked.

Angela nodded. "So long as you pick your things up after invaders leave. If not, I sell your things next yard sale."

CHAPTER 37

IT HAD BEEN worrisome when the Cendy fleet blockading Triumph sortied most of their fighters to reinforce the mothership while the Taskforce Red's strikecraft were less than an hour into their 30-hour flight towards 30 Skeksis.

But then someone on the surface of Triumph used that as an opportunity to launch a massive torpedo strike against the Cendy fleet.

Several flashes near Triumph marked where torpedoes got close enough to their targets to detonate, and the detection of debris showed that there was at least some damage done to the Cendy fleet. Enough that the fighters sent to reinforce the mothership all reversed course to return to the fleet to protect it from further torpedo strikes launched from Triumph.

That just left the ships guarding the mothership, which were still considerable.

The Monolith herself made no efforts to change position, either unable or unwilling to detach herself from 30 Skeksis.

Instead, the Fusiliers and Katyushas formed a defensive hemisphere between the asteroid and 30 Skeksis and waited for the strikecraft.

And that's all that happened over the next 24 hours. While Taskforce Red burned at a leisurely 1g directly for Triumph, the strikecraft rocketed ahead at a far harder 10g cruising burn.

Gradually, the strikecraft squadrons approached closer and closer, their speed dropping during their tail-first braking burn towards the Cendies.

The flag bridge was tense and silent as Jessica sat in a jump seat behind Admiral Moebius. The admiral and her assembled officers all stared into the holotank as they waited for the engagement to begin. The icons shifted as the strikecraft slowed to attack speed and started spreading out into combat formations, the Lightnings moving ahead to shield the Conquerors.

"It's starting soon," Vice Marshal Singh said.

"It's already finished," Admiral Moebius said, leaning forward to plant her elbows on the edge of the holotank, resting her chin on her steepled fingers. "Light lag is infuriating."

The massed formation of Federal fighters and bombers dwarfed the small Cendy fleet guarding the Monolith like a predatory swarm about to swoop down on larger, slower prey.

The Cendy fighters remained close to their Fusiliers, opting to augment their point defenses rather than challenge Lightnings unsupported. The Katushas fired the first shots, launching a massed wave of interceptors at the Federal strikecraft, missile tracks extending like tentacles away from the concentration formation.

"Not holding back," Admiral Moebius said.

"As we anticipated," Vice Marshal Singh said.

A few squadrons of Lightnings lit their drives and pushed ahead at maximum acceleration, breaking away from the main formation of fighters.

On her personal console display, Jessica summoned an infographic showing the loadout of the fighters. Vice Marshal Singh had assigned a part of his fighter squadrons to suppressing the interceptors of the Katyushas. To that end, each Lightning assigned to interceptor suppression carried a full external load of eight Stiletto pods each.

The leading Lightnings formed into a flat shield, each fighter spaced so that the tiny bubbles of their Stiletto engagement envelopes overlapped.

Seconds before the interceptors reached the lead Lightnings, a massed volley of tiny Stilettoes erupted from all the spread-out fighters. A few seconds later, tiny flashes of missile-on-missile impacts flashed on the screen, punctuated by the larger flashes of interceptors hitting Lightnings. Like a breakwater, the Lightnings blunted the wave of massed interceptors, losing ten percent of their number in the process.

The surviving Lightnings immediately changed course, their engines burning at full power to heave their vectors away from the Cendy fleet. The remaining interceptors were cleaned up by the Lightnings in close formation with the Conquerors. The Cendies had taken their first swing, and Taskforce Red's squadrons had managed to block the attack.

"Our turn," Vice Marshal Singh said.

The Conqueror bombers accelerated ahead with their Lightnings escorts, pushing over 10gs.

Finally, the Cendy Outriders broke formation with their starships to intercept the bombers and disrupt their formation before they released their ordinance. A brief, violent engagement saw the Conquerors blow through the Cendy fighters with the help of the escorting Lightnings, scattering the wreckage of dozens of strikecraft from both sides.

The Conquerors continued through on their attack runs, and then suddenly broke formation, leaving icons representing the estimated tracks of their bombs to continue for the Cendies.

The bombers pushed their drives to emergency power as they burned hard to move their vectors away from the Cendy fleet with a punishing 18gs.

Jessica watched with anticipation as the bombs drifted at high speed towards the Cendies, slowly expanding as they closed. Fusiliers and Katyushas fired their drives at full power, attempting to evade the stealthy bombs as they approached. Point defense guns fired, spitting walls of metal in the path of the bombs. Then, just as the bombs merged with the Cendy fleet, both disappeared in the glare of multiple nuclear detonations.

"Damage report coming in the squadron leader of Regulator squadron," said one of the staff officers on the flag bridge. "Twenty enemy starships destroyed; all remaining enemy ships showing heavy damage. Hussar and Demolisher squadrons are setting up torpedo runs to finish off the crippled ships. Undertaker squadron is preparing to make their bombing run against the mothership."

Jessica focused on Undertaker Squadron's Conquerors. They had been specifically reserved to attack the mothership and had full loads of bombs. They didn't fly directly for 30 Skeksis but approached at an angle to stay out of range of any interceptors or other weapons that might be protecting the mothership. Then, as soon as the Undertakers got line of sight on the mothership, they fired their main drives hard, until their vector crossed just above the crater where the mothership rested and released their bombs.

The Undertakers relit their drives to burn away from 30 Skeksis while momentum carried the bombs towards their target. The bomb's vector would not directly impact the mothership, instead passing just over it.

The bombs flew a kilometer above the surface of 30 Skeksis, surface defenses opened fire, and the bombs flashed out of existence.

But the angle of the attack did not give the Cendies enough time to kill all the bombs. A simultaneous detonation of the remaining bombs lit up the space over the mothership like a dozen small stars, their directional warheads blasting the surface with deadly radiation.

On the feed from the Undertakers, Jessica could see wisps of vaporized rock rise from the surface. Then the glare cleared, giving her a good look at the aftermath.

"Oh, bloody hell," she said.

The mothership was still there, amid the partially molten surface of the crater, her once light gray hull charred black. But there were no apparent points were the hull had been penetrated.

"Blimey, they make those things tough," Jessica said.

"Any indication that thing is still alive?" Admiral Moebius asked.

"Still waiting for the battle-damage report from Undertaker Leader, Admiral," Vice Marshal Singh said. "Regulator Leader says all remaining enemy starships have been knocked out. Undertaker leader is going in for a closer look."

The lead Conqueror broke off from the rest of Undertaker Squadron, burning on a highspeed flyby vector of the mothership.

Jessica watched as the high-res feed came in from the bombers' scopes. Where the crater wasn't glowing, it was blackened by the intense heat of multiple nuclear detonations. Up close, she could see where rock and metal had fused the mothership to the crater. Switching to thermal scans, Jessica noted that the mothership was cooler than the surrounding rock.

"Undertaker Leader reports that emissions from the Monolith are consistent with the ship still being active, sir," Vice Marshal Singh said. "It appears that the blast effects welded the ship to the asteroid."

"So, they're alive but not going anywhere," Admiral Moebius said. "How many munitions do the strikecraft have left?"

"All squadrons have reported they've exhausted their anti-starship munitions, sir," Vice Marshal Singh said.

"Then there's nothing we can do about that mothership anyway. Bring our pilots home. It's time to get ready for the big fight waiting for us over Triumph."

CHAPTER 38

Angela rolled a rugged mountain bike with thick tires and aggressive treads into the living room. It was a far cry from the lightly built bicycles Mason used to get around Starport Armstrong as a kid.

"You know how to ride?"

Mason nodded. "Yeah. Though this is, uh, more complicated than I'm used to."

"You learn, I think. To fill tires, use air pump here." She patted the tubular device clamped to the bike's frame. "Will put water and food in rear basket."

Mason gave the tires a pinch, feeling the firm rubber give slightly. All the bikes he used had foam tires. "What if I pop a tire?"

"There is patch kit in basket with instructions," Angela said.

"Guess that will have to do," Mason said.

The dogs in the living room sniffed the bicycle, briefly interested before returning to where they had been lounging.

A helmet rested on the back of the bike. Mason grabbed it and pulled it on.

It was a little tight, but the cushioning had enough give for him to fully seat the helmet on his head.

"Thank you, Angela. I'll check in on you when all this is over," Mason said. "I'll try to get you some supplies as soon as possible."

Angela nodded. "Ride safe, Mason."

Mason rolled the bike out the front door. Angela waited at the threshold, the heads of several dogs peeking out from behind her legs.

Mounting the bike, Mason waved Angela goodbye and started pedaling down the road. Wobbly at first, his balance became surer as he gained speed. The navigation app on his brainset projected a line for him to follow against the road. It was the most direct route back to Citadel 44, right through Cendy forces.

Hopefully, a guy on a bike wasn't sufficiently threatening to the Cendies. Otherwise, he doubted they'd have much trouble shooting him off his bike. And there was nothing to say he might not catch a stray bullet or find himself under a falling bomb just through sheer happenstance.

Mason forced himself not to worry about things he had no control over. All he could do was keep pedaling uphill towards Citadel 44.

The road was relatively clear, only the occasional wrecked military vehicle or abandoned civilian car on the side of the road. He was pleased to see that there were a few civilians wandering around, which he hoped would deflect attention from himself. He spotted the still-burning wreck of a Planetary Defense tank, the turret blown off the hull and resting a few meters away from the side. There was no sign of the crew, and Mason doubted what was left of them would do his psyche any good if he found them.

As the hours passed, he started to hear the sharp, rapid-fire cracks of small-arms fire. He couldn't pinpoint where the gunfire was coming from. Or, more precisely, it seemed to come from everywhere in front of him. He heard the beat of dozens of feet running up behind him. Looking over his shoulder, he saw a column of Cendies charging down the road at a full sprint.

The shock caused him to lose his balance, and he rode the bike into a ditch, tumbling over the side of the road. He fumbled for the gun he left behind at Angela's house as the collective footfalls of running Cendies caused the ground to vibrate.

For several minutes, Mason just lay in the ditch as he watched hundreds of Cendies run by him. Not a single faceless head turned his way.

If they were packing themselves into the roads like that, it meant they weren't too worried about an air or artillery attack here.

Mason decided to adjust his navigation app to take him off the roads, through the woods leading to Citadel 44. It would be much slower, but he wouldn't have to worry about getting trampled by a column of charging Cendies again.

Twigs and dead leaves cracked under the mountain bike's thick tires, and the uphill climb over rough terrain started to take its toll. Mason's legs burned from the exertion, and he had to take frequent breaks to drink water and rest.

As the day grew dark, he saw the first sign of friendly activity—a Lightning flying between peaks at subsonic speeds, the roar of its engines reverberating off the sides of the mountains. From his vantage point, Mason watched as the Lightning dropped a string of bombs, and then banked hard while dropping flares.

The bombs cut a line of fire through the woods when they impacted. Mason stopped his bike and covered his ears before the sound of the bombing reached him. A series of thunderous booms rumbled his rib cage.

If Lightnings were dropping bombs ahead of him, then somewhere beyond was a friendly ground element providing targeting data.

Mason mounted his bike again and started pedaling, the prospect of seeing friendly faces giving him motivation to push through the pain in his legs. He didn't want to try sleeping out in the woods while the Cendies were prowling around.

He spotted groups of Cendies in the woods, but their attention was directed skywards, some aiming missile launchers at the darkening sky. The Cendy soldiers carrying the tubes seemed bigger, more muscular than the ones who carried rifles, but also less armored. On their backs they had half a dozen reloads of their tubes.

Mason took a snapshot with his brainset as he rolled by.

A buzzing sound drew his attention overhead. Looking up, he saw a small drone with counter-rotating rotors flying between the treetops. It was a Federal spotter drone. Mason waved to it, hoping that would get the operator's attention.

The drone came to an abrupt stop.

"That's right. Come on, down here!"

The drone descended towards him, getting close enough to the ground to start blowing leaves away. As the optical sensor looked at him, Mason got a near-field communications request on his HUD.

Mason accepted.

"Squadron Leader Grey, is that you?"

"Sergeant Cane? It's good to hear your voice," Mason said.

"Yeah, I bet," Cane said. "Where the hell did you get that bike?"

"Local gave it to me," Mason said.

"And your hardsuit and uniform?"

"Left it with her," Mason said. "Cendies are ignoring civilians, hence the disguise. Could you guide me to your position?"

"I'm uploading now," Sergeant Cane said. "It's a good thing I spotted you. There are Cendies crawling all over the area. I was about to call in one of your pilots to bomb your position."

"Then help me find you before something ironic happens, Sergeant," Mason said.

A waypoint two thousand meters ahead of him appeared on Mason's HUD. He immediately started pedaling in that direction.

The drone climbed back up to the top of the trees, the sound of its rotors fading against the ambience of several distant gun battles going on at the same time.

After fifrteen minutes of careful pedaling, Mason reached the waypoint, but didn't see anything.

"Uh, hello?" Mason called out.

A Federal trooper in a full combat hardsuit appeared, active camo shifting as she moved. "Over here, sir!" She waved him over.

As he approached, he saw the outline of an APC concealed under a camouflage tarp.

Sergeant Cane lifted the edge of the tarp. "Leave the bike, sir."

Mason propped the bike against the side of the tree and marked the location in his brainset for later, just in case he ever got a chance to return it to Angela.

Following Sergeant Cane under the tarp, Mason entered a torrid sauna with a wheeled APC inside.

"Hot in here," Mason commented.

"Thermal camo is basically a blanket, sir," Sergeant Cane said.

"How long have you been out here?"

"We've been staying just ahead of the frontline calling in strikes for days, sir."

As they entered the rear hatch, Mason found the interior cramped passenger compartment with control consoles on either side. Beyond the passenger compartment was the bottom of a turret basket separated from the passenger compartment by a metal grating.

The legs of one PD soldier dangled from the turret.

"Let me introduce you to the crew of this vehicle," Cane said. She indicated the small woman seated at one of the consoles. "That's Sergeant Lachman. She's in command of this vehicle. The guy on the other console is Technician 1st Class Bryce; he helped me adapt my drone to their system. Real whiz kid. Glad he's on our side. The pair of legs you see angling from the turret is Corporal Vinter, the gunner. Saw her dust a Cendy at three thousand meters with one shot from the autocannon, so stay on her good side."

The enlisted PD nodded as they made their greetings. Even the gunner, Corporal Vinter, stuck her head below the lip of the turret to say hi.

"The driver, Corporal Moors, is in the front. Nice guy, terrible driver," Sergeant Cane said.

"Hi, everyone. Got room for one more?" Mason asked.

"Of course, sir. It was starting to feel lonely in here with all the empty space. You don't even need to sit in someone's lap," Sergeant Lachman said "The horror," Mason said, sitting down in a fold-out seat next to Sergeant Lachman.

"Hey, Bryce, get the new Federal patched into comms so he can talk to his pilots," Sergeant Lachman said. "I'm going back outside to pack up the camo net."

"We're moving?" Mason asked.

"Cendies are too close. We'd be on the move already if we weren't waiting for you," Lachman said.

Sergeant Lachman and Sergeant Cane disappeared from the passenger compartment to collect the camo net.

Technician Bryce turned away from his console towards Mason. "Sir, I have Osiris 5 online if you want to talk with her," he said in perfect Federal.

"Please," Mason said.

"Hauler, I'm glad to hear you're still alive," Zin said. "I was sure you were dead when I saw the assault shuttle break up."

"Got thrown from the wreckage," Mason said. "Hardsuit kept me alive on the way down."

"Couldn't have been easy sneaking past the Cendy lines," Zin said.

"Actually, it was not that hard. Just had to disguise myself as a civilian," Mason said. "Cendies don't seem to pay any attention to non-combatants. How's the rest of the squadron?"

"Same number of pilots and Lightnings as there were before you got shot down," Zin said. "Everyone will be relieved to hear you're alive."

"Well that's heartwarming," Mason said. "How are things with Taskforce Red?"

"They finished their strikecraft attack on the Cendy mothership, and are still headed our way," Zin said. "But it's not all good news. Cendies have been making extra efforts to take down Triumph's planetary defenses before Taskforce Red arrives. Heavy Missile Base 20 went dark ten hours ago, leaving Citadel 44 the only installation left on the continent. All Planetary Defense still active on Stoneland are converging on Citadel 44 for a last stand."

"Understood, Shutdown," Mason said. "I'll leave you to your bombing. I'll try to return to base as soon as possible."

Sergeant Lachman returned with Sergeant Cane following close behind, the camo net tightly packed into a sack under her arm. She struck the button on the rear hatch and it started to close.

Sergeant Lachman walked past Mason towards the turret. "Take my seat, Cane. I'm going to the turret." The small woman squeezed around the rim of the turret basket and climbed up inside to join the gunner.

Moments later, the APC began lumbering slowly forwards.

CHAPTER 39

Mason hadn't realized how much he depended upon the anti-nausea drugs his hardsuit pumped into him until he found himself bouncing around inside an APC without them.

"You're looking a bit green there, Squadron Leader," Sergeant Cane remarked.

Mason nodded, electing not to speak out of fear of decorating the APCs interior with the half-digested remains of the food Angela had given him.

"Contacts front!" echoed Sergeant Lachman's voice through the bottom of the turret.

The APC rumbled to a halt, throwing Mason into Sergeant Cane and the armored plates of her hardsuit.

"Ouch!"

As Mason righted, the APC started to reverse while the autocannon's muzzle blast banged the hull like a drum, and he lurched into Sergeant Cane again.

Barely audible over the sound of the thumping autocannon were the pings of small-arms fire bouncing off the armor.

"Fuckers must have gotten around us," Sergeant Cane said.

"They're swarming all over the damn mountain," Lachman said. "We'll need air support to get to the defense line."

"I'm on it," Sergeant Cane said.

"Need some help, Sergeant?" Mason asked.

"Yeah, I got a couple of your pilots overhead. You can coordinate with them while I work with the League gunships," Sergeant Cane said.

"Can do," Mason said. On the tactical display, Zin was still overhead leading her two-ship element from Osiris 5.

"Osiris 5, this is Osiris Leader. We're taking fire directly ahead of my position. Request immediate air support, danger close," Mason said.

"Making our runs now, Osiris Leader," Zin said.

Sergeant Cane was barking orders in Exo almost too fast for his brainset to translate. Along with the Lightnings, a four-ship flight of League tilt-rotor gunships were inbound to provide support.

A thunderclap drowned out the whine of the APC's engine and thump of the autocannon. On the external feed, Mason saw the rising clouds of three simultaneous detonations.

"Moors, drive us right through where those bombs just hit!" Lachman barked through the intercom in Exo.

"On it!"

The APC lunged forward again, driving into the still-rising clouds of smoke left by the explosion.

Debris kicked up by the detonation rained down on the APC, pinging off the armored roof over Mason's head.

New contacts appeared on the tactical overlay just before Mason heard the whine of the turret's traverse motors as Corporal Vitner swung the cannon around to engage.

More Cendies were climbing up the ridgeline in loose formation. Several stopped to fire their rifles at the APC even as Vitner lit them up. Explosive shells from the cannon detonated like grenades among the Cendies, causing several to drop to the ground.

A puff of white smoke was the only warning Mason had before something exploded a few meters short of the APC, the detonation rocking the vehicle.

"Active defenses just knocked down a rocket," Technician Bryce said.

"I saw," Lachman said. "Moors, evasive maneuvers. Active defenses can only knock down so many missiles at once."

"Got it, Sergeant."

The APC started swerving as it bumped along the ground, doing nothing for Mason's motion sickness, but that seemed preferable to getting blasted by a Cendy anti-armor rocket.

"Vitner, waste that fucker!" Lachman called out.

The turret traversed a few degrees, and the autocannon barked, lighting up the area where the rocket came from.

"Osiris 5, this is Osiris Leader, I've marked an area filled with hostiles," Mason said. "Engage at will."

"Roger that, Osiris Leader, rolling in," Zin said.

The roar of their engines preceded the Lightnings as they made their subsonic attack runs.

They flew overhead and left trails of bombs falling behind them, cutting across the ridge the Cendies were climbing over.

From the direction of Citadel 44, a volley of rockets streaked over the APC to impact areas of Cendy movement. The tilt-rotor gunships hovered over the tree line as they cut loose with their chin turrets, peppering the ground on the far side of the APC with explosive shells.

The Cendies Mason saw on the thermal scanner disappeared as the explosions kicked up dirt and blew trees apart.

The deep thumping of the autocannon was replaced by the sharp chatter of the coaxial machine gun as Vitner sprayed into the woods, laying down suppressing fire over any Cendies that had survived the air attack.

The APC continued to roll up the side of the mountain, passing broken and burning trees as well as the shredded remains of Cendies caught in the Lightnings' bombing runs.

The once pristine forest was now a blackened hellscape cast green in the image intensifier. It was then that it hit home to Mason just how messy ground combat was. Not just the blood and guts, but dirt, mud, and shredded vegetation churned up by the liberal distribution of high-explosive ordinance.

And this little skirmish was just a sample of the fighting going on around the mountain. Above the tree line, Mason could see smoke rising from all around him. There soon wouldn't be any trees left standing. Just burnt earth, broken branches, and ragged stumps.

The APC finally rolled up to one of the auxiliary entrances to the base, rolling over the disguised pavement between two heavily dug-in infantry positions that flanked the entrance.

Mason saw the heads of League PD soldiers peeking over the rim of the sandbag wall, the barrels of rifles and machine guns sticking out from under the sandbags like the spines of an agitated porcupine.

The APC rolled through the entrance, and into the dim tunnel beyond.

"I didn't know you were returning to base," Mason said.

"Just passing through, sir," Sergeant Cane said. "This side of the mountains is saturated with Cendies, as you may have noticed. We're driving through the base to get to the far side of the mountain. We'll drop you off along the way."

"Well, thanks for the ride, Sergeant," Mason said.

"Just remember who picked you up when you're prioritizing air-support requests, sir," Sergeant Cane said with a grin.

Mason chuckled. "Will do, Sarge."

The APC's tires squeaked as it came to a stop on the smooth floor of the main base after traversing through the tunnel.

Following Sergeant Cane out of the back of the APC, Mason stretched to full height, working out cramps that had formed from hours hunched over inside the vehicle.

"Mason!"

Mason turned just in time to get enveloped in a massive hug by Zin. The other pilots of Osiris Squadron were there too. Sabal and Dominic sporting huge smiles on their faces as they watched Osiris Squadron's XO welcome their commanding officer back from the dead.

Zin was still smiling when she let Mason go. "I admit, I thought that was it for you when I saw your assault shuttle go down."

"You and me both, Zin," Mason said.

"Squadron Leader Grey."

Mason turned to face Colonel Shimura as she approached.

"Sir," Mason said, snapping a salute.

Colonel Shimura walked up to Mason until the toes of her boots were just centimeters from Mason's. She looked him up and down with a flat expression.

"You're out of uniform," Colonel Shimura said.

"Uh, yes, sir. But I have a good explanation!"

Then Colonel Shimura smiled and took Mason's hand in a firm handshake, grabbing Mason's shoulder firmly in her free hand.

Mason guessed this was about as close as Colonel Shimura ever got to giving a hug.

"It's good to have you, back, Squadron Leader. You've quite the talent for survival," Colonel Shimura said.

"Cendies have given me a lot of opportunities to practice, sir," Mason said.

"And there's more to come, I think," Colonel Shimura said.

"Oh, belts and zones!" Mason said.

"I know you'd like to get some rest, but I'm afraid events aren't about to give us a break just yet."

"What's happening, sir?"

"Taskforce Red's closing into firing range of the Cendy fleet."

"Oh," Mason said. "Can I take some time to get a shower and a fresh uniform?"

"Yes," Colonel Shimura said. "Get some food and a shower, Squadron Leader. But I expect you in the Command Center the moment you're ready."

⁘

After taking a hot shower and pulling on a fresh uniform, Mason walked into the Command Center feeling like a complete human being again.

Ahead of him was the familiar sight of Colonel Shimura and Commander Serova standing at the front of the Command Center, looking at the giant display on the wall. Mason walked past the rows of stations occupied by chattering controllers to join them.

The icons on the holotank showed the Cendy fleet gathered into a single concentrated formation while Taskforce Red itself was divided into several dispersed formations. League icons and labels in Exo made it hard for Mason to digest all the information, but after his brainset translated some of the labels, he stopped in his tracks and stared up at the screen.

"Something amiss, Squadron Leader?" Colonel Shimura asked.

Mason pointed to the screen as he walked up to her. "Yeah, *Independence* is way out in front of the rest of the fleet. The Cendies are going to focus all their fire on her."

"I think that is the idea, Squadron Leader," Colonel Shimura said. "I expect the Cendies to start launching torpedoes any moment now."

"Torps aren't what I'm worried about, sir," Mason said. "The bulk of the Cendy fleet's killing power is going to be the spinal guns of their Fusiliers."

"That's what I wanted to talk to you about, Squadron Leader. There's scant little we can do to help Taskforce Red with the missiles, but we might be able to disrupt the Fusiliers before they start firing." Colonel Shimura said. "Commander Serova was able to contact the remaining active Planetary Defense Forces. We're currently formulating a plan to launch a strikecraft attack against the Cendy fleet right about when Taskforce Red enters kinetic range."

"We've used all our torpedoes already, sir," Mason told her.

"But squadrons flying out of Citadel 30 and Citadel 22 have not, Squadron Leader Grey," Commander Serova said. "They're loading up their fighters with all the torpedoes they can carry. All remaining fighter squadrons will launch to provide escort for them."

"Then I think this might be a good time to break out the Raiden Cannons again," Mason said.

"It is. Especially since Citadel 44's not going to be here for much longer," Colonel Shimura said.

"We're not going to hold the base?"

Commander Serova shook her head. "It's only a matter of time before the Cendies breach the tunnels, even if we collapse them. They'll just dig them out. We're already in the process of evacuating the base's personnel. As soon as our fighters launch, our ground crews will evacuate via air transport."

"What about the ground troops guarding the base?"

"They'll evacuate to the coast where PD Maritime Forces will recover them."

"Will you be flying out, Colonel?"

Colonel Shimura shook her head. "I'll be with the ground forces to help our troopers coordinate with the League. But don't worry. I have no intention of making a heroic last stand here."

"Citadel 44's has just about served its purpose," Commander Serova said. "Soon, there will only be one thing to do with this base."

"And what is that, Commander?"

"Deny it to the enemy, Squadron Leader."

CHAPTER 40

Admiral Moebius nodded to Jessica as she entered the flag bridge, and then turned her attention to the communications officer who was approaching her.

"You're on in thirty seconds, sir," he said.

Jessica took her seat and brushed down the front of her jumpsuit.

"Did you get your jumpsuit pressed, Lieutenant?" Admiral Moebius asked.

"I figured I should look my best for your big speech, sir," Jessica said.

Admiral Moebius nodded, "Very thoughtful of you, Lieutenant." She then turned to face the camera resting on a tripod near her seat.

On a nearby console, Admiral Moebius's face appeared, showing Jessica what everyone else in the fleet was seeing. A middle-aged woman with mid-length brown hair in a Fleet-blue jumpsuit and four stars on her collar.

"To the officers and enlisted personnel of Taskforce Red, my fellow spacers, this is Admiral Julia Moebius. I am addressing you today not to inspire you or dishonestly state how victory is certain when it is not.

"I'm here to tell you what the stakes are. Our victory here will not end the war. Losing it will. If we don't defeat the Ascendency fleet marauding Triumph and secure the fuel reserves of 61 Virginis, the 1st Fleet around Sol will run out of fuel and the Ascendency forces around Jupiter will roll over them to take Earth and the habitats of the inner solar system.

"After that, the Earth Federation will no longer be able to continue the war. We will have lost too many ships, too much of our fuel infrastructure, and too much industrial power to continue.

"On Federal Station, in the locked drawer inside the President's desk, is a letter that is only to be read if we fail here. In that letter is the unconditional surrender of the Earth Federation to the Ascendency. That is what's riding on our mission. Those are the stakes. We are here, far from our homes, fighting to save the capital system of our oldest enemy in order to protect our people and preserve the Earth Federation.

"But we're fighting for more than just the preservation of a political institution. We're fighting to protect the right of all humans, everywhere, to travel through space. The Ascendency wants to take that from us. They want to be the ultimate authority over who gets to reach the stars. To that, I have one thing to say. Over my dead body.

"We're still days out from engaging the enemy. Spend that time getting your affairs in order and preparing yourselves for battle. I do not expect the impossible, but I do expect excellence from everyone wearing the uniform.

"Admiral Mobius, out."

❧

The Cendy fleet broke orbit and entered into a pyramidal battle formation, with Fusiliers concentrated in the front and Katyushas spread out across the rear. Squadrons of Outriders screened ahead of the fleet in a loose wall of strikecraft.

Taskforce Red was divided into a long train of discrete formations, one following behind the other. The leading formation centered on *Independence*. Admiral Moebius had placed the flagship well ahead of the main formation of battleships. Surrounding her were over half of the destroyer and cruiser squadrons of Taskforce Red. The destroyers spread themselves out in a loose hemisphere ahead of *Independence*, while the cruisers formed a vertical halo around and behind the battlecarrier.

Behind *Independence*, the nine battleships formed into a vertical diamond formation, with a Saturn-class battleship at each point while lighter Jupiter-class vessels filled in the gaps between them.

Another formation of destroyers loitered around the space between

Independence and the battleships, an additional layer of defensive firepower the Cendies would have to penetrate in order to hit the battleships.

Further behind them were Taskforce Red's ten carriers and their cruiser escort formed into a well-spaced line.

Finally, Lightning squadrons formed a shield between Taskforce Red and the Cendy fleet.

Any outside observer in 61 Virginis with a half-decent scope would see the vast collections of deadly hardware arrayed against each other, waiting for the moment to clash. What no one could see, other than Jessica from behind her console in the Flag bridge, was a collection of malignant software at her disposal to frustrate Cendy attempts to bring harm to the ships and crews of Taskforce Red.

Jessica had firsthand knowledge of just how effective *Independence*'s electronic warfare systems were. *Independence* was a massive starship, with proportionality massive amounts of armor and firepower. She also had a disproportionately large powerplant that could feed not only the weapons and long-burn drives, but her vast arsenal of dazzle lasers and jammer arrays.

She had used those very jammer arrays to hold off dozens of Cendy warships sent to pursue *Independence* after the battlecarrier had launched from its hidden dock inside Amalthea.

This time *Independence* had a fleet backing her up, and Jessica's fingers tingled in anticipation at unleashing the battlecarrier's power against the Cendies once again.

"Lieutenant Sinclair, how are things looking from the flag bridge?" Commander Veracruz asked, the head of *Independence*'s Electronic Warfare section.

"I have a clear view of everything, Commander," Jessica said. "Looks like your people know what they're doing."

"I'm glad my people are performing to your satisfaction, Lieutenant," Commander Veracruz said. "We're about to start blasting the Cendies with focused jamming. I could use your help picking targets."

Jessica focused her display on the Cendy fleet, narrowing her focus onto the arsenal ships forming the base of the enemy battle-pyramid. "The Katyushas should be the focus of *Independence*'s jammers, Commander.

With all the sensors they need to guide their missiles, we'll get the most value out of our energy budget."

"Understood. We'll start blasting them one at a time," Commander Veracruz said. "I'll give you control of jammer array 3. Just highlight a target on your screen and my crews will do the rest."

"Thank you, Commander," Jessica said.

Independence's emissions increased as they reached half a light-minute from the Cendy fleet. A tight cone of disruptive energy reached out from the battlecarrier towards the massed Cendy starships.

Commander Veracruz had picked a Katusha at the upper-right rear corner of the wedge formation to blind with his jammers.

Jessica focused a long-range scope on the ship and read the emissions coming from it as the time to impact reached zero.

A minute after *Independence* started beaming disruptive photons at the Katusha, Jessica saw the ship sparkle with tiny visible light flashes. A quick analysis from the sensor AI told her what the flashes were all about. The Katyusha must have had all her passive sensors dialed to full sensitivity as she prepared to fire her missiles, and the sudden blast of electromagnetic radiation from *Independence* caused them to overload and burn out.

Without firing a shot, Commander Veracruz had landed the first strike, by doing what was the space-combat equivalent to throwing sand in the enemy's eyes.

Commander Veracruz immediately redirected *Independence*'s sensor AI to lower the sensitivity of the battlecarrier's sensor arrays, going so far as to shut down several receivers. This blunted the Cendy electronic counterattack as over a hundred Katushas focused their own powerful jammer arrays against *Independence*.

The Cendy fleet fuzzed-out on *Independence*'s sensors, but there were no devastating overloads like what had happened on the first Katyusha.

And while *Independence*'s passive sensors were dialed down to minimum, the active jammers and dazzle lasers continued to work. The next Katyusha to fall under the glare of *Independence*'s jammer arrays didn't start sparking like her sister. Instead, its own electronic assault halted. Blinded by *Independence*'s weaponized light show, it could no longer keep its jammer arrays focused on the battlecarrier.

Following *Independence*'s lead, the cruisers and battleships powered up their own jammers and formations of Conqueror bombers, equipped not with torpedoes but with large jamming pods, added their voices to the vicious chorus.

For several minutes, the Battle of Triumph was fought just with disruptive light as Taskforce Red closed the range. Then the Katushas launched their torpedoes. It was a full volley. Seemingly every tube along the sides of each arsenal ship erupted with heavy missiles.

And every minute, those tubes fired again, and again, and again, until Jessica was certain that the Cendies had launched their entire torpedo stockpile.

The Cendies understood the stakes just as well as Jessica did. If they won this battle, victory over both Earth Fed and the League was theirs. There was no point in holding back.

Though fired in separate volleys, the Cendies directed their torpedoes to gather into a concentrated tidal wave of warheads.

Jessica felt a flutter of anxiety quiver in her artificial stomach. The vast number of torpedoes burning towards her could wipe out all of Taskforce Red even if a fraction of them got through.

She didn't waste her time trying to disrupt the torpedoes just after they launched. In their cruising phase, the torpedoes' seeker heads would be dormant and immune to jamming. Instead, Jessica focused her attention on the Katyushas guiding them.

First, she had to separate the real contacts from the fraudulent ones. Back at Jupiter, the Cendies had created phantom ships for her to waste her efforts trying to jam.

Sure enough, several Katushas were false contacts, though not complete ghost ships. It seemed the Cendies had taken a page out of the Federal Space Forces' playbook and started disguising Fusiliers as Katyushas.

The Fusiliers had similar emissions since they shared common drives and hull layouts. But they were different enough that once Jessica told the sensor AI what to look for, it quickly cleared the false contacts away.

"Commander, I've isolated the real Katushas from the false ones," Jessica said.

"I see it. Good work, Lieutenant. I'm directing jammers against them now," Commander Veracruz replied.

The concentrated wave of torpedoes started to lose cohesion as they lost guidance from their launch platforms. Where Jessica had used *Independence*'s systems to subtly misdirect the Cendy torpedoes, Commander Veracruz used brute force.

Coordinating with the other ships, they concentrated on a few Katyushas at a time and blasted them with every kilowatt they could spare.

Gradually, the torpedoes spread apart as several Katyushas were forced to shut down their sensors to avoid being blinded. The remaining arsenal ships lacked the reserve bandwidth to guide the hundreds of suddenly orphaned torpedoes.

"Torpedoes are going active!" Commander Veracruz said.

Almost as one, the torpedo icons changed course. Half the torpedoes locked onto random targets, picking them in the absence of guidance from their launch ships.

The rest locked onto *Independence*, and the already concentrated formation of torpedo icons converged on the battlecarrier.

"Oh blimey, this is rather familiar," Jessica said under her breath. She was finding herself aboard ships targeted by masses of torpedoes more often than she cared. The fact that the number of torpedoes flying her way always seemed to escalate did nothing to make her feel better about it.

"Start spoofing torps along the perimeter. Let the fighter screen deal with the center mass," Commander Veracruz ordered.

Multiple beams on the tactical screen radiated from *Independence*, tight cones of malignant electromagnetic emissions reaching outward to burn out seeker heads.

Torpedoes along the edges of the swarm started falling out of formation, some slightly drifting off course, others spinning out of control as *Independence*'s jammers fried their electronic brains.

The center mass of icons continued towards *Independence*—hundreds of warheads all capable of individually crippling the battlecarrier.

The Lightnings moved to intercept, placing themselves directly between the incoming torpedoes and the battlecarrier. They didn't fire their Javelin interceptors as they entered range. Instead, they maintained their position, each fighter evenly spaced apart in their formation.

When the torpedoes were just about to pass the Lightnings, each fighter erupted with dozens of the Stiletto interceptors. Their small short-burn drives only had enough fuel for a few seconds of thrust, but it was more than enough for them to position themselves directly in the path of the incoming torpedoes.

The torpedoes attempted to evade the Stilettoes, but the lumbering torpedoes couldn't outmaneuver the tiny interceptors.

The heart of the Cendy torpedo volley flashed and disappeared, leaving a scattered ring of torpedoes and a few lucky survivors that got through the fighter screen to proceed.

Destroyers started launching Javelin interceptors, joined soon by *Independence*'s own as the remaining torpedoes closed the range.

Torpedo icons winked out of existence as interceptor icons merged with them. The torpedoes thinned out as they approached. Just forty got past the destroyers.

Interceptors from *Independence* and the cruiser escorts continued to savage the Cendy torpedoes, forty became twenty, then a dozen. Then the point defense guns opened fire.

Hundreds of point defense guns fired tens of thousands of rounds a second, throwing up a storm of hot and fast metal into the path of the remaining torpedoes.

The Cendy torpedoes winked out of existence as they tried to push through the storm in little flashes of light on the tactical display that belied the violence of the impacts.

In all the excitement, Jessica had lost track of the torpedoes that weren't homing in on *Independence*.

Just as the last torpedo locked onto *Independence* died in a hail of converging point defense fire, explosions lit up space around the battle-carrier. The icons of three cruisers turned gray, indicating they were no longer combat effective and had started falling out of formation. Two unfortunate destroyers simply disappeared, vaporized by sprays of nuclear fire unleashed by detonating Cendy torpedoes.

Though Taskforce Red had made the first strike, the Cendies had drawn first blood.

"Cruisers Winnipeg, Shanghai, and Pretoria are reporting extensive damage and are unable to maintain formation," announced a junior officer on the flag bridge.

"Advise *Winnipeg*, *Shanghai*, and *Pretoria* to abandon ship. We cannot commit other vessels to protect them," Admiral Moebius said.

Moments later, icons spawned from the cruisers as a flurry of escape pods and a few shuttles launched.

"Shall I direct search and rescue craft to pick up the survivors, Admiral?" Vice Marshal Singh asked.

"No. We'll recover them after the battle," Admiral Moebius said.

The cruisers and their escape pods fell out of formation, being left alone in space to fend for themselves. Jessica wondered if there would be anyone to rescue them when the battle was over.

She turned her attention back to the Cendy fleet. They had yet to bring out their most dangerous weapons, the spinal-mounted guns of the Fusiliers.

While the Katyushas had engaged Taskforce Red with torpedoes and jammers, the Fusiliers had maintained their tight formations, their emissions running high as they kept the capacitors of their spinal guns charged and ready for firing.

Jessica let out a calming breath as she felt a shudder run through her body. The first volley would be the most devastating. Two hundred Kinetic Kill Vehicles, most, if not all, likely to be targeted on *Independence*, were about to be fired while Taskforce Red was still too far away to reply with their own guns.

Then new contacts appeared on the screen. The drive plumes of dozens of strikecraft. Jessica leaned forward towards her screen, forgetting her own peril for the moment.

It looked like someone on Triumph had noticed that the League's attention was diverted away from them and was taking the chance to stab the Cendy fleet in the back.

CHAPTER 41

After the last weapons were mounted and all the pre-flight checks were completed, Chief Rabin and the League ground crew scrambled away to the waiting assault shuttles and tilt-rotors. The chief turned to give Mason a salute. Mason returned the salute from the top of his open cockpit, then descended into the cockpit and closed the opaque canopy.

"Osiris Leader is powered up and ready to go," Mason said.

"We copy, Osiris Leader. Auto tractors on their way. We're bugging out now. Good luck out there."

"Likewise, ATC," Mason said.

The tractors rolled up and attached themselves to the front wheels of his Lightning, others similarly attaching themselves to the other ten active Lightnings in Osiris Squadron.

Mason spent the ride down the tunnel to one of the remaining auxiliary vertiports running diagnostics, not because he didn't trust Chief Rabin's work, but to distract himself from the coming fight. Over and over again, everything came up green and in the clear.

The tractors rolled the Lightnings onto the hidden tarmac, and then rolled to park in a neat line off to the side, not returning to the tunnel like before. There was no point. There wouldn't be a Citadel 44 to return to after much longer.

"All fighters prepare for takeoff," Mason said. With the ATC crews evacuating, there was no one to ask for takeoff clearance.

After all his pilots gave their affirmatives, Mason opened the throttle and lifted his Lightning off the ground.

He glanced down the open tunnel, feeling a strange sense of nostalgia. Citadel 44 had been his home since he came to Triumph. And he was leaving it for the last time.

As Mason turned and transitioned to level flight, the other Lightnings lifted off. Further away, Asps streamed from the other bases, forming up as they climbed towards the overcast sky concealing their takeoff from the Cendy fleet above. Mason doubted the Cendy fleet was paying that much attention to what was happening on Triumph now. Not when they had a Federal fleet bearing down on them.

As they climbed, something detonated inside Citadel 44, and the entire mountain collapsed in on itself before disappearing behind an expanding cloud of dust.

"No going back," Mason said.

Mason's squadron datalink merged with that of the League fighters. And those further merged with other League Asp squadrons that ascended to orbit. Over a hundred strikecraft across the planet climbed to orbit.

The Cendy fleet hung over the horizon in a dense formation, a cloud of deadly starships. Beyond them burned the collective long-burn drives of the warships of Taskforce Red. *Independence* positioned well ahead of the rest of the fleet, all but daring the Cendies to focus their fire on her. Fighters, destroyers, and cruisers formed layers of defense between the battlecarrier and the two hundred spinal-mounted guns of the Cendy Fusiliers.

Mason cut the drives as he entered low orbit. As the other fighters of Osiris Squadron formed up around him, Mason opened a communications channel with his League counterpart.

"Osiris Leader, Centurion Leader. We're formed up in orbit and about to begin our approach burn for the enemy fleet," Commander Serova said.

"Copy that, Centurion Leader. Osiris Squadron is ready for action," Mason said.

"I hope you are, Osiris Leader," Commander Serova said. "We'll have a hard time getting past those Katyushas if you can't disable some of their interceptor batteries."

"We'll deal with the Katyushas, Centurion Leader," Mason said. "Just keep their Outriders off our backs."

"That we can do, Osiris Leader. Initiating departure burn in ten seconds."

Mason nodded. As soon as the countdown finished, he activated his drives at the same time as the rest of the fighters orbiting over Triumph did, 10gs instantly crushing him into his seat. But he was barely aware of the sensation, his attention focused on what was going on outside of his fighter.

Over a hundred drive plumes lit up in low orbit over Triumph. The exhaust reacted with the trace atmosphere in low orbit, creating faint blue trails behind each fighter as it ascended towards the Cendy fleet a light-second from the planet.

It was clear that the Ascendency saw Taskforce Red as a greater threat than the partially conquered Triumph. Even as over a hundred strikecraft lifted off from the planet on an attack trajectory, the Cendy fighter screen remained positioned in front of the Cendy fleet, screening against the approaching Federal fleet.

The Cendies seemed confident that the Katyushas, with their immense interceptor armaments, would be more than adequate for deflecting any opportunistic attacks launched from Triumph.

And they might have been right, if Osiris Squadron wasn't among the forces rising from Triumph.

The Cendy fleet was accelerating, maintaining 1g of acceleration on a tangential course in the direction of Taskforce Red, moving in a relatively straight line. It would not be hard for Mason's combat AI to calculate a firing solution for the Raidens.

It would take about a minute for the Raiden's penetrator rounds to reach their targets from maximum effective range. Enough time for Mason to empty the Raiden before the first penetrator struck.

<Osiris Leader,> called Commander Serova, <engage the Katyushas at the top-right corner of the enemy formation. If you can disable their interceptors, that should provide a gap for the torpedo-armed Asps to punch through.>

<Understood, Centurion Leader. Moving into firing range,> Mason responded.

<Good luck, Osiris Leader.>

The priority targets appeared on Masson's screen. A vertical column of Katyushas that formed the top-left corner of the Cendy formation.

Mason summoned a detailed schematic of the Cendy arsenal ships, and marked the locations were the interceptor batteries were located.

Interceptor launchers were concentrated into clusters around the rear of the ship, just forward of the drives, forming a belt of tightly packed missile tubes around the ship's outer hull.

<Shutdown, I have a plan,> Mason said.

<Those can be dangerous in the wrong hands, Hauler. Please share,> Zin said.

<We'll attack directly from behind so our rounds will cut through as many interceptor tubes as possible,> Mason said. <With luck, that can cause a chain reaction as propellant cooks off inside the tubes.>

<That's going to rely on a lot of precision, sir. Those Katushas might not be able to evade our shots, but they can certainly spoil our firing solutions enough to keep our penetrators from hitting their interceptor batteries.>

<I have a solution for that. We're going to start jamming the Cendies with everything we have. With a little luck, they'll think we're just trying to blind them before the Asps enter range and not notice the two of us shooting at them.>

<Right. Seems as good an idea as any. I'll follow your lead.>

Mason passed the orders along for his pilots to start priming their jammers.

He then flipped over his fighter and burned retrograde until he just about matched the speed of the Cendy fleet. Just outside of effective interceptor range, he turned around and cruised at 1g. His sensor AI was hard at work blasting the Cendy Katyushas with jammers and dazzle lasers, though the wattage his fighter could generate would do little more than add a bit of static to the Cendy sensors.

From the rear, where the Cendy sensors were their weakest due to having to see around the exhaust plumes of the engines, that would be enough to conceal the shots he was about to take. Or so he hoped.

Mason deployed his Raiden cannon and the massive gun descended from the weapons bay, extending to its full length as he powered up the capacitors.

Zin armed hers as well, and Mason saw on the tactical display her combat AI had firing solutions for all her targets. Each shot aimed at the rear of the ship was aligned almost parallel to the hull to hit the maximum number of interceptor tubes. The interceptors were primed and ready for launch, in their most active state as the Katyushas waited to wipe out the incoming strikecraft attack.

<Shutdown, fire on my command,> Mason said.

<Acknowledged, Hauler,> Zin responded.

<Fire!>

Mason squeezed the trigger, and his Lightning lurched under him as it sent a tungsten-cored penetrator towards the Cendies.

Maneuvering thrusters pulsed as the combat AI adjusted the fighter's attitude to lay on the next arsenal ship in the firing queue and fired as soon as the weapon finished charging.

After less than a minute, ten penetrators were flying through the abyss towards the Cendy Katyushas, who were making no efforts to evade.

Mason brought up the magnified image of the first Cendy Katyusha, largely concealed by the glow of its drive exhaust, and held his breath.

He saw a flash on the side of the ship, and a second later, a plume of white-hot gas spewed out of the hull.

Then the side of the ship blew out, and a chain of explosions circled around the starship. The drives winked out as the arsenal ship fell out of formation.

More explosions followed at five-second intervals as the other penetrators struck their targets.

The entire formation started to evade, but it was too late to save the targeted vessels. The penetrators punched through the thin rear armor of the ships, turning into jets of metallic plasma that cut through missile tubes, igniting propellant as they went.

None of the Katyushas were destroyed outright by the explosions, but they were crippled and rendered combat ineffective, opening a gap in the Cendy rear guard's missile coverage.

The Asp flared their drives to exploit the gap before the Cendies could close it.

<All fighters go full burn and follow the Asps in,> Mason said before pushing the throttle forward, multiplying the gs weighing down on him.

A hundred Asps flew past the Katyushas without resistance, the bulk of the undamaged ones still evading from the surprise attack that had crippled ten of their fellows.

The Fusiliers saw the danger and started to evade, turning away from Taskforce Red to bring their armored prows to bear against the League's torpedo attack.

Asps started launching short-burn torpedoes in a single coordinated volley, throwing almost five hundred at the Cendy fleet.

Point defense fire erupted all around the Cendy fleet, filling the space around with streams of deadly projectiles while Outriders launched interceptors.

Most of the torpedoes disappeared in flashes of light as interceptors and point defenses took their toll. A few did get through, though, getting close enough to detonate their directional warheads.

Mason's sensors lost track of the Cendy fleet, blinded by multiple nuclear detonations. When the glow faded, several Fusiliers were falling out of formation, some crippled, others smashed to pieces.

Six Fusiliers had been destroyed outright, with twice as many damaged. But the casualties weren't the main source of damage. It was the loss of cohesion just as Taskforce Red entered range of their spinal guns.

It was then that Mason saw several squadrons of Outriders had broken off to engage the Asps and Lightnings, three times as many Cendy fighters as there were League and Federal. It wasn't the smartest move. Without torpedoes, the Asps and Lightnings from Triumph were only a limited threat to the Cendy starships.

But the Cendies seemed to be keen on destroying them anyway.

<All fighters follow my vector,> Commander Serova ordered, turning her fighter away. <We'll draw away those fighters as far as we can before they can engage us. Keep them from being able to support their starships.>

<Osiris Squadron is taking up the rear guard, Centurion Leader,> Mason said. <Our Stilettoes can shield your fighters from the Outriders' interceptors.>

<Understood, Osiris Leader,> Commander Serova said.

Following Mason's orders, Osiris Squadron split into two-ship elements to cover the retreating Asps as the Outriders moved to engage. The Outriders did not have the residual velocity of an approach burn to overcome and were accelerating harder than the Asps and Lightnings. There was no question of escape. Just a question of time and distance.

<Set Stilettoes to full-auto with self-defense as priority. We're not going to do anyone any good by sacrificing ourselves,> Mason said.

The Cendy fighters launched their interceptors in a massed volley as soon as they entered range.

Mason replied by firing his four interceptors over-the-shoulder. The interceptors ejected from the inner-wing pylons, flipped around, and ignited their drives to accelerate in the direction of the enemy.

All the other fighters around him did the same, sending out a powerful counter volley of guided munitions against the Cendies. It was smaller than the Cendy volley, but still a lot to face off against.

And at least for Osiris Squadron, all the large interceptors they fired were targeted at enemy fighters. The Stilettoes gave them that option.

Mason had several Cendy interceptors bearing down on him and his wingmate.

<Going defensive!> Mason called as he turned and redlined his drive, pushing close to 20gs as his sensor AI worked to jam and dazzle as many interceptors as possible while the combat AI picked targets for the Stilettoes.

A couple of seconds before impact, Stilettoes rippled-fired from their pods on the outer-wing pylons, and all the interceptors coming Mason's way disappeared in flashes of kinetic impact. His Stiletto pod ripple-fired two more times before emptying itself, going after interceptors directed at his wingmates and then at interceptors trying to fly past him to engage the Asps.

Blunted by Osiris Squadron's Stilettos, the Cendy interceptor volley only managed to hit Asps.

Over fifty Outriders dropped off the tactical display when the retaliatory interceptors hit. A good trade, but one that still left the Asps and Lightnings outnumbered by close to two to one.

<Jettison all expended pods and weapons, including the Raidens, Shutdown. We're going to be in for a hell of a gunfight,> Mason said. He jettisoned the empty Stiletto pods from his wings, letting them fall behind him as he opened the weapons bay to do the same with his Raiden cannon.

If they survived the battle, maybe they could be recovered later.

<All fighters arm guns and turn to engage!> Commander Serova ordered.

Mason's cannon was already armed as he flipped his fighter over and redlined his drives.

The Outriders were burning straight for them, the estimated velocity at merger at several kilometers a second.

Mason's combat AI gave him a list of targets, and he selected the one with the highest threat rating to shoot first. He then started jerking the stick, randomizing his movements to throw off the firing solution of the Cendy fighters. It wasn't enough to throw off the aim of his combat AI. It would only need a fraction of a second of control to lay the gun on his target and fire.

Mason squeezed the trigger on his stick, giving his combat AI control authority to aim and fire the gun. His Lightning lurched under the pulses of the maneuvering thrusters and spat out half-second burs.

An Outrider flashed and broke apart from multiple impacts. Near misses streaked past Mason's Lightning, while several friendlies flashed and died around him, including two of his own Lightnings.

Mason the loss yet more of his pilots of added a little extra pressure on top of the crushing acceleration. He flipped his fighter over, maintaining full thrust to re-attack.

The Outriders were down to half their original number, but it was still a hefty sum to be jousting with.

Mason turned sideways to the Cendies and maintained his 20g acceleration, moving himself out of direct line of fire with the Cendies. Keeping the narrowest profile of his fighter facing towards the enemy, he jinked and juked with random pulses of his maneuvering thrusters. Then at the last moment, he snapped around and fired, catching an Outrider in the fuselage, shattering the fighter into a cloud of dust and metal shards.

The jousting turned into a confused furball as the two groups of fighters matched velocities. Fighters paired off into deadly dances, spinning around each other like co-orbiting planets, firing away with their guns.

As Mason did his best to survive the dogfight, a massive electromagnetic spike signaled the firing of the main guns of a starship. But it didn't come from the Cendy battlecruisers. *Independence* had closed the range and opened fire.

CHAPTER 42

Jessica's seat rumbled from the immense recoil of eight terajoule-class kinetics firing at once.

Eight KKVs flew true under *Independence*'s guidance. The Cendies responded with a blistering barrage of dazzle lasers and ECM to break the lock, but *Independence*'s powerful sensors burned through the electromagnetic haze.

As the KKVs reached the midpoint of their flight, the first of the Cendies opened fire. With their formation disrupted by the strikecraft attack from Triumph, their firing was staggered rather than simultaneous, sending a stream of KKVs *Independence*'s way.

Jessica immediately got to work using her portion of the battlecarrier's ECM system to disrupt the lock of at least a few of the inbound KKVs.

She picked up the guidance signals the Cendies were transmitting to their KKVs. Already, other members of *Independence*'s electronic warfare team were sending powerful bursts of electromagnetic radiation to overwhelm and knock out the guidance antennae. But every time they knocked out one Cendy guidance system, another Fusilier took over, keeping the KKVs flying true.

Jessica decided on a different approach, collecting the data from the various guidance emissions from the Cendy ships.

Independence rumbled again with another volley from her main guns, thirty seconds after the first.

The Cendy signals were encrypted, of course, but she wasn't trying to decode them. She fed the signals into the sensor AI, ordering it to compare them to the return signals from Cendy KKVs. What Jessica came up with would be, at least in theory, a good copy of the KKV guidance signal.

Independence let off a third volley as soon as she was ready to begin her attack. The first volley of Cendy KKVs were just about to enter interceptor range.

Jessica started breaming false KKV signals back to the Cendies.

"Yes!" Jessica said as a few of the Fusiliers took the bait, locking onto her ghost KKVs to guide them, abandoning the real ones. Twenty-four Cendy KKVs stopped firing their maneuvering thrusters to track *Independence*, their course straightening out, their computed trajectories taking them out of the system without hitting anything along the way.

The rest continued to fly true, and the Lightnings started launching interceptors.

KKVs flashed and disappeared into clouds of hypervelocity metal vapor, far enough away that the deadly clouds would disperse enough to cease being a threat to *Independence*.

About half the remaining KKVs blew through the fighter screen, only to run into a wall of interceptors thrown up by the destroyers.

Independence and her cruiser escorts started launching their own interceptors as soon as the first wave of Cendy KKVs flew past the destroyers, turning more and more of them into plasma.

Six survived long enough to enter entered point defense range.

Independence's forward point defense guns opened fire, joined by those of the cruisers, hosing incoming KKVs with multiple streams of hypervelocity death.

In quick succession, the KKVs vaporized, their debris continuing forward from their own momentum.

A metallic bang echoed through *Independence*'s hull as dense clouds of metallic vapor struck the inclined frontal armor of the starship's prow. Multiple minor damage alerts appeared. Sensors and PD turrets were knocked out of action, but the main armor had not been breached. Which was good. A solid KKV could punch through the armor and travel the length of the battlecarrier before exiting through the engine bells.

Lightnings clashed with Outriders as the fighter screens ranging ahead of the two belligerent fleets merged. Exhaust trails of interceptors and the flashes of hypervelocity impacts filled the shrinking volume of space between the fleets.

Independence's KKVs penetrated through the Cendy occupied fighter screen, only to venture into a torrential hail of interceptors fired from the Katyushas. None of the KKVs in the first volley made it through, nor did the second, nor the third.

But *Independence* continued to drive straight towards the center of the Cendy formation, the layers of defenses absorbing the fire from the Fusiliers.

More hits registered against the hull. Both light glancing blows and direct hits by the vaporized remains of KKVs that did not quite make it all the way through to *Independence*'s point defense guns.

Minor damage piled up, sensors and point defenses getting knocked out with every hit, systems deeper in the hull suffering from the repeated shocks of impact. But the armor itself held together, and as the Cendies continued to pour fire into Taskforce Red's shield of interceptors and point defense guns, the sword of Taskforce Red's battleships came into reach.

Ten Federal battleships opened fire at the same time as soon as they entered effective range of their KKVs, launching a hundred of them in the first volley. They fired two more volleys before the first entered point defense range of the Cendy fleet.

By then, Taskforce Red's Lightning squadrons had scattered the Cendy fighter screen, and the massed interceptors of the Katyushas were split between dealing with the KKVs and Conqueror bombers launching torpedo at in coordination with the battleships.

Only four KKVs in the first volley hit, striking three separate Fusiliers. The two that took one hit apiece went dark as their engines failed. The one that took two hits broke in half.

As the range closed, the superior rate of fire and heavy armor of the Federal battleships started to show their advantage. Admiral Moebius' strategy, combined with the well-timed attack by strikecraft from Triumph, had succeeded in robbing the Fusiliers of their range advantage.

The range continued to close; cruisers opened fire with their main guns, adding their lighter, faster firing guns to the mix, multiplying the number of KKVs the Cendies had to fend off.

Then they got into range of the primary guns of the destroyers and the secondaries of *Independence* and the other heavy starships.

A rain of small, unguided projectiles from hundreds of rapid-fire gun barrels tore into the Cendy starships. Ships that weren't taken out by the knockout blow of the capital-class kinetics were subjected to a death of a thousand cuts as they faced hundreds of small impacts, far more than their point defenses could handle.

Cruisers and destroyers blew apart as they took close-range hits from Cendy Fusiliers.

The tactical screen registered a hit on FSFV *Tau Ceti*, and the battleship went dark and started drifting out of formation.

"What is *Tau Ceti*'s status?" Admiral Moebius asked.

"She's not responding to hails, sir. FSFV *Titan* reports that a Cendy KKV struck solid against *Tau Ceti*'s frontal armor and exited through the drive section."

"Sortie rescue shuttles to the wreck when it's safe to do so," Admiral Moebius said.

Independence flew through the Cendy fleet at several kilometers per second, firing in all directions, savaging the Cendy ships around her.

And then she was on the other side, leaving a trail of dead enemy starships behind her.

The rest of Taskforce Red followed behind her, passing through the Cendy fleet, guns blazing.

The Cendies continued to fire their weapons even as they took hits to their vulnerable flanks, focusing their fire on the precious battleships.

FSFV *Deimos* took a hit that punched diagonally through her drive section, snuffing out her drives before she drifted through the enemy fleet, still firing on the Cendy starships.

FSFV *Neptune* took a direct hit to her frontal armor, and the battleship instantly went gray on the tactical display.

"What's the status of *Neptune*?" Admiral Moebius asked.

"Whatever hit her broke her in half, sir. I'm detecting escape-pod launches. Looks like her crew are abandoning ship."

"Sortie destroyers to pick them up. What's the status of *Deimos*?" Admiral Moebius asked.

"Heavy damage, main drive is offline. Captain Henke reports she has attitude control and is working on restoring at least one of the long-burn drives."

"What's her trajectory into the system?"

"She'll fly by Triumph at 30 thousand klicks and proceed into the inner system on a parabolic trajectory, sir.'

"Something for the fleet tenders to catch up with, then. What are the Cendies up to?"

"We're detecting launches from crippled ships consistent with escape pods. The rest of the fleet is continuing to accelerate away from us, sir. It looks like they might be quitting the system. Should we send ships to pursue?"

"Negative, we've lost enough ships already. Recall all strikecraft for rearmament and tell the tankers their path into the inner system is clear. The rest of the fleet is to enter the orbit of Triumph and prepare to provide orbital fire support."

CHAPTER 43

Just like that, it was over.

The remaining Outriders turned to rejoin the battered Cendy fleet, and Mason's squadron was in no condition to chase them. Two Lightnings on his tactical display were bright red. Destroyed. Osiris Squadron was down to seven strikecraft.

"Flight leads, report," Mason said.

"Shutdown here, Hauler," Zin said. "Stacker's fighter got hit. Bottles and I are checking to see if they're still alive."

"Hardball reporting. Turntable is gone."

A nauseous feeling crept into Mason's stomach that antiemetics could do nothing about.

"All fighters, rendezvous with Shutdown's flight," Mason said.

"Centurion Leader to Osiris Leader, report," Commander Serova asked.

"I'm down two ships and out of missiles," Mason said. "How about you?"

"Lost four Asps from my two squadrons," Serova said. "No interceptors left. Doesn't look like we'll be needing them."

"No, it doesn't look like it, Centurion Leader," Mason said.

Already, Taskforce Red's fighters were returning to their carriers, no doubt to rearm with air-to-ground munitions while the starships burned tail-first towards Triumph, slowing to orbital velocity.

"Shutdown here, Stacker is dead," Zin said.

"Roger that, Shutdown," Mason said. "Standby for orders." Whatever those might be.

"Osiris Leader, this is Vice Marshal Singh, strikecraft commander for Taskforce Red. Report your status."

"This is Osiris Leader, sir. My squadron is down to eight pilots and seven active strikecraft," Mason said.

"Understood, Osiris Leader. Once *Amazon* enters orbit, you're to dock with her and await further orders."

"Roger that, sir. Please note that one of my pilots and a couple of tech crew are still groundside on Triumph."

"I'll see about recovering your people, Osiris Leader," Vice Marshal Singh said. "And before I forget, Admiral Moebius sends her compliments. You did good work today."

"Thank you, sir," Mason said. The admiral's gratitude did nothing to lighten the burden of eight pilots dying under his command.

Amazon was with the carriers in the rearmost formation, flying tail-first as she slowed to enter orbit over Triumph. She was about an hour out from inserting herself into orbit.

"All fighters, form on me. We'll take position near *Amazon*'s expected arrival point," Mason said.

"Nice to land somewhere familiar for once," Hardball said.

"Osiris Leader to Centurion Leader, we'll be joining up with Taskforce Red. Looks like this will be goodbye, for now," Mason said.

"Understood, Osiris Leader," Commander Serova said. "It was a privilege flying with you. I hope it will not be too long before we meet again."

"Likewise, Centurion Leader," Mason said. "Likewise."

Serova's Asps lit their drives and started burning back towards Triumph.

"All ships in the vicinity, this is Admiral Moebius. Taskforce Red will begin an orbital strike against Cendy ground targets momentarily. All ships are advised to clear the firing lanes between Taskforce Red and Triumph. Admiral Moebius, out."

"You heard the lady, time to move," Mason said.

"Roger that, Hauler," Zin said.

Mason ignited his drives and pushed his Lightning at 1g to high Triumph orbit.

Still burning retrograde, flying backwards relative to Triumph, *Independence* and the surviving battleships of Taskforce Red all traversed their main gun turrets over the starboard sides, aiming them "over the shoulder" at Triumph.

In a rippling volley of dozens of terajoule-class guns, Taskforce Red's battle line opened fire, flinging KKVs towards the planet.

The KKVs gradually diverged as they approached the planet, vectoring on the Cendy landing sites. The KKVs cut white hot lines through Triumph's atmosphere as they descended towards their targets. Defenses around the landing site erupted with defensive fire as masses of kinetics and guided missiles rose to attempt to stop the KKVs.

Those defenses, which proved impenetrable to air attacks by the League, were helpless against the kinetic strike launched by Taskforce Red.

All the KKVs struck ground within a second of each other, and impact flashes lit up Stoneland. Expanding thermal plumes rose from craters where the Cendy landing sites and their Turtleback landing ships used to be, leaving the Cendy armies in the field cut off from reinforcements.

CHAPTER 44

Amazon opened her hangar bay doors to welcome Osiris Squadron's return as soon as she slotted into orbit.

"Osiris Leader, your fighters are cleared to dock with assigned hangar bays," *Amazon*'s space traffic controller said.

"Roger that, *Amazon*," Mason said. "Osiris Squadron, dock in reverse sequence. That means your flight docks first, Hardball."

"Understood, Hauler. See you aboard," Sabal said. She and her wingmate pulsed their maneuvering thrusters to drift towards *Amazon*.

Zin's flight fired their maneuvering thrusters a minute later, and Mason's flight followed hers in turn.

As his half-strength squadron of eight fighters drifted towards *Amazon*, the rest of Taskforce Red took position in multiple orbits over Triumph.

The other capital ships of Taskforce Red, the carriers, surviving battleships, and *Independence*, formed a long, curving line following *Amazon*'s orbit like beads on a bracelet. Far below, Taskforce Red's cruisers were slotting into low orbit, their guns firing a steady stream of kinetic death towards Cendy armies in the field. Squadrons of Lightnings loaded with air-to-ground munitions flew below them, entering the atmosphere to provide air support for Triumph's defenders.

The siege of Triumph was over. All the violence happening below was cleanup.

The battered remains of the Cendy fleet were still burning hard for the jump limit. Where they intended to go, Mason did not know, nor did he care. He was just glad that they weren't his problem anymore.

Osiris Squadron landed one by one, leaving Mason's Lightning the last outside of *Amazon*.

He lined up with Hangar Bay 4 and folded his wings before giving his Lightning a light kick from the maneuvering thrusters. He drifted into the hangar bay until the maglocks on his landing gear activated and pulled the fighter to the docking pad. He depressurized his cockpit and ran through the shutdown cycle, spooling down both reactors while the pressure dropped to near zero.

He popped open his cockpit and found a swarm of hangar techs in orange pressure suits floating towards his fighter. They ignored Mason as he pushed himself out of the cockpit and towards the airlock. The techs seemed intent on reacquainting themselves with the fighter that had left *Amazon* without them.

Mason flew through the outer hatch and grabbed a handhold to stop himself just short of the inner hatch. The door closed, and the chamber pressurized until it matched the pressure inside. Then the inner hatch opened, and he floated into the corridor that connected all the hangar bays together.

Mason removed his helmet and breathed in the air of the old troopship. Without a battalion of sweaty Special Purpose Branch troopers or a squadron of Lightnings to maintain, the air lacked the smell of sweat, lubricant, and sealant that Mason had come to associate with *Amazon*. The ship just smelled sterile, which made it seem unfamiliar, despite the worn high-traction coating on the deck looking the same as it did when he had departed.

Zin waited outside the hardsuit storage room wearing her jumpsuit, her hardsuit already stored, Mason presumed.

"Where's everyone else?" Mason asked.

"Sent them ahead for food and rest," Zin said.

"Why are you waiting here?"

"Making sure my CO does the same. Even at the cost of delaying my own warm meal and hot shower."

"I won't hold you any longer," Mason said. He floated to his assigned alcove and locked the boots of his hardsuit into clamps on the deck. As soon as his suit was secure, he sent a command through his brainset and the entire hardsuit split open, pulling itself away from his body.

Mason pulled himself out, shivering as cool air passed through the fabric of his jumpsuit to kiss his skin underneath.

"Squadron Leader Grey, report to the bridge."

"Belts and zones, I just got here!" Mason sighed. "Thanks for waiting for me, Zin. But it looks like it'll be a little longer before I can call it a day. You go ahead to the hab ring."

"I'll make sure there's something warm waiting for you in the wardroom," Zin said.

"Thanks, Zin. I'll let you know what this is all about," Mason said. "I don't think Captain Alvarez missed me that much."

When Mason reached the bridge a few minutes later *Amazon*'s XO directed him to the captain's waiting room adjacent to it.

"Squadron Leader Grey reporting as ordered, sir," Mason said.

"I apologize for delaying you from your well-deserved rest, Squadron Leader, but I'm afraid your presence is required," Captain Alvarez said.

"Understood, sir. I assume there's a mission?" Mason asked.

"There is. We just need to wait for Colonel Shimura to get connected. She's currently overseeing the withdrawal of Federal personnel from Triumph's surface."

"Aren't the Raiders providing fire control, sir?" Mason asked.

"Controllers from Taskforce Red are already en route to relieve them, Squadron Leader. And after the kinetic strikes against the Cendy landing sights, the Cendy offensive has ground to a halt. Currently, League's Planetary Defense is containing the Cendies while our cruisers pulverize them from orbit."

"When will Colonel Shimura return to *Amazon*, sir?"

"Two hours, Squadron Leader," Captain Alvarez said. "Under normal circumstances, I'd have waited at least until Colonel Shimura was back aboard before holding a mission briefing, but Admiral Moebius wants to get the ball rolling immediately."

"Rolling on what, sir?" Mason asked.

"On capturing the Cendy mothership that Taskforce Red crippled on their way in-system," Captain Alvarez said.

"Belts and zones!" Mason exclaimed.

Captain Alvarez tilted his head to one side, like he was listening to whispers from a ghost. "Ah, Colonel Shimura's assault shuttle has dusted-off. She should be connecting with us as soon as they break atmosphere."

A few minutes later, Captain Alvarez nodded to him. "She's connected now. I'll invite you to the group call."

A notification on Mason's HUD invited him to join a group call. He accepted.

Colonel Shimura's portrait appeared in his HUD the same time as her voice echoed in his ear. "Greetings, Squadron Leader Grey, how are things aboard *Amazon*?"

"Feeling empty without you and the ground pounders, sir," Mason said. "How are Flight Lieutenant Dominic and Chief Rabin and his people?"

"Flight Lieutenant Dominic is currently asleep in the seat across the cargo hold from me, Squadron Leader," Colonel Shimura said. "He kept himself quite busy while the rest of Osiris Squadron was fighting. Chief Rabin and his techs are aboard another assault shuttle. They should dock with *Amazon* before I do."

"Good to hear they made it," Mason said. "How were the troopers' casualties?"

"Light. The Raiders have mostly been involved in providing fire control rather than frontline fighting. The raider battalion is still at ninety-five percent fighting strength. Which is good, given what Admiral Moebius has planned for us."

"Speaking of which, she just connected via tightbeam from *Independence*," Captain Alvarez said. "She's joining the call now."

Admiral Mobius' portrait appeared, the four stars on her collar clearly visible.

"Colonel Shimura, Squadron Leader Grey, you have a pile of commendations coming both your ways after the fine work did on Triumph," Admiral Moebius said. "Unfortunately, the first reward I have for your good work is yet more work."

"Nothing out of the ordinary for us, sir," Colonel Shimura said. "I understand you want us to capture the Cendy mothership that you welded into an asteroid in the local belt."

"Yes. Though I should start by saying that 30 Skeksis is not just any asteroid. It's a shard of a shattered planetary core. A big chunk of metal that the Cendy mothership appeared to be turning into Turtlebacks to support the invasion of Triumph. With it disabled but still intact, we have a unique opportunity to capture it. And it just so happens that I'm speaking with people who have the most experience boarding and capturing Cendy warships."

"Do we know why the Cendies haven't scuttled the mothership if it can't escape yet?" Colonel Shimura asked.

"The strikecraft attack on the mothership also wiped out all the escorts, so there aren't any nearby warships left to destroy the mothership," Admiral Moebius explained. "And the remains of the main Cendy fleet are making no effort to divert towards the mothership to try to destroy it."

"So, they decided whatever is on the mothership isn't worth the risk of losing more ships trying to protect," Colonel Shimura said.

"That is one potential answer, Colonel," Admiral Moebius said.

"It could also be that the potential losses the mothership could inflict on us might outweigh anything we gain from trying to capture her," Mason said.

"That is another potential answer," Admiral Moebius said. "Lieutenant Sinclair's conclusion is both, based on what our observation of the mothership since our attack seems to indicate. From what we're seeing through our probes, it appears the mothership's crew are digging in, turning the rock into a fortress that will cost us dearly to attack."

"Admiral, that sounds like it might be better for us to just pound that asteroid from a distance with our battleships," Colonel Shimura said.

"It might come to that if boarding proves to be untenable, Colonel, but right now, I want to at least make an effort to take that ship intact," Admiral Moebius said. "The potential intelligence gain from capturing a mothership cannot be overstated."

"Understood, sir," Colonel Shimura said. "What support will we have?"

"The cruiser *Burlington* and a squadron of destroyers will provide escort for *Amazon*," Admiral Moebius said. "I'm also sorting replacement pilots and Lightnings to bring Osiris Squadron back to full strength. As well, I will have an assault shuttle sent over with specialist personnel."

"What kind of specialists, sir?" Colonel Shimura asked.

"Along with a crew of engineers, Lieutenant Sinclair will be with them to provide on-site analysis," Admiral Moebius said.

Mason felt a quiver in his chest at the prospect of seeing Jessica again, but kept his face impassive.

"It will be good to work with her, again, sir," Colonel Shimura said.

"That's not all, Colonel," Admiral Moebius said. "Lieutenant Sinclair will also have… an associate with her. One Miriam Xia."

"Uh, which Miriam Xia would that be, sir?" Mason asked.

Admiral Moebius chuckled over the comm. "Exactly the one you're thinking of, Squadron Leader. It will make sense when you meet her."

⁂

Jessica's assault shuttle and the replacement Lightnings caught up with *Amazon* thirty minutes after the assault ship lit her long-burn drive to break orbit.

Mason felt like a new man standing in the hangar level under 1g of thrust gravity. He had managed to get a shower and a nap while he waited for Jessica to arrive. He even got a fresh haircut and a shave.

He heard the blasts of their landing engines and felt the deck rumble as the Lightnings and assault shuttle made powered landings inside *Amazon's* spare hangar bays.

Mason looked down at his black uniform, pulling out a crease in the middle before straightening his posture, trying not to bounce with excitement at the prospect of seeing Jessica again. He forced himself to calm down when he heard heavy footsteps approaching.

The first to come around the corner was not Jessica, but a female pilot with shockingly blue hair, lumbering down the corridor in her hardsuit. The spring in her step and her bright eyes told Mason that she was quite happy to be aboard *Amazon*.

"You must be my new boss," she said, snapping Mason a salute. "Flight Lieutenant Sienna Armitage reporting. Callsign's Marbles."

Mason shook her gauntleted hand. "Squadron Leader Mason Grey, Hauler. Glad to make your acquaintance. Thank you for volunteering."

"I should be thanking you for letting me join your squadron, sir," Marbles said. "I always wanted to fly with the special forces."

"We'll see if you still feel that way after our next mission, Marbles."

The three other replacement pilots rounded the corner soon after. Mason greeted them in turn, trying not to be too blatant about looking over their shoulders for Jessica.

Finally, a group of spacers from the assault shuttle walked around the corner. A group of personnel in Fleet-blue uniforms with the badging of engineering officers, a tastefully sexy mobility rig, and Jessica herself, walking with the mobility rig, chatting with her like they were old friends.

When she saw Mason, her smile grew wide, showing her perfect white teeth against her soft brown skin.

"Oh, hey, I know you!" Armitage said.

"Marbles! Seems you haven't seen the last of me," Jessica said.

"I'll take it as a good sign. Being around you has been some of the most fun I've ever had in my career," Armitage said.

"Uh, I take it you two have worked together?" Mason asked.

"I gave her a ride around Inner Sol just before my carrier joined up with Taskforce Red," Marbles explained. She pointed to the mobility rig. "She got to ride from Earth in my fighter stuffed in the cargo hold."

"Thank you for reminding me of that, Flight Lieutenant," the mobility rig said. Presumably Miriam Xia.

Jessica walked up to Mason. "I'm relieved to see you're all right, Mason." Her words were formal, but her eyes expressed a hunger that made Mason's breath catch.

"So am I," Mason said, his own eyes just as expressive. "You're, uh, taller."

"Yes, a bit of an adjustment I made for my new body," Jessica said. "Do you like?"

"Yes,' Mason said.

"Would this be the same Mason you've been talking about, Jessica?" the mobility rig asked.

"Yes, indeed," Jessica said. "Mason, this is Miriam Xia."

"I take it you've heard of me," she said.

"Uh, yeah," Mason said. "Including the part about your being dead."

"True, but incomplete," Miriam said.

"I gather as much, given that you're here," Mason said, scratching his head in puzzlement. Jessica spoke up. "Miriam was a backer of the Pinnacle Foundation, the people we believe created the Cendies. She knows more about them than anyone and has come along to provide her expertise."

"Oh, I see," Mason said. "You've been busy."

"As have you," Jessica said. "Couldn't have been easy keeping Triumph out of the Cendies' hands."

"What's one more impossible mission?" Mason said.

Jessica smiled. "Seems you and Colonel Shimura have a way of making things work."

"So, sir, where do we report?" interrupted Marbles.

"My XO should be resting, along with the rest of my pilots, so I'd hold off on introductions. Get your quarters squared away and use this time to relax. I'm sure you haven't had any more chance to rest than I have."

"It'll be nice to have a break," Armitage said. "Glad to meet you, sir."

Mason nodded. "Welcome to Osiris Squadron."

As the new pilots departed, Mason was left standing in the corridor with just Jessica and her new friend.

"I take it you weren't here just to make introductions to your new pilots?" Jessica asked.

"I admit to having an ulterior motive, yes," Mason said.

"Oh, are you going get that coffee he asked you for?" Miriam asked.

Mason glanced at the mobility rig. "Pardon?"

"Never mind her," Jessica gave Miriam a hard look. "So, would you mind escorting me and my companion to the habitat ring, Squadron Leader Grey? My assigned quarters are uploaded to my brainset."

Mason caught a broad smile on Miriam's face as he turned to lead her to the habitat ring.

They had the elevator to themselves as it descended several decks down to the ring section. It was one of the large elevators designed for carrying masses of troopers to the assault shuttles.

Mason caught Jessica looking at him as they waited for the elevator to complete its journey. She smiled at him.

He smiled back, not caring if Miriam noticed.

Once the elevator reached the habitat ring level, they walked down the spokes leading to the edge of the ring.

The ring had been spun down before *Amazon* ignited her long-burn drives; all the modules that formed a chain around the ring had rotated to keep their decks facing towards the pull of thrust gravity. They proceeded to a module dedicated to officer accommodations.

Jessica pointed to an empty cabin. "That's yours, Miriam. There're charging ports compatible with your mobility rig in there."

Miriam nodded. "In that case, I think I'll get settled in. Probably enter a sleep cycle… with my auditory sensors turned off."

The mobility rig walked through the open door and closed it behind her, leaving Mason alone with Jessica for the first time since they had rescued *Independence*.

Mason took a calming breath and looked Jessica in the eyes. "So, you still want to get that coffee?"

Jessica gave him a lopsided grin with a hungry look in her eyes. She tossed he duffel bag through the open door to her cabin, where it hit the far wall.

"How about we skip the bloody coffee and get to the part I think we both want to happen after the coffee," Jessica said.

"I could do that," Mason said.

Jessica gripped the collar of his jumpsuit and pulled him down for a kiss.

The first was light and tender, as was the second. The third was more earnest as Mason felt an electric buzz run through his body.

After the fourth, Jessica rested her head on Mason's chest.

"Bloody hell, it's finally happening," Jessica said. "I can't tell you how much I've been looking forward to this."

Mason wrapped his arms around her and rested his cheek on the top of her head. "I think you just did. Belts and zones, it's good to see you again, Jessica."

Jessica chuckled. "I hope you like my new look."

She withdrew, standing in front of Mason with his arms on her shoulders and hers at his chest.

Aside from her height, she looked the same as when he first met her. Near-perfect face. Smooth dark skin, black hair pulled back into a ponytail.

Her height was closer to his. He used to be head and shoulders taller than her, but now her nose was at the same level as his chin.

"I love it," Mason said.

"So, it will be four days before we reach the mothership," Jessica said. "And it just so happens that your cabin is adjacent to mine."

"Not a coincidence I take it," Mason said.

"No." Jessica took Mason's hand and started pulling him gently into her stateroom.

Mason followed her in, and kicked the door shut behind him.

CHAPTER 45

The four days travel to 30 Skeksis had been uncharacteristically blissful for Jessica, with nightly visitations from Mason, where they spent much of their time exploring each other's bodies.

Mason had no shortage of compliments on the smoothness of her skin, or the tone of her artificial muscles, or how it felt to be inside her.

His body, by contrast, had countless little flaws that did nothing to detract from his attractiveness. Several small, evenly distributed scars covered his body. Leftovers from the multiple surgeries done to reinforce his body against the g-forces a Lightning could subject him too.

There was one scar that wasn't the faded straight line of a surgical cut, but an ugly, jagged scar on his right thigh. Jessica traced her finger down the scar on his leg as they lay together on a gel bed too small for the two of them together.

"That tickles," Mason said.

"Does it now?" Jessica asked as she pulled up to kiss him. "I'll need to remember that for later."

"Keep it up and I might have to get it removed," Mason said.

"You wouldn't dare do such a thing. I like your battle scar."

"Battle scar, eh?"

"That's what it is."

"Strange, I don't recall much of a battle. Just a big fucking explosion that almost launched me into orbit."

"You'd be the most handsome of Jupiter's irregular moons."

"I kinda like where I've ended up," Mason said. "Save for the multiple close brushes with death."

Jessica rested her head on his chest. "You've had more than your fair share."

"I'd say I'm in good company," Mason said, wrapping his arms around Jessica and squeezing her tightly to his chest.

Jessica let out a happy sigh as she was pressed against his warm body. "Fair, our careers have been far too adventurous."

"Yeah. I hope I get some leave time after this," Mason said. "The longest vacation I've had in the past year was in the brig of a League cruiser."

"I'll put in a word with Admiral Mobius," Jessica said. "She's already considering you for a medal."

"Great. Just what I need, more attention from her," Mason said.

"What's wrong with that?" Jessica asked.

"I'll probably be near the top of her list of people to call on for the next hideously dangerous mission," Mason said.

"Admiral Moebius doesn't waste spacers' lives," Jessica said.

"No, she spends them," Mason said. "And I'm not sure that makes much of a difference to the dead."

"You need to talk about it?" Jessica asked.

Mason shrugged under her. "I lost almost half the pilots I started with when I put Osiris Squadron together. Three pilots have died flying off my wing. Death seems to have trouble catching me, but not the people who are near me. It's starting to bother me."

"Good," Jessica said. "It means your human."

"Not sure how many more dead pilots I can take, Jessica," Mason said. "Every time one of them dies, I feel like there's a little bit of me that goes with them."

"Sounds like you really need that leave," Jessica said.

"Yeah, yeah, I fucking do."

An alarm in Jessica's brainset started buzzing in her head.

"Time to go to work," she said, sliding off Mason and bringing her feet to the deck. She stretched out. Mason's eyes traced up and down her naked body.

"I could get used to this," he said.

⌘

Mason left to return to his cabin to get ready for duty. By the time Jessica had washed and put a fresh jumpsuit on, an announcement passed through the ship that the long-burn drives were about to shut down.

Amazon was about to match orbit with 30 Skeksis.

Jessica braced herself down on the deck for when thrust gravity disappeared.

Moments later, the deck jostled as the habitat ring spun up, and the module Jessica stood in tilted until the bottom faced away from the center of the ring, gradually speeding up until a one-third standard g of spin gravity pulled her down.

Jessica walked out of her stateroom and over to Miriam's room, the next door spinward from hers.

She only had to rap on the door once before Miriam opened it.

"Good morning, or whatever happens to be the time on this ship," Miriam said. "Off to the briefing?"

"That we are," Jessica said. "We're close enough now to get real-time data from the mothership. See what insights you might have now that we're up close."

"Then let's not waste any time," Miriam said. "I'm curious to see if this mothership is as similar to *Ascension* as she seems."

Miriam followed Jessica three modules anti-spinward to the module where the briefing was being held, in one of *Amazon*'s war rooms.

Just outside, she ran into Mason, who gave her a warm smile as she approached.

"Good morning, Lieutenant," Mason said.

"Good morning, Squadron Leader."

"It's adorable the way you two are acting like you're not fucking," Miriam said.

Jessica shot Miriam a hard look. "Not so loud."

"Oh, *I'm* being loud? I never said anything about all the noise you've been making the last four nights," Miriam said. Then she smiled. "It's nice to see such passion in people so young."

Jessica sighed, and looked at Mason, his face flushed with embarrassment. She chuckled. "Aw, I never took you for bashful."

"It's just an awkward thing to speak about while my commanding officer is on the other side of the hatch," Mason said.

"Well, you'd better do something about all that color on your face, then," Jessica said, before proceeding inside the war room with Miriam in tow.

Colonel Shimura, Captain Alvarez, and Lieutenant Major Thorne were already inside when Jessica walked in.

Hovering over the holotank was an image of the mothership resting on the surface of the lumpy asteroid it had been mining when Taskforce Red arrived.

"Lieutenant Sinclair, Squadron Leader Grey, Miss Xia, good to see you up this morning," Colonel Shimura said. She gestured to the holotank. "Probes released by Captain Alvarez before *Amazon* completed her breaking burn are feeding us data on the mothership right now."

"Taskforce Red sure did a number on her," Mason said. "Are we sure there are still Cendies alive in there?"

"Yes," Colonel Shimura said. The image zoomed in on the line where the mothership and asteroid touched.

Across the line, points of blue-white light shimmered in the shadow of the ship.

"What are those?" Mason asked.

"Cutting torches," Colonel Shimura said. "They're trying to cut themselves free of the asteroid."

"Belts and zones!" Mason said. "I take it we're still going to try to board it?"

"Yes, Squadron Leader," Colonel Shimura said. "But first, Miss Xia, any insights you'd be willing to share?"

Miriam walked up to the holotank, resting her hands on the edge while she looked up at it.

"Could you zoom out, so I can get a view of the whole ship?" Miriam asked.

Colonel Shimura nodded, and the image expanded until the full length of the mothership hovered before Miriam.

"She sure does look like *Ascension*, just a lot bigger and meaner," Miriam said.

"Any idea why the Ascended would model their mothership on *Ascension*?" Colonel Shimura asked.

"Good design, fundamentally," Miriam said. "The only thing they needed to change was the scale."

"So, the interior layout might be similar to that of *Ascension*?" Colonel Shimura asked.

"That would be a fair guess, though without actually seeing what's inside that ship, I can only speculate," Miriam said.

"Then we work with what we have," Colonel Shimura said. "Based on how the hull weathered the blasts from the space bombs, we can safely assume the hull is too thick for our assault shuttles to try to cut through, so ingress will be limited to the existing openings in the hull."

The image shifted position and zoomed down to a low hill near the mothership.

"Is that spoil?" Miriam asked.

"Good catch, Miss Xia," Colonel Shimura said. "How did you know?"

"I dug a lot of holes on Luna when I was biological," Miriam said. "I know spoil when I see it. Judging by the size of that spoil, I'd venture there are a lot of tunnels dug into that asteroid."

Colonel Shimura nodded. "Indeed. And that presents an opportunity."

"You want my troopers to get into the mothership using the mines under it?" Lieutenant Major Thorne asked.

"It seems the best available option," Colonel Shimura said.

"Do we have any idea what's down there?" Thorne asked.

"Not as of yet," Colonel Shimura said. "We'll need to get a seismic sensor on the surface to map out the tunnels under the mothership."

"Cendies aren't likely to let us prospect that asteroid in peace," Mason said.

"Not to mention if they detect our sonar pings through the rock, they'll figure out we intend on attacking through the tunnels," Captain Alvarez said.

"How does one normally detect tunnels in an asteroid?" Jessica asked, glancing at Miriam.

"Either with an explosive charge buried under the surface or with a kinetic impactor," Miriam said.

"We don't exactly have a shortage of kinetic impactors, now, do we?" Jessica said.

"So, we get a seismic sensor on the surface and let it use the impacts from our weapons to map out the tunnels under the ship?" Mason asked.

"Indeed," Jessica said.

"How do we get a sensor down there without the Cendies noticing?" Captain Alvarez asked.

"A sustained kinetic bombardment from *Amazon* would be quite the distraction," Colonel Shimura said. "And the Cendies will be expecting us to bombard them anyway, so it's unlikely they'd notice us taking seismic measurements."

"So how do we get a sensor on the surface without the Cendies noticing?" Mason asked.

"Well…I might have an idea," Jessica said. "Someone goes down and plants it."

"A person in a pressure suit would probably be detected, Lieutenant," Colonel Shimura said.

"That would be true of most people," Jessica said. "But I wasn't suggesting just anyone try."

"Who were you suggesting, Lieutenant?" Colonel Shimura asked.

"The only person in this room who can, Colonel," Jessica said. "Me."

CHAPTER 46

"Blimey, this was not one of my better ideas," Jessica said as she fell very, very slowly towards 30 Skeksis.

She had been falling towards the dense lump of shattered planetary core for six hours. It loomed before her larger than any mountain on any planet she had ever set foot on, tumbling end over end. The landing site of the Cendy mothership was right in the center of rotation.

30 Skeksis' irregular shape reminded her of Amalthea. But while Amalthea was reddish in color due to contamination from her larger sister moon, Io, 30 Skeksis was a light gray object that seemed to glitter in the sunlight. The bright spots were where the surface dust had been blown away by impacts, exposing the naked metal below. It was one of those spots where Jessica needed to go.

A large seismic sensor was clamped to the back of her thruster rig. Though 30 Skeksis was quite dense, it was covered in a thick layer of dust collected over the eons, and that dust would insulate the seismic sensor from any soundwaves traveling through the asteroid. So, she had to place it on exposed metal.

Once she planted the sensor and activated it, all she would have to do was wait for *Amazon* to start her bombardment, and then read off the data produced by the shockwaves of the assault ship's kinetic impacts.

As she closed to within three hundred meters of the surface, she activated her ink suit's active camouflage system.

The black surface shimmered to mimic the stars around her. Any

Cendy looking at her would just see more stars. Not even a shadow against the backdrop of space.

As for thermal, Jessica solved that by running her artificial body in an extreme low power state. Only the systems needed to keep her brain alive were active, minimizing her thermal signature to barely more than that of a bit of rock warmed by the light of 61 Virginis. Of course, it also meant she was deaf, blind, and paralyzed, her perception of the world coming only from her remote connection to the sensors of Mason's Lightning loitering hundreds of kilometers away from the asteroid.

And what she sensed wasn't a direct visual feed, but a projection. Her ink suit made her practically invisible to even a Lightning's optics. All she saw of herself was a simple blue icon following a projected trajectory that just barely grazed 30 Skeksis.

<This is the strangest feeling,> Jessica said though the same tightbeam connection feeding her data from Mason's fighter.

<Strange how?> Mason asked. <Are you still doing okay, Jessica?>

<Oh, I'm fine. It's just I keep forgetting that the icon I'm watching fall towards the asteroid is me.>

<I haven't forgotten,> Mason said.

<That's sweet of you, my dear,> Jessica said. <Next time talk me out of one of these crazy plans, will you?>

<Maybe don't start with how you're the only one who could do the job,> Mason suggested.

<Yes, I guess I played myself there a bit.>

<Not as bad as you will play the Cendies,> Mason said. <Just a few more minutes.>

Jessica would have nodded if she wasn't completely paralyzed. Her thrust rig included a grapnel launcher that would fire a pair of lines into the asteroid as she flew close to the surface and pull her in.

Her trajectory and relative velocity had been closely matched with the larger end of the tumbling asteroid. Slow enough that she should be able to safely land without having to use thrusters to slow down.

It wasn't the most challenging way to get someone onto an asteroid, but her paralysis gave her an uncomfortable and familiar sense of helplessness as she fell as she fell.

<You're about to reach the closest approach, Jessica,> Mason said. <Grapnels should launch any second now.>

If Jessica could still move, she'd have her fingers crossed.

The bulbous end of 30 Skeksis swung up beneath her icon in its three-hour long rotation.

Jessica didn't feel the grapnel lines launch. She just saw a prompt appear on her icon informing her that the grapnels had fired. The only clue she got that they had hit was when the lines went taut and her velocity suddenly changed. Winches on her thruster rig activated and started to slowly reel her in, feet-first towards the surface.

<Looks like you got a solid connection, Jessica,> Mason said. <No Cendies in line of sight of your landing zone.>

<Booting my body up now.>

It wasn't a simple matter of just flipping her artificial body on. The startup process first involved heating up her body's artificial blood, which would be viscous at several degrees below zero centigrade.

Once her blood was warmed up and flowing, her artificial muscles started to unlock. Jessica started wiggling fingers and toes; her muscles felt as stiff as rolled-up paper.

She was barely ten meters above the surface when she could move her arms and legs again. In any real gravity she doubted she'd be able to walk, but with Skeksis' practically non-existent gravity, her biggest problem would be remaining on the surface without kicking herself into orbit.

By the time her boots touched down on the surface of Skeksis, Jessica's arms and legs were mostly back under her control.

The ends of the grapnel lines were embedded in the dust to either side of her, the winches maintaining a light tension on the line, giving her enough pressure to stand.

She had landed just about where she intended to, just at the rim of the crater at Skeksis' larger end. Below, the bowl of the crater disappeared into darkness, the bottom shadowed by the rim. It would only get darker for the next hour and a half as the crater swung away from 61 Virginis.

Hopefully, the darkness and her ink suit would keep her from being detected by any Cendies who might be patrolling the rock.

"I've touched down on the surface," Jessica said through stiff jaws.

"Copy that, Lieutenant," Colonel Shimura said. "Take your time getting down to the crater's interior. Surveillance shows no signs the Cendies are aware that you're there."

"And hopefully they will remain that way," Jessica said.

There wasn't any real way someone could walk across the surface of an asteroid like 30 Skeksis, especially on the surface farthest from the center of rotation, where the spin partially canceled out the already pitiful gravity. Instead, Jessica would have to climb.

From her belt, she grabbed a pair of asteroid axes. They were similar in design to classic mountaineering axes, but with one difference. Instead of a point, the ax head was leaf shaped, like a gardening shovel.

Squatting down under the tension of the grapnel lines, Jessica swung the ax in her right hand down. The head buried itself fully into the dust, throwing up a puff of particles that drifted up and away, the impulse from the ax enough to send the particles into orbit around Skeksis.

She would have to be careful not to kick up too much dust, lest she draw the attention of the Cendies.

Pulling herself up, she dug the toes of her boots into the regolith and, once secure, she sent a command through her brainset, ordering the thruster rig to jettison the winches.

They practically floated next to her. Not willing to wait for Skeksis' gravity to pull them away, Jessica knocked the winches away with light taps from her free ax.

Once clear, she started climbing down the side of the crater, towards the bowl at the bottom.

Five hundred meters untethered climbing would be almost suicidal on Earth. On 30 Skeksis, it was merely tedious. Her artificial body didn't fatigue; it was just a matter of chopping one ax into the regolith after the other, careful to dig in her cleated boots with every step to keep her from kicking herself upside down.

As she worked her way to the center of the crater, she felt the point of her ax strike something hard under the regolith, which she recognized as the nickel and iron that made up the vast majority of 30 Skeksis.

"I'm at the bottom of the crater," Jessica said. "I'm going to start setting up the sensors."

"You're clear, Jessica," Mason said. "Cendies don't seem to suspect a thing."

"They bloody well better stay that way," Jessica said.

Pulling herself up, she pulled out a magnetic anchor and placed it on the first clear spot of metal. The magnet stuck fast, and Jessica put her axes away, securing them from floating away from the asteroid.

Then she pulled the seismic sensor from her back. It was a cylinder as tall as her torso, and as wide as the palm of her hand. She hit a button on the side, and four spring-loaded legs popped out, each tipped with an electromagnet.

The magnets activated as soon as they touched the exposed metal, and from the bottom of the cylinder, probes extended to touch the surface.

Jessica checked the data, and saw the seismic sensors picking up vibrations inside the asteroid.

"Seismic sensors are secured and streaming data," Jessica said.

"I see it, Lieutenant," Colonel Shimura said. "Standby and hold tight. *Amazon*'s preparing to open fire."

"Understood," Jessica said, pulling her anchor tight so that it kept her all but pressed against the bottom of the crater. Things were about to get bumpy.

On her tactical overlay, *Amazon* didn't move. She had been in firing position for hours.

A few minutes later, Jessica got a broadcast from the assault ship herself.

"This is Captain Alvarez to all ships; *Amazon* is opening fire."

Jessica had line of sight with the starship when she opened fire. The ship was too far to be visible as any more than a bright dot even to Jessica's eyes, but the icon that surrounded the dot made her stand out against the starfield behind her.

The dot flashed, and the icons of her KKVs came tearing through space.

Amazon's guns, though powerful, were much lower velocity than those used by frontline warships. Her KKVs were made to use mass rather than velocity to do damage, as heavier, slower projectiles preserved their velocity traveling through atmosphere better than lighter and faster conventional KKVs.

Against an asteroid, the heavy, slow-moving KKVs struck like hammer blows.

She felt Skeksis tremble beneath her. Each hit sent sound waves echoing through Skeksis' core that were picked up by the seismic sensors and beamed back to *Amazon*, where AIs were using the raw data to construct a map of the suspected tunnel complex under the Cendy mothership.

Jessica opened a window in her HUD to see what the AIs had found.

With each hit, the seismic sensor gathered more data, and the picture became clearer. It looked like the Cendies had vastly expanded the original mining chamber under the surface, digging out a volume as large as the immense mothership herself.

As bombardment continued, and the resolution continued to improve, Jessica saw smaller tunnels radiating from the central chamber. Some were old mining tunnels leading down towards veins of valuable minerals. Others, clearly dug by the Cendies themselves, sloped towards the surface.

"Well, the Cendies sure have been busy," Jessica said.

"No doubt turning a lot of what they dug up into Turtlebacks," Colonel Shimura said. "The main chamber's ceiling looks relatively thin."

"If ten meters of rock can be considered thin, sir," Jessica said.

"Thin enough for the tools we have," Colonel Shimura said. "Your mission is complete, Lieutenant. Launch off that rock and wait for pickup."

"Roger, Colonel. I'm jumping off now."

Getting her feet under her, Jessica used the tension from her anchor line to keep her standing. She then primed her suit thrusters and squatted down. She hit the release on her anchor lines at the same time as she leapt, launching herself into space. Firing her suit thrusters for extra velocity, Jessica soon exceeded 30 Skeksis' escape velocity and was floating away from the rock.

"Jessica, Kodiak 6 is inbound on your position for pickup. Skies are still clear. I think the Cendies are too occupied by *Amazon*'s bombardment," Mason said.

"Good to hear it, Mason," Jessica said. "Stay safe out there."

"You do the same," Mason said. "Osiris Leader out."

Minutes later Jessica spotted Kodiak 6 as it approached her.

"I have visual on you, Lieutenant. Prepare for pickup," the assault shuttle pilots said.

"I'm not going anywhere," Jessica said.

Kodiak 6 executed a slow flip as it approached her, stopping its rotation with a pulse from the maneuvering thrusters. The assault shuttle's tail ramp opened, revealing the illuminated interior and the armored Raiders inside. A group of them stood near the ramp, ready to catch her.

Strong hands grasped her as she floated into the assault shuttle's cargo bay and guided her to the wall covered in webbing that she could grab hold of.

"Welcome aboard, Lieutenant," Sergeant Cane said. "How was the prospecting?"

"I survived it," Jessica said.

"Let's get you strapped in. Orders from *Amazon* said to get ready to begin landings."

Jessica nodded, and climbed up the webbing until she reached the first unoccupied acceleration seat and strapped herself in. She quickly linked her brainset to the assault shuttle, gaining access to the vessel's sensors, and to the larger datalink it was part of.

There was only one thing that would consider ten meters of rock thin, and Jessica was very glad Colonel Shimura ordered her off 30 Skeksis before using it.

"All ships be advised—nuclear strike is imminent. Prepare to turn all sensors away from 30 Skeksis," Captain Alvarez said.

A pair of torpedoes launched from FSFV *Burlington*, igniting their short-burn drives and rocketing past *Amazon* even as she continued to pour fire into the asteroid.

Jessica tracked the torpedoes until they disappeared behind 30 Skeksis. A second later, two bright flashes went off in rapid succession.

"Strike successful, damage report pending," Captain Alvarez said.

As the gas and dust thrown up by the nuclear-shaped charges dissipated, Jessica tapped into the datalink and got a view through one of *Amazon*'s scopes as it peered at the mothership.

Through the haze, Jessica saw a hole almost a hundred meters across, the edges glowing bright red.

CHAPTER 47

"Holy shit, the Special Purpose Branch sure knows how to make an entrance!" Armitage said.

"Cut the chatter, Marbles. Save the commentary for after we get back," Mason said.

"Understood, Hauler," Marbles said.

"Osiris Leader, I need one of your fighters to make a close pass of the hole *Burlington* just punched into the asteroid," Colonel Shimura said.

"Understood, sir. I'll check it myself," Mason said. "Marbles, stay close. Engage any Cendy contacts you detect."

"With pleasure, Hauler," Marbles said. "I've got your six covered."

"Zin, you and the rest of Osiris Squadron take overwatch positions over the mothership," Mason said.

"Roger that, Hauler," Zin said.

Mason ignited his drives and pushed his throttles forward until 5gs weighed down on him like a sumo wrestler sitting on his chest.

He flipped at the halfway point and accelerated in the opposite direction until he was closing with 30 Skeksis at just over 300 meters per second.

His vector would take just over the surface, and he would emerge just over the rim of the depression the Cendy mothership rested in. Mason kept an eye on his threat display, waiting for his sensor AI to alert him to any hostile contacts as the mothership's landing site came into view. With a brief, violent pulse of 10gs of acceleration, he leveled his vector with the mothership, aiming to pass directly over the landing site. Armitage matched his maneuver with immaculate precision.

As the mothership came into view, Mason gained an appreciation for the sheer scale of the thing. The size of a fleet base, the length of the mothership nearly spanned the width of 30 Skeksis.

The hull was blackened by the nuclear attacks launched by Taskforce Red that had welded it to the asteroid. A hole punched through 30 Skeksis' surface by *Burlington*'s torpedoes glowed across the EM spectrum a few thousand meters away from it.

"Making closest approach now," Mason said. "That hole is pretty damn hot."

"I can see that on the datalink. It looks like temperatures are dropping fast, though. That asteroid's basically a giant heatsink with all that iron it has," Colonel Shimura said. "As soon as temperatures reach a safe level, Squadron Leader, I want a pair of Lightnings to enter the hole and secure the chamber below."

"Sir, any Cendies in there will be ash," Mason said.

"And don't think for a moment the Cendies won't set up defenses as soon as that chamber is cool enough, Osiris Leader," Colonel Shimura said. "Get fighters in there and keep the Cendies at bay until I can get assault shuttles in there."

"Roger that, sir," Mason said. "Marbles, we're the closest, so we're going in first. Zin, I want another flight ready to relieve us as soon as I call for it. I think we're going to use up our munitions quickly in there."

"Roger that, Hauler," Zin said. "Good luck."

"Eyes open, Marbles. Blast anything that moves in there," Mason said.

"Will do, Hauler," Marbles said, giggling as she said it.

"Belts and zones!" Mason said as he reversed his vector, placing himself on an approach course with the breach.

As the colonel predicted, the breach cooled rapidly as heat migrated from the breach deeper into the iron-rich asteroid. The temperature was just about safe for him to enter, so long as he didn't get too close to the sides of the breach.

"Osiris Leader going in," Mason said.

The hole was large enough for ten Lightnings to fly through with room to spare. He powered up his fighter's external lights, illuminating the far side of the chamber, a patch of partially melted rock and iron.

Mason fired his braking thrusters and pitched his nose up towards the mothership above.

The beams of his fighter's spotlights barely cut through the darkness of the chamber in the visible spectrum. With the help of light amplification, Mason saw a vast chamber hollowed out of the asteroid. Several thousand meters ahead of him, in the ceiling of the chamber, was a circular opening right where the mothership rested.

There were already groups of Cendy soldiers floating out of it, like motes of dust out of a vent.

"Hostiles spotted. Engaging!" Mason said, firing a pair of Hammers set to proximity detonation.

The missiles flew across the chamber, their engines lighting up the darkness as they went, and detonated among the Cendies swarming out of the mothership.

"Marbles, I'll engage the Cendies coming out of the mothership, you get the ones who get past me," Mason said.

"Roger that," Marbles said, firing a pair of Hammer missiles towards the chamber walls were Cendies were already trying to dig in.

Mason fired another proximity-fused Hammer towards the entrance to the mothership, turning another group of Cendies into white mist.

"Colonel Shimura, Cendy reinforcements are attempting to retake the chamber," Mason said. "Osiris 2 and I are holding them off for now, but we're expending munitions rapidly doing so."

"Roger that, Osiris Leader," Colonel Shimura said. "The first assault shuttles are two minutes inbound."

Before Mason could respond, he got a warning from his sensor AI just in time to lurch his Lightning out of the way as a missile fired from one of the branching tunnels.

Mason launched a Hammer into the tunnel, where it detonated at the mouth, sending debris flying across the side of the chamber.

"Marbles, we got Cendies coming from the side tunnels," Mason said. "Hold off the reinforcements from the mothership while I deal with them."

"Roger that, Hauler. I won't let any of the little bastards get past me," Armitage said.

The ambient heat in the chamber made it all but impossible for him to spot the Cendies using thermal imaging, and the dust and debris kicked up made active sensors ineffective.

Instead, Mason just blind-fired Hammers into the mouth of each branching tunnel, assuming all of them had Cendies in them.

The explosions threw more dust and rock all around the chamber, and gravel pinged off the exterior of his fighter as he maneuvered.

"Osiris Leader, Kodiak 6 is inbound," said the pilot of the first assault shuttle.

"Watch your velocity, Kodiak 6, there's debris floating all around the chamber," Mason said. "Keep an eye to the branching tunnels. I have no way of telling if I got all the Cendies in them."

"We'll keep our eyes open, Osiris Leader," Kodiak 6's pilot said.

Kodiak 6 dropped through the opening, its chin-mounted turret blazing away. The assault shuttle swept the stream of shells across the bottom of the chamber, cutting through Cendies who had survived Marbles' attention.

The miniguns under each of Kodiak 6's wings spewed fire into the nearest tunnels. With all the dust and debris, there was no way they could see what they were shooting at, but the stream of bullets would discourage any surviving Cendies from trying to peek out to launch another missile.

Mason kept up firing Hammers every time Cendy reinforcements tried to push through. With no cover, the Cendy soldiers caught floating through the chamber or trying to crawl along the ceiling were easy pickings.

More assault shuttles followed Kodiak 6, adding their own cannon fire to the barrage of weapons.

Kodiak 6 hovered just a meter off the ground, still firing away as the tail ramp opened, and a platoon of Raiders started jumping out.

"This is Kodiak 6. Passengers are dropped off. Any way we can be of help, Osiris Leader?"

"If you take position next to the mothership's entrance, your guns will be very helpful in keeping Cendy reinforcements at bay," Mason said.

"Roger that, Osiris Leader," Kodiak 6 said. "We'll cover the entrance until our guns run dry."

"Speaking of running dry," Mason said. "Marbles, weapons status?"

"Just launched my last Hammer, Hauler," she said.

"Head back outside. I'll follow you out as soon as I fire my last missiles. Mind oncoming traffic," Mason said.

"On my way out," Armitage said.

"Shutdown, it's almost your turn," Mason said.

"We're hovering just outside the breach, Hauler," Zin said. "Just give the word."

Another wave of Cendies attempted to push through, weathering the barrage of fire coming from Kodiak 6.

Mason locked his last two Hammers on them and launched. The missile detonated, turning the clump of Cendy soldiers into an expanding cloud of white mist and body parts.

"The word is given, Shutdown," Mason said. "I'm on my way out."

CHAPTER 48

As soon as Mason's Lightning flew out of the breach, another pair of Lightnings flew into the chamber, taking up station well away from the mothership entrance to provide heavy ordinance.

The Raiders had formed a perimeter around the landing zone, but there were no Cendy soldiers for them to fight. The Lightnings and assault shuttles had done too good a job preventing the Cendies from retaking the chamber after *Burlington*'s nukes burned them out.

Jessica looked up at the entrance to the mothership, noting the web of tubes running along the ceiling and down the sides and radiating towards the tunnels branching out the sides of the main chambers. At several points, the tendrils were melted into the rock, probably by the heat of the nukes or blasted open by stray fire from the Lightnings.

But it was clear looking at the remains what the tendrils were—conveyors that fed ore mined from deep inside 30 Skeksis to the mothership's production facilities.

"This is Osiris 5, the Cendies have stopped trying to send reinforcements into the chamber."

"Roger that, Osiris 5, remain on station," Colonel Shimura called out over the command channel. Over a private channel, she connected to Jessica. "Lieutenant Sinclair, you're my eyes on the ground. What are your thoughts?"

"Well, sir, I don't have to tell you that bottlenecks work both ways," Jessica said.

"Yes, and we don't know what's waiting for us in there," Colonel Shimura said. "I want you to take Sergeant Cane's squad and approach the mothership entrance. From there, I want you to guide a swarm of recon drones into the mothership. Hopefully, enough of them will last long enough for us to get a good idea what's waiting for us in there."

"Understood, sir," Jessica said. "Sergeant Cane, your squad ready to do some reconnaissance?"

"Sure thing, sir," Cane said. "It's boring just standing here watching the flyers have all the fun."

"I'll handle controlling the drones; you just make sure there aren't any Cendies waiting to ambush us," Jessica said.

Sergeant Cane brought her battle rifle up to a ready rest. "Nice to get to play soldier again." She turned to the troopers behind her. "1st Squad, on me. Time to go for a walk."

Walking wasn't really something the troopers could do in 30 Skeksis' gravity. The weak pull was good for little more than establishing what direction down was. Instead, the troopers moved outside the perimeter with short jumps, launching airborne with their legs, and pushing themselves back down with their suit thrusters.

Their jumps were staggered. No more than four troopers were moving forward at any one time; the others were firmly on the ground with their weapons held ready.

Jessica followed them a few meters behind, keeping up with Sergeant Cane's hops. She kept her carbine latched across the front of her ink suit. The last thing Sergeant Cane's troopers needed was an overly excited officer trying to fire a gun over their heads. Her HUD's tactical display fed her what the Raiders of Sergeant Cane's squad were seeing, with overlapping cones of awareness fanning out ahead of her. More information poured in on the datalink at large; an icon representing 1st Squad slowly traversed from the landing zone to the access tunnel.

All the while, assault shuttles and Lightnings hovered around the mouth of the access tunnel like moths hovering around a light, careful not to expose themselves to whatever weapons might be trained on the entrance. From their position on the ground, Jessica and 1st Squad would be the first ones to get a look at what was inside the mothership.

She didn't hear the shot that hit one of Sergeant's Cane's troopers. She just saw a shot punch clean through the hardsuit, leaving a misty trail of blood behind the trooper's body.

Jessica used her suit thrusters to push her down into a depression as her HUD lit up with weapon-fire alerts.Looking up, brackets on her HUD marked where the fire was coming from. Just over the lip of the access tunnel, Cendy soldiers were firing down on Cane's squad below them.

Cane herself yanked the wounded trooper down, while the others returned fire, their weapons flashing silently in the vacuum.

"Bloody hell!" Jessica said. "This is Lieutenant Sinclair, 1st Squad is taking fire from the rim of the access tunnel. I have the enemy's position locked on the datalink."

"This is Osiris 5. I have the position locked and I'm about to launch. Standby."

Moments later, one of the Lightnings loitering overhead launched a pair of missiles that flew below the access tunnel, and then pulled up hard to enter the tunnel mouth, detonating a few meters away from where the Cendies were shooting from.

"Good hit, Osiris 5!" Jessica said.

"Got more where that came from," Osiris 5 said.

Jessica broke cover to walk up to Sergeant Cane's position. Cane was fixing her wounded trooper down with an anchor jammed into the rock. On Jessica's HUD, the stricken trooper was badly wounded but stable thanks to the medical systems of their hardsuit.

"Do you want me to call in a medivac, Sergeant?" Jessica asked.

"Not while we're in line of sight of the Cendies in the mothership," Sergeant Cane said. "Do you think you could guide the recce drones in from here, sir?"

Jessica glanced up at the access tunnel in the ceiling of the chamber, getting a glance at the interior of the Cendy mothership. "I think I can make it work."

"Then I'll keep an eye on my guy while you do that," Sergeant Cane said. "The rest of my squad will keep you covered."

"Thank you, Sergeant," Jessica said before opening her drone control panel.

There were hundreds of idle drones resting in crates in the LZ waiting for the command to go into motion.

With the way the Cendies were guarding the chokepoint, there weren't any clever tricks Jessica could think of to sneak a drone through. So instead, she opted for brute force.

She started programming instructions into the drones' collective AIs. Once she executed the program, the drones would handle the work of flying in and gathering data. All Jessica had to do was watch. But she had to make sure that the instructions she gave were good ones.

"I've got the drones programmed," Jessica said.

"Don't wait on my account, sir," Sergeant Cane said.

Jessica started transmitting on the mission channel. "All craft in the vicinity, I'm about to launch our recon drones. Maintain at least fifty meters altitude and clear the area around the access tunnel. That space is about to get crowded."

On the tactical display, the assault shuttles nearest to the access tunnel started backing off. Once Jessica felt they had cleared the airspace enough, she activated the drones, and turned around to watch her work. Hundreds of softball-sized drones streamed out of the crate and scattered around the landing zone, gathering into a dark cloud before flying towards Jessica. She resisted the urge to duck as the drones flew three meters above her, hugging close to the floor of the chamber as they headed in the direction of the access tunnel.

The Cendies started firing as soon as the drones entered line of sight. Shots from the access tunnel rained down on the drones, destroying several before flying directly below the access tunnel.

Then the drones rose into a spiraling column that ascended rapidly towards the access tunnel. The spiral sparked with small explosions as Cendy fire tore through it, growing more intense as the drones pushed closer and closer to the tunnel. The swarm left a trail of broken drone parts raining below them as they ran the gauntlet.

As the drones entered the access tunnel, the Cendies concentrated their fire, wiping out the drones at the front. The swarm grew thinner and thinner even as data started streaming in, building a map of the access tunnel's throat on Jessica' s HUD.

Then the drones penetrated the mothership herself.

"Oh blimey," Jessica breathed.

The access tunnel led to a massive empty cylinder inside the mothership, with just the axis of the drive keel running through the center of it. Along the walls were Turtleback landing ships in various stages of construction, apparently halted by the attack that had disabled the mothership in the first place.

The stream of data rapidly degraded as drones disintegrated and there were fewer to capture and relay data back to Jessica. Within twenty seconds, Jessica lost her real-time view of the mothership's interior. But it had been enough.

The drones had identified where most of the fire was coming from—several mostly complete Turtlebacks towards the front of the mothership. Any force trying to assault through the access tunnel would be slaughtered by the powerful point defenses of the Turtlebacks.

But now they knew were the guns were, it was just a matter of finding a way of knocking them out.

CHAPTER 49

THE HANGAR TECHS aboard *Amazon* wasted little time in removing the empty Atlatl pods. With no thrust gravity to complicate matters, they simply attached cables to the empty pods before popping them off the hardpoints and winching them away towards the back of the hangar where they could be secured and reloaded.

Mason surveyed the activity from his cockpit. He didn't bother with trying to leave his fighter. Doing so would only add an unnecessary delay to returning to 30 Skeksis and the troopers who would need all the fire support they could get when the time came to board the mothership herself.

While the hangar techs were starting to load fresh Atlatl pods onto his wings, a direct call came in from Colonel Shimura.

"Squadron Leader Grey."

"Yes, sir?"

"We just got reconnaissance data from the interior of the mothership. I'm uploading it to your fighter now."

Images of the interior of the mothership appeared on Mason's HUD. Someone had already taken the time to highlight the main area of interest: the Turtlebacks towards the front of the starship's massive interior. In the images, he saw the point defenses blazing away at the drones that took the picture.

"Looks like a production line in there, sir," Mason said.

"And some of the Turtlebacks are complete enough to fight," Colonel

Shimura said. "It looks like they make up the bulk of the firepower inside the mothership."

"That could be a challenge, sir," Mason said. "I've seen firsthand just how good Turtleback's point defenses are."

"And I'm sorry I have to further complicate things for you by stating that we need to limit what damage we do to the mothership," Colonel Shimura said.

"Since you're speaking with me, I take it you intend for my fighters to deal with the Turtlebacks," Mason said.

"Fighters are the only thing we have that have both the precision and the firepower to neutralize the Turtlebacks without causing excessive damage to the mothership," Colonel Shimura said.

Mason sighed. "I'm going to lose more pilots, sir."

"I know, Squadron Leader," Colonel Shimura said. "I hate placing you in a position to risk more lives. But that is the responsibility of command."

"I know, sir," Mason said. "And it is my responsibility to choose who goes in first."

"Yes, it is, Squadron Leader," Colonel Shimura said. "I leave it to you to make the wisest choice."

Mason sighed, then opened a channel with Chief Rabin. "Chief, change of plans. I need you to rearm me and Osiris 2 with Slugger torpedoes, full load."

"Roger that, sir," Chief Rabin said.

Like a switch being set in reverse, the hangar techs started pulling Atlatl pods off Mason's wings.

"Hey, Hauler, why are the hangar techs stripping weapons off just as they got them on?" Flight Lieutenant Armitage asked.

"New mission, Marbles," Mason said. "We're going to go inside the mothership and use Sluggers to take out the active Turtlebacks inside."

"Oh, that sounds dangerous, sir. When do we fly out?"

"As soon as Chief Rabin's people finish their job."

"Understood, sir. Guess I'll just wait here, then."

Mason routed through *Amazon*'s communications system and connected with Zin's fighter.

"I hear you, Hauler," Zin said. "What's changed?"

"Colonel Shimura wants us to fly in and neutralize the Turtlebacks," Mason said. "How's our ordinance looking?"

"We still have ninety percent of our Hammers in total, Hauler," Zin said. "Though those aren't going to be enough to deal with Turtlebacks."

"No, but they'll be enough to saturate the point defenses for a few seconds," Mason said.

"A few seconds to do what, Hauler?" Zin asked.

"Marbles and I are loading up with Sluggers as we speak," Mason said. "I want you to save the rest of the squadron's Hammers until we arrive. It will be the job of the rest of Osiris Squadron to get us through the access tunnel and cover us until we launch our Sluggers."

"That's going to be a tight fit, Hauler," Zin said. "We're going to take losses."

"I know, Shutdown," Mason said. "And you're going to have to make sure Marbles and I stay covered until we launch our Sluggers."

"We'll keep you two safe, Hauler," Zin said. "Please be quick about knocking out the Turtlebacks."

"We will, Shutdown."

"I'll set up the queue."

"No, Shutdown, I'll do that."

"Hauler, it's no problem," Zin said. "I can handle this."

"I don't want you to handle this," Mason said. "I'm the one who's putting us into danger. I'm not going to pass off the responsibility of picking who's going to go in first."

෴

By the time Mason launched from *Amazon* and made the short flight to 30 Skeksis, he had completed selecting the order in which his squadron would try to force their way through the access tunnel.

The selection had been random, selecting the order where two-ship elements would go in. As much as Mason wanted to lead from the front, it would only endanger the success of the mission.

Whatever happened, he and Marbles had to survive long enough to deliver their payloads.

As he drifted towards the still cooling hole blasted into 30 Skeksis, he took one last look at the Cendy mothership.

"That bitch better be worth it," he muttered.

The fourteen other fighters of Osiris Squadron hovered inside the massive chamber cut into the rock below the mothership.

The Cendies had ceded the lower chamber to the Federals. A reinforced regiment of Raiders had set up firing positions all around the access tunnel in the ceiling, ready to use their hardsuit thrusters to fly up the throat and move into the mothership as soon as Mason and his squadron could give them an opening.

"Silverback, you're on point," Mason said. "The Cendies are going to fire at you first, so go in hard and fast and launch all your Hammers on the pre-programmed course."

"Roger that, Hauler," Dominic said. "I always wanted to be first at something."

Mason doubted this was quite what Dominic had in mind, but Mason wasn't going to contradict him. The man and his wingmate were taking a terrible risk. It would be cruel to discourage his attempts at coping.

"Hardball, your flight is in next. Silverback is going to be the focus of a lot of Cendy fire, so you do your best to draw fire away from him," Mason said.

"It'll be my pleasure to save Silverback's ass, sir," Sabal said.

"I'll take up the rear and pick up the slack," Zin said. "We'll leave a corridor open for you and Marbles."

"Thanks, Shutdown," Mason said. "Prepare to engage on my mark."

Mason glanced at his weapons display one last time. All sixteen Sluggers were armed and ready, as was his fighter's main cannon. He took a series of deep breaths, gathering the nerve to utter the next order.

"All fighters—execute," Mason said.

The four fighters of Dominic's flight ignited their drives and flew straight towards the access tunnel, Sabal's flight following a couple of seconds behind. Zin and the six fighters with her followed behind them in a line of two fighters abreast. The access tunnel was large enough for four Lightnings to fly abreast with enough room to maneuver, and maneuver they had to.

Dominic's fighters came under fire as soon as he flew into the access tunnel, flying through a storm of small-arms fire that was quickly suppressed by a volley of Hammer missiles just before they broke out into the interior of the mothership.

Precise, heavy-point defense fire from the frontal area greeted Dominic and his wingmate as they loosed all their Hammers at the Turtlebacks, giving the Cendies far more targets to deal with.

Sabal's flight pushed into the chamber not long after and launched yet more Hammers into the Turtlebacks. The missiles weren't powerful enough to punch through the armor of the landing ships, but they were an effective distraction.

As soon as Zin flew into the mothership, Mason pushed his throttles forward and started his own run. He pulled up into the tunnel, and almost flew into the debris of a ruined Lightning falling back down into the tunnel.

"Shit!"

A hard burst of the port-maneuvering thrusters punched Mason to the side as he evaded the falling fighter. Dust and debris battered his fighter as he rose into the tunnel mouth.

As soon as they entered the tunnel, Mason's sensor AI got to work jamming every targeting sensor it detected. With the rest of Osiris Squadron serving as a distraction, the Cendy Turtlebacks did not immediately turn their fire towards Mason and Marbles.

Armitage broke formation with Mason and turned towards the Turtlebacks while Mason continued straight up, flying around the drive keel that ran through the middle of the mothership's interior.

"Sluggers away!" Marbles announced as Mason turned just short of the top of the mothership and prepared to make his run. He hit the launch button, and the eight slugger torpedoes on his wings launched at the same time, ejected off the hardpoints by explosive bolts and then igniting their short-burn drives a half-second later.

The rotary launcher in his fighter's belly emptied itself in four seconds, the last leaving the launcher just as Marbles' torpedoes detonated.

Sluggers were essentially kinetic cannons with engines. The recoil of their guns firing shattered them, but not before sending a heavy penetrator flying toward the target.

The Turtlebacks didn't have time to react as the Sluggers detonated, and penetrators drove clear through their hulls. From the Turtleback they had managed to temporarily capture, Mason knew exactly where the penetrators needed to go to disable them.

Two Sluggers were sent against each active Turtleback, and the penetrators punched through their main fusion reactors, silencing the vessels and their murderous point defenses.

The only remaining weapons fire inside the mothership came from the small arms of the thousands of Cendy soldiers scattered around the mothership's interior, but their fire was met with Hammer missiles and cannon fire from the other Lightnings of Osiris Squadron—what was left of them.

"This is Osiris Leader. All Turtlebacks are neutralized, assault force is clear to enter," Mason said before finally glancing at his squadron status display. Half his fighters were coming up red, including Zin's.

"Understood, Osiris Leader," Colonel Shimura said. "Lieutenant Major Thorne, begin the assault."

"Copy that, we're go for assault," Thorne said. "Fireteams are taking off now."

"Hauler, the Cendies just stopped shooting at us," Armitage said.

Mason turned his attention to his tactical display. The sensor AI still showed a multitude of threats spread throughout the interior of the mothership's cylinder, but there was no warning of missile launchers, nor pot shots from small-arms fire.

"Keep alert, Marbles," Mason said. "The Cendies might be up to something."

Just as he finished his sentence, a powerful unencrypted broadcast echoed throughout the interior of the mothership.

A vaguely feminine, strangely accented voice crackled in Mason's ears.

"This is Emissary Gia to all Federal Forces, we request parley."

CHAPTER 50

"Well, this is a bloody surprise," Jessica said.

"Wonder what they're playing at," Sergeant Cane said.

"I'm not sure they're playing at anything," Jessica said.

"This is Colonel Shimura. I will accept nothing less than an unconditional surrender."

"I'm afraid that could be complicated, Colonel," Emissary Gia said. "The warforms were only just outvoted."

"Outvoted? You can't just order them to surrender?" Colonel Shimura asked.

"I'm afraid that is not how things work with us, Colonel," Emissary Gia said.

"Their soldiers still want to fight. I can respect that," Sergeant Cane said.

Jessica squatted down and opened her direct line to Colonel Shimura.

"This better be good, Lieutenant," Colonel Shimura said.

"Yes, sir. I was thinking we should perhaps make use of the specialist that we brought along," Jessica said.

"What does she have to offer?" Colonel Shimura asked.

"Well, given that her friend created the Cendies, her word might carry weight that yours does not," Jessica said.

༄

The assault shuttle carrying Colonel Shimura and Miriam set down in the landing zone near the breach.

Jessica had traversed from Sergeant Cane's observation position to the landing zone by herself.

She waited as the assault shuttle's tail ramp descended, and the suited figures of Colonel Shimura and Miriam Xia walked down.

Jessica snapped a salute. "Welcome to 30 Skeksis, Colonel."

"Thank you, Lieutenant. I'm glad to see you're well," Colonel Shimura said.

Miriam looked around, taking in the scenery of glassed rock inside the vast darkness of the chamber. "Well, this is desolate. Is this typical of the places the Special Purpose Branch takes you, Jessica?"

"As of late, yes," Jessica said. "Are you ready to meet with the Ascendency?"

"No, but why should that delay anything?" Miriam said.

"I hope you're prepared for a walk, Miss Xia," Colonel Shimura said. "It's a three-thousand-meter hop to the meeting point."

"It will be nice to stretch my legs."

With the gravity of 30 Skeksis being what it was, they more flew than walked towards the meeting place, jumping over dozens of meters with each skip.

They came to a stop at Sergeant Cane's forward observation post. A few hundred meters ahead, a group of figures stood in the center of the circle of light cast down through the access tunnel of the mothership.

"Anything to report?" Colonel Shimura asked.

"One emissary and half a dozen soldiers standing out in the open," Sergeant Cane said. "No funny business as far as I can tell."

"Keep your sights zeroed on the soldiers just in case, Sergeant." Colonel Shimura turned to Miriam. "All right, Miss Xia, it's your time."

Miriam chuckled. "I think my time is long past, Colonel. But I'll see if I can't get one more negotiation out."

"You still want to do this, Lieutenant?" Colonel Shimura asked.

"I think Miriam and I are the best qualified people here to negotiate the surrender of the Cendies, sir," Jessica said.

"Then here we go," Miriam said. "I guess I'll go first."

"We'll go together, Miriam," Jessica said.

It took just over two minutes to traverse from the observation post to the meeting point. Jessica glanced up at the brightly lit interior of the mothership, the top of the main chamber barely visible even to her eyes.

The Cendy soldiers were still armed, but their weapons were secured across their chests. Jessica was quite sure that if they reached for their weapons, Sergeant Cane's troopers would gun them down before they had a chance to shoulder them.

Jessica hoped it wouldn't come to that.

Despite the lack of air, Emissary Gia did not have a suit. Just the shimmering gray robes of an emissary. How they were able to keep the robes from flapping about in the low gravity was a mystery.

"I am Emissary Gia," the emissary said over near-field comms, lips unmoving. "Are you the negotiators?"

"Yes," Jessica said. "I'm Lieutenant Jessica Sinclair." She gestured to Miriam. "This is Miriam Xia. I'll be assisting her with the negotiations."

"Miriam Xia?" Emissary Gia turned to Miriam. "Would you be related to the Miriam Xia who founded Xia Spaceworks?"

"I'm not related to her," Miriam said. "I am her. Or her digital construct in any case. I believe I might have been friends with one of your creators."

"Visionary Marr," Emissary Gia said.

"He was always just Julian to me," Miriam said.

Emissary Gia's expression changed, from the bland expression of neutral benevolence, to something approaching awe. "How?"

Miriam nodded to Jessica. "She's the reason I'm here. It seems her theory that Julian had a hand in creating you was right."

Gia glanced at Jessica, then back to Miriam. "She is correct."

"So, let's get to business. You voted to surrender, but only over the objections of your soldiers," Miriam said.

"Yes, the warforms wish to fight to the end, but we feel the cost of continued fighting would not outweigh the attrition we'd inflict on your forces with continued resistance,' Gia said.

Jessica glanced at the blank, faceless soldiers, the warforms, as they stood in a semi-circle behind Gia.

"I don't suppose you could explain to me what their issue is. Is it a matter of martial honor not to surrender?" Miriam asked.

"No, it is a matter of purpose. Warforms are made to fight. Just as I am made to communicate with humans," Gia said.

"And surrendering would be counter to their purpose," Miriam said.

"It is," Gia said.

"Hrmmph." Miriam turned to Jessica. "Anything you would like to add, Jessica?

"I did have a question, if you would humor me," Jessica said.

"You may ask any question you wish, Lieutenant," Gia said. "Though I might not answer them all."

"I just have the one. Cendies have never tried to surrender before," Jessica said. "Why is this instance different?"

"You mean, why didn't we destroy our home?"

"Your home?" Jessica asked. "That's why you didn't scuttle your mothership?"

"What did you think our ship was, Lieutenant?" Gia asked.

"A giant factory ship," Jessica said.

"It is much more than that," Gia said. "There are hundreds of thousands of beings aboard the mothership. Destroying her would cost too many Ascended lives for too little in return."

"Now I understand," Miriam said. "It sounds like Julian's utilitarianism has had a strong influence on your sense of ethics."

Gia nodded. "We seek the greater good, not just for us, but for all."

Jessica cocked her head to one side. "How–"

Miriam stopped Jessica with an outstretched hand. <Now is not the time for that,> she subvocalized, then turned back to Gia. "Are your warforms also motivated by serving the greater good?"

"They are," Gia said. "They believe any attrition they inflict on your forces will help our war effort, and thus serve the greater good."

"I see," Miriam said. "Might I make a proposal, then?"

"Of course," Gia said.

"The Federal Space Forces, as you are aware, is bound by strict rules for treatment of prisoners of war," Miriam said.

"We are aware of the Liberty Accords," Gia said. "We're not bound by it."

"No but bear with me for a moment. There's a minimum level of treatment that the Earth Federation must provide any prisoners of war. Which means that each prisoner adds a level of burden to the resources of the Earth Federation."

"Go on," Gia said.

Miriam looked to one of the warforms. "They're listening?"

"They are," Gia said.

"Well, caring for prisoners over the long term would put more a drain on the Earth Federation than any attrition the warforms might inflict here," Miriam said. "Surrender and imprisonment will serve the greater good more than any needless sacrifice."

"That is… an interesting proposal. Could you give us a moment to come to a consensus?" Gia asked.

"Take all the time you need," Miriam said.

Gia turned around to face the soldiers. If she was conversing with them, there was no way to tell other than trying to hack into their near-field communications, and Jessica wasn't about to do that just yet.

Miriam walked over to Jessica. "So, what do you think?"

"Not the first surrender you've negotiated, I take it?" Jessica asked.

"It's not all that different from buying out a rival company," Miriam said.

Emissary Gia turned around. "The warforms have accepted your proposal. They, and the rest of the Ascended will surrender to the Federal Space Forces, so that we may tie up resources that would otherwise be used for fighting."

"I'll take it," Miriam said.

CHAPTER 51

Mason set down next to Zin's crashed Lightning, atop the remains of a half-finished Turtleback.

He hit the release button and his canopy opened, blowing out the cockpit's inert atmosphere. Jumping out of the cockpit, Mason used his suit thrusters to push himself towards Zin's broken fighter.

The crash had partly buried the Lightning in the Turtleback's hull, leaving it crumpled and broken. But the cockpit canopy looked intact. He allowed himself to hope.

Mason landed just to the side of the Lightning, pulling open a panel to expose the external emergency opening lever. He grabbed the lever and pulled it down, holding it a few seconds. Explosive bolts blew the canopy off, sending it flying up to the top side of the mothership's chamber. Mason scrambled up to the cockpit, trying to connect with Zin over nearfield communications, but getting nothing in return.

He found her in a gimbaled seat, unmoving. Her chest plate was perforated in multiple places.

"No, no, no!" Mason tilted her seat back, looking into her visor. Her eyes were open, staring off at nothing.

Something cold and heavy settled in Mason's chest, as he stood there, looking down at his dead friend.

"Hauler, what's Shutdown's status?" Dominic asked.

"She didn't make it," Mason said.

"I know the Cendies have surrendered and everything, but I would feel a lot better if you got back into your fighter, sir," Dominic said. "We can tag her for recovery later."

Mason looked down at Zin's body. "No, we're taking her back with us."

Releasing the bolts holding her to her seat, it was a simple matter of lifting her out of her seat and flying out of the cockpit under power of his suit thrusters.

He landed directly in the cockpit of his fighter, and secured Zin's body to the passenger seat in the rear of his cockpit.

"She's secure," Mason said. "Let's head back to *Amazon*. I don't think they need us here anymore."

Departure from the mothership and 30 Skeksis could not be more different than entering it, and not just because no one was shooting at his fighters.

Groups of Cendies stood still watching his fighters descend into the access tunnel. Exiting into the chamber below, Mason saw squads of troopers gathering on the ground below the access tunnel preparing to board the mothership.

Upon exiting 30 Skeksis, Mason sent a message to *Amazon*.

"*Amazon* control, this is Osiris Leader, we're inbound. Request clearance for docking."

"Roger that, Osiris Leader. You're cleared for direct approach."

"Thank you, *Amazon*. And make sure you have a mortuary detail ready. I'm bringing a dead pilot home."

"We'll be ready when you touch down, Osiris Leader," *Amazon* control said.

After the short flight from 30 Skeksis to *Amazon*, the assault ship's hangar doors were opened in preparation for recovering Osiris Squadron.

Mason brought his fighter to a stop and lined up with one of the open hangars, folding his fighter's wings and extending the landing gear as he did.

A one-second pulse of the maneuvering thrusters sent his fighters drifting towards the hangar bay.

He glided through the open door, his landing gear close enough to the pad that as soon as he powered the electro-magnets on the bottom, they pulled his fighter down to the deck.

After going through the shutdown procedure, Mason opened the cockpit and turned around to get Zin out of her seat.

It was an awkward process getting her out of the cockpit as her limbs flopped around. But soon there were hangar techs helping him pull her out of the fighter and guiding Zin's body to a stretcher flanked by a pair of medics.

They strapped her into the stretcher and bore her off towards the airlock.

Mason kicked off to follow them into the airlock.

The medics were wasting no time in getting Zin inside. They would take her directly to the med-bay where Zin could be extracted from her hardsuit before rigor mortis set in.

When the inner hatch opened and the medics maneuvered Zin's stretcher out, Mason received a notification on his brainset.

"Squadron Leader Grey, please report to the bridge at your earliest convenience," said the message from Captain Alvarez.

Mason sighed. He just wanted to get to the habitat ring and fall into bed.

He passed through the airlock after Zin's body and the medics carrying her, but as soon as the inner hatch opened, the medics went in the opposite direction from where Mason needed to go to get to the bridge.

He popped off his helmet and headed to the nearest ladder.

Mason felt like he had a weight resting in the pit of his stomach, despite the complete lack of gravity. It seemed grief paid no mind to physics.

After passing through several decks, he arrived at the command level and proceeded to the bridge. The hatch to the bridge was open, and only occupied by a partial command crew. No one inside was wearing pressure suits. It seemed Captain Alvarez had stood down his ship from battle stations after the Cendies surrendered.

Captain Alvarez floated in the air on the other side of the holotank from Mason. He spotted Mason through the display and pulled himself around the holotank.

"Thank you for making good time, Squadron Leader. I'm sorry to order you to the bridge when you're probably desperately wanting to get some rest."

Mason shrugged. "Bridge is on the way to the habitat ring, sir."

"I will try not to delay you any longer than necessary," Captain Alvarez said. "I have orders waiting for you and I wanted to convey them in person rather than via brainset. You're being transferred over to *Independence*."

"When, sir?"

"Within the next forty hours. Enough time to get some rest before you board your fighters."

"What's *Amazon* going to be up to without us?" Mason asked.

"We'll be providing support for Colonel Shimura as she secures the Cendy mothership," Captain Alvarez said. "I think we're going to be in 61 Virginis for a while."

"I don't envy the task of figuring out what to do with all the Cendies on that rock, Captain," Mason said.

"I can already see the signs of the mess brewing," Captain Alvarez said. "The Leaguers have made it clear that they do not want any Cendy prisoners flown down to Triumph."

"Can't blame them after what they've been through," Mason said. "Is there anything else, sir?"

"No, Squadron Leader. You're dismissed. Get some rest," Captain Alvarez said.

"Thank you, Captain."

Mason headed to the nearest ladder well and descended from the command deck to the habitat-ring level. After a slow elevator ride to the ring, he proceeded to the gimballed pod where his pilots were berthed. Pilot country was quiet, the doors to each cabin closed shut. No doubt his surviving pilots were fast asleep.

Mason headed directly to his private cabin, activating his shower as soon as the door closed behind him. It wasn't until after he finished showering and brushing his teeth that he decided to check his inbox on *Amazon*'s network. He had one message from Triumph, belonging to a Planetary Defense officer.

When Mason opened the message, he was surprised to see Angela staring into the camera.

"Hello, Mason. Lieutenant Okoye said she would pass a message along to you." She pointed to one side, and the camera panned to show a pair of

Planetary Defense personnel manhandling his hardsuit into a hand truck under the watchful supervision of her dogs. Judging by the sweat on their brows, it looked like they had carried the thing by hand up the stairs from Angela's basement.

The camera panned back to Angela. "As you can see, your hardsuit is being returned. Also, my dogs and I are doing okay. Planetary Defense has been dropping off supplies. Thank you for letting them know I was here so they would not bomb my house. Good luck up there."

The message ended, leaving Mason feeling a profound sense of relief. He hadn't realized until now how worried he'd been about Angela and her pack.

Mason decided to delay going to bed to open a connection to Jessica. He expected to connect to her automated inbox but instead got an instant response.

"Hey, Mason, give me a moment to get in front of a camera."

Mason took that time to sit down at his desk and activate the camera on it.

Jessica's face appeared in a box on his HUD. "Hello there, Mason."

"Hi, Jessica. Thanks for taking the time to take my message directly. I'm sure you must be buried up to your ears in work."

Jessica smiled. "Interesting phrasing given I'm underground. I'm right now in a bit of a lull. The troopers are busy securing the mothership before they'll let us aboard to start picking it for intelligence. Your timing could not have been better."

"Yeah, so about timing," Mason said, taking a breath. "My squadron's been re-assigned to *Independence*. We're due to transfer over to her in 40 hours."

"So, no leave for you?" Jessica said with an undertone of worry. "No leave for me yet."

Jessica nodded. "I guess it would be a waste to keep Osiris Squadron loitering here now that the Cendies are gone."

"What's left of it," Mason said. "There are probably some unfortunate pilots waiting for me on *Independence* to replace my losses."

"Blimey, Mason, I don't have the words to express how sorry I am for what you have to deal with," Jessica said. "This war has cost me a lot of friends," Mason said. "And will probably claim more before it's over. Assuming I live that long."

"Well, in my absolutely selfish opinion, I encourage you to survive whatever hell the Cendies put you through, so you can come back to me," Jessica said.

"It could be a while before we see each other, Jessica. You sure you'll want to pick up the thread where we left it?"

"Of course, love," Jessica said. "Assuming that's what you want."

"More than anything," Mason said.

"Then you keep yourself alive so I can jump you the next chance I get," Jessica said.

Mason chuckled. "I'll make every effort. You stay safe as well, Jessica."

"Thank you, love," Jessica said, smiling sadly. "Best of luck with whatever is in store for you aboard *Independence*. I think you're going to need it."

CHAPTER 52

It felt like it had been years since Mason had last been aboard the *Independence*, though it had only been a few months. They had both been through a lot.

During his docking approach, the battlecarrier sparkled with the light of hundreds of welders and cutting torches repairing the damage sustained during the Battle of Triumph. Upon boarding *Independence*, Mason encountered multiple repair teams flowing through the starship's corridors seeking damage hidden within the guts of the ship.

Independence's habitat ring had escaped any battle damage, so Mason and his pilots were able to get settled in .3gs as they recuperated from the attack on the stranded Cendy mothership.

Somehow the battlecarrier, though fully crewed, felt empty. Jessica and Colonel Shimura were busy studying the captured mothership, while Zin was in a refrigerated box aboard *Amazon*.

Mason had survived the whole siege of Triumph with only a few bruises, and yet he felt like there was a gaping hole left inside him.

And it didn't look like he was going to get much time to patch that hole.

Osiris Squadron was once again below full strength after the attrition suffered in the last mission. No doubt Vice Marshal Singh and Admiral Moebius already had replacements lined up, possibly already aboard *Independence*.

But there was one replacement that was Mason's job to handle.

"Silverback, a moment of your time?" Mason asked.

The shorter, older man nodded. "It's yours, Hauler."

"I'll get straight to it. I need a new executive officer and I would like that to be you," Mason said.

"You're giving me big shoes to fill, Hauler," Dominic said.

"I know, but they need filling, and I would rather fill them with someone who has been with Osiris Squadron from the start," Mason said.

Dominic sighed. "You know, I figured I'd get sick of this job before I had to take any real responsibilities. That or die a spectacular death. The Cendies have thus far failed to oblige me with the latter."

"You could always refuse," Mason said.

"Nah, that would just be shifting responsibility to someone else." Dominic said. "Not that I have any problem serving directly under you, Hauler."

"I know I'm offering you a job you would rather not have," Mason said. "Truth be told, commanding my own squadron has lost its attraction. Too many people have died under my command."

"And plenty have survived, sir," Dominic pointed out. "You weren't coy about the fact that what we're doing is dangerous. And I'm not under any illusion that you, me, or anyone in Osiris Squadron has desirable odds of seeing the end of this war. But in exchange we get something that few get to have."

"And that is, Silverback?" Mason asked.

"We get to make a difference, Hauler," Dominic said. "And, given the ship we've been assigned, I think we're going to keep doing just that."

*

The troopers guarding the entrance into the flag officers' pod inside *Independence*'s habitat ring stopped Mason just long enough to scan his brainset before letting him through.

Inside the main room was the central holotank with a display of the 61 Virginis system inside the radius of the system's jump limit.

Triumph was surrounded by the icons of Federal starships, many in low orbit providing fire support to League ground forces busy cleaning up the scattered remains of the Cendy invasion force.

Vice Marshal Singh was on the other side of the holotank, looking up at the translucent images of 61 Virginis' inner gas giants and the tankers from Taskforce Red on a cruising burn towards them.

Mason walked around the holotank and snapped a salute to the highest-ranking Federal pilot in the system.

"Squadron Leader Grey reporting, sir," Mason said.

Vice Marshal Singh returned the salute. "Welcome aboard *Independence*, Hauler. I'm guessing these are familiar surroundings for you?"

Mason looked around the war room. "Actually, sir, this part of the ship is new to me. Spent most of my time on the bridge when I was last aboard *Independence*."

Singh nodded. "I guess your duties didn't give you much time to explore the ship. In any case, Hauler, you did fine work on Triumph. I cannot overstate the contribution you and your pilots made to our victory there."

"Thank you, sir," Mason said. "Though I admit the price is heavier than I would have liked."

"That is usually the way it is in special operation squadrons, Hauler. My advice it to get promoted out of squadron command before you burn out."

"Is that what you did when you flew spec-ops, sir?" Mason asked.

"I skipped the command part," Vice Marshal Singh said. "When I got my Squadron Leader bars, I transferred out of the Special Purpose Branch to take command of a regular squadron and didn't look back."

"Sounds smart, sir," Mason said.

"More like good timing," Vice Marshal Singh said. "We weren't in a major war at the time. Do you still feel up to the task?"

"After-battle psych-eval said my stress levels were still in the normal range, sir," Mason said.

"I know that, Squadron Leader. But what do you think? There's no shame in admitting that the job is getting to you."

Mason sighed. "I think I have at least one more mission in me before I'll need a long leave, sir."

Vice Marshal Singh nodded. "Good enough." He waved for Mason to follow and walked up to the holotank. He pointed to the icons representing Federal starships on a braking burn for the third planet from 61 Virginis. "That is over half of all the Space Forces' fleet tankers on approach for the strategic reserve over Ember. Once those tankers get their fill and head back for the jump limit, *Independence* and four carriers will join the escort and proceed to Sol."

"What about the battleships?" Mason asked.

"Taskforce Red's being split up, Hauler. The ships that are staying are either being repaired or will reinforce the defenses in 61 Virginis to secure the fuel reserves here. We are reshuffling squadrons to make sure *Independence* and all the carriers with us will have full strikecraft complements."

"Two hundred and forty strikecraft won't be enough to drive out the Cendy fleet over Jupiter," Mason said.

"It was never the plan to have Taskforce Red knock out two invasion fleets, Squadron Leader," Singh said. "Our job will be to get as many of the tankers through Cendy opposition as possible and reach Earth, where they can replenish the 1st Fleet's fuel reserves and hold off further Cendy aggression against Inner Sol."

"So, we're not liberating Jupiter, sir?" Mason said.

The Vice Marshal shook his head. "Not much left to liberate after the Cendies threw all the stations down orbit. Fact is that our victories haven't yet overwhelmed the advantage the Cendies took when they first invaded Outer Sol. We still need to resupply the 1st Fleet before we fully stabilize the situation in Sol. Then we can think about taking the fight to the Cendies."

"Can we expect any support from the League battlefleet?"

"Beyond letting us clear out their strategic reserve, no, Hauler. They're fully committed to defending their own territory. Saving Inner Sol will be a purely Federal operation."

"So how are we going to get our tankers through the Cendy blockade, sir?"

"We have between now and when those tankers jump out for Sol to figure that out, Hauler."

"I'm not sure if I should be disgusted or impressed," Miriam said.

"Why not both?" Jessica asked as they both stared at the lattice work of transparent tubes that wrapped around the core of the spherical compartment like the strands of a cocoon.

Some Federal personnel had made crude analogies comparing the viscous white substance inside the tubes to seminal fluid, but Jessica knew better.

She had seen it before in the veins of dissected Cendies. It was blood.

Miriam sighed. "Julian always went on about how inefficient life was at utilizing energy. Looks like he greatly streamlined the nutrient cycle for them."

"Yes, he did a very good job optimizing all the fun out of being alive," Jessica said.

"Yes, probably explains why they like to spend so much time in virtual," Miriam said.

Jessica's eyes traced thicker tubes running from the cocoon to the walls of the bloodworks. The darker fluid was depleted Cendy blood being fed into the lattice work to be replenished, while fresh blood was pumped to the neighboring compartments that wrapped around the bloodworks.

In what passed for sleeping quarters were hundreds of thousands of coffin-like pods filled with acceleration gel. Most of the pods were filled with numerous variants of Cendy workers, along with a smattering of emissaries and what was left of the mothership's soldiers. After their surrender, the mothership's crew had gone into their pods, leaving the rest of the vessel deserted.

"So, what do you think is waiting for you inside their virtual world?" Jessica asked.

"My guess would be something not nearly as fun as the virtual worlds I've been spending my time in for the last couple of centuries," Miriam said. "Though it must mean a great deal to the Ascended if they were willing to surrender to keep us from destroying it."

"Shall we see if they're ready to receive you?" Jessica asked.

"Let's. I've learned all I need to about this place," Miriam said.

In the low gravity, it was an easy jump to get into one of the corridors connecting the bloodworks to one of the sleeping chambers.

Inside, Colonel Shimura and a team of techs stood around the disassembled remains of a Cendy sleeping pod, bundles of wires spilling out and feeding into a jump seat taken off an assault shuttle.

"Miss Xia, I trust you're ready to interface with the Cendy virtual network?" Colonel Shimura asked.

"As ready as I'll ever be, Colonel. Have you finished splicing into it?"

"We have, though my techs have yet to get a good idea of what's waiting for you in there. Their encryption is annoyingly robust."

"I can understand why they might not want uninvited guests showing up in their simulated paradise," Miriam said, glancing at Jessica.

"In my defense, it was a desperate situation," Jessica said.

Miriam smiled. "And the start of a grand adventure." She turned to the chair. "And it seems I'm about to embark on another one."

"How long do you plan to be inside?" Colonel Shimura asked.

"I don't know," Miriam said. "I somehow suspect the Ascended aren't too worried about our timetables."

"I wouldn't be surprised if they're running an underclocked simulation," Jessica said. "It could be a while."

"I'm sure we'll have plenty to do examining the rest of this ship while Miriam's on the inside," Colonel Shimura said.

"Well, no time to waste," Miriam said. "Let's get me hooked up to this contraption and see what's inside."

Jessica helped Miriam into the jump seat, where she reclined into her pressure suit.

Miriam looked up at Jessica through her visor. "I suppose this is goodbye, for now."

"I suppose," Jessica said. "So close yet so far away."

"There's more to distance than raw kilometers." Miriam reached out with her hand. "Good luck with your work, Jessica. I hope to see you when I wake up."

"Me too, Miriam." Jessica took Miriam's hand and squeezed it. "I look forward to hearing about what you find."

Miriam nodded, and looked to Colonel Shimura. "I'm ready, Colonel."

Colonel Shimura nodded, and turned to the techs. "Plug her in."

"Yes, sir," said one of the techs, tapping on the screen of a tablet.

Miriam closed her eyes and her grip went slack.

"Good connection," the tech said. "She's in."

"Good, make sure there's someone monitoring her at all times," Colonel Shimura said. "I want to know the moment she wakes up."

Jessica let go of Miriam's limp hand and stood back. She didn't look so much asleep as she did vacant.

"You all right, Lieutenant?" Colonel Shimura asked.

"I'm just wondering what's she's seeing in there," Jessica said. "And if she's going to be okay."

"I know the feeling," Colonel Shimura said. "All we can do is do our jobs while we wait for her to come back out."

"Yes, I suppose," Jessica said. "Bloody hell, I'm not used to being this worried."

"Good, it means you care," Colonel Shimura said. "I sure as hell have never got used to the worry."

"That's not exactly comforting, sir," Jessica said.

"You're in the wrong line of work if you're looking for comfort, Lieutenant," Colonel Shimura said.

"I suppose," Jessica said. "So how do you want to handle trying to digest an entire mothership's worth of intel?"

"The same way you eat an elephant, Lieutenant," Colonel Shimura said. "One piece at a time."

The End.

Printed in Great Britain
by Amazon